Jack Sheffield grew up in the tough environment of Cipton Estate, in north-east Leeds. After a job as a 'pitch boy', repairing roofs, he became a Corona pop man before going to St John's College, York, and training to be a teacher. In the late seventies and eighties, he was a head-teacher of two schools in North Yorkshire before becoming Senior Lecturer in Primary Education at Bretton Hall College of the University of Leeds. It was at this time he began to record his many amusing stories of village life as portrayed in *Teacher, Teacher!*, *Mister Teacher*, *Dear Teacher*, *Village Teacher*, *Please Sir!*, *Educating Jack*, *School's Out!*, *Silent Night*, *Star Teacher* and *Happiest Days*.

Starting Over is his eleventh novel in the *Teacher* series and continues the story of life in the fictional village of Ragley-on-the-Forest.

In 2017 Jack was awarded the honorary title of Cultural Fellow of York St John University. He lives with his wife in Buckinghamshire.

Visit his website at www.jacksheffield.com

Also by Jack Sheffield

Teacher, Teacher!
Mister Teacher
Dear Teacher
Village Teacher
Please Sir!
Educating Jack
School's Out!
Silent Night
Star Teacher
Happiest Days

For more information on Jack Sheffield and his books,
see his website at www.jacksheffield.com

STARTING OVER

A Ragley story 1952–53

Jack Sheffield

CORGI BOOKS

TRANSWORLD PUBLISHERS
61–63 Uxbridge Road, London W5 5SA
www.penguin.co.uk

Transworld is part of the Penguin Random House group of companies
whose addresses can be found at global.penguinrandomhouse.com

Penguin
Random House
UK

First published in Great Britain in 2018 by Bantam Press
an imprint of Transworld Publishers
Corgi edition published 2019

A CIP catalogue record for this book
is available from the British Library.

ISBN 9780552174039

Typeset in 10.4/14.2pt Zapf Calligraphic 801 BT
by Jouve (UK), Milton Keynes.
Printed and bound in Great Britain by Clays Ltd, Elcograf S.p.A.

Penguin Random House is committed to a sustainable future
for our business, our readers and our planet. This book is made
from Forest Stewardship Council® certified paper.

MIX
Paper from
responsible sources
FSC
www.fsc.org   FSC® C018179

1 3 5 7 9 10 8 6 4 2

For all my friends in the village of Medstead in Hampshire and, in particular, the church community of St Andrew's.

Contents

Acknowledgements

I have been fortunate to have had the support of my editor, Bella Bosworth at Penguin Random House, who came up with the idea of a prequel to the *Teacher* series. Since then, assistant editor Molly Crawford has worked tirelessly to bring this novel to publication. Thanks also to the excellent team, including Larry Finlay, Bill Scott-Kerr, Jo Williamson, Hannah Bright, Brenda Updegraff, Vivien Thompson and fellow 'Old Roundhegian' Martin Myers.

Special thanks as always go to my hardworking literary agent and long-time friend, Philip Patterson of Marjacq Scripts, for his encouragement, good humour and the regular updates on the state of England cricket.

I am also grateful to all those who assisted in the research for this novel – in particular: Mary Adams, ex-student of Royal Holloway College, retired teacher and author, Four Marks, Hampshire; Helen Carr, primary-school teacher and literary critic, Harrogate, Yorkshire; Tony Greenan, Yorkshire's finest headteacher (now retired), Huddersfield,

Yorkshire; Ian Haffenden, ex-Royal Pioneer Corps and custodian of Sainsbury's, Alton, Hampshire; John Kirby, ex-policeman, expert calligrapher and Sunderland supporter, County Durham; Roy Linley, Lead Architect, Strategy & Technology, Unilever Global IT Innovation (now retired) and Leeds United supporter, Leeds, Yorkshire; Susan Maddison, retired primary-school teacher, proofreader and maker of excellent cakes, Harrogate, Yorkshire; Elke Pollock, German translator and gardening enthusiast, Medstead, Hampshire; Dudley Skinner, 25th Bomb Disposal Company, Living History Group, Medstead, Hampshire; and all the terrific staff at Waterstones, Alton, including the irreplaceable Simon (now retired), the excellent manager Sam, plus Scottish travel expert Fiona.

Finally, sincere thanks to my wife, Elisabeth, without whose help the *Teacher* series of novels would never have been written.

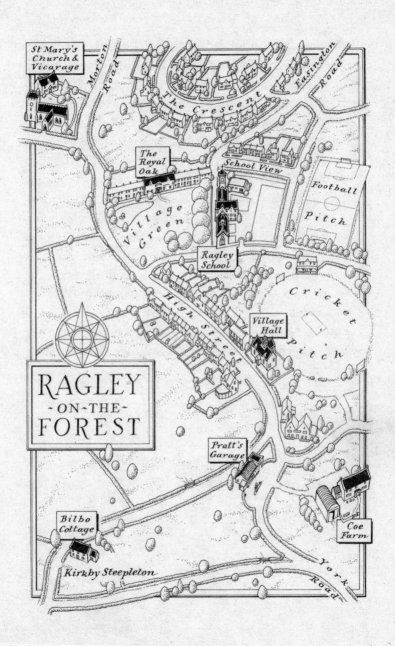

St Mary's Church & Vicarage

Morton Road

The Crescent

Easington Road

The Royal Oak

School View

Football Pitch

Village Green

Ragley School

Cricket Pitch

High Street

Village Hall

RAGLEY
-ON-THE-
FOREST

Pratt's Garage

Coe Farm

Bilbo Cottage

Kirkby Steepleton

York Road

Prologue

Promises.

Many are made, but some are broken.

So it was in the late summer of 1952 when a young woman took a creased black-and-white photograph from her handbag. She looked around at the other passengers on the bus. No one had noticed and after a brief glance she replaced it carefully in her bag. As she stared out of the window a smile flickered across her face. The past was receding and a new life stretched out before her. A promise had been made and a secret was safe. Her earlier life lay concealed behind a closed door. There was no going back and she would not speak of it.

William Featherstone's cream-and-green Reliance bus trundled through the quiet, picturesque countryside of North Yorkshire until it reached a pretty village ten miles north of the city of York. The road was flanked by high grassy verges and cottages with pantiled roofs and tall chimneys.

'Ragley High Street,' announced William as he slowed

down next to a parade of shops. He pulled on his hand-brake, opened the door, skipped down the steps and stood to attention on the pavement. His wartime army background was there for all to see and, as a survivor of Dunkirk, he valued life and loved his job. In his neatly pressed navy-blue three-piece suit, peaked cap, clean white shirt and regimental tie, William took a pride in his appearance. 'Cleanliness is next to godliness,' his mother had told him and he had never forgotten.

The young woman stepped down and William touched the neb of his cap and smiled. 'Morning, Miss. Would you like some 'elp with y'case?'

'Thank you . . . but I'll be fine.'

She put down her brown suitcase on the pavement, tugged on her leather gloves and took in the scene. The first shop on the High Street, the General Stores & News-agent, was already busy with early-morning trade. Next door, behind the window of Piercy's butcher's shop, a burly man in a striped apron and straw hat was arranging pairs of pigs' trotters. He smiled as he glanced up at her standing on the pavement. *Nice-looking lady*, he thought.

The village Pharmacy was about to open and a portly man in a white coat was sticking a poster on the door advertising:

ANDREWS LIVER SALTS
4 oz tin for 1/6d
'for INNER CLEANLINESS'

He waved a friendly greeting. 'Good morning, Miss,' he called out, wondering who the attractive newcomer might be.

Next in line was Pratt's Hardware Emporium, where, outside on the forecourt, a slightly built youth in a cut-down brown overall was arranging a display of galvanized buckets and scrubbing brushes with infinite care. He paused before polishing a bright sign next to the window that read 'ATLAS LAMPS', then he hurried back inside, full of nervous energy.

The bus stop was right outside an imposing shop above which an ornate sign read 'DORIS CLUTTERBUCK'S TEA ROOMS' in bold capitals. It appeared to cater for the discerning customer, as the sign on the door read:

HORNIMAN'S DISTINCTIVE TEA
Rich and fragrant
The blend for the connoisseur

Meanwhile, Wigglesworth's Hair Salon had different illusions of grandeur, with photographs of Loretta Young, Marilyn Monroe and Joan Collins in the window. Finally, the village Post Office, with a bright-red telephone box outside, propped up the end of the row.

William took off his cap and mopped his brow with a large white handkerchief. When he returned to his seat he studied the young stranger keenly. Her looks were striking. Her slim figure, smart two-piece grey suit and dark-brown wavy hair reminded him of the film star Vivien Leigh. A picture of the vivacious Scarlett O'Hara in *Gone with the Wind* came into his mind and he stared after her as she headed purposefully up the High Street towards the village green.

The young woman crossed the road, walked past a

white-fronted pub, The Royal Oak, and stepped under the shade of an avenue of recently planted horse chestnut trees. There before her, behind a wall of Yorkshire stone, amber in the flickering sunlight, stood the village school. It was a Victorian building of weathered reddish-brown bricks, with a steeply sloping grey slate roof and a high arched window in the gable end. The sign on the stone pillar next to the gate read 'Ragley-on-the-Forest Church of England Primary School'.

As she walked up the cobbled drive she glanced up at the bell tower, where two rooks circled and cawed menacingly. She took a deep breath and paused in the entrance porch. Above her head the year 1878 was carved deep into the lintel and the giant oak door creaked on its hinges as she opened it. Opposite her in the dark corridor was a door with a small brass plate that read 'John T. Pruett, Headmaster', and she knocked gently.

A bespectacled man just short of his fortieth birthday opened the door. He smoothed his hair and gave a gentle smile as recognition dawned. 'I'm John Pruett,' he said, 'and you're right on time. Welcome to Ragley.'

The young woman put down her suitcase, carefully removed her gloves and shook hands formally.

'Good morning, Mr Pruett,' she said. 'I'm Lily Briggs, the new teacher.'

Chapter One

First Day for Miss Briggs

It was nine o'clock on Wednesday, 3 September and the bell of Ragley-on-the-Forest Church of England Primary School rang out to announce to everyone in the village that the academic year 1952/53 had begun.

The headteacher, John Pruett, tied the bell rope to the metal cleat on the wall, walked across the entrance hall and opened the ancient door. Then he smiled as he surveyed the boys and girls playing in the bright sunshine. For the past seventy-four years the children of the village had scampered up the worn stone steps at his feet. John had been the headteacher since 1946 and this was his seventh year in charge. After serving in the Royal Engineers during the war he had taken a short course at the college in York and arrived at Ragley School when the previous headmistress retired. A man of average height and unremarkable appearance, he lived alone in his cottage on the Morton road and loved his job.

He took a deep breath, raised a whistle to his lips and gave two brief blasts. Everyone stopped, then the older children grabbed the hands of the new starters and formed two lines, boys in one and girls in another. The pupils were well drilled and John nodded in satisfaction – until he spotted two boys sliding down the pile of coke outside the boiler-room doors.

'David Robinson,' he shouted, 'and Malcolm Robinson – go and stand by my desk!'

The two boys, one very tall for his age and the other a foot shorter and diminutive in comparison, looked up in horror. They were cousins and as always it was ten-year-old David, or Big Dave as he was known to all the other children, who spoke first. 'Oh 'eck . . . yes, sir.'

'And be quick about it,' added John Pruett forcefully.

'Yes, sir,' echoed nine-year-old Malcolm. He spat on his grimy hands and wiped them on his grey shorts. The two boys were inseparable friends and Malcolm looked up expectantly at his giant cousin.

'C'mon, Malc,' whispered Dave, 'we're for it now,' and they trudged into school to await their fate.

The school caretaker, forty-six-year-old Edna Trott, was leaning on the school gate watching the scene unfold. 'Them two Robinson boys'll be the death o' me,' she muttered with a wry smile. Edna had packed away her yard broom and finished her morning's work. It had been a busy summer preparing the school building for another year and her bones were beginning to ache.

'Ah blame t'parents!' exclaimed a voice from over her shoulder. 'They let 'em run wild these days.'

Edna turned to see the ample figure of twenty-eight-year-old Deirdre Coe, viewed by many as the most unpopular woman in the village.

'There's nowt wrong with t'Robinson family,' Edna retorted firmly. 'Them Robinson brothers would give a 'elpin' 'and to anybody an' their sons tek after 'em. It's jus' 'igh spirits, Deirdre. Boys will be boys.'

'Well, my Stanley is allus 'avin' t'chase 'em off 'is pig farm. 'E sez' 'e'll give 'em a good 'idin'.'

Edna gave Deirdre a knowing look. 'An' ah've no doubt their dads would return t'favour. So you tell Stanley t'watch 'is step,' and with that she strode down School View to her home on the council estate.

'Nowt but a cleaner-upper,' muttered Deirdre, 'an' livin' on t'never-never if what ah've 'eard is true. Not got two ha'pennies t'rub t'gether.' Then she leaned on the school wall. There had been talk in the village of a new lady teacher and Deirdre was keen to see her for herself.

Elsie Crapper, the timid twenty-eight-year-old church organist, arrived at the school gate. She had volunteered to play the piano in morning assembly prior to walking up the Morton road to St Mary's Church. Elsie was on the church cleaning rota and the team of ladies known affectionately as 'the Holy Dusters' did not take kindly to latecomers. Consequently, Elsie appeared nervous and agitated. 'Good morning, Deirdre,' she said quietly.

'Nowt good that ah can see,' muttered Deirdre as she eyed up the new teacher. 'She fancies 'erself, does that one.'

Elsie was in no mood to continue the conversation and scurried up the cobbled drive like a church mouse. Meanwhile Deirdre gave the school a final withering glance and set off for the General Stores to buy cigarettes for her brother.

*

Lily Briggs took a deep breath. *This is where it begins*, she thought.

'Now girls,' she said, 'walk smartly into school and show the boys how it should be done.'

John Pruett gave her a wry smile. *Good start*, he thought.

The girls looked up in awe at their new teacher, who smiled at each one of them as they stepped into school. She appeared very different to Miss Flint, the severe part-time teacher who used to help Mr Pruett and teach the little ones.

'Now, boys,' said John Pruett sternly, 'it's your turn. Show Miss Briggs how smartly you can walk into school and then sit down in the hall.' He turned to Lily. 'I'll just have a word with the Robinson boys and then I'll join you.'

Big Dave and Little Malcolm were standing next to the headteacher's huge oak desk. On it were a magnificent brass inkstand, a collection of broad-nibbed pens and a tall stone bottle full of black ink. On the sloping lid a Manila attendance register lay open at the first page.

The boys looked anxiously around them. John Pruett had written 'Wednesday, 3rd September 1952' on the blackboard with a stick of chalk in careful cursive writing. The loop beneath the letter 'y' and the descender below the letter 'p' were exactly the same length. Mr Pruett believed good handwriting was important and many hours of practice stretched out before the children in his care. On the shelf under the blackboard was a large stick of chalk, a board rubber and a one-yard-long wooden ruler.

Also, hanging ominously from a hook on the wall was a bamboo cane. Little Malcolm stared up at it and began to tremble. Big Dave put an arm around his shoulders. 'Don't worry, Malc,' he whispered reassuringly, 'it'll be all right . . . Mr Pruett won't cane us on t'first day.'

Lily was about to follow the last child into school when a lady suddenly appeared at her side carrying a small shopping bag.

"Scuse me, Miss Briggs. Ah'm Mrs Poole. My Veronica 'as jus' started t'day.' She pointed to a small, freckle-faced, ginger-haired girl who was clutching a rag doll, and then lowered her voice. 'Ah know she's five now, but she still wets t'bed when she gets agitated. So ah've brought some spare pants. 'Ope y'don't mind.'

She handed over the bag and Lily glimpsed a pair of baggy navy-blue knickers.

'Don't worry, Mrs Poole,' she said with a reassuring smile, 'I'll keep an eye on her.'

'Thank you kindly, Miss,' said Audrey Poole with a relieved sigh. 'Ah were frettin' summat awful las' night an' worryin' 'bout 'ow she'll cope.' She cast a final look at her daughter, who was sitting happily on the hall floor showing her doll to seven-year-old Daphne Cahill.

John Pruett looked at the Robinson boys and noticed how much David had grown during the summer holiday. Their ruddy, sunburned faces were streaked with dust and their spiky hair made them look as though they had been pulled through a hedge backwards – which they probably had.

'Now, boys,' he said, 'what have you to say for yourselves?'

The two boys looked up with sheepish expressions.

'Sorry, sir,' mumbled Big Dave. He nudged Little Malcolm. 'Sorry, sir.'

'So you should be. Mrs Trott works hard to keep that coke pile tidy. You must apologize to her. Any more misbehaviour and it will be the cane.'

'Yes, sir,' said Big Dave, and Little Malcolm nodded.

John studied the two of them. *They're not bad lads*, he thought. 'Fine, make sure you understand. Remember, boys, you must do as you're told. I'm just trying to keep you safe. It's for your own good. Now wash your hands, quick as you can, and hurry into the hall.'

Elsie Crapper bashed out the opening line of 'The King of Love my Shepherd Is' on the piano and the older children who could read began to sing. The younger ones knew a few of the words, while five-year-old Frank Shepherd wondered why they were singing about him.

John Pruett and Lily Briggs were sitting on chairs at the front of the hall facing the children. 'Now, boys and girls,' said John, 'this is a special day for Ragley School. Hands up if it is your first day here.' A few of the bigger brothers and sisters encouraged their younger siblings to raise their hands. Then Lily raised hers and the children laughed.

'That's right,' said John. 'We're welcoming some new boys and girls into our school and I want you older ones to make sure they are safe and happy.' There were knowing nods from the nine- and ten-year-olds. 'It's also the first day for Miss Briggs. She has come all the way from the south of England to teach the younger boys and girls. So I want you to show our new teacher what a lovely school we have here. Be good and work hard. Now, I'll ask Miss Briggs to lead us in the Lord's Prayer.'

'Hands together, eyes closed,' said Lily.

Back in her classroom Lily distributed the modest collection of books and sat down next to six-year-old Bertie Stubbs. He was staring in dismay at his new reading book in the *Janet and John* series. The title was *I Went Walking* and it featured a pretty little girl carrying a doll and an umbrella.

'What's the matter, Bertie?' asked Lily.

Bertie shook his head. 'Ah'm not keen on girls an' ah don't like dolls, Miss.'

Lily studied the little boy and considered the content of his reading book. It was clearly inappropriate for this son of Yorkshire. 'We could make our own book, Bertie,' she said. 'What are you interested in?'

'Int'rested?'

'Yes, what do you like?'

'Pigs, Miss,' answered Bertie without hesitation.

'Pigs?'

'Yes, Miss, ah 'elp m'dad wi' farrowin' an' feedin' an' muckin' out an' suchlike.'

Lily looked at this eager, stocky little boy with a short-back-and-sides haircut that could only be described as brutal. She selected a piece of white paper and a tin of crayons from the shelf next to the blackboard and placed them next to him. 'Bertie, I would like you to draw a picture of some pigs and then we shall make up a story about them.'

'Cor, thanks, Miss!' said Bertie. 'Ah luv pigs,' and he picked up a crayon and began to draw as if his life depended on it.

*

In John Pruett's classroom there was absolute silence as the children copied out their seven times table in their new mathematics exercise books.

The desks were in rows and the children bowed their heads and gripped their pencils fiercely. 'Stop chewing the end of your pencil, Edward Brown,' Mr Pruett called out suddenly. Ten-year-old Eddie Brown looked up in dismay and wondered how the teacher could see what he was doing while writing on the blackboard. The room was bleak and the walls were almost bare. John didn't encourage distractions. There was only a huge map of the world next to the blackboard. Many of the countries were coloured pink to show the vastness of the British Empire.

Also, in the corner of the room was the bane of Mrs Trott's life: namely, a shiny black tortoise stove – a cylindrical black monster resembling a cast-iron post box and so named because of its output of 'slow but sure' heat. Installed in 1910, it was beginning to show its age and John hoped the Ragley caretaker would be able to coax it back into life when the cold months began.

However, on this sunny September morning all seemed well and he pondered on the new colleague who had arrived to share his professional life. The letter from her previous headteacher in Buckinghamshire spoke of a dedicated and hard-working member of staff. She was disappointed that Lily had left with her family to live in Yorkshire, but their loss was Ragley's gain.

John Pruett smiled to himself. It had been an excellent appointment. Miss Briggs was just what the village needed – a young woman with new ideas who would help with the school's growing numbers. After the war the council estate had expanded. Soldiers had returned to their previous jobs and married their girlfriends. In consequence, there had been a boom in the birth rate. In fact, ten more five-year-olds had enrolled last year, hence the advertisement for a new full-time teacher. His previous assistant teacher, Miss Valerie Flint, who firmly believed that children should be seen and not heard, did not want a full-time commitment. She had taken up a new part-time teaching post in the neighbouring market town of Easington.

'Very well, children,' he said, 'all together now: one seven is seven, two sevens are fourteen . . .'

At morning playtime Lily leaned against the school wall and watched the children playing. There had once been metal railings on top of the wall, but these had been removed during the war to build Spitfires and support the war effort, so now only their stunted stubs protruded. There was talk of replacement railings but the funds had yet to be found.

A group of girls were chanting out a popular skipping rhyme:

> *Red, white and blue,*
> *The Queen's got the flu,*
> *The King's got the tummy ache,*
> *And don't know what to do.*

Two ten-year-olds, Winnie Pickles and Edie Stubbs, were winding an old washing line while nine-year-old Celia Etheringshaw jumped nimbly in and out. Lily marvelled at her agility and skill.

Eddie Brown looked on. He was known as 'Fat Eddie' to the other children, as he was the only overweight pupil in the school. Unlike Eddie, all the other boys and girls were whippet-thin owing to huge amounts of exercise and a limited, sugar-free diet. In complete contrast, Eddie was a sedentary boy and fed by his mother on a regular supply of sticky buns.

Winnie Pickles was the girl of Eddie's dreams and he always sought out opportunities to talk to her. As his mother worked at the local chocolate factory in York, Eddie had decided to give some of the sweets she brought home to Winnie. She was unimpressed with the lazy, not-very-bright Eddie; however, she was happy to succumb to his chocolate charms.

On the far side of the playground ten-year-old Billy Icklethwaite was playing conkers with nine-year-old Norman Fazackerly, while Daphne Cahill was teaching Veronica Poole how to play hopscotch. Veronica was still clutching her doll. It had a dress made from scraps of old material and the child held it close to her. Lily smiled. It was a busy scene and the children were happy in their private world, where friendships were formed, the days were long and everyone thought they would live for ever.

As she watched, Lily noticed the occasional loner. Sitting away from the hubbub of the noisy games and reading a comic was eight-year-old Reggie Bamforth, a studious boy who loved mathematics. He was wearing hand-me-down, scratchy grey flannel shorts and long woollen socks with a ruler pushed down the leg, which, at a moment's notice, could become a sword, a rifle or a telescope.

Unlike his willowy, fair-haired sisters, Reggie was stocky

and strong with a mop of curly black hair. There was talk
that his father had been an American airman, but such conversations were never held within earshot of his mother . . .
and definitely not of Mr Bamforth.

Ragley School was fortunate in that it had a kitchen and at
lunchtime a meal of Spam fritters and beans followed by
jam roly-poly pudding and custard was served. After
devouring second helpings, the children ran out on to the
playground and the school secretary, Vera Evans, was
enjoying a cup of tea in the staff-room with Lily. Vera had
just passed her thirtieth birthday and cut a tall, elegant
figure. Her official title was 'clerical assistant' but Vera
preferred 'school secretary'. She worked three half-days a
week, on Mondays, Wednesdays and Fridays. Single and
sister of Joseph Evans, the local vicar, Vera was content
with her life. It revolved around the church, Ragley School
and keeping the beautifully furnished vicarage in the
grounds of St Mary's Church, which she shared with her
younger brother, looking spick and span. Their parents
had retired to the east coast and left them a tidy inherit-
ance, so for Vera it was a relatively comfortable life in
times of austerity.

Vera sipped her tea thoughtfully and smiled at her new
colleague. 'How are you settling into Kirkby Steepleton?'

'Fine, thanks, Vera,' said Lily. 'It's handy being only three
miles away and the bus stops right outside the cottage.'

'William provides an excellent bus service. Always on
time. And how is your mother? Florence, isn't it?'

'Yes,' replied Lily, putting down her cup and saucer. 'It
was a wrench for her leaving Buckinghamshire, but she

loves her new home. I left her making bedroom curtains this morning.'

'I heard she is a talented seamstress,' said Vera with enthusiasm. 'Perhaps she might be interested in our cross-stitch club. My friend Millicent Merryweather is a member and lives in your village. I'm sure she could offer a lift.'

'That's kind, Vera. I'll mention it to her. She has more time now that my little brother has started school.'

'Mr Pruett mentioned you have *two* brothers.'

Lily had noticed that Vera always referred to John as *Mr* Pruett. 'Yes, George is nineteen and doing his National Service, and little Freddie is just six. He started today at Kirkby Steepleton Primary School.'

Vera nodded in approval. 'He will be fine there.'

'Sadly, my father only knew him for a short time,' added Lily.

'Oh dear,' said Vera. There was a moment's silence. 'I heard in the village that it was pneumonia.'

'Yes, last year,' said Lily with a sigh. 'It was a terrible time. I miss him.'

Vera saw the pain in her face. 'I'm sure you do,' she said quietly.

Lily stared out of the window. 'Then we decided on a fresh start. So we sold our house and moved to Yorkshire when I was appointed to Ragley.'

'I'm sure the school will benefit,' said Vera, 'and do remember I'm always here to help.'

Lily felt it was the beginning of a special friendship as they stood side by side drinking tea and watching the children playing on the school field.

*

A few minutes before one o'clock the oldest boys went into the school hall and erected a line of folding camp beds. It was the norm for the five- and six-year-olds to rest for half an hour in complete silence. Many were puzzled by this enforced rest, as they had boundless energy, but they understood that school life had its own set of customs, ranging from regular doses of cod liver oil to frequent episodes of corporal punishment.

Afternoon school began with a contrast between the two classrooms. In John Pruett's the eight-, nine- and ten-year-olds made a list of the kings and queens of England. Again there was silence and John wondered why lively noises could be heard from Lily's class.

Her five-, six- and seven-year-olds were enjoying a painting lesson. Lily had torn the pages from an old wallpaper sample book and mixed up some of the powder paint she had found in a dusty corner of the stock cupboard. Bright pictures were emerging and Lily reflected on the wonderfully imaginative artwork that young children could produce, only for it to be crushed into conformity in later years.

When afternoon playtime came, Lily carried a cup of tea on to the playground for John. They leaned against the wall, warm against their backs, and watched the children enjoying their games of hopscotch and leapfrog. John nodded towards the Robinson boys, who were playing marbles on a rough piece of ground at the edge of the school field.

'Do you know,' he said, 'I don't think I've ever heard Malcolm Robinson utter a full sentence. His cousin does all the talking for the two of them.'

'Let me have a try,' said Lily with a grin and set off towards the two boys.

John called after her, 'If you get a sentence out of him it will be a miracle.'

Big Dave and Little Malcolm looked up anxiously when Lily spoke to them.

'Hello, boys. Are you enjoying your first day back in school?'

'Yes, Miss,' said Dave cautiously.

'Yes, Miss,' echoed Malcolm.

Lily crouched down so that she was the same height as Malcolm. 'Tell me, Malcolm, what will you be doing when you get home?' She spoke slowly and clearly, smiling gently.

Malcolm looked up at his cousin for support but none was immediately forthcoming. His brow furrowed in concentration. There was a long pause. 'Choppin', Miss,' he said.

'Shopping?' Lily was pleased to receive a reply.

Dave realized it was time for him to make his presence felt. 'No, Miss, 'e means *choppin'* – y'know – choppin' wood.'

'Oh, I see.' Lily stared hard at Little Malcolm and tried a new tack. 'And tell me, Malcolm, what do you most enjoy about school?'

'Dinner, Miss,' replied Malcolm without hesitation.

Lily was encouraged. 'Anything in particular?'

'Plums, Miss.'

'Anything else?'

'Custard, Miss.'

Lily decided to seek a different direction. 'Malcolm, tell me something else about school that doesn't involve eating.'

18

Malcolm thought hard. This was a difficult question. Finally he nodded. 'Rusks, Miss.'

'Rusks?'

'Yes, Miss.'

'But you can eat rusks.'

'No, Miss.'

'Why not?'

''E gives 'em t'me,' added Dave helpfully, ''cause 'e dunt like 'em.'

At that moment John Pruett came to stand beside them. 'Excuse me, Miss Briggs, but it's time for the bell.'

'Thank you,' said Lily. 'I'll ring it.'

When she turned back the boys had gone.

At the end of school the children stood behind their chairs and said a prayer, then ran outside. The freedom of the local woods beckoned and there were trees to climb.

Lily stared at her desk. Books for marking, slates, chalk, thick pencils and a pot full of raffia needles. After tidying up she walked into the ladies' cloakroom, took a mirror from her handbag, checked her appearance and reapplied her favourite bright-red Max Factor lipstick, then thought better of it. With a small lace handkerchief she wiped her lips until only a faint trace remained.

It was just before five o'clock when she was standing by the bus stop outside the village hall. A burly man in a flat cap suddenly stopped his Land Rover across the road. He was towing a trailer stacked high with straw bales.

'D'you want a lift, luv?' he shouted.

'No thank you,' replied Lily.

'Not seen you 'round 'ere.'

Lily didn't answer and turned to study the bus timetable.

'Bus might not be 'ere for a while. Y'might as well jump in an' ah'll tek you t'where y'goin'.'

Lily stared back at the unwelcome villager. A cigarette hung from his fleshy lips. 'I'm fine, thank you, and don't need a lift.'

'Ah'm Stan Coe. Who are you then?'

'If you don't mind I don't want to have a conversation with you across the street,' said Lily in a voice that brooked no argument.

'Ah can come over there then.'

'No thank you.'

At that moment a little black police car pulled up outside the General Stores and a policeman got out. He paused and stared at Stan Coe, then glanced at the attractive young woman.

'Everything all right, Miss?' he called.

Lily smiled at the newcomer. He was a tall, broadshouldered policeman with sergeant stripes on his sleeves. She pointed towards the leering Stan Coe. 'This gentleman was trying to engage me in conversation.'

Stan glowered at the policeman and drove off quickly.

'Not any more by the look of it,' said the young man with a smile.

'Thank you,' said a relieved Lily.

'A pleasure, Miss,' he said and carelessly brushed a lock of wavy black hair from his eyes.

'I'm waiting for the bus,' she added by way of explanation.

'Here it comes now,' he said as the bus appeared on the Morton road and drew up next to Lily.

She climbed aboard, found a seat and glanced through

the window. The policeman was standing across the road outside the General Stores and, as the bus pulled away, he smiled.

Florence Briggs had prepared a plate of boiled beef and potatoes and was sitting in her tiny kitchen with Lily and young Freddie. She looked quizzically at her daughter. 'So, have you had a good day?'

'Yes, Mother – eventful, but I survived.'

'And how was Mr Pruett?'

'Kind and helpful. I'm lucky to have him as a headteacher.'

'What about the children? How are they?'

'A wide variety, as you would expect. Reading will be a challenge, but I've got plans to improve that.'

Florence looked thoughtful. She felt at ease to see her daughter so animated and apparently enjoying her new job.

It was after Lily had put Freddie to bed and they were sitting at the kitchen table drinking tea that Florence probed further. 'So, did you meet any of the villagers?'

'Yes, definitely a mixed bag . . . a few anxious parents, a farmer who was obnoxious and . . . oh yes, the local policeman.'

'Policeman?' questioned Florence with a hint of concern.

'Yes,' said Lily. She stared down at a few stray tea leaves in the bottom of her cup . . . and smiled.

Chapter Two

The Harvest Bicycle

Pale shafts of early-morning sunshine lit up the back road from Kirkby Steepleton to Ragley and Lily felt a sense of freedom as she sped along on her new bicycle. At dawn an autumnal mist had descended like an undertaker's shroud over the plain of York. However, now only patches remained and Lily slowed as she approached each bend.

Made of steel, her bicycle was a modern Raleigh, painted bright red and with state-of-the-art technology – namely, a three-speed Sturmey-Archer gear hub. Her handbag and gloves were nestled neatly in the saddle bag and the children's books she had marked the previous evening were in the straw basket attached to the handlebars. It was Friday, 26 September and a busy day lay ahead. The annual Harvest Festival had arrived for the folk of Ragley village and there was much to do.

As she approached a copse of sycamores on a sharp bend there was still a hazy view of the distant fields. In spite of the mist a fine day beckoned and, with the breeze in her hair, Lily felt a sense of adventure. The last field was being harvested, marking the end of another season, and over the hawthorn hedgerow the sinuous motion of the ripe corn was a living rhythm of burnished gold. Lily had quickly grown to love this corner of 'God's Own Country', as the locals called it, and she breathed in the sharp moist air.

In spite of the fact that Lily's mother had protested vehemently, saying it was dangerous for a young woman to cycle on lonely roads, her bicycle was proving ideal for Lily's journey to school. When the winter weather and dark nights returned she would, she had decided, catch the local bus, but for now she was enjoying her new-found freedom.

Suddenly a large rusty vehicle hurtled round the bend on the wrong side of the road straight towards her and Lily took evasive action. Her front wheel crashed into the hedge and she toppled headlong over the handlebars.

Through the leaded windows of the vicarage a shaft of sunshine pierced the mist and lit up the entrance hall as Vera prepared to leave for school. She checked her appearance in the hall mirror, smoothed her skirt and fingered the Victorian brooch above the top button of her silk blouse.

An important day lay ahead for the Ragley School secretary. Her new typewriter was due to be delivered and the bright modern technology of the early 1950s awaited her. She had promised to type a selection of Harvest Festival notices for the various noticeboards in the village and her new typewriter would be perfect for the task.

She set off at a brisk walk down the Morton road

towards Ragley's village green. Early-morning shoppers appeared like wraiths in a ghostly world through the golden hue of swirling mist. It was only when she reached The Royal Oak and walked across the village green that the sun broke through once again and the familiar sight of Ragley School came into view.

Meanwhile, on the south side of the village, a black Ford Prefect was leaving the forecourt of Victor Pratt's garage after filling up at the single pump. Two large policemen occupied the front seats and Victor waved a cheery farewell to the local bobby, twenty-eight-year-old Sergeant Tom Feather, and the young trainee police constable, Harry Dewhirst.

'It's a farm, Sergeant,' said twenty-one-year-old Harry, glancing down at his notebook. 'The cattle are getting out through a broken fence on the way to Kirkby Steepleton.' He was a second row forward for the York Railway Institute rugby union team and the small car was uncomfortable for his huge frame. However, Harry was content with his life. Having completed two years of National Service, he had achieved his boyhood ambition and joined the police force.

The stoic Tom merely nodded and concentrated on the journey ahead. Mist kept drifting across the road and on occasions visibility was difficult. Also, he knew all the local farmers and this call was simply routine, but as he drove along he was aware that this visit would provide useful experience for his enthusiastic colleague.

Cut, scratched and shaken, Lily sat up on the grassy bank and stared after the hazy shape of a large vehicle as it raced away into the distance. She had caught only the briefest glimpse of it before she was bundled into the hedgerow.

She got to her feet unsteadily and looked down at her torn stockings. 'Blast!' she muttered. Her shoes were scuffed and there was a small tear on the sleeve of her jacket. Then she looked at the road ahead. All was silent and there was still a mile to go. With a sigh she collected her books, which had scattered on the road, then she took a small mirror out of her handbag and checked her appearance. Her hair was bedraggled and there was a scratch on her cheek from her collision with the hawthorn hedge. It was only when she retrieved her bicycle that she realized the extent of the damage. 'Oh no,' she shouted out loud. The front wheel was buckled.

However, moments later, help unexpectedly arrived. A black car pulled up alongside Lily and two policemen got out. The sergeant looked concerned as he weighed up the situation. 'Can we be of assistance, Miss?'

Lily immediately recognized the handsome young officer who had intervened when she was being bothered at the bus stop after her first day at school. Suddenly embarrassed, she covered the scratch on her face with her hand and looked up into his blue eyes. 'Oh, yes please. Thank you for stopping. I've had an accident.'

'Are you hurt?' he asked, studying her carefully. *Nothing obvious*, he thought.

'Just shaken up, I think. I was forced off the road and finished up in the hedge.'

'Forced off the road?'

'Yes, a vehicle came straight at me and I had to swerve. I didn't see the driver. It all happened so fast.'

Tom gave a knowing look to his partner, who nodded in acknowledgement. 'We may know who it might be,' he murmured, staring back up the road. 'In the meantime, Doctor Davenport lives only a mile away. Let me take you there.'

Lily hesitated. 'No – please, I'll be fine.'

'Just a wise precaution, Miss,' said Tom firmly.

She looked at her wristwatch. 'I have to get to school.'

'School?' The penny dropped and Tom smiled. 'Of course – you must be the new teacher.'

'Yes, that's me,' said Lily quietly, thinking that she must look a sorry state.

'Well, I'm pleased to meet you. I'm Tom Feather and this is PC Dewhirst.' Harry leaned against the car and nodded. He was enjoying observing a gentle side to his tough colleague that rarely surfaced.

'And I'm Lily Briggs.'

Tom reached forward and took hold of Lily's elbow gently. 'May I?'

'Of course,' she said thankfully as he guided her on to the passenger seat.

'The doctor is on our way,' Tom assured her. 'Better to be safe than sorry. Then I'll drop you off at school if he says you're fine.'

Lily breathed out slowly. It made sense to follow the advice.

'Harry, put the basket and books on the back seat.'

PC Dewhirst gathered up Lily's belongings. 'What about the bicycle?'

'I want you to take it to the hardware shop. Young Timothy Pratt will fix it.'

'But it won't fit on the back seat,' said a bemused Harry.

'You're a big lad,' replied Tom with a grin, 'you can carry it.' And he drove away smoothly, leaving the perplexed police constable by the roadside.

Tom cast an appreciative glance at Lily. 'So you're working with John Pruett – a good man.'

'Yes, he's been really supportive.'

'I call in occasionally to speak to the children. Y'know, the usual stuff about Stranger Danger and not stealing birds' eggs.'

'That's good,' said Lily. She had relaxed at last. 'Then I'll be able to say thank you once again.'

Tom settled back to concentrate on the winding road and reflected that sometimes the unexpected made his job interesting.

Dr Davenport recognized a determined young woman when he saw one and, after a brief examination, Lily was declared fit for duty. Tom drove her back to school and carried her books into the office. After a word with John, and satisfied all was well, he drove off.

In the staff-room Vera prepared a cup of sweet tea for Lily and it was agreed she would stay with her until morning break. John took all the children into the hall for an extended assembly, after which the Revd Joseph Evans arrived for more Bible stories with the younger children while John taught his own class.

During morning break Vera took out her 'Emergency Repairs' tin from the cupboard in the staff-room and sewed the torn sleeve on Lily's jacket.

'Thank you, Vera,' said Lily, 'it's good as new. Everyone has been so kind.'

'It was lucky Sergeant Feather came along,' remarked Vera.

'Yes, he handled the situation very professionally. He seemed to think he had an idea who the driver might have been – but he didn't mention any names.'

Vera pursed her lips and kept her thoughts to herself.

'The sergeant arranged for my bicycle to be repaired, so I'll collect it later, probably next week. He really couldn't have been more helpful.'

'Tom Feather is a good man,' said Vera with gravitas. 'By all accounts during the war he fought with distinction, but he rarely speaks of it.' She stared out of the window and watched a flurry of fallen leaves swirl in the breeze. 'He lives with his mother, Gracie, on the road to Easington. Sadly, their house in London was bombed in the Blitz. Tom's father was killed and his mother was injured and still uses a walking stick. After the war they came to Yorkshire to start a new life.'

'Oh dear,' said Lily, 'I'm so sorry.'

'Yes, Gracie is a kind lady, always supports the church. She will be at the Harvest Festival on Sunday.'

'Looking forward to it,' said Lily. 'I'll be there with my mother and Freddie.'

It was then that a battered 1940 Vauxhall 10 that had clearly seen better days trundled up the drive and stopped in front of the boiler-house doors. A short, stocky, bald man with a handlebar moustache climbed out and lifted a heavy box out of the boot.

'Ah, it's here!' said Vera. 'My new typewriter, all the way from Leicester.'

Lily returned to her classroom while Vera hurried to the school door and held it open.

"Ello, Miss,' panted the red-faced man as he staggered into the entrance hall with the box. 'I'm Clarence Tingle – we spoke on t'telephone.'

'Good morning, I'm Miss Evans. And this is my new typewriter, I presume.'

He placed the package on Vera's desk and removed the cardboard cover. 'Well 'ere it is, Miss Heavens, a state-of-the-art, bran' new, 1952 Imperial typewriter. It's a 'uge step forward in typewriter technology.'

Vera did not like effusive men, particularly ones who dropped their aitches and compensated by inserting others in the wrong place. However, there was no doubt that the typewriter was very impressive. Originally the brain-child of typewriter genius Arthur Pateman, she had been reassured it was the brand backed by the government, particularly for use in the public sector.

'Thank you, Mr Tingle,' she said. 'And is there an instruction booklet?'

'It's right 'ere, Miss Heavens,' said Clarence, dabbing beads of perspiration from his brow with a handkerchief that Vera thought had seen better days and had clearly never been ironed. 'All y'need t'know is standin' before you.'

'Pardon?'

'I 'ave all t'knowledge y'might want.'

'Really?'

'Yes,' said Clarence as he moved seamlessly into demonstration mode. 'Your Good Companion Model Sixty-five replaced the Model Sixty this year, so it's right up t'date an' easy t'repair an' service. Jus' remove two screws – the ones holding t'ribbon spools cover in place – an' bingo.'

'Bingo?'

'Yes, Miss Heavens, an' not f'gettin' a detachable carriage t'change y'fonts.'

'May I?' asked Vera. She sat down, took a deep breath, swept the arm of the carriage return and immediately fell in love with the *ker-ching*.

It was lunchtime and after a school dinner of fish and chips and mushy peas, followed by a bowl of something that resembled frogspawn with a blob of jam to make it edible, John Pruett joined Vera, Joseph and Lily in the staff-room.

Vera was reading an article in her newspaper under the headline 'A Woman's Place'. It said that in 1952 the average age for marriage was twenty and 75 per cent of women were married. It came as quite a shock to those women who had worked in the war.

'Oh dear,' said Vera, 'it says here a woman's place is in the home.'

John absent-mindedly nodded in agreement and Lily frowned.

'That's right,' agreed Joseph.

The Revd Joseph Evans, as well as being the local vicar was also chairman of the school governors.

Vera looked up sharply at her younger brother. 'What was that you said, Joseph?'

'Well, it would appear that in an ideal world men would go out to work and women would stay and look after the house and children.'

'What rubbish, Joseph!' exclaimed Vera.

'Surely you can't deny that is the natural order of things?' replied Joseph defensively, his cheeks becoming red.

Vera shook her head and returned to her newspaper. 'I'm surprised at you, Joseph. I do hope you don't mention anything like that during the Harvest Festival.'

Suitably admonished, Joseph left quietly to return to the vicarage.

During afternoon break on the playground a group of girls led by Winnie Pickles decided they wanted to play kiss-chase. However, it required the involvement of at least one boy who was willing to run around after them and plant a kiss on the cheek of whoever was caught.

Eddie Brown looked up expectantly but, to his great chagrin, he was bypassed.

'We're playing kiss-chase, Dave,' said Winnie, looking admiringly at the tallest boy in the school. 'Do you want t'play?'

Dave ignored the request. He didn't speak to girls.

'What about you, Malcolm?'

Little Malcolm went bright red and looked towards Dave for reassurance.

'Get lost,' shouted Dave. 'We don't play wi' no bloody girls.'

It was unfortunate that Lily appeared on the play-ground at that exact moment.

''E swored, Miss,' shouted five-year-old Lizzie Butter-shaw pointing at Big Dave.

For a moment Lily was undecided whether to correct the use of the past tense or press on with an investigation into who had uttered the expletive.

'So, David,' she said, 'did you use a swear word?'

Dave was an honest boy. 'Yes, Miss.'

'But it weren't 'is fault, Miss,' shouted Little Malcolm.

Lily frowned. 'There's no need to raise your voice, Malcolm.' Then it dawned . . . Malcolm Robinson had uttered a complete sentence and she couldn't wait to tell John Pruett. 'Having said that, Malcolm, I do understand why you feel you need to support David.'

'Yes, Miss, it's 'cause them girls wanted us t'play kiss-chase an' we don't play games like that.'

Another even longer sentence, thought Lily. *Wonders never cease.*

At the end of school Vera stayed on to practise on her typewriter and complete her Harvest Festival notices. There was the rattle of a galvanized bucket in the entrance hall and Vera was surprised to see Ruby Smith in the open doorway clutching a mop.

'Oh, hello, Ruby,' said Vera.

'Mrs Trott asked me t'come an' clean, Miss Evans, an' m'mother's lookin' after our Andy.'

'So where is Mrs Trott?'

'Gone t'see Doctor Davenport wi' 'er bad back.'

'I see. Well, thank you for coming in, Ruby,' said Vera. 'I do hope it's nothing serious.'

'She said she did it liftin' a new fire distinguisher.'

'Yes, Mr Pruett is very safety conscious,' said Vera, refraining from correcting Ruby's unique use of English.

'She's tried 'avin a 'ot bath.'

'Did it work?'

'Dunno, Miss Evans, but m'mother gave 'er some goose grease. She said that never fails.'

Vera watched the young woman hurry towards the toilets singing Vera Lynn's 'We'll Meet Again' in a beautiful soprano voice, and she admired her fortitude.

It was Saturday morning and Vera was busy in the vicarage kitchen preparing to make something special for the Harvest Festival – a coffee and walnut cake. As always, Vera made sure all her ingredients were weighed accurately and arranged neatly. She studied her mother's spidery cursive writing in the family recipe book. It was a recipe she had completed many times. Vera loved baking and as she greased an eight-inch-square cake tin Joseph watched in admiration.

'The secret is I weigh the eggs first,' said Vera. 'Three eggs weigh approximately eight ounces, so then I add the same weight of margarine and caster sugar. Also I flavour it with a teaspoon of Camp Coffee. It never fails.'

'I don't know how you do it with all the rationing,' said a bewildered Joseph.

There were some secrets Vera preferred to keep to herself.

'Ah well,' continued Joseph, 'God loveth a cheerful giver.'

'Two Corinthians, chapter nine, verse seven,' replied Vera without looking up from her mixing and Joseph reflected that his sister's knowledge of the Bible had always been better than his.

Vera decided to change the subject and pointed towards a large tin of Nescafé. 'I bought that for the staff-room.'

'That makes a change,' said Joseph with enthusiasm. He picked up the tin and stared at the label. It said it was a soluble coffee product and you simply had to put a spoonful in a cup and add hot water and milk. It sounded a good idea. 'I imagine it will catch on with the modern generation.'

Vera walked to the sink and filled the kettle. 'Yes, apparently Miss Briggs seems to prefer it.'

'Different times, Vera.'

'In fact, even Mr Pruett is beginning to change his habits.'

'Really?'

'So, Joseph, would you like a hot drink?'

'Yes please,' said Joseph and he handed her the tin.

Vera put it in the cupboard and closed the door firmly. Joseph frowned. Then she lifted her large earthenware teapot decorated with a pattern of flowers and placed it on her silver teapot stand.

'Tea,' she said firmly as she collected a pair of china cups and saucers, two teaspoons and a tea strainer.

'Oh,' said Joseph, 'not coffee then?'

'No,' said Vera firmly in a tone that brooked no argument. 'We shall drink *tea*, Joseph – coffee is for *Americans*.'

On Saturday afternoon Vera arrived in the butcher's shop as Tommy Piercy was cleaning his window.

'I'm here to collect my order, Mr Piercy,' she said. Tommy replaced his sponge in a bucket of soapy water. 'I thought Mr Wainwright cleaned your windows.'

'Not any more, Miss Evans. 'E did a moonlight flit,' said Tommy. 'Up an' went, 'e did.'

'Why was that?'

'Couldn't pay 'is rent no more, so ah 'eard.'

'Where did he go?'

Tommy shook his head forlornly. 'Lancashire . . . poor so-an'-so. 'E must 'ave been desp'rate.' As far as Tommy was concerned, the Wars of the Roses ran deep and Lancastrians, like vegetarians, reawakened his deep-seated prejudice.

'I have *friends* in Lancashire,' said Vera evenly.

Tommy sighed. He knew when to keep quiet. 'There's y'sausages, Miss Evans.'

On Sunday morning Millicent Merryweather left her home at Bilbo Cottage in Kirkby Steepleton in her 1947 Standard Vanguard and drove to a small cottage on the High Street. Florence Briggs was standing in the sunshine in her best tweed suit at the garden gate and waved as Millicent parked outside. Lily appeared in the doorway in a bright floral dress with a reluctant Freddie in his Sunday best and a school cap on his head.

'Good morning, everybody,' said Millicent. 'What a lovely day for the Harvest Festival. Just pile in and don't mind the basket of plums on the back seat.'

Millicent and Florence had become friends through their shared interest in cross-stitch and they chatted happily as they sped along the back road to Ragley. As they drove past Twenty Acre Field they saw that the first of the hayricks had been thatched to protect the precious straw from the ravages of winter.

'Freddie might like one of the plums, Florence, don't you think?'

The young boy didn't need asking twice and picked up a juicy plum.

At the entrance to St Mary's Church they were welcomed by the imposing and graceful figure of Vera, who was giving out the hymn books. Her crisp blouse was buttoned to the neck, where her Victorian brooch was pinned. It was a precious family heirloom and one of Vera's special treasures. She was acting as sidesperson along with Aloysius Pratt, the fifty-year-old owner of Pratt's Hardware Emporium and the local garage.

Millicent pointed out an empty pew to Lily and she sat down with Freddie and her mother. She noticed Tom Feather in a pew near the front. He was out of uniform, wearing a smart pinstriped suit and sitting next to a grey-haired lady.

Many of the locals were arriving with bags full of carrots or onions. It was the custom for the villagers to bring gifts of produce and these were displayed in front of the altar to be distributed later to those in most need.

Derek 'Deke' Ramsbottom, the local farmhand who supplemented his income by singing cowboy songs in the local pubs, had brought in a sheaf of corn, which he propped next to an orange pumpkin and a large marrow. As always, Deke had removed his favourite Stetson hat when he entered the church.

During his sermon Joseph was on good form and thanked the Lord for the bountiful harvest, while Elsie Crapper was on cue for the first bars of the offertory hymn. The villagers were in fine voice and followed Elsie's lead on the organ with 'We plough the fields and scatter', after which Aloysius read one of the lessons in a deep, sonorous voice. Following the final prayer, the congregation gathered outside church in little groups. It was a time to swap stories, catch up with the local gossip and rekindle friendships.

Aloysius Pratt approached Vera and Lily while Freddie ran off round the back of the church. He was spotted by Tom Feather, who left his mother talking to a group of ladies from the Women's Institute. Like all the other boys in his school, Freddie carried a penknife. Each day he hoped there would be an opportunity to whittle some sticks or even use the attachment that was supposed to remove stones from a horse's hoof.

Tom walked along the grassy bank that led to the cemetery and watched young Freddie with interest. The boy was holding his knife by the blade, then flicking it towards a clump of dandelions next to a gravestone. He was remarkably skilful.

A voice startled him. 'Careful with that, young man.'

Freddie hastily put his penknife away and stared up at the giant policeman. 'You need to go back to your mother before there's an accident,' said Tom with a grin. Freddie nodded and they both returned to the gravel drive in front of the church.

Lily was aware of Freddie suddenly standing alongside with Tom Feather. 'Freddie, what have you been up to?'

'Nothing to worry about, Miss Briggs,' said Tom. 'He was just playing round the back of the church,' and he winked at Freddie.

'Hello, Tom,' said Aloysius. 'I was just telling Miss Briggs that her bicycle is ready for collection.' Aloysius was a large, genial man with a booming voice. He had built up his empire in the village with his thriving hardware shop and had installed his son, Victor, in his garage as the local mechanic. He was also grooming his other son, Timothy, to take over the Hardware Emporium in a few years' time. Meanwhile his daughter, Nora, had her heart set on being an actress. Aloysius was a kindly soul and had decided to support her even though he held out little hope of her achieving her dream.

'That was quick,' said Tom.

'Our Timothy fixed it,' said Aloysius with pride. ''E's good at repairing things.'

'I'm very grateful, Mr Pratt,' said Lily. 'If you will let me have the bill I'll call in after school tomorrow.'

'No charge, Miss. It kept our Timothy busy yesterday an' 'e enjoys doin' jobs.'

'That's very kind of you.' She looked down at the gangling teenager. 'And thank you, Timothy. You are a very clever young man.'

'An' very *particular* is our Timothy,' added Aloysius with satisfaction. 'Allus does things in t'right order.'

Tom stepped forward. 'I could deliver it back to your house if you like,' he offered. 'It's no trouble, and then you could ride it to school tomorrow.'

Lily smiled. 'That's very kind.'

Vera looked at the two of them with a new interest.

It was a perfect evening and Lily wheeled her bicycle into the garden shed. It had been a surprise when Tom Feather had offered to deliver it back to her home. As she locked the door she sighed. Around her the air was soft as the light finally began to die. Above her head the vast sky over the plain of York was turning purple, studded with myriad stars.

The Harvest Bicycle

She had begun to enjoy being part of the local community and hoped to make new friends. As she walked back towards the bright lights of the cottage she reflected that it had been an eventful few days – and largely because of her new bicycle.

Chapter Three

A Surprise for Ruby

It was a cold autumn morning on the first day of October as nineteen-year-old Ruby Smith stared out of her bedroom window. In her arms she held her son, Andy, now a year old, and welcomed his warmth against her winceyette nightdress.

Beyond the untidy garden at 7 School View on the council estate, the distant hills were shrouded in a blanket of mist. The season was changing and the trees stood like spectres in the grey dawn, while fallen leaves covered the land like scattered souls. Trails of wood smoke drifted from the nearby chimney pots and Ruby shivered. She felt unwell again, but another demanding day lay ahead and her child needed feeding.

The bedroom door creaked as she walked out on to the landing.

Her husband, Ronnie, stirred. 'Bring us a nice cup o' tea, luv.'

'Tell 'im t'get 'is backside out o' bed,' shouted a strident voice from the hallway.

Ruby's mother, thirty-nine-year-old Agnes, was putting on her threadbare coat before catching the early bus into York. She worked at the Rowntree's chocolate factory and over the years had become an expert in hand-decorating fine chocolates. She waited to give her grandson a kiss on his forehead before setting off and then looked at Ruby. 'Y'look a bit peaky this mornin',' she said. 'Try an' get some rest.'

An' pigs might fly, thought Ruby as she lifted Andy's little hand so he could wave goodbye.

The bell above the door of the General Stores rang and Vera walked in.

'Good morning, Vera,' said Prudence Golightly. Prudence was the thirty-five-year-old owner of the shop and a dear friend of Vera's. The diminutive shopkeeper mounted the next wooden step behind the counter to be on the same eye level as Vera.

'Good morning, Prudence. Just some sugar for the staff-room, please.'

'And how's the new typewriter?'

'Perfect,' said Vera. 'I've got used to it now. As you know, I'm not keen on change simply for the sake of it, but this really makes such a difference.'

'I know what you mean,' said Prudence. 'I've just got some new weighing scales. It's important to be *exact* these days, especially with all the food rationing and particularly with sweet things.' She stared knowingly at the bag of sugar.

Vera smiled. 'Mr Pruett likes two spoonfuls in his tea and he needs the energy to teach those children.'

'Yes, he's a good man,' said Prudence and there was silence between them as she stared out of the window.

Vera guessed she was thinking of another good man – the love of her life. Jeremy, the brave Spitfire pilot, had been engaged to be married to Prudence, but in 1940 he had perished during the Battle of Britain when his plane crashed into the English Channel. Not a day went by without Prudence recalling their brief and happy courtship and mourning his passing.

'Well, must get on, Prudence,' said Vera, breaking the spell.

As she left the shop she saw Ruby Smith pushing a battered old pram and carrying a shopping bag.

'G'mornin', Miss Evans,' said Ruby.

Vera noticed that Ruby's rosy cheeks were a little more red than normal and she looked as though she had been crying.

'Good morning, Ruby, and how is Andrew?' Vera peered down and looked wistfully at Ruby's little bundle of joy.

'Growin' up fast, Miss Evans,' said Ruby, recovering quickly from her dark thoughts, 'an' feedin' for England.'

Vera thought for a moment. 'If you call by the school later, we always have a few rusks left over.'

Ruby frowned and pushed her wavy chestnut hair from her face. 'Ah don't want no charity, Miss Evans, but thank you kindly.'

Vera smiled gently. 'But it's a *gift*, Ruby. It's not charity – and you can't say no to a gift for your beautiful son.'

Ruby stared up at this confident lady. She was the most sincere person she knew.

'Thank you,' she said at last.

'Call in this morning if you can,' said Vera.

Ruby nodded in appreciation. 'Ah'll be there in two shakes of a cow's tail,' she said.

Lamb's tail, thought Vera, but she said nothing as Ruby hurried into the shop to buy a loaf of bread.

At 7 School View Ronnie Smith sat up in bed. He was a short, skinny man with a big opinion of himself. Ruby described him as 'seven stones drippin' wet'. He had begun smoking Wills Woodbine cigarettes at the age of twelve, and now he lit up another, leaned back and reflected on his life.

Two years ago Ronnie had received a buff envelope on which OHMS was printed in bold letters. Enclosed were his call-up papers for National Service and he was sent to Winchester in Hampshire.

The NCOs – namely, the sergeants and corporals – soon appreciated that Ronnie was their laziest recruit. They took away his Brylcreem and marched him to the barber, where his long, slicked hair was reduced to a short back and sides. Rumour had it among the recruits that the barber had been a sheep shearer in an earlier life! The initial training lasted six weeks, during which time it appeared the aim was to stamp out any hint of individuality. For Ronnie life became a living hell.

He had been issued with three cotton vests, three itchy shirts, a uniform that didn't fit and a beret with a cap badge. He spent hours 'bulling' his boots so that his toecaps had a glassy shine. As a young man Ronnie had been used to being sewn into his underwear at the beginning of winter and remaining in his thermal cocoon until spring. So early-morning physical training followed by cold showers did not come naturally to him. In consequence, he was a regular on sick parade.

Predictably, Ronnie had difficulty learning to march and was given punishment known as 'Jankers', or restrictions of privileges. It became a way of life for him. Meanwhile, the bromide in his tea had no effect when he returned home on leave: his amorous advances towards Ruby continued unabated.

After his basic training he managed to secure a cushy job as a pay clerk for the Training Company. Each soldier had a pay book and Ronnie authorized payment of twenty-six shillings per week. Out of this the soldiers had to purchase their own Blanco, Brasso and dusters. During the remainder of his time he learned very quickly that 'If it moves, salute it; if it doesn't, paint it.' It wasn't until the ordeal was over and he returned home to Ragley village that he was able to resurrect his old life and once again became known as 'Brylcreem Boy'.

Now he looked at the clock beside the bed. It was half past eight and he hoped that by nine o'clock Ruby would have prepared a cooked breakfast. After all, he thought, apart from looking after Andy and doing a bit of cleaning at The Royal Oak, she didn't have much else to do. He lay back, lit another cigarette and stared at the ceiling.

When Lily's bicycle had been returned to her home in Kirkby Steepleton by Tom Feather, her mother had remarked that she thought it was above and beyond the call of duty. It had been repaired, oiled and polished, and Lily had been impressed by this tall, understated man. There was clearly a gentle, caring side to his nature that wasn't always apparent when he was going about his police duties. Also, she couldn't help but recall how handsome he was with his wavy black hair and strong physique, and the effortless way he had lifted her bicycle out of the hedgerow.

The cold autumn breeze flushed her cheeks as she cycled past Coe's Farm and Pratt's garage and approached Ragley High Street. The hedgerows were thick with brambles and wild blackberries, while robins were busy claiming their territory. Lily's thoughts wandered as she turned past the village green and in through the school gates. It would be a full day, including a visit to school assembly by Tom Feather, and Lily couldn't resist a smile.

Meanwhile, in the Robinson household Little Malcolm was not happy. His mother dipped a rough flannel into a basin of soapy water and gave his face a quick wipe.

'Ow!' exclaimed Malcolm. 'That 'urts.'

'Don't be so soft, y'big girl,' replied his mother.

Malcolm grimaced at the perceived insult and was pleased Big Dave was not within earshot. He stood back from the sink, assuming the ordeal was over.

'Now stand still – ah've got t'do your mucky ears. They're like black 'oles o' Calcutta.' Gertie Robinson twisted a corner of the flannel and poked it in each ear. 'There, that'll 'ave t'do. Now look sharp an' get t'school afore Mr Pruett gives y'what for.'

'All right, Mam,' said Malcolm, sprinting towards the back door.

Mrs Robinson shouted after him, 'An' don't forget you're 'avin' a bath t'night. It's first o' the month.'

Malcolm froze in the doorway. 'But Mam – ah 'ad one las' month.'

Mrs Robinson, sloshing the dirty water down the sink, chose not to listen and Little Malcolm slammed the door. 'Bloody 'ell,' he muttered.

At nine o'clock Ruby wasn't cooking Ronnie's breakfast. Instead she was the first customer in the village Pharmacy. When she walked in, Herbert Grinchley was unpacking boxes of Pond's Skin Cream and Pepsodent toothpaste. The portly fifty-year-old chemist had owned the local Pharmacy since the end of the war and he knew everybody's business. He was also willing to share it with discerning customers. Ruby approached tentatively and stood by the counter. There were burn marks along the edge where Herbert regularly balanced his lighted cigarette while he was serving someone.

'Good morning, Ruby,' he greeted her. 'And how is young Andy this morning?'

''Ello, Mr Grinchley. 'E's comin' on an' ah'm tryin' m'best t'feed 'im like Doctor Davenport said.'

'That's good to hear, Ruby. An' what's it to be?'

'A bottle o' Seven Seas, please,' said Ruby, handing over her note from the doctor.

Herbert selected a bottle from the shelf behind him. 'Y'can't beat a bit o' castor oil,' he said. 'Strong bones and teeth, one teaspoon a day,' he added for good measure.

46

Ruby picked up the bottle thankfully. To buy it would have cost her 1/6d, but for expectant mothers and young children it was free.

'It comes in capsules as well, Ruby, but better t'stick wi' what y'know.' Herbert studied her quizzically. 'And how are *you*, Ruby?'

Ruby sighed. 'Ah'm seein' Doctor Davenport this afternoon. Ah've been a bit sickly lately.'

'Well, let me know what he says.'

'Thank you, Mr Grinchley,' she said. She tucked young Andy under an ancient shawl and hurried out of the shop.

Meanwhile Herbert looked through the window at the slim, attractive young woman and wondered why she had finished up with a man like Ronnie Smith.

It was shortly after ten o'clock when the children gathered in the school hall for morning assembly. At six feet two inches tall Sergeant Feather appeared like a giant to them as he stood in front of their upturned, eager faces. He seemed aware of this and knelt down on the wood-block floor.

'Boys and girls, this talk is called "Stranger Danger" and the aim is to keep you safe.' His voice was soft and persuasive, and the children hung on to every word. They were not the only ones. John Pruett sat back in his chair and watched the children carefully to ensure they were well behaved, while Lily studied the tall policeman with a new interest.

It was a talk Tom had given many times to the various schools in the Easington catchment area and he was used to the questions that might come his way.

'Is it safe t'talk to anyone in a uniform?' asked ten-year-old Celia Etheringshaw.

'Good question,' said Tom and proceeded to give examples of policemen and nurses.

At the end, John Pruett asked the children to join him in reciting the traditional school prayer:

> *Dear Lord,*
> *This is our school, let peace dwell here,*
> *Let the room be full of contentment, let love abide here,*
> *Love of one another, love of life itself,*
> *And love of God.*
> *Amen.*

John turned to Tom and spoke quietly. 'Could you do me a favour before you leave?'

Tom glanced at his watch. 'I've got time.'

John looked up at the sky. The sun had broken through the clouds. 'Just a thought, Tom, but while you're here could you take a photograph for me? I take one each year of the children and staff.'

Tom smiled. 'At your service.'

'Miss Briggs, could you gather the children outside on the playing field? And we'll need three chairs for the staff.' He hurried into the office and opened the bottom left-hand drawer of his desk. On top of the school logbook was the popular camera of the day, a Box Brownie in its case of wood and leather. Vera followed him outside, feeling slightly flustered at the short notice and buttoning up her cardigan.

John was seated in the centre, flanked by Lily and Vera.

The younger children sat cross-legged on the grass and the older ones stood in a line behind them. Vera had chalked '1952' on a slate board and it was propped in front of the toecaps of John Pruett's highly polished black leather shoes.

'Right everyone, look at the camera and smile please,' said Tom and the class of '52 froze for their special moment in time.

Everyone did as they were told and looked at the camera . . . except Lily. She was looking at Tom.

Later, Lily was on playground duty and pretending to watch the goldfinches in the hedgerow pecking at the ripe seeds while keeping one eye on Tom as he walked down the steps of the entrance porch.

He smiled when he saw her. 'Miss Briggs, how's the bicycle?'

'Perfect,' said Lily, touching her cheeks and hoping she wasn't blushing. 'It's running well. Mr Pratt's son did an excellent job, but after half-term I shall catch the bus.'

'Probably wise with the darker days coming up.'

They both leaned back against the school wall. Around them the hedgerows were rich with wild fruits. A feast of jams and jellies was in store for the villagers of Ragley as autumn shifted towards winter.

'That was a wonderful talk, Sergeant Feather,' said Lily. 'Thank you for that. The children gained a lot from it.'

Tom nodded. 'It's important to keep them safe.' Then he looked around. Children were running, skipping and kicking a football. None was within earshot.

'Perhaps you could call me Tom when I'm off duty?'

It was Lily's turn to smile. 'Very well.'

He glanced at his wristwatch. 'Anyway, things to do, must press on.'

As he turned away, Lily called out, 'I'm Lily, by the way.'

He waved as he closed the school gate. 'I know,' he said.

Off duty, mused Lily.

It was half past nine and Ruby was in her steamy kitchen washing nappies. It was a messy, smelly business, as Andy went through six nappies every day. She stood next to a huge tub and pounded the posser stick up and down in the soapy water. As she worked, beads of sweat formed on her brow. She was turning the handle of the mangle when Ronnie walked in.

'Where's m'breakfast?'

'You'll 'ave t'wait, luv,' said Ruby.

He sat down at the kitchen table. 'Well, don't be long – ah'm sweatin' cobs in 'ere.'

'Ah'll 'ave t'feed Andy soon,' said Ruby. 'Can you get y'self some toast?'

'Man can't survive on bread alone,' quoted Ronnie.

'Ah'll do an egg after ah've seen to Andy,' she said in a tired voice. 'Ah think there's one left.'

Soon Ruby was feeding her son. She had been advised by the health worker to wean Andy at four months and feed him on bone broth. Her mother, Agnes, had supplemented this with some tripe, as she said it was high in iron and wasn't rationed. Naturally, Ruby followed her mother's advice.

There was a pattern to the week for the womenfolk of Ragley village and they wore a headscarf and a pinny as a form of universal uniform. Monday was washday, followed by ironing on Tuesday. Wednesday and Thursday involved lots of polishing and dusting, and Friday was the day the menfolk brought home their wages. Saturday was 'Big Shop' day, with possibly a visit to the cinema, and Sunday was a time for best clothes and church.

However, even though it was Wednesday, Ruby had nappies to wash. Also, it was rare for Ronnie to give her any money for housekeeping and the money from her part-time cleaning at The Royal Oak was barely enough to pay the rent and put food on the table. Times were hard for Ruby.

At eleven o'clock she recalled Miss Evans's offer of a few Farley's rusks and set off for school. Vera was a member of the Church Toys for Children Committee and she had passed on to Ruby a knitted teddy bear with long, straggly legs. Andy loved chewing one of the legs at every opportunity and Ruby was pleased it kept him both quiet and happy.

Vera saw her coming up the drive and went out to meet her. 'Hello, Ruby, I'm glad you came. Come round the back to the kitchen door.'

In the kitchen, Vera collected the leftover rusks and brought them out to Ruby.

'Perfec' for our Andy wi' a bit o' warm milk,' said Ruby. 'Ah'm grateful, Miss Evans.'

With Andy chewing on his teddy, they walked back down the drive and Vera wondered what would become of this hard-working young woman.

At lunchtime John Pruett and Lily were inspecting the children's hands before they sat down for their meal.

'You'll have to wash your hands, Malcolm,' said Mr Pruett.

Dave always stood up for his diminutive cousin. 'But they'll only get mucky again, sir.'

John nodded sagely. 'Yes, David, I expect they will . . . but we don't want any germs, do we?'

Dave paused. 'Germs?' Then his face lit up with realization. 'Ah, Germans . . . y'reight there, sir, 'cause we gave 'em a proper good 'idin' in t'war.'

'You shouldn't say things like that, David,' said Lily sternly.

Dave looked puzzled. 'Yes, Miss,' and he ran off.

John grinned. 'Actually, he does have a point.'

Lily turned away abruptly and didn't reply.

It was mid-afternoon when Ruby's mother, Agnes, arrived home from the chocolate factory in York. She took off her coat, picked up Andy and gave him a cuddle. 'How's my little soldier?' she asked.

Then she winced and went red in the face with the effort of lifting her sturdy grandson. Agnes was the proud owner of a pair of cami-knickers made from parachute silk. These were fine, but she also insisted on wearing a peach-coloured corset with severe bones, which, after a couple of hours of decorating chocolates, felt like an instrument of medieval torture. In consequence, it made breathing very difficult. Ruby had tried to encourage her to purchase a rubber roll-on corset, but to no avail.

'Tek y'corset off, Mam, an' 'ave a cup o' tea,' said Ruby.

Agnes looked at Ruby and a crease of worry appeared on her forehead. 'You look proper peaky. What's matter?'

'Ah'm all at sixes an' sevens t'day,' said Ruby.

'Mebbe you ought t'fill that brain o' yours wi' summat useful, Ruby,' said Agnes with feeling, "cause empty cans mek most noise.'

'Ah'm too busy, Mam.'

'Y'need t'go an' learn summat useful.'

'Mebbe ah will.' Ruby glanced at the clock. 'Ah'll 'ave t'go, if y'don't mind lookin' after our Andy. Ah've got an appointment wi' Doctor Davenport.'

'What's up?'

'Nowt . . . jus' not feelin' m'self,' and with that she hurried out.

She passed their next-door neighbour, Mrs Cuthbertson, in the doorway. Betty Cuthbertson was known as the local scrounger. She knocked on the door and walked straight in. No one on the council estate locked their back doors and it was the norm for neighbours to arrive unannounced.

"As tha got a cup o' sugar, Agnes luv?' She sat down heavily on a chair. 'Tea in t'pot?' she enquired.

It was well known that Betty's four children drank out of jam jars as she only owned two old pottery mugs. As usual, she had sent them to school with a slice of bread and dripping.

'So what's matter wi' your Ruby?' asked Betty, who was never backwards in coming forwards.

Richard Davenport's surgery was on the Morton road, in the front room of Elderberry Cottage, where he lived with his wife, Joyce. He was a kindly twenty-seven-year-old, who had recently qualified and had grown used to the village community with its wide variety of ailments and problems. Often he could be seen hurrying out with his little black bag and bottles of strange-smelling medicine and jumping into his Morris Minor.

On occasions, home visits were requested by telephone, but more often than not there would be a knock on his door and an eager face would look up with the urgent message, 'M'mam's been tekken badly, Doctor.'

'Oh dear, do you know what's wrong with her?'

'Women's troubles.'

Dr Davenport would nod knowingly and reach for his black bag.

When Ruby Smith arrived at his surgery, it didn't take long for him to realize the young woman needed time and reassurance, and their conversation was lengthy.

Half an hour later Ruby walked slowly to the village green, deep in thought, and sat down on the bench under the weeping willow tree.

All was quiet until, above her head, a skein of honking geese flew in perfect arrow formation across a gunmetal sky over the school bell tower and into the distance. She watched as they disappeared over the horizon and envied their freedom.

Vera was coming out of her meeting in the village hall when she caught sight of Ruby sitting alone. Ruby looked tired and her eyes were red with tears once again.

'Hello, Ruby,' said Vera. 'Is there something wrong?'

'It's 'appened,' said Ruby.

'What has happened?'

'Ah've *fallen* again, Miss Evans,' explained Ruby. She looked concerned and chewed her knuckles.

'Fallen?'

'Yes, ah'm expectin' m'second.'

'I see,' said Vera evenly. 'And did you *want* another child, Ruby?'

'Not speshully, but ah'd no choice.'

'No choice?' It was Vera's turn to look concerned.

'Well ah were allus told it were *men* what took care o' that side o' things.'

Vera frowned. 'Who told you that?'

'M'mother, Miss Evans.'

Vera was aware that access to contraception was extremely limited. 'Well I wish you well, Ruby, and do come to me if you need anything.'

Ruby couldn't bring to mind anything the tall, elegant spinster could do for her, but she recognized the gesture. 'Thank you kindly, Miss Evans,' she said and set off for the butcher's to request a scrag end and a few spare bones to make some stock.

Vera stared after her and said quietly, 'There is surely a future hope for you, and hope will not be cut off.'

If her brother had been there she wondered if he would have added 'Proverbs, chapter twenty-three, verse eighteen' . . . but she doubted it.

It was six o'clock and Agnes had set off for the weekly Bingo session in the village hall while Ruby was preparing Ronnie's evening meal. She had a large cast-iron pan with a wire frying basket inside. It was perfect for cooking chips and, in the butcher's shop, Mr Piercy had told her that if you saved up enough lard and cooking fat you could make a healthy meal. Ruby had done just that and she shook the basket and smiled. Ronnie would be pleased when he came home.

The radio was on and she was humming along to Vera Lynn's bestselling record 'The Homing Waltz' when he came in smelling of beer and smoking a cigarette. 'What's f'tea?' he shouted.

'A bit o' meat from Mr Piercy an' some chips. He said our Andy needed feedin' up.'

'Well 'urry up – ah'm starvin'.'

Ruby sighed. 'Can y'light a fire, Ronnie? It's comin' in cold again.'

Ronnie walked into the front room, flicked cigarette ash on to the brown linoleum and tripped over the brush and shovel next to the hearth. 'Bloody tip in 'ere,' he grumbled and sat down on the single armchair.

A few minutes later Ruby put Ronnie's meal on the table. Ronnie had lit up another cigarette and had begun to doze in the chair. Ruby began to get frustrated. 'C'mon Ronnie, y'slow-coach,' she shouted, 'y'tea's ready. Buck up an' show willin'.'

'Allus naggin',' muttered Ronnie. He staggered into the kitchen, took a final drag of his cigarette and sat down heavily. As he began to eat the chips with his fingers Ruby returned with Andy in her arms and sat down opposite.

'Ah've got some news, Ronnie,' she said quietly.

Ronnie didn't look up.

'Ah'm expectin' again.'

'Y'what?'

'Another baby, Ronnie. Doctor Davenport said so.'

Ronnie pushed away his plate. 'We can't 'ave no more babies. Y'don't earn enough as it is.'

'If you get a job things'll be better.'

'Y'daft ha'porth – jobs are 'ard t'come by.'

'Well, there it is, ah'm havin' another an' there's nowt we can do about it.'

Ronnie took out another cigarette and rummaged in his pocket for his box of matches. 'Mebbe there's another way, luv.'

'What d'you mean?'

'Y'could get shut of it.'

That night Ruby wept silent tears as a cold wind swept away the rags of clouds to reveal a gibbous moon.

Chapter Four

Little Malcolm's Butterfly

The church clock up the Morton road was ringing out. It was 8.00 a.m. and, impervious to the cold weather, the two Robinson cousins, Big Dave and Little Malcolm, had left home early to climb trees in the private wood at the back of Mrs Uppington's cottage. It was a forgotten backwater of the village and their secret playground. In the hedgerow the red hips of dog roses were providing much-needed food for hungry voles, while the morning dew, like untouched diamonds, sparkled in the early-morning sunlight. The earth was cooling and the nights were beginning to draw in, but it mattered little to these intrepid sons of Yorkshire. Making a hole in the hedge had been difficult, but the tough Robinson boys were not easily daunted by prickly hawthorn.

With scratched knees they emerged on to the cinder track next to a row of old dilapidated thatched cottages that led to Chauntsinger Lane and the blacksmith's forge. A washing line hung across the track between the cottages and they ducked under the flapping sheets.

To their surprise, Mrs Phyllis Uppington was collecting a bucket of water from a rainwater butt at the back of her cottage and she waved in acknowledgement. She ran a dubious bed and breakfast frequented in the main by itinerant farmworkers seeking seasonal employment. On the garden gate was a painted sign reading 'B&B – No Blacks or Irish'. In Mrs Uppington's world, prejudice was the norm.

'Hello, boys,' she called out. 'I saw you go into my wood.'

'Oh, 'ello Mrs Uppington,' said Dave. His mother had told him that this strange lady was 'soft in the head', so he chose his words with caution. 'Sorry, we were jus' climbin' trees.'

Phyllis Uppington was sixty-five years old and, with the exception of the occasional visitor, a recluse. Many thought her strange. She held up a shawl that, once upon a time, had been white. 'I'm going to wash my shawl,' she said. 'It used t'be beautiful.'

'It's still lovely,' said Dave generously. 'We like that shade o' grey, don't we, Malc'?'

Malcolm nodded.

Her hair was like fine thistledown, silver-grey now and cascading down her back in gentle waves. 'Did you know my two grandchildren used to climb in this wood?'

Dave looked through the open doorway. 'Where are they now?'

'In heaven.'

''Eaven?'

'Yes . . . and they'll be dancing.'

'Dancing?' repeated Dave and Malcolm in unison.

'Yes, they were a proper little Fred Astaire an' Ginger Rogers.' She filled the bucket and walked back inside, seemingly at peace in her world.

'C'mon, Malc,' said Big Dave, 'let's play conkers,' and they raced off to school.

In the vicarage Vera was in her kitchen listening to the radio. She sighed. A panel of experts was discussing the recent news. Britain had become the third member of the nuclear power club, along with the USA and Russia. In a far-off lagoon in the uninhabited Monte Bello islands off Australia's north-west coast, a twenty-five-kiloton plutonium implosion device had exploded and left behind a crater over three hundred yards in diameter on the sea bed. Vera was so shocked she almost forgot to time her boiled egg with her usual precision.

'Operation Hurricane' had been seven years in the making since in 1945 the then prime minister, Clement Attlee, had set up a Cabinet committee to explore how we could develop our own atomic bomb. The radio reporter declared it was an act of independence and defiance, but for Vera it felt like the beginning of the end.

'Oh dear,' she murmured.

Fortunately the next discussion item dispelled the gloom. A few weeks ago the silent movie star Charlie Chaplin had returned to England for the first time in twenty-one years, to promote his latest film, *Limelight*, and he had been cheered in the streets of London.

Finally, Vera turned off the radio, put her magazine in her bag and called to her brother. 'Joseph, I'm leaving now.'

He appeared in the doorway, a tall, almost skeletal figure in a clerical collar.

'I'll see you in school later this morning,' he said enthusiastically. 'I'm giving a talk to Mr Pruett's class.'

'Oh yes,' said Vera cautiously. Joseph was always at ease with his Sunday morning congregation, but completely at a loss with young children. 'What's the theme?'

'Creation,' said Joseph.

And the best of luck, thought Vera as she set off for school at a brisk walk.

On the school field Big Dave and Little Malcolm were playing conkers. Dave was so much taller than Malcolm that he had to crouch each time it was his turn. Even so, it was the diminutive Malcolm who shattered Dave's conker and sent it crashing to the ground.

Dave was puzzled. 'Y'beat me ev'ry time, Malc,' he said as they sat down on the grass.

'It's 'cause of m'dad.'

"Ow d'you mean?' asked Dave.

"E soaks 'em in vinegar an' then bakes 'em in t'oven.'

'Flippin' 'eck, Malc,' said Dave in admiration, 'no wonder you allus beat us.' He looked around furtively. 'Ah've got summat f'you.'

Malcolm looked up curiously at his best friend. Dave rummaged in the pocket of his baggy grey shorts and pulled out two cigarettes and a box of matches. 'One f'you, Malc, and one f'me.'

'Thanks, Dave!'

'Let's 'ope m'dad doesn't notice ah nicked a couple,' Dave mumbled.

Malcolm's eyes lit up and he smiled at his giant cousin. 'Where to, Dave?'

'Be'ind t'bike shed,' said Dave knowingly. 'Ol' Pruett'll never see us there.'

A minute later they were leaning back against the wall of the cycle shed, puffing away contentedly. Dave took out a torn scrap of paper from his crumpled jacket. "Ave a look at this, Malc.'

It was a page from a magazine with a photograph of Stanley Matthews. The Blackpool and England footballer was smiling while smoking a cigarette. Malcolm stared at the picture in awe. 'M'favourite footballer, Dave, Stanley Matthews. Ah wanna be like 'im.' His ruddy face screwed up in concentration. 'Big words. You read it. What's it say?'

Dave took a final puff of his cigarette and tried unsuccessfully to blow a smoke ring. Then he studied the tiny print. 'It sez 'ere that t'wizard of t'dribble smokes Craven A cigarettes f'smooth, clean smoking.'

Malcolm nodded. 'Ah'm gonna smoke Craven A when ah'm bigger.'

'So am I,' replied Dave. 'Mind you, ah'm bigger now.'

Riding her bicycle on the back road from Kirkby Steepleton, Lily passed Twenty Acre Field. Two men were completing the thatching of the hayricks to protect the precious straw over winter. The season was changing and the villagers were checking their woodpiles in preparation for a long, cold North Yorkshire winter.

It was Wednesday, 15 October and in the hedgerows teardrop cobwebs shivered in the bitter wind and the red hips of dog roses were a forerunner of darker days ahead. Lily's face glowed with health as she raced along and, as she cycled towards Ragley High Street, russet leaves blew across the road, while goldfinches pecked at the seeds of the tall teasels.

Lily dismounted at the school gate and walked up the cobbled drive. As she parked her bicycle the Robinson boys appeared, smelling of cigarettes and looking guilty.

'Have you been smoking?'

'Oh 'eck . . . yes, Miss,' confessed Dave.

'Well, at least that's an honest answer.'

'Yes, Miss,' agreed Dave.

'You know what Mr Pruett will do, don't you?'

'Yes, Miss.'

'What did he say about smoking?'

'It'll be t'cane, Miss,' said Dave. Secretly he was thinking there was a rule for teachers and a rule for pupils. He recalled seeing the headteacher smoking by the open window of his office.

'We wanted t'be like 'im, Miss,' said Malcolm forlornly, holding out the magazine cutting of the England footballer looking relaxed with his cigarette.

Lily took it from him, studied it and considered the power of advertising.

'Boys, on this occasion, if you promise not to smoke again, I'll let you off.'

'Thank you, Miss,' said Dave and Malcolm nodded vigorously.

'Come to my classroom at playtime and I'll give you some work to do.'

The boys breathed a sigh of relief and ran off.

In John Pruett's class, after the children had chanted their tables, it was time for handwriting practice. John poured the precious black ink into twenty inkwells and made sure every child had a wooden pen holder with a broad metal nib. Then everyone was issued with a square of blotting paper and a sheet of lined paper.

'Now I want you to copy this poem in your best handwriting.' The children stared at the blackboard. The lines of William Wordsworth's famous 'Daffodils' had been written neatly in white chalk. 'I wandered lonely as a cloud,' it read, 'that floats on high o'er vales and hills.'

Reggie Bamforth put up his hand. 'Please, sir.'

'Yes, Reggie?'

'What's a vale please?'

Edie Stubbs shot her hand in the air. 'Please, sir!'

'Yes, Edie?' said John, encouraged by the girl's positive response.

'It's what m'big sister 'ad t'cover 'er face when she got married.'

Good try, thought John.

For the next half-hour the children toiled laboriously over their attempts at copperplate writing. They all knew to take extra care. Pushed in the wrong direction, the nib would spray tiny spots of ink over their work, so they wrote a single word very carefully and then dipped the pen in the inkwell once again. Using blotting paper was fun. After pressing it on the damp ink, the writing appeared reversed. Mr Pruett told them if they held it up in front of a mirror they could read it again the right way round. Sadly, there were no mirrors.

During the few minutes before morning playtime there was time for a few more demanding mental arithmetic problems. The various units of imperial measures were chanted repeatedly. 'Sixteen ounces in a pound,' they chorused, 'twenty-two yards in a chain, eight furlongs in

a mile,' and so on. Finally John collected his cup of tea and
went out on the playground to supervise playtime.

In the staff-room Vera had prepared a pot of tea. News
of the end of tea rationing at the start of October had been
well received and meant unlimited 'cuppas' for the first
time in twelve years. Major Gwilym Lloyd George, the
Minister of Food, had announced an improvement in sup-
plies of tea since the end of the war. However, rationing
would continue for sweets, eggs, butter and sugar.

Vera settled down to read her *Woman & Home* magazine. It had been a shilling well spent and came complete
with articles on sewing, embroidery, knitting and crochet.
There were exciting transfers between the middle pages
on the theme of fairies and she wondered how she might
use them. Vera also wondered why Lily had not arrived
for her morning beverage.

Lily gave Dave and Malcolm a large sheet of paper, a pencil and some coloured crayons.

'Now, boys, I want you to draw something interesting
you have done today . . . and that doesn't include smoking,' she added, resisting a smile.

Dave looked forlorn. He was hopeless at drawing,
whereas Malcolm was thrilled. He loved art and the detail
in his sketches was always a joy to behold.

'I'll be back at the end of playtime,' said Lily and
walked out.

'Bloody 'ell,' muttered Dave.

'Hooray!' said Malcolm, picking up his pencil with a
smile. He knew exactly what to draw. That morning, high
in one of the tallest trees near Mrs Uppington's house, he

had spotted something that looked like a tiny alien space-craft. It was hanging from a topmost branch and completely out of reach. He had wondered what it might be.

It was almost twelve o'clock and Joseph had completed his lesson with the older pupils. His talk on 'Creation' had proved demanding, but at least the persistent Edie Stubbs appeared animated.

'Well, ah believe in God an' 'eaven an' suchlike,' she declared.

'That's wonderful,' said Joseph with a beatific smile. Perhaps the lesson hadn't been a failure after all.

Edie frowned. 'Jus' that – y'know . . .'

'What?' asked a perplexed Joseph.

'Y'said 'E created t'whole world in less than a week an' that teks some believin'.'

'Oh dear,' said Joseph, 'and why is that?'

'Well, m'dad's pigeon loft took over a fortnight.'

Joseph's shoulders slumped.

'An' there's summat else, Mr Evans,' added Norman Fazackerly.

'Yes, Norman?' asked Joseph a little wearily.

'Where do babies come from?'

A flurry of hands went up. 'Ah know,' shouted Eddie Brown. 'My mam says t'stork delivers 'em.' He held up a picture from his reading book. It showed a stork flying among fluffy clouds in a sunlit blue sky. In its bright-yellow beak it was carrying a new-born baby wrapped in a big white blanket.

'Well, my dad sez 'e found me under a gooseberry bush,' said Celia Etheringshaw with utter conviction.

Norman looked concerned. 'Ah wouldn't like that wi' all them thorns an' sharp prickles,' he retorted.

'Well, ah *know* where they come from,' said Winnie Pickles with an assured smile, 'an' 'ow they mek 'em.'

The bell rang and Joseph hoped his sister had made a pot of camomile tea.

It was lunchtime and Lily was showing Malcolm Robinson's drawing to Vera. 'He has a wonderful talent, don't you think?'

'Definitely,' agreed Vera. 'Mr Pruett, do look at this excellent drawing.'

John put down his fountain pen and picked up the colourful sketch.

'It's Malcolm's impression of Chauntsinger Woods this morning. Apparently the boys climb trees there,' said Lily.

John studied it carefully and then stood up suddenly. His face was ashen.

'Vera, Lily, please don't be alarmed, but I have to go out of school.' He was staring at the drawing. 'This may be urgent.' He glanced up at the clock. 'Lily, please ring the bell and gather all the children in the hall.' He turned to Vera. 'And the registers need to be checked to ensure everyone is present. Keep them together and don't let anyone leave until I return.'

'Of course,' said Vera, immediately recognizing the seriousness of the situation but not knowing what it might be.

John took out a notebook from the top drawer of his desk and riffled through the pages, then picked up the receiver.

'Where are you going?' asked Lily.

'To Chauntsinger Woods.' He held up Malcolm's drawing and pointed to the carefully drawn shape in the treetop. It looked like a tin can with metal wings.

'This is exactly the shape of a wartime explosive device.'

Lily stepped back. 'You mean . . . a bomb!'

'Yes,' said John. 'If this drawing is accurate – and, knowing young Malcolm, I suspect it is – then this is a *butterfly* bomb.'

Without another word, Lily and Vera hurried out as John dialled a number.

'Bob – John Pruett here, and this may be urgent.'

Captain Bob Hastings immediately recognized the voice of his old colleague. 'Good to hear from you again, John. How can I help?'

'There is a possibility two of my pupils have come across an SD2 in the local woods.'

'An SD2? A butterfly bomb?'

'Exactly.'

'It's inevitable there are still a few scattered around in inaccessible places.' There was a pause. 'John, I'll muster a couple of my team and we'll be with you in thirty minutes. What's the location?'

'Here in Ragley village, the woods at the end of Chauntsinger Lane.'

'I know it. Beyond the blacksmith's.'

'That's right. In the meantime I'll contact the local police to cordon off the area.'

Tom Feather answered his telephone on the second ring and listened intently to John's message. 'I'll come now with

Harry and I'll need the two boys to tell me the exact location.'

The children were gathered in the hall getting on with writing and drawing. Vera had checked off every name and the school cook, Mrs Irene Gubbins, was helping to supervise.

'So are you saying that during the war John was in bomb disposal?' asked Lily.

'Yes,' said Vera, 'he was in the Royal Engineers, a member of the bomb disposal section. It's well known in the village, but he tends to keep the details to himself.'

'It sounds to have been very dangerous work,' said Lily.

Vera looked thoughtful. 'I remember reading that the life expectancy during the war for these men was sixteen weeks.'

Suddenly Lily was seeing the quiet, unassuming head-teacher in a new light. 'So we're lucky he survived,' she said quietly.

'Yes, we are,' said Vera. 'I remember being up at Morton Manor a few years ago and Captain Forbes-Kitchener mentioned that in nineteen forty there were ten thousand involved in this work and almost five hundred were killed. Apparently the anti-handling devices dropped by the Luftwaffe were deadly.'

Out of the high arched window Lily could see John at the school gate talking to Tom Feather and Harry Dewhirst. The constable was making careful notes while Tom and John questioned Dave and Malcolm. The two boys were pointing towards the High Street. Finally, John walked with the Robinson boys back up the school drive and into the hall, where he left them with Lily and Vera, then he rejoined the policemen and set off towards Chauntsinger Lane.

'Please let them be safe,' whispered Lily.

Vera squeezed her hand gently. 'Don't worry – good will prevail.'

PC Dewhirst began knocking on doors and Mrs Uppington was taken away with the other residents as Captain Bob Hastings arrived with two members of his bomb disposal team. John told them the location and they made their way into the wood. The boys had given perfect directions and soon the men were staring at a rusted metal canister high in the trees.

'It's been out of sight for years,' said Tom.

John looked thoughtful. 'They keep turning up, like bad pennies.'

Captain Hastings took out his powerful binoculars and studied the device carefully. Then he passed them to John Pruett. 'Like old times, John.'

There was a serious expression on John's face as he stared up into the branches. He nodded briefly. 'An SD2, Bob, no doubt – but which type? That's the question.'

'Usual procedure,' said Bob in a matter-of-fact tone. He turned to his colleagues. 'Get the sandbags and two lengths of the thin rope.'

The two young soldiers leaped into action.

'What can I do?' asked Tom.

'You need to go back to help Harry,' said John, 'and make sure no one approaches.'

Tom realized it was sensible advice and walked away.

Captain Hastings turned to the Ragley headmaster. 'John, you don't need to stay.'

'You might need me,' he replied quietly.

Bob looked at his former colleague and recognized the determination in his face. There had been many times in the past when their lives had hung by a thread. 'You of all people know the risks,' he said.

John nodded towards the two men stacking a circle of sandbags under the tree. 'Do they?'

'They're the best I've got.'

John said quietly, 'They look so young.'

Bob put his hand on John's shoulder. 'We were once.'

John closed his eyes for a moment and recalled the horrors of war. The faces of friends long gone flashed through his mind. Then he sighed. 'I'm staying,' he said simply.

It was a matter of minutes for the athletic soldiers to climb the tree and, with the greatest care, tie a length of string to the spindle above the casing of the bomb. It was a well-rehearsed procedure. Next, a second string with a noose in the free end was looped around a branch. The first string attached to the bomb was then threaded through the noose. Then the two soldiers stood at the base of the tree, one of them holding the taut string as if his life depended on it . . . which of course it did.

The critical moment had arrived.

'Our turn now,' ordered Bob Hastings in a commanding voice.

There was a moment's hesitation as the two young men realized their captain and the quiet, unassuming civilian were about to complete the most dangerous part of the procedure.

With infinite care John grasped the string and took the weight of the bomb. 'Mine now,' he said. The soldier released his grip and took a step back.

Bob Hastings stared up as the bomb swayed above their heads. 'You two stand back,' he said quietly to the soldiers beside him. With infinite patience John lowered the bomb towards the ground while Bob guided the descent inch by inch. They knew that one slip now would be their last.

There was a moment when the string snagged on a branch and the bomb revolved like a spinning top, but John's grip never wavered until finally it was lowered gently to the circle of sandbags. From a distance the two soldiers watched with grudging respect as the quiet man in the three-piece suit completed the operation with consummate skill.

'Back ten,' murmured Bob, and he and John retreated to a safe distance with careful, measured steps. All was silent apart from the crunching of leaves beneath their feet, while a shaft of sunlight flickered through the treetops. Then came a controlled explosion, with everyone at a safe distance, and by mid-afternoon all was calm and back to normal.

Bob Hastings told Tom Feather that it would be wise to cordon off the area while a thorough search was completed. Then he shook hands with John. There were few words, merely a shared respect and harsh memories of a conflict that had taken its toll. Both men had ended the war clearing British beaches of emplacement mines that had been put there in case of invasion.

Harry Dewhirst was left to guard the cordoned area while Tom and John walked back to school. 'Eventful

times, John,' said Tom. 'Now back to the day job,' he added
with a grin.

'What time do you get off duty?' asked John.

'Five o'clock,' said Tom.

'That's an hour before opening time at The Oak. We
could celebrate with a drink.'

'You're on,' said Tom. 'See you then.'

At the end of school Lily telephoned Mrs Merryweather
in Kirkby Steepleton to ask her to let her mother know she
would be late home. Millicent offered to drive to Ragley to
give Lily a lift rather than have her cycle in the dark. Lily
said she would let her know. She also telephoned Vera,
but couldn't persuade her to set foot in a public house.
However, she did ask Lily to congratulate John Pruett on
his action and commended the brave bomb disposal team.

Meanwhile, news had travelled around the village and
Big Dave and Little Malcolm had become local heroes. A
reporter from the *Easington Herald & Pioneer* appeared on
their doorstep for an interview and photograph. In Ragley
it was destined to be the main topic of conversation for
weeks to come and Malcolm's drawing was exhibited in
the village hall.

At six o'clock Lily walked with John across the village
green, where the welcoming lights of The Royal Oak
shone brightly. Tom, now out of uniform in baggy flan-
nels and a thick sweater, was waiting outside. The three of
them found a quiet table by the bay window and John
bought two pints of Chestnut and a gin and tonic.

Lily sipped her drink and felt the tension ease. 'So
what's a *butterfly* bomb?' she asked.

John supped deeply on his pint, sat back in his seat and sighed. 'Well, there are three types. The first one explodes on landing, the second has a thirty-minute timer and the third explodes five seconds after the slightest disturbance.'

'Oh dear, what was this one?'

'Simply one that misfired – so not too dangerous.'

'If you know what you're doing,' added Tom with a wry smile.

'And why is it called a *butterfly* bomb?' asked Lily.

John gripped his pint tankard and stared into his beer. 'It doesn't look like a conventional bomb, not like a rocket with fins. It has a cast-iron cylindrical body about the size of a baked bean tin. Then they're covered with a pair of curved flaps that resemble a butterfly's wings.'

'But that would attract children – just like David and Malcolm,' said Lily.

'Yes, they were often brightly coloured for that reason. However, this one was worn with age and simply looked like a rusty can.'

'That's horrific!' said Lily.

'That's war,' murmured Tom.

There was silence while the enormity soaked into Lily's consciousness.

John lowered his voice. 'The Germans used them to bomb Cleethorpes and Grimsby. They dropped dozens of them in a container from an aircraft. At a pre-set height they all fell out, then the force of the rushing air opened up the wings. After that they revolved like sycamore keys and floated to the ground while a turning screw activated the bomb. Inside there's about four and a half pounds of high explosive.' He took another drink of beer and looked down at the tabletop. 'The killing radius is about eighty feet.'

'I heard they were almost impossible to diffuse,' said Tom.

'Yes, it was difficult,' agreed John. 'So we made sure the whole town was closed down and there was a news black-out. We didn't want the Germans to be aware of the dreadful impact of this kind of bombardment.'

For a while they sat in silence until, after Tom had bought another round of drinks, they relaxed.

Lily looked at her wristwatch. 'Millicent Merryweather offered me a lift.' She stared out of the window at the darkness beyond. 'I shall have to telephone her. I don't want to cycle back in the dark.'

'I can take both of you back home,' said Tom. 'It's the least I can do.'

John looked across at Lily, a hint of disappointment on his face. 'That's kind, Tom, but I can walk – and one day I may own a car of my own,' he added with a forced smile.

The three left together, each with their own thoughts.

The following morning Lily stared out of her window at the trees and fields beyond Kirkby Steepleton as the dawn light crested the distant hills. Spiders had spun their webs outside her bedroom window. Beads of moisture hung from the silken threads and glistened in the sunlight, while in the hedgerows harvest mice were weaving their nests. The tiny creatures of the land were busy on this autumn morning.

For Lily another day of teaching stretched out before her, but the man she worked alongside was now different in her eyes. He was clearly a brave man. However, it was Tom who was beginning to fill her thoughts. Last night when they parted he had asked if she would like to go to the cinema.

She had smiled and said simply, 'Perhaps.'

Chapter Five

Goodbye Mr Hitler

It was Friday, 7 November and a reluctant light spread across the land. As Lily stared from the window of William Featherstone's bus a cloak of mist shrouded the fields beyond the hedgerows. A tractor was in Twenty Acre Field, ploughing neat furrows and making a pattern of chocolate-brown lines over which cawing birds swooped noisily.

As the bus entered Ragley village liquid rainbows reflected in the oily rainwater on the forecourt of Victor Pratt's garage. On this iron-grey morning Lily had private thoughts and almost by habit she opened her handbag and took out a familiar creased black-and-white photograph. Finally she gave a sigh of contentment. There were still bright promises on a distant horizon.

Lily stepped down from the bus on to the pavement and looked up as a parliament of rooks stared down from the high elms behind the village hall. Suddenly, as one, they flew off up the Morton road towards the tower of St Mary's Church and Lily stared after them. Then she turned up her collar and strode purposefully towards school.

It was the day before the village bonfire and there was eager anticipation for this annual event. A crowd of children had gathered in front of the window of the General Stores. On the shop door was a large notice:

The Village Hall Committee
RAGLEY VILLAGE BONFIRE
Saturday 8th November 1952
7.00 p.m. The Old Field
Bring your own fireworks.
Hot Soup & Tea (courtesy of Doris Clutterbuck)

In the window, large boxes of fireworks were on display under a sign that read 'Light up the sky with Standard Fireworks', along with a vast collection of loose fireworks on the shelf below.

'Cor, look at 'em, Malc,' said Dave Robinson. 'Catherine wheels, rockets, Roman candles, snow fountains, jumping jacks . . . an' bangers!'

'An' sparklers,' contributed Malcolm.

'F'little uns,' said Dave disdainfully, 'an' girls,' he added for good measure.

Malcolm nodded. He understood that, as in life, there was a pecking order to fireworks.

'Y'reight there, Dave.'

During morning break Lily was on the playground watching Norman Fazackerly and Reggie Bamforth exchanging cigarette cards that featured film stars and footballers.

There was some serious bargaining going on and Reggie was insisting that a single Nat Lofthouse was worth three of Joan Collins. Meanwhile Lily was thinking how she might capture this interest in a mathematics lesson.

It was then that a familiar police car pulled up alongside the avenue of horse chestnut trees just outside school and the tall Tom Feather emerged, stretching tired limbs. He was in his uniform and he pressed his large hands on the wall of Yorkshire stone and gave a cautious smile towards Lily.

She walked across the playground, wondering what to make of this man. There had been many silences between them, as if he weighed words carefully before he spoke them. He also had kind blue eyes and a gentle smile.

'Just checking,' he said quietly, as if he didn't want the children to hear. 'Still fine for tonight?'

'Yes, looking forward to it.'

He stretched his long arms and rubbed the back of his neck. 'Sorry, late shift last night.'

'So what time?'

'I could pick you up at six thirty. That gives us time to drive to York, park in Micklegate and walk to the cinema.'

'Fine, see you then,' said Lily and looked around anxiously. 'And I'm on duty, so must go.'

He waved as he climbed back into his car.

'Sit up straight, arms folded and silence, please,' said Lily.

It was lunchtime in the school hall and the children were staring at their plates. Mrs Gubbins had prepared her famous pease pudding. The split peas had been soaked overnight and she had served it up with a thick slice of boiled beef. A feast for most of the boys and girls.

'Now let's say grace. For what we are about to receive . . .'

In the staff-room Vera and John were drinking tea when Lily joined them after completing her dinner duty. Vera was reading a newspaper. 'Dear me,' she said, 'have you heard that average house prices in London have shot up to one thousand eight hundred pounds?'

'That's worrying,' said John, head bowed over some paperwork. 'Out of my range.'

Lily shook her head. 'Well, *I'll* never afford a house of my own on a teacher's salary,' she said.

Vera weighed her words carefully. 'Perhaps one day you may have a *partner* to share the cost.' It was meant to be a helpful addition to the conversation.

'I doubt that,' said Lily a little too sharply, and John looked up in surprise.

There were a few quiet moments while Vera riffled through the pages and John continued to read a lengthy document from County Hall about reducing winter temperatures in schools by conserving coal and coke.

Lily thought she ought to make amends. 'By the way, Vera, I've offered to help Mrs Gubbins in the kitchen tomorrow.'

'That's good news,' said Vera. 'Thank you. It's always a busy evening.'

'She says Mrs Clutterbuck is providing soup.'

'That's right,' said Vera, 'she always does. No doubt she will have her Saturday assistant with her.'

'Nora Pratt?' said Lily. 'I've spoken to her – a lovely girl.'

'It's such a pity she can't pronounce the letter "R",' said Vera.

John looked up. 'Yes, she was always like that – nothing we could do about it.'

Vera closed her newspaper and looked at Lily. 'When I was in the Tea Rooms, Mrs Clutterbuck mentioned you were going to the cinema with Sergeant Feather.'

It was a mini-bombshell.

Lily's cheeks flushed slightly and John stopped reading but didn't look up. 'I didn't realize it was open knowledge,' said Lily. 'It was only yesterday I said I would go.'

'And where were you at the time?'

'Outside the Pharmacy.'

Vera nodded. 'That explains it. Was the door open? If so, Mr Grinchley would have heard, so it will have been all round the village in no time.'

'I see,' said Lily quietly.

'Anyway, do have a lovely time,' said Vera, 'and I'll see you tomorrow.' She picked up her dinner-money tin, tidied her desk and collected her coat from the passage-way that linked the staff-room to the office.

John was very quiet, so Lily left him to it and walked into the hall to prepare for the afternoon music lesson.

Over the years John Pruett had scraped together a large collection of musical instruments and the Friday after-noon music lesson was always a treat for the children of both classes. They all assembled in the hall and the instru-ments were distributed among the older children while the younger ones were encouraged to clap their hands. For John it was a way of ending the school week in a posi-tive way and, literally, on a high note.

However, a pattern had developed regarding the allocation of instruments, with the boys *always* playing the drums and cymbals while the less popular triangles were left for the girls. Lily was determined to change this but had to overcome stiff resistance.

'But girls don't play drums, Miss,' protested Dave Robinson.

'They do now, David,' said Lily firmly and Winnie Pickles proceeded to show everyone why.

There was no pianist, but fortunately Lily had a sweet voice and she sang the first verse of 'The Skye Boat Song'. Within minutes the children knew the words. 'Over the sea to Skye' they sang with gusto.

Billy Icklethwaite put up his hand. 'Ah saw t'sea when we went t'Bridlington, Miss.' He was full of excitement at the memory. 'It went on for ever – right far out – 'til it got to t'sky.'

It was at moments like this that Lily felt she had the best job in the world. *Teach well*, she had been told during her training, *and you will touch lives for ever.*

The bell rang for the end of the school day and the one-week half-term holiday was about to start. The children walked out to the cobbled drive, excited at the thought of dark nights, fireworks and the annual village bonfire. John was standing in the entrance hall saying goodbye to the children.

'Have a good holiday, boys,' he said as Dave and Malcolm walked out of the door.

'Thank you, sir,' said Dave. 'We're goin' to t'pictures tomorrow morning.' The Saturday morning children's cinema was a huge attraction, with an admission charge of sixpence.

'And what are you going to see?'

'Loads, sir. There's Roy Rogers an' 'Opalong Cassidy an' Zorro an' cowboys fightin' Indians.'

'An' Tom Mix an' Flash Gordon,' added Malcolm.

'An' there's a comic album coming out at Christmas wi' 'em all in,' continued Dave.

'Well, enjoy it, boys,' said John and the cousins ran down the drive, galloping like Roy Rogers' famous horse Trigger.

Lily was a few minutes late and hurried out into the darkness where Tom was waiting. 'Sorry, it's been a bit hectic. I had to help get Freddie's tea. Mother was busy finishing some curtains for Mrs Merryweather.'

'Not a problem,' said Tom. 'We're in good time.'

Lily glanced at him as he opened the passenger door for her. He had brushed up well in a collar and tie, thick V-neck pullover and belted gabardine raincoat. There were knife-edge creases in his grey flannel trousers and the toecaps of his shoes shone like black glass. Against the fashion of the day, Tom disregarded Brylcreem and his wavy hair blew gently in the breeze. Lily approved of the natural look.

'I'm not sure I like being picked up in a police car,' she said with a mischievous smile. 'What will the neighbours think?'

'Probably that their local bobby is a lucky man.' He looked content as they set off for their ten-mile journey to York. 'You look lovely, by the way.'

'Thanks.'

'And you're right about the car.'

'I didn't mean to criticize.'

'Actually, I'm thinking of buying a car. I've been saving since the end of the war, a little bit each week. I should get there soon.'

'That's wonderful, Tom. What sort of car?'

'An Austin A30,' he said proudly. 'It was launched last year at the Earls Court Motor Show. I've seen all the pictures. They called it the New Austin Seven.'

'Impressive,' said Lily, although it meant little to her.

'Yes, and over sixty pounds cheaper than the Morris Minor, so it's a bargain.'

'Sounds ideal!'

Tom was becoming effusive. 'Yes, and there's plenty of room. It's a four-door family car.'

The silence that followed was deafening.

Tom parked near Micklegate Bar and they walked under the most westerly gate of York's city walls. The Odeon cinema was in Blossom Street and they joined the queue.

'What's the film?' asked Lily.

'Angels One Five,' said Tom.

'What's it about?'

Tom looked surprised. 'Sorry, I thought you knew. It's really popular and got great write-ups in the *Herald*. It's set during the Battle of Britain.'

Lily bit her bottom lip. 'Oh, I see,' she said quietly. 'A *war* film.'

The Odeon cinema was stylish, with an art deco interior, and Tom bought seats in the dress circle. It had opened in a blaze of publicity in 1937 when all 1,484 seats were sold out in ninety minutes. Lily was unaware that the fifteen-year-old Vera had attended on that opening night with her father and collected for the Poor Children Fresh Air Fund. On that long-ago evening it had cost sixpence for a cheap seat in the stalls. Two shillings for one of the best seats in the dress circle was considered an extravagance by her father.

Lily settled down to watch one of the most popular British films of 1952 as a dense pall of cigarette smoke drifted up to the ceiling. Tom explained that *Angels One Five* referred to an altitude of radar contact of fifteen thousand feet. The plot centred on a young fighter pilot immediately before and after the Battle of Britain in 1940. John Gregson's character, 'Septic' Baird, was mortally wounded and in a dramatic finale crashed to his death. Jack Hawkins played a fiercely patriotic group captain, 'Tiger' Small, while the other two stars were Michael Denison and Dulcie Gray. Lily had read a recent issue of *Picturegoer*, the national film weekly, and recognized these two. She whispered to Tom, 'They're married in real life. You can tell by just looking at them,' and Tom wondered why. The film also featured a beautiful young actress, Veronica Hurst. 'Her hair is like yours,' said Tom when the lights went up.

A fish and chip shop was across the road from the cinema and Tom took Lily's hand. 'Let's finish the evening in style,' he said with a grin.

'You know how to treat a lady.'

'Last of the big spenders, that's me,' joked Tom as they hurried inside. 'Four pennyworth of fish and chips twice, please.' He leaned over the counter and flashed a smile at the young assistant. 'With a few scraps, please.'

Lily smiled at the request.

The girl, red-faced from the heat of the boiling fat, shovelled an extra scoop of the batter bits from the pan and added them to the feast. Then she folded the two portions expertly in newspaper and handed them over the counter. 'Let's eat them in the car,' said Tom.

He put the parcel inside his coat to keep it warm and, on this cold night, he appreciated the heat on his chest. The car windows steamed up as they enjoyed their supper, while Lily recalled days long ago in the Land Army when a fish supper with all the girls was a special treat.

Back in Kirkby Steepleton, Tom walked Lily to her front gate and immediately spotted the twitching curtain.

'I think your mother is on lookout duty.'

Lily frowned. 'At my age that's embarrassing.'

'Anyway, thanks for coming,' said Tom. 'I hope you enjoyed it . . . and sorry if I picked the wrong film.'

'It was lovely,' said Lily without conviction. In truth she had hated the film and the glorification of war.

'Perhaps we can do it again sometime?' suggested Tom hopefully.

There was a silence as Lily pondered this new situation. He was a lovely man, but . . .

'And you can select the film,' added Tom.

Lily wanted desperately to say yes. 'It's complicated,' she said quietly.

'Oh well, the offer is there,' said Tom, not sure of where the conversation may be heading. 'Goodnight, Lily.'

There was an awkward moment as they stood facing each other. Finally Lily said, 'Goodnight, Tom.'

She hurried up the path and Tom watched her open the door. For a moment her slim figure was silhouetted in the bright light of the hallway, then the door was closed. The curtains twitched again as he turned and drove away.

It was Saturday morning and Lily had put on her warmest coat and was about to catch the bus into Ragley. She called upstairs, 'I'm leaving now, Mother. See you later at the bonfire.'

'Very well,' said Florence curtly. 'So it's up to me to bring Freddie this evening, I suppose.'

Lily had grown used to her mother's dark moods and unkind words. She recalled that her father had once said to her, 'Your mother is quick to chide and slow to bless.' That had been in happier times, when her father kept the peace in a troubled household. She pulled on her woollen hat and scarf and called out, 'I'll buy some fireworks for him, Mother, and keep them safe in school.'

When she reached Ragley, Big Dave was standing outside the General Stores next to a wheelbarrow in which a reclining figure was displayed and trying desperately to keep still.

'Penny for the guy, Miss,' he called out.

Lily studied the so-called guy and noted it looked remarkably like Little Malcolm in his father's cast-off boiler suit, thick gloves and a papier-mâché mask under a large balaclava.

Lily smiled. 'A wonderful guy, David,' she said. 'Pity

Malcolm isn't here to see it,' and behind the mask Malcolm's eyes blinked in surprise.

Dave rattled an old cocoa tin and Lily dropped in a coin. 'There,' she said, 'that should be enough to buy a firework for each of you.'

'Thank you, Miss,' said Dave.

'Thank you, Miss,' echoed the guy.

Emerging from the shop doorway was Prudence's delivery boy, fifteen-year-old Peter Miles-Humphreys. He had just loaded up the large basket on the front of his bicycle. Peter was a willing boy and Prudence knew her customers would make allowances for his unfortunate stutter, which added minutes to every transaction. He smiled shyly at Lily as he wheeled his heavy bicycle towards the road.

Lily walked under the green canvas canopy above the shop window and skirted round the pair of old wooden carver chairs that Prudence always put out for elderly customers. 'Good morning, Miss Golightly,' she said.

Prudence stepped up on to the next wooden step behind the counter. 'Good morning, Miss Briggs. A fine dry day for the bonfire. Exciting times for the children. Now what can I do for you?'

'A box of fireworks, please,' said Lily and Prudence stepped down and produced a selection from the shelf behind her.

With a box of Standard fireworks under her arm, the bell rang merrily above the door as Lily walked out and across the road towards the school.

On the village green PC Harry Dewhirst was working with the Ragley Scout troop under the supervision of the imposing figure of Captain Rupert Forbes-Kitchener.

They were busy making a guy for the village bonfire. The young policeman had become a popular figure in the village and the boys never misbehaved for the huge rugby player. He believed in the old-fashioned remedy of cuffing lads around the ears if they misbehaved. In this way he kept order and parents always welcomed his intervention as well as his unorthodox methods.

Meanwhile, in the vicarage Vera was making bonfire toffee apples. The radio was on and, while she dipped the apples into the sticky toffee, she hummed along to the heartbreaking opening of Schubert's Fantasie in F minor, one of her favourite piano duets. On the wall above the work surface was a colour picture of the Queen, neatly framed and taking pride of place in her kitchen. Vera was an ardent royalist and she recalled that wonderful moment in 1949 when she had been in the crowds that lined Stonegate in York. Princess Elizabeth had walked by close enough to touch as she toured the city accompanied by the mayor and, of course, the handsome Duke of Edinburgh. They were on the third day of their tour of the West Riding and it was etched for ever in Vera's memory.

Meanwhile, as she stood each toffee apple upside down to set on greaseproof paper, she wondered how the other members of the Women's Institute were faring in support of the Village Hall Committee. It was important that everyone pulled their weight in times of need.

In Morton Manor, another member of the Women's Institute, Alexandra Forbes-Kitchener, wife of the captain, was reading one of her old *Woman & Home* magazines. The recipe for vol-au-vent had worked perfectly, which merely left her wondering whether she should fill them with creamed chicken. While this was more to Rupert's taste, she thought something a little less exotic would be a more palatable choice for the evening soirée at the village bonfire.

After the birth of their daughter, Anastasia, Alexandra had been unwell frequently and she was not looking forward to venturing out on a cold evening. Meanwhile the vol-au-vent decision would not go away.

Her husband, Rupert, was in the General Stores. 'Half a dozen rockets, please, Prudence, and a few sweets for the young lads helping with the guy.' He put a ten-shilling note on the counter.

Prudence produced a bumper box of fireworks and two bags of sweets. 'There we are, Captain. That should keep them happy – liquorice torpedoes and mint imperials.'

He held up one of the rockets. 'We need to get the bonfire off with a good show, don't you think?'

'Of course, Captain.'

Next to him Vera Evans had arrived and was studying the headlines of the newspapers on the rack next to the counter.

'Look at that,' said Rupert, 'the population of Britain has gone up to fifty million.'

'A huge number,' said Vera. 'Hard to imagine.'

'We'll be too full if they let all these Jamaicans in,' said Rupert a little too forcefully.

Vera frowned. 'I'm sure they're fine, hard-working people,' she said.

'Ah well, er . . . yes, Miss Evans, I'm sure they are . . . as long as they have jobs and aren't a burden.'

'And they must feel the cold terribly,' added Prudence for good measure.

Tom Feather was on his way to the Pharmacy. He had spent the last hour working in the bonfire field with local farmhand Derek 'Deke' Ramsbottom.

Deke had arrived on his tractor, towing a trailer piled with old pieces of timber collected from various outbuildings in the village. There was enough for a huge bonfire and a few of the menfolk had gathered for this annual task. Deke had taken on the role of lead bonfire builder and, in his Stetson hat, leather waistcoat and sheriff's badge, he looked the part.

It was well known that the film star John Wayne was Deke's hero. He had been to the cinema twice recently, once to see *Rio Grande*, in which his favourite cowboy appeared alongside the smouldering Maureen O'Hara, and then to watch *She Wore a Yellow Ribbon*, filmed in glorious Technicolor. Deke tried hard to imitate John Wayne's famous walk, but only succeeded in looking as though he had an acute case of piles. Even so, the hard-working cowboy was giving his all to the cause of the village bonfire.

Sadly, Tom was struggling with a sore throat, hence his visit to the Pharmacy.

'Some throat sweets, please, Herbert,' he said.

'Of course, sir,' said Herbert. The Ragley chemist was always polite to the local law enforcement. He was also aware that Tom had taken the new teacher to the cinema. It was the talk of the village, mainly thanks to him.

'And ... maybe something for the weekend, sir?' he added in a conspiratorial whisper.

'Pardon?'

Herbert tapped the side of his nose. 'Y'know, Sergeant. Might come in 'andy.' He pointed up towards the boxes of Durex on the highest shelf.

Tom frowned and shook his head. 'Just the throat sweets, please.'

Herbert knew when a potential sale had died a death and passed over a packet of Victory Vs.

After helping Mrs Gubbins, Lily decided to take a break and walked across the road to Doris Clutterbuck's Tea Rooms. She was impressed with the genteel tidiness of the place. Small circular tables were covered with white tablecloths, a folded napkin had been placed under a dessert fork and next to a bowl of sugar with a silver spoon was a clean, shiny ash tray. A radio played in the background, as Doris thought it added a certain ambience to the tea-drinking experience.

She was served by the Saturday assistant, fourteen-year-old Nora Pratt. Nora was excited, but not about the bonfire. In her *Girl* magazine it said the first British singles chart was to appear next week and would list the most popular records. Nora loved music and dreamed of being a singer or an actress.

'Just a light snack, please,' said Lily.

'Well, ah'm sowwy, Miss Bwiggs, there's not much left,' said Nora. 'We've 'ad a wush on . . . but there's a beetwoot salad an' some fwesh bwead.'

Lily looked at the display cabinet. 'Just tea and a cake, please, Nora.'

Nora returned with a large teapot, a china cup and

saucer and a tea strainer. 'Fweshly bwewed,' she said enthusiastically, 'an' 'ere's a Swiss woll.'

There was a pile of old magazines on the table next to Lily and she picked up a *Woman's Own* and flicked through the pages. It looked expensive at 4½d, but there was a chance to win a guinea on the Letters page. Lily considered what she could buy with £1.1s – a huge sum. Then she read the winning letter and decided not to bother. A conscientious lady explained in detail how a broken button could be mended with sealing wax prior to making fresh holes with a needle. *I'd rather buy a new button*, thought Lily, and she sipped her tea while wafting away the cigarette and pipe smoke that drifted towards her. Everyone seemed to smoke and she wondered why she was different. It simply didn't appeal to her.

Doris Clutterbuck was regaling a group of ladies at the counter with a story about watercress. She had just cooked it for the first time.

What's watercress? thought Nora, who could of course *imagine* the letter 'R' in her thoughts without a problem.

It seemed as though the whole village had turned out for the bonfire. Freddie was waving a lighted sparkler while a concerned Florence and a delighted Lily looked on.

'I'll get a soft drink for him before the bonfire is lit,' said Lily and hurried over to the refreshment tent.

Tom was there and he came over to talk to her. 'Would you like a cup of tea?'

'I'm just getting a drink for Freddie.'

Tom saw the little boy standing next to Florence. 'I'll bring over two cups for you and your mother.'

Vera was at the other end of the trestle table with Doris

Clutterbuck, serving soup, and she looked up at Tom and Lily. As they walked away into the darkness Vera thought she was beginning to see Lily in a new light: perhaps this was the beginning of a shy attraction. *Who can tell how love begins?* she thought. *A glance, a touch, a smile, a word.* She wondered if it would ever happen to her and how Joseph would cope without her. Her brother was an innocent in a guilty world and she knew he wouldn't survive without her guiding hand.

Outside the refreshment tent Edna Trott and Irene Gubbins were sharing their thoughts.

'She's not backwards in comin' forwards, is that Miss Briggs,' said Edna.

'Y'reight there, Edna, y'wouldn't mess wi' 'er.'

'An' Mr Grinchley said 'e saw 'er wi' that nice-lookin' policeman what drives 'is own police car.'

'Fancy that,' said Irene.

''E reckoned 'e'd 'eard they were goin' to t'pictures in York.'

'Were they 'oldin' 'ands?'

'Ah think it's a bit early f'that, don't you?'

Irene recalled her courtship days. 'Not if 'e's owt like my 'Enry.'

In the circle of villagers standing close to the bonfire, Billy Icklethwaite was talking to Freddie. Lily returned with a cup of orange juice and Tom followed on with two mugs of tea.

'For you, Mrs Briggs,' he said with a smile.

Florence studied the tall policeman for a moment and offered a hesitant 'Thank you.' She frowned at Lily with a warning glance.

Suddenly Captain Forbes-Kitchener thrust a flaming

torch into the bonfire and the flames roared up towards the guy. The papier-mâché face with its black toothbrush moustache was an excellent likeness.

'Cor, look at that!' said Billy. 'It's 'Itler.'

'So it is,' said Tom.

Billy stared up at Lily. 'My dad 'ates Germans, Miss. 'E said 'e were captured an' put in a constipation camp.'

Lily looked thoughtful. '*Concentration*, Billy.'

Billy considered this for a moment. 'But ah am concentratin', Miss.'

Tom gave Lily a knowing smile.

'Do *you* 'ate Germans, Miss?' enquired the persistent Billy.

Lily sighed. 'Well . . . not *all* of them. There's good and bad everywhere in the world.'

'Are y'sure, Miss?'

'Yes, I think so.'

'Ah thought teachers knew ev'rythin', Miss.'

Lily smiled. 'No, not *everything*,' but at that moment her mind was elsewhere.

'Well, fancy that,' said Tom. 'Hitler on our bonfire.'

'Everything changes,' said Florence darkly.

There was a silence, broken only by the crackle of flames and the whoosh of a rocket.

'Except memories,' said Lily with a sad smile.

Tom moved a little closer to her. 'So it's goodbye Mr Hitler.'

Lily simply stared into the flames and thought of different times.

Chapter Six

Mr Pruett's Poinsettia

It was Friday, 12 December and Lily looked out of her bedroom window in Kirkby Steepleton. The first snow of winter had fallen and the distant land was covered in a white shroud. It curved in graceful folds over the combed ridges of the ploughed fields and all sounds were muted. A bitter wind rattled the wooden casements and frost patterns covered the panes. She pulled her dressing gown a little tighter and shivered as cold draughts seeped into the house. An eventful day lay ahead with the rehearsal for the school Nativity play, a hair appointment after school and the small matter of her twenty-seventh birthday.

Lily smiled and thought of previous birthdays during the war when she had been in the Land Army. They had been riotous times alongside young women who had since gone their separate ways, some to become GI brides in America, others to return to the towns and cities of England. Lily sighed as she recalled the many months of hard toil interspersed with a few days of joy. However, her silent reverie was soon broken as an excited Freddie ran into her room clutching a parcel.

'Happy birthday,' he shouted and jumped on to the bed.

Florence was standing in the doorway wearing a thoughtful expression. 'He couldn't wait, poor thing. He's been awake for the last hour waiting to come in.'

Lily gave Freddie a hug that seemed to last for ever and then she looked at her mother, whose face remained impassive and cold. No words were spoken, but a brief nod of acknowledgement passed between them. Florence walked in and sat beside Freddie on the bed. Lily ruffled his fair hair tenderly. 'Go on,' she said, 'open it for me. I know you want to.'

Freddie needed no second invitation to untie the string and rip off the brown paper. It was a woollen cardigan. 'Try it on, try it on!' urged the excited boy.

Lily took off her dressing gown and slipped it on over her nightdress.

'It's lovely, Mother. Thank you so much.' She stroked the soft wool and admired the pattern of flowers on the sleeves. 'I didn't see you making it. How on earth did you find the time?'

'When you were at school,' Florence stared down at her work-red fingers, '. . . and in the evenings when you were meeting *that policeman*,' she added pointedly. 'I suppose you'll be seeing him again tonight.'

Lily's jaw set in a determined fashion. It was a look Florence had come to know over the years. 'Yes, Mother, he said he would call by.'

Florence was becoming angry. 'So – are you going out

with him? You know that's the last thing you should be doing.'

'No, Mother, nothing is planned. I'm having my hair done after school as a treat and then I'm coming home to see you and Freddie – but I may choose to pop out later.'

Florence got up to leave. 'As long as you know what you're doing. Remember you have responsibilities here rather than fraternizing with a strange man.' She stopped by the door and wagged her finger. 'Don't forget. There will be a cake when you come home. You know how much Freddie enjoys blowing out the candles.'

The little boy looked up at Lily and she held him close.

'Candles!' he said and there was excitement in his eyes.

John Pruett stared out of his kitchen window at his new car. The previous week he had dipped into his savings and bought a 1946 Ford Anglia. It was a black two-door saloon and he had spent the weekend polishing it to a glassy shine. He was disappointed that it was now covered in snow.

The car was his pride and joy, and he was sure Miss Briggs would be impressed. He had given this much thought over the past few weeks. Above all he wanted her to see him as *more* than simply a professional colleague. In other words, he hoped he might be Lily's *friend* and, with a car, there was a chance he could compete with Tom Feather for her affections.

This was a new experience for John – a nagging ache that he didn't understand. *It can't be love*, he thought. That would be ridiculous – this was a feeling more akin to indigestion. Even so, he was aware that Lily had brought light into the shadows of his quiet life, colour into his mono-chrome existence. After school and away from his headteacher's desk he was occasionally tongue-tied in her presence and he didn't know why.

Also, it was her birthday and he had an idea. Even though the first snow had arrived during the night and the sky was an ominous grey, he thought of a way to brighten this special day. He would buy her some flowers.

Meanwhile, further down the Morton road, Joseph and Vera were in their kitchen eating toast liberally covered with Vera's prize-winning marmalade. The radio was burbling away in the background.

'That's interesting,' said Vera, suddenly animated by the latest piece of news.

'What is?' asked Joseph. His mind was elsewhere. After seeing the latest rehearsal of the school Nativity play he was concerned about the perceived lack of Christian con-tent. Billy Icklethwaite as the outspoken innkeeper had told the Virgin Mary, 'Sling yer 'ook sharpish 'cause my pub is full an' ah don't want no donkey crappin' in my tap room.' Perhaps a word in the ear of Miss Briggs would help, as John Pruett seemed preoccupied these days.

'It's at the Ambassadors Theatre, Joseph,' said Vera, 'and it sounds really good.'

'What does?' asked her brother through a mouthful of toast.

'The stage play of Agatha Christie's *The Mousetrap* has opened in London. We could book tickets in the new year after your busy Christmas schedule.' Vera was clearly excited at the prospect.

'What's it about?' asked Joseph with affected interest as he reached for a third slice and wondered if Vera had noticed.

'Well, a group of people gather in a remote part of the countryside and discover there's a murderer in their midst.'

'Oh dear,' said Joseph. 'Not very Christmassy.'

'But it's a *cultural* experience,' insisted Vera, 'and we could visit the museums as well.'

'Very well,' Joseph murmured through a mouthful of crumbs.

Vera got up to clear the table. 'And by the way, Joseph . . . that's your *third* slice.'

It was a quarter past eight and John and Lily had met in the staff-room to discuss the forthcoming Nativity play while Vera made a pot of tea. On the table was Vera's newspaper with a photograph of the Duke of Edinburgh, who had opened a £1.25 million extension to the Raleigh bicycle factory in Nottingham. Vera sipped her tea and read the article as she admired the handsome features of her perfect man, the Duke. 'It says here that bicycles are the transport of the future,' she remarked.

'We just need some cycle lanes,' said John, 'particularly with Stan Coe driving like he does.'

Lily looked up sharply. 'So was it Mr Coe who ran me off the road?'

John pursed his lips. 'Not proven, Lily . . . but very likely. I had a word with Tom and he said that Deirdre Coe would insist her brother was elsewhere on that morning.'

'I suppose she would,' said Lily.

'Well, they weren't riding their bicycles in London earlier this week,' said Vera. 'All those poor people under that blanket of thick smog.'

A week ago a killing combination of smoke and fog had descended on the capital, lasting for five days and causing thousands of deaths, while ambulance men and firemen had to walk in front of their vehicles.

'We need cleaner air,' said Lily. 'The government ought to control the way we pollute it. It's bad enough here, but in a city the size of London it's catastrophic.'

'I agree,' said John, 'but how do people keep warm in winter? What's the alternative?'

There was silence as they pondered the question.

Finally, Vera said, 'Well, regardless of the dreadful weather, I've brought in a small cake to share after lunch to celebrate Lily's birthday.'

John Pruett smiled. 'Well done, Vera, we'll certainly need it after the rehearsal.' Vera and Lily looked puzzled. However, they had yet to experience Billy Icklethwaite's contribution as the innkeeper.

At lunchtime John put on his coat, scarf and trilby hat and walked across the road to the General Stores, where Prudence Golightly was always pleased to see the local headteacher.

'Good afternoon, Mr Pruett. I imagine the children are pleased to see the first snowfall.'

'Yes, Prudence,' said John, 'they're loving it.'

'How can I help?'

'I should like to buy some flowers.'

'Of course,' said Prudence.

'Nothing too ostentatious,' he added nervously.

'I presume your sister is coming to visit?'

'Well, er . . . not until nearer Christmas.'

Prudence was rarely surprised by the requests of her customers, but this was the first time John Pruett had asked for flowers. She assumed they were intended as a gift for a relation, or perhaps a friend in hospital, but she didn't wish to intrude. 'Yes, while this is not the best time of the year for flowers, I may have the perfect solution. I order a delivery of these each December from the market in Easington and was just about to put them in the window.' She went into the back room and returned with a bushy plant in a pot. 'Here we are – it's a poinsettia.'

'Perfect,' said John.

Prudence smiled. 'It's a Mexican shrub and the ideal houseplant for Christmas. It should last into the New Year if it's looked after.'

'I'll take it, please.'

The tiny shopkeeper put it in a tall cardboard box and covered the leaves carefully with brown paper. 'There – that should keep it safe until you get it home.'

When John returned to school he put the plant on the passenger seat of his car to keep it away from prying eyes. He would give it to Lily at the end of school.

In the village hairdresser's Sylvia Icklethwaite was having her weekly shampoo and set and Diane Wigglesworth puffed on a cigarette while she sorted her box of rollers.

"Ow about a nice cuppa tea?' she suggested.

Soon two steaming mugs of tea were placed on the shelf beneath the big mirror and next to Diane's ash tray.

'So, any news, Di?'

'Well, ah've got Miss Briggs, t'new teacher, comin' in as m'last appointment t'day.'

'She's good,' said Sylvia. 'She sorted out my Arnold an' didn't 'ave t'use a cane.'

'Ah wonder what she does instead.'

'Keeps 'em interested wi' drawin' an' plays an' suchlike. In fac', my Billy's gorra big part in t'Nativity.'

'What's 'e like at actin'?'

Sylvia shook her head. 'Jus' like 'is dad.'

'As bad as that?' Diane looked in the mirror. 'So what's it t'be this week?'

Sylvia had picked up an old copy of *Woman's Own* from the pile of magazines and newspapers on the shelf next to the big mirror. It was the October edition and on page 21 a woman was having a luxurious facial involving creams and massage. 'What's a *facial*, Di?' she asked.

'Dunno,' said Diane. 'Sounds summat medical. Anyway, what d'you fancy?'

Around the edge of the mirror was a collection of front covers from *Picturegoer* magazine. They had been stuck on the wall with strips of brown sticky tape. Sylvia pointed to a photo of the shapely Joan Collins. 'Like 'er, please, Diane.'

A little while later Diane had sprayed Yorkshire Pale Ale as a setting lotion on Sylvia's hair and stood back to admire her creation. 'There y'are,' she said as she lit up another cigarette. 'Joan Collins.'

Sylvia nodded with obvious satisfaction. 'Ah saw t'eadmaster buyin' a fancy plant in the Stores,' she revealed.

'That's not like 'im,' said Diane.

'Ah got t'thinkin' it were probably 'is sister comin' t'stay.

She often does nearer Christmas an' gives 'is 'ouse a proper tidy-up.'

Diane nodded. 'That mus' be it.'

Half an hour later Diane's next customer arrived. Mrs Violet Fawnswater was a newcomer to the village. She had arrived from Leeds with her husband and seven-year-old daughter, Phoebe, an overindulged little girl with a passion for pretty dresses. Violet believed in turning out her daughter every morning to look like the child film star Shirley Temple. In fact, she had made the tuneless Phoebe practise singing 'The Good Ship Lollipop' until she was word-perfect.

Violet had moved from the Quarry Hill Flats development in Leeds city centre, where the Victorian slums had been replaced with a modern housing development including a shopping centre, nursery school and even a built-in refuse-disposal system. In consequence, she thought she was a cut above the country yokels in Ragley. Her husband had secured a management position, or so she described it, at the Rowntree's chocolate factory in York. She was also convinced Phoebe would be the obvious choice for the part of Mary in the school Nativity play.

'So, what's it t'be, Violet?'

Violet gave an extravagant sigh. 'Something different . . . something unique . . . something just me,' she said, almost bursting into song.

Bloody 'ell, thought Diane, *I've got a right one 'ere.*

The rehearsal for the Nativity play went surprisingly well. Lily had made sure all the children had a part, including five-year-old Lizzie Buttershaw, who was, literally, the star.

Phoebe Fawnswater had arrived with a beautiful blue dress and headscarf in order to be the perfect Mary. Billy Icklethwaite was delighted to be demoted from innkeeper to third shepherd and enjoyed giving Bertie Stubbs as fifth sheep an occasional thwack with his crook. Veronica Poole's rag doll was the stand-in baby Jesus and Reggie Bamforth, wearing a tea towel on his head and one of his mother's old dresses, made a sincere and convincing Joseph. Although a nervous Malcolm Robinson as the back half of the cow had to keep going to the toilet, it mattered little as only the front half, namely Big Dave, had to speak – or, to be more precise, moo.

'Thank you, Lily,' said John as the children returned to their classrooms. 'It looks like being the best yet,' and Lily wondered what previous performances must have been like.

Outside the General Stores, Vera was pleased to see that Aloysius Pratt and Tommy Piercy had cleared the footpath of snow. Even so, after buying a packet of tea for the staff-room she stepped carefully on to the frosty forecourt, where a large black hearse had just drawn up.

'May I 'elp you, Miss Evans?'

It was Septimus Bernard Flagstaff, the local funeral director, looking like a plump magpie in his black coat and gloves. Vera had always been intrigued by the name Septimus and had discovered he was the seventh child of a seventh child. Meanwhile, Septimus had made it clear that he worshipped the ground that Vera walked upon and Vera had politely rebuffed him at every turn.

'I'm fine, thank you,' she replied.

'Ah could give you a lift to t'vicarage, Miss Evans, if ah
may be so bold.'

'A lift?'

Septimus took out a large spotted handkerchief from
his coat pocket and polished a chrome headlamp with an
exaggerated flourish. 'Isn't she a beauty?' he said with
obvious satisfaction. 'She's the pride of our fleet, a nineteen thirty-seven Rolls-Royce Silver Wraith. Only the best
for Flagstaff and Flagstaff.'

'You have a *fleet*?' asked Vera.

'Well, er . . . we 'ave another 'earse, an old un.'

'I see. Well I appreciate the offer, but the walk will do
me good.'

'You would be very comfortable. It 'as a beautiful bench
seat. All t'coachwork were done by Alpe and Saunders
down in London. Top quality.'

'Well, I'm very pleased for you.'

Septimus saw his opportunity to impress. 'Ah'm tekkin'
this business t'places it's never been before. We packed in
'orse-drawn funerals after t'war an' came up t' date so
t'speak an' now ah'm a member o' t'National Association
o' Funeral Directors and t'Cremation Society.'

Vera was singularly unimpressed.

'M'busy time's comin' up,' he added eagerly. 'Winter
months are our bread an' butter when t'killin' cold sets in.
Old folk start droppin' like flies.'

'How very sad.'

'Not many people know this, Miss Evans, but ah'll tell
you as a personal friend.'

Vera frowned. She did not consider herself to be a *personal friend* of this loquacious little man. Also, her feet

were getting cold, but Septimus was on a roll. 'Ah'm a member of t'Stag Beetle Society an' one day ah may be president.'

'Stag beetles?'

'Yes, they're wonderful creatures.'

'I'm sure, like all God's creatures, they are indeed a blessing.'

'So would y'like t'see my collection?'

'Your collection? Are they dead?'

Septimus looked puzzled. 'Dead? Yes, o' course they're dead. Ah 'ave t'stick pins in 'em for m'display.'

'Oh dear,' said Vera, visibly shocked. 'In that case, no thank you.'

'Never mind, Miss Evans, ah know women can be a bit squeamish.'

Vera was beginning to feel unwell. 'Anyway, I need to get back to school, so goodbye, Mr Flagstaff.'

Septimus stared at the woman of his dreams as she walked briskly across the High Street. 'M'friends call me Bernie,' he said quietly to himself. It was then that he looked in the window of the General Stores and had an idea.

In Doris Clutterbuck's Tea Rooms Nora Pratt had returned from school and was in the kitchen polishing spoons. She had spent 3½d on a copy of *Picturegoer* magazine. The latest issue featured the film star Janet Leigh wearing nothing but a bath towel and Nora wondered if she could adopt the same pose.

Also, something new and exciting had happened in Nora's young life. The publication of the first UK singles chart in mid-November had been every bit as good as

Nora had hoped and she was pleased that the first number one, 'Here In My Heart' by the American jazz singer Al Martino, still held that position four weeks later. She was also happy that Vera Lynn had three records in the Top Ten, including Nora's favourite, 'Forget Me Not'.

She flicked through the pages and, after considering the various merits of Rock Hudson, or 'Mr Beefcake' as Mrs Clutterbuck preferred to call him, alongside David Niven, the debonair English actor, she decided the handsome American was her favourite. Nora still dreamed of acting stardom, though she knew her inability to pronounce the letter 'R' was a significant setback. However, Doris, as the president of the Ragley Amateur Dramatic Society, believed Nora's enthusiasm deserved some reward so had put this apparent impediment to one side and given her a part in the annual village pantomime.

For Nora it was the first step to stardom.

At the end of school John Pruett was walking through the entrance hall on his way to collect his gift for Lily from his car. Through the open door of the staff-room he saw Lily and Vera looking at a familiar plant and discussing it. He walked in and stared. 'It's a poinsettia,' he said in surprise.

'Yes, an ideal plant for Christmas,' said Vera with cautious enthusiasm. 'Mr Flagstaff called in and gave this to me. I don't wish to take it home . . . it wouldn't be appropriate. So I thought it would brighten up the staff-room.'

'I dread being given plants,' said Lily.

'Really?' asked John, suddenly crestfallen.

'Yes, I had one last Christmas and all the leaves fell off. I vowed never to have one again.'

'Never mind,' said Vera. 'Perhaps you just haven't got green fingers.'

John stared forlornly out of the window towards his car.

'Anyway, must rush,' said Lily. 'I'm getting my hair done and then my mother is preparing a birthday tea.'

Lily was aware that John appeared as if there was something important he wished to say. On occasions during recent days she had noticed him looking at her, just a glance, never a stare. In her presence he spoke less and smiled often. Although he kept his distance, he was never far away. It occurred to her that John had become a reassuring presence, a trusted friend – but, of course, never more than that.

'Enjoy your evening,' said Vera.

'Yes, happy birthday, Lily,' said John quietly.

It was a hasty farewell and after Vera had departed the school was silent. John sat at his desk and took out the school logbook. He unscrewed the top of his fountain pen and began to record the events of the day. There was no mention of a poinsettia.

The hairdresser's was empty apart from Diane when Lily walked in. Diane was sitting on a chair by the closed window smoking a cigarette. 'Hello, Miss Briggs,' she said. 'Come and sit down.'

'I get "Miss Briggs" all day at school,' said Lily with a grin, 'so please call me Lily.'

Diane stubbed out her cigarette and smiled in the mirror. 'Right then, Lily, what's it t'be?'

'Nothing special – just a trim. It's down to my shoulders now, so perhaps an inch or so.'

'You've got lovely 'air,' said Diane. 'I could do with your

picture up there.' She gestured with her hairbrush towards the collection of film stars.

'Thanks,' said Lily. 'Fortunately I don't have to bother with it much.'

'You're lucky. Most of my customers would pay a fortune for a 'ead of 'air like this.'

Lily settled back in the chair, enjoying the freedom from small children pulling at her skirt while she repaired kings' crowns and shepherds' crooks. Diane brushed her hair gently and then got to work with her comb and sharp scissors.

'So, how's Sergeant Feather these days?'

Lily knew the hairdresser's was famous for its village gossip. 'He's certainly a good policeman – so I've heard.'

Diane smiled. 'He's still a man though, Lily, an' they're all alike.'

It was Lily's turn to smile. Tom Feather was not like other men. *He was different.*

When Lily got off the bus in Kirkby Steepleton and walked home to Laurel Cottage a happy occasion was in store. Florence had worked hard with meagre rations to produce a fine party tea. Also, Freddie had made a card. It had a crayoned picture of himself holding hands with Florence and Lily.

'I wanted to draw Dad, but I couldn't remember what he looked like.'

Florence walked to the mantelpiece and took down a photograph in a frame. It was Arthur and Florence on their wedding day in 1924. 'He was a wonderful man, but Jesus wanted him to go and live with the angels in heaven.'

'Will Jesus send him back?'

'No, dear,' said Florence. 'He'll always be in heaven.'

'Will I get to see him again?' asked Freddie.

Suddenly there was a knock on the door.

Florence looked sharply at Lily. 'I think I know who that might be.' She glanced at the clock and shook her head. 'Late for a visit.'

Lily opened the door and Tom stood there in his uniform. 'Come in out of the cold,' she said.

'Only for a moment,' he said. 'Happy birthday.' He handed over a sealed envelope. 'Your card,' he added with a smile.

'Thank you,' said Lily and looked over her shoulder. 'We're just about to cut the cake. You're welcome to come in.'

'Sorry, I'm on late shift, but I wondered if you would like to go somewhere tomorrow, maybe the cinema again? There's a good film on. It's called *My Wife's Best Friend*.'

'What's it about?' asked Lily.

'I read the review in the *Herald*. It got a good write-up. Apparently, Macdonald Carey and his wife, Anne Baxter, are in a plane that is about to crash and he tells her he had an affair with a friend because he didn't want to die without confessing the truth . . . dramatic stuff.'

'That sounds terrible!' said Lily.

'Well, the good news is the plane lands safely.'

'So I suppose the moral is never tell the truth on your deathbed,' said Lily.

Tom sensed her disapproval and glanced at his watch. 'I'll have to go, Lily. We could go for a drink instead if you like.'

'Yes, the film's not really my cup of tea, so come round tomorrow evening.'

'Fine, see you then.'

There was the usual pause while he waited for Lily to make the first move, but her mind seemed elsewhere.

'Save me some cake,' he said with a smile as Lily opened the door and he went out into the darkness.

Back in the front room Florence and Freddie were sitting by the log fire.

'It was Tom,' said Lily simply and stood his card unopened on the mantelpiece.

'Thank goodness you didn't invite him in,' said Florence gruffly. 'Now, let's light the candles.'

When Freddie was about to blow out the candles Lily crouched down beside him. 'You should make a wish, Freddie . . . something nice.'

Freddie closed his eyes, then smiled and blew them out. 'I hope it comes true,' he said.

Lily stroked his hair tenderly. 'Don't tell us what it was, because then it might not.'

Freddie stared at the guttering candles. 'I hope it does, 'cause it was about Dad.'

For a few moments there was only the crackling of the fire as Lily hugged Freddie and a preoccupied Florence cut the cake.

Late that evening John Pruett was sitting in his favourite armchair reading a novel. The dying embers of the fire gave a solemn light to his sparse sitting room and he put down his book on the table. It was the recent novel *The Catcher in the Rye*, by J. D. Salinger, which had taken the book world by storm following last year's publication. John was enjoying the story and could relate to the issues of innocence, belonging and loss – never more so than on this lonely night.

On the small table by the window his new pot plant stood on a saucer. He had watered it thoroughly. Miss Golightly had said it would be fine if it was looked after. *Perhaps I care too much*, he thought.

He stared at his poinsettia and sighed as a scarlet leaf fell gently to the carpet beneath.

Chapter Seven

A Christmas Secret

It was Friday, 19 December, the last day of the autumn term, and the world had changed. When Lily looked out of her bedroom window more snow had fallen and the land was cloaked in silence. The countryside was still as stone and the prints of a midnight fox had patterned the smooth crust on the garden. In the distance the boughs of a mighty oak shook in the bitter wind.

She shivered in her dressing gown. There was so much on her mind – issues from her past, hidden now, a new man in her life and a job that she had begun to love. Freddie appeared settled and was content at Kirkby Steepleton Primary School. He had made friends and seemed a happy little boy. Meanwhile, another difficult journey to school lay ahead and she hoped William Featherstone's bus could negotiate the hazardous roads.

The final school day of 1952 in Ragley promised to be a special treat. There was to be a Christmas party and the children had been invited to bring in games to play during afternoon school. Lily looked in her wardrobe for her bright-red dress and Christmas cardigan. It was important for the children to see her looking cheerful. As she stared at her clothes she heard Florence's voice calling to Freddie. There was always an underlying tension in her mother. Lily felt there were problems that could never be resolved.

Half an hour later she was standing in the open doorway saying goodbye to Florence. In her thick coat, woollen scarf, hat and leather boots she was well protected from the cold. The cumbersome shopping bag she carried contained her party dress and shoes, plus some cards for the children in her class.

'Well, just look at that,' said Lily with a smile.

A familiar Ford Prefect had pulled up outside the cottage, clouds puffing from the exhaust pipe. Tom got out and swept fresh snow from his rear window with a gloved hand.

'Thought you would appreciate a lift on party day,' he called.

Lily smiled and waved back. 'Yes, please.'

'He's keen,' said Florence with a knowing look. 'Too keen.'

Lily blushed and raised her eyes. 'Oh, Mother. Tom is just being a good neighbour. It's merely a kind gesture.'

Florence said nothing and returned to the kitchen to help Freddie with his bowl of warm porridge. She scraped the bottom of the bowl and kept her thoughts to herself. Lily was either fortunate to have such a helpful friend or she was playing with fire.

Tom parked in Ragley High Street and Lily walked

across the village green. Her breath steamed before her as she reached the school gate and paused to take in the sight. Ragley School looked like a Christmas card, with a fresh fall of snow on the roof, frost patterns on the windows and icicles hanging from the eaves. Excited children were rolling snowballs, making snowmen on the field and sliding on the icy playground. No one seemed to mind the cold. These were hardy country children, used to an outdoor life.

Mrs Trott, in a coat and a headscarf, was sweeping the entrance steps. The biting wind appeared to have no effect on this tough lady.

'Mornin', Miss Briggs,' she said. 'Ah've turned 'eatin' up for y'party.'

'Thank you, Mrs Trott,' replied Lily and hurried into the relative warmth of the school.

It was a busy morning in her classroom and the children were excited. Above their heads paper chains stretched across the room. Earlier in the week Lily had brought in a small Christmas tree and every child had made a paper decoration to hang on the boughs.

Suddenly Bertie Stubbs called out, 'Look, Miss, a robin!'

John Pruett had erected a bird table just outside the window and the children stood on their chairs to get a better view. Mrs Trott had put a few scraps from the kitchen on to the table that morning and a bright-eyed robin was pecking at a crust. The children watched in fascination.

"E's 'avin' a good breakfast, Miss,' said Lizzie Buttershaw.

'Ah wonder if birds 'ave Christmas presents like us, Miss,' mused Daphne Cahill.

'What do you think, Daphne?' asked Lily, pleased that this shy girl had spoken.

Daphne blushed slightly, suddenly the centre of attention. 'Well, if they do, ah reckon they'll be different.'

'That's right, Daphne,' said Lily. 'Well done.'

'Like worms, Miss,' said five-year-old Arnold Icklethwaite.

'Or mebbe a mince pie,' suggested Veronica Poole.

Suddenly everyone was shouting out.

'Let's make a list on the blackboard,' said Lily.

After morning break John gathered all the children in the hall. He had been in the loft to bring out the old wooden Christmas post box.

'Now, children,' he said, 'we're all going to write a letter to Father Christmas and post it in our special post box,' and some of the older children shared secret smiles. 'All your letters will go to Santa at the North Pole.'

The children returned to their classrooms and were each given a sheet of paper and a pencil. Lily had written on the blackboard, 'Dear Santa, please may I have ...' and the children had copied it carefully followed by their requests.

Lizzie Buttershaw had asked for a dolly's tea set. Daphne Cahill showed her individuality and wrote, 'Dear Santa, there is a black doll in Woolworths. Please may I have one?' Veronica Poole requested a Noddy annual.

Phoebe Fawnswater had asked Santa for one of the new Rosebud dolls. She had seen one in York in a shop window and on the side of the box it read 'The World's Most Beautiful Doll'. For Phoebe, nothing less would do.

Meanwhile the older boys and girls in John's class were

a little sceptical about writing to Father Christmas but went along with the writing exercise. Reggie Bamforth spent a long time on his letter. He had set his heart on a model of the famous oceangoing liner, the steam ship *Queen Mary*, for 2/6d. He had drawn a wonderful picture and added, 'It's a bargain, Santa, for half a crown.'

Reggie was a true supporter of Father Christmas. When he had finished his letter he handed it with significant solemnity to John Pruett and declared, 'Ah know that Santa is real 'cause las' year ah got a bike an' my mam an' dad couldn't afford anything that expensive.'

All the letters were posted with great ceremony, followed by John Pruett insisting that only *good* boys and girls would receive a gift on Christmas morning. Finally, the morning ended with a newspaper-folding exercise resulting in every child wearing a pointed hat like a pirate.

At lunchtime Lily sat at a table next to Phoebe Fawnswater and Reggie Bamforth, who were keen to share their news.

'We're going to London at Christmas, Miss,' said Phoebe.

'That's wonderful,' said Lily. 'What will you do there?'

'We're going to see Bertram Mills Circus.'

'And Phoebe's mum has got one of those new television sets,' said Reggie, 'and she lets me go and watch.'

'That's good, Reggie,' replied Lily. She wasn't surprised that Mrs Fawnswater encouraged her daughter to play with this well-behaved and polite boy. 'What's it like?'

'It's really good, Miss, just like the cinema – but smaller and always in black and white. There's something called *The Flower Pot Men* that started last Monday – but they don't talk sense. Phoebe likes *Muffin the Mule* . . . but you can see his strings,' he added as an afterthought.

It was well known in the village that Mrs Fawnswater now spent many hours in front of her television and never missed the opportunity to watch *Come Dancing* and *What's My Line?*

A new world of entertainment, thought Lily. *It could catch on.*

In the afternoon the party was a lively affair. Elsie Crapper played Christmas songs on the piano and a group of mothers arrived to serve the crab paste sandwiches, biscuits and home-made lemonade. Ruby Smith had come in to help Edna Trott wrap a tiny gift for every child. They used tissue paper, pink for girls and blue for boys, then hung them with thread on the Christmas tree.

They played Statues, Musical Chairs and 'What's the Time, Mr Wolf?' amidst much screaming and shouting. By half past two the children were exhausted and the afternoon ended with them playing games in the school hall, mainly Lotto and draughts and with dolls' tea sets. Lily noticed these were now made of bright modern plastic instead of Bakelite.

After they had cleared up at the end of the day, John offered to take Lily back to Kirkby Steepleton and she accepted. When she got out he said, 'Happy Christmas, Lily,' and she wondered why he looked so sad.

It was Saturday morning and Vera was in her kitchen listening to the radio and wondering what it would be like to have a television set. She couldn't imagine life without her radio. Two years ago she had listened to the thousandth episode of *Woman's Hour* and last year had become an avid listener of a new programme called *The Archers*. She had no interest in other entertainment programmes such as Kenneth Horne's radio comedy *Much Binding in the Marsh*. These were trivial as far as Vera was concerned, while *The Goon Show* appeared incomprehensible. She had also listened to the ventriloquist Peter Brough with his puppet Archie Andrews in *Educating Archie*.

However, of much more concern than entertainment was the fact that she had noticed that in the vicarage they were running out of tea.

Sylvia Icklethwaite had called into the General Stores.

'Good morning, Sylvia,' said Prudence.

"Ello, Prudence. Ah'd like some o' them new triangle cheeses, please. My kids luv 'em.'

Kraft Dairylea Cheese Spread was a new product on the market and Prudence had soon discovered that eager shoppers were queuing up for them.

'It's all change these days, Sylvia – hard to keep up. I even heard from Mrs Fawnswater that they have *launderettes* in London.'

'Launderettes!' exclaimed Sylvia. 'That's a poor do,' she muttered, 'when them southerners can't do a proper Monday wash.' Her muscles flexed as she spoke. 'Anyway, must rush. We're busy on t'farm an' ah've got some castratin' t'do.'

Prudence winced visibly as the burly farmer's wife hurried out; she hoped she was talking about the livestock.

It was Christmas Eve and winter gripped Ragley village in its iron fist, while the land was still and silent. The boughs of elm and sycamore bent under the weight of the fresh fall of snow and the hedgerows sparkled with frost. Wolf-grey clouds hung heavy over the Hambleton hills with the promise of more snow, while a grudging light filtered through the skeletal branches of the trees and a new day dawned.

Ragley High Street was soon busy with the early-morning shoppers and Vera was collecting her Christmas order from the butcher's shop.

"'Ere's y'sausage meat, Miss Evans,' said Tommy. 'Finest sausage meat on God's earth,' he added without a hint of modesty.

'Thank you, Thomas,' said Vera cautiously, 'I'm sure it is.'

'You'll be at Midnight Mass no doubt,' said Tommy. 'Allus a special time.'

'Yes, I shall be there, although this snow makes it a little more difficult.'

Tommy shook his head. 'This is nowt but a dustin', Miss Evans. In t'winter o' forty-seven ah were up to me armpits shovellin' snow.'

Vera offered a gentle smile towards the curmudgeonly Yorkshireman who always believed that everything in his native county was bigger and better – or, in this case, deeper.

Next Vera called into Pratt's Hardware Emporium, where Aloysius served her with some new light bulbs. His son, Timothy, was in the back room. He had written a detailed letter to Santa via his parents requesting the prompt delivery of an Airfix construction kit of Sir Francis Drake's famous sailing ship the *Golden Hind* from Woolworths. It would be his big present, and he presumed it would be supplemented by a satsuma, some sticks of liquorice and a bag of nuts. He decided to list these as well. 'Success is in the detail,' his father had told him and young Timothy, if nothing else, was always thorough.

By five o'clock darkness had settled over the vast plain of York and the folk of Ragley village were gathering for their annual 'Carols on the Green'.

Tom had collected Lily in his car and Vera was delighted to welcome them both. She had been trying to encourage Lily to join the church choir. As a mezzo-soprano with a sweet, clear voice she would be welcome.

On the village green Captain Rupert Forbes-Kitchener had deployed some of his staff to erect a huge Christmas tree. It was his annual gift to the village and now it had been decorated with garlands of silver and a variety of colourful baubles. A circle of straw bales had been arranged around the tree to provide seating for anyone who needed it. Snow was falling as the carol singers gathered and the pantile roof of The Royal Oak was covered in wavy patterns.

Most of the men in the church choir had lamps on long poles, which they brought out every year. Tom Feather was holding a trimmed ash branch on which hung a hurricane lamp, which cast a flickering light on Lily's face. His lusty bass voice rang out and Vera smiled when she caught a glimpse of Lily standing alongside him. Clouds of silver mist hovered around their heads as they launched into the opening verse of 'In the Bleak Midwinter'.

It wasn't long before Mavis Higginbottom, the buxom barmaid from The Royal Oak, came out with a plate of mince pies and another with slices of cake, each topped with a sliver of Wensleydale cheese. Clarence, her husband and owner of the pub, followed behind with a huge jug of steaming mulled wine and a collection of cracked tumblers.

The carol singers gathered round and enjoyed the welcome treat.

'Lovely singing, Miss Evans, as always,' said Clarence.

'Thank you for your generosity,' said Vera, 'and you'll forgive me if I don't partake of your magnificent punch.'

Clarence was aware that no drop of alcohol ever passed Vera's lips and he smiled in acknowledgement. 'As long as you have some cake. Mavis makes a smashin' bit o' cake.'

Lily and Tom were enjoying the hot mulled wine and wondering what Clarence had added to give it a kick like a mule. 'Cheese with cake?' Lily wondered aloud, picking up a slice.

Tom grinned. 'It's a Yorkshire thing. You know what they say – fruit cake without the cheese is like a kiss without a squeeze.'

Lily opened her eyes wide in mock astonishment, but she was secretly pleased at the thought.

A few minutes later 'Hark the Herald Angels Sing' rang out around the village green.

At 11.15 p.m. it seemed as if the whole village was on the move, trudging through the frozen snow towards the bright lights of St Mary's Church.

Whirling snowflakes pattered against the huge oak door as Tom and Lily walked in. The pews were soon filled and a candle flickered on each of the ledges of the stone pillars. Green holly with bright-red berries had been attached to the lectern and Elsie Crapper played 'Away in a Manger' as the congregation settled down. Finally, the chief bellringer, Archibald Pike, tied off his bell rope and took his usual seat at the back of the church. Aloysius Pratt closed the door and a calm silence descended.

Then, unaccompanied, Mary McIntyre, a young soprano, sang the first verse of 'Once in Royal David's City' and the choir entered, each member carrying a candle as they walked down the aisle towards the choir stalls. Tom and Lily joined in the second verse and she smiled up at him. It was a fine Yorkshire Christmas occasion, with local farmers singing alongside members of the Ragley Women's Institute. Lessons were read and custom acknowledged: the pattern of the age-old service was woven into the tapestry of this special time.

Following messages of goodwill from the congregation, Tom drove slowly and carefully back to Kirkby Steepleton. It was a strange, eerie journey through countryside emptied of wildlife and still as stone. Eventually the car crunched to a halt a short distance from Lily's gate and they sat there in silence. The beech tree next door to Laurel Cottage meant that the car could not be seen from Florence's bedroom window and Lily smiled at Tom's forethought. Steam covered the windows and it was as if they were in their own private cocoon.

'Thanks, Tom. I appreciate the lift.'

He turned to face her. 'Any time.'

'My first Christmas in Yorkshire,' she said.

Tom rubbed the steam from the windscreen and stared out. 'I love living here.'

'Same here,' said Lily. 'It's my home now. I've moved on.'

'I'm glad you did,' said Tom softly.

'This time of year is so special,' said Lily and she shifted in her seat so she could look up at him. 'You'll be with your mother tomorrow.'

'Yes. Her brother, my uncle Don, and his wife are coming over from Scarborough. It's always the same – turkey, home-made crackers and paper hats. My mother loves it and slaves away all morning preparing the meal.'

'I'll be with my mother and Freddie, just the three of us. At times like this I miss my dad.'

He leaned towards her and stroked her hair. 'I understand.'

They sat in silence, each with their own thoughts, while outside ragged clouds drifted across the sky. The moon cast a cold pallid light and ghostly shadows danced on the walls of the cottage. It was a hunter's moon, bright and big, when the moon was closest to Earth.

'There's something I want to say,' said Lily and then there was a pause, followed by an imperceptible shake of the head. 'Perhaps another time.'

Her face tilted up towards Tom and he wanted to kiss her, but something held him back.

He wasn't sure.

Does she want to be kissed? he wondered.

If not now it may be never.

He stooped closer and she responded. Her lips brushed against his, light and gossamer-soft. He held her a little tighter, and finally there was an urgency to his kiss. In that moment Tom felt a new understanding between them. As snow began to fall once again, they held each other with the need of lovers.

On Christmas morning a rim of golden fire caressed the eastern hills and light raced across the frozen land with the promise of a clear, cold day ahead. Freddie had risen at the crack of dawn and was soon playing with his clockwork train set with Lily sitting alongside. Last night Tom had given Lily a parcel. As she opened it Florence looked on with undisguised interest. It was the new novel *The Borrowers* by Mary Norton, a children's fantasy.

'What a lovely gift,' said Lily.

'A children's book?' retorted Florence, clearly unimpressed.

'Yes, but it can be read by adults as well. It's just won the Carnegie Medal as the year's outstanding book by a British author. It's an excellent choice. How unexpected!'

After Christmas dinner Lily and Florence went into the lounge and switched on the radio.

'Well, this is it,' said Florence. 'I wonder if she's nervous?'

Queen Elizabeth II was about to make her first Christmas speech to the Commonwealth.

'Possibly,' said Lily, 'but no doubt she will take it in her stride.'

'Everyone in the land gathered round their radio sets – good luck, Your Majesty,' said Florence.

Lily looked at the clock. It was seven minutes past three and the reporter had said the speech would be coming live from Sandringham House. You could have heard a pin drop as the Queen began to speak in a calm, clear voice.

'Each Christmas, at this time, my beloved father broadcast a message to his people in all parts of the world. Today I am doing this to you, who are now *my* people.'

'Very regal,' whispered Florence.

'What's regal?' asked Freddie.

'Ssshh, I'll tell you later. Go and play with your train in the kitchen,' said Lily.

Freddie was happy to oblige.

'As he used to do,' continued the Queen, 'I am speaking to you from my own home, where I am spending Christmas with my family.'

'Isn't it wonderful, Lily?' said Florence. 'It's as though she was here in our front room.'

The Queen went on to ask for people to pray for her on Coronation Day next summer and, finally, the broadcast came to an end and the radio was switched off.

'A job well done, Your Majesty,' murmured Florence.

That evening Lily and Florence sat by the fire after Freddie was tucked up in bed. Two tall white candles stood on either end of the mantelpiece with sprigs of variegated holly at their base. Bright-red berries twinkled in the candlelight.

'Another Christmas, Mother,' said Lily quietly.

'Will we be happy here?' asked Florence. Her hands were gripped around her cup of tea.

'I think so,' said Lily guardedly. 'We know where we stand.'

'You mean we know what can be said and what must never be said.'

'How could I forget?'

'As long as we understand each other,' said Florence. Her glance was keen in the firelight. 'Remember our secret, Lily. Never forget it.' There was a hint of menace in her voice.

Lily stared into the flames . . . and thought of Tom.

Chapter Eight

Doris Clutterbuck's Alpine Corset

It was New Year's Eve and in the apartment above the Tea Rooms Doris Clutterbuck looked critically at her new figure-enhancing garment. On the leaflet inside the parcel it read, 'Alston's Rubber Reducing Body Garment'. As the star of the village pantomime, Doris was determined to look shapely and she knew her purchase would be perfect. At £2.2s it had definitely been expensive, but she knew that quality came at a price and so she read the instructions carefully. It said that the girdle had a nine-inch zip for 'the fuller figure', and Doris stared at her reflection and smiled. She had sent her waist and hip measurements and enclosed an extra threepence for swift postage, so it had arrived just in time.

The annual pantomime was only a few hours away and excitement was building for Ragley's Amateur Dramatic Society – but especially for Doris. With the help of her new body garment she knew that, even at the age of fifty-five, her Cinderella would be her *tour de force*.

However, once she had struggled into it she could barely breathe. Then came the moment of truth. Over the top she added her magnificent Alpine leather corset. While last year it had proved a snug fit for her Snow White, it had clearly shrunk over time. She couldn't fasten up the toggles and threw it back in the wardrobe in despair.

For fourteen-year-old Nora Pratt, it was also an important day. This was her first step towards stardom. Nora had been a member of the Ragley Amateur Dramatic Society for two years and her promotion from ensemble non-speaking parts in previous performances was well deserved. She never missed a rehearsal, and as she cleaned the tables and folded the napkins in the Tea Rooms she rehearsed her two lines. She had been given the part of Fairy Nuff, assistant to the Fairy Godmother, and she had to run on and say:

> 'Fairy Godmother! Fairy Godmother!
> Here comes Cinderella.'

Unfortunately, when Nora ran on in rehearsal to utter her two lines, she always recited:

> 'Faiwy Godmothe'! Faiwy Godmothe'!
> He'e comes Cindewella.'

However, Nora knew not only her own lines but everyone else's as well. She had lived and breathed this performance of *Cinderella* and could recite every scene. In consequence, her moment of stardom was about to arrive in an unexpected way.

*

In the Kershaw household on the council estate all was not well. Fred, the local coalman and the Ragley Rovers centre forward, had injured his left knee in the recent game against Thirkby United.

'Ah can't stand up, Mam!' he cried out as he limped into the front room and lay down on the sofa.

'Shurrup, y'big soft jessie,' yelled his father from the kitchen.

Alfie Kershaw, the Ragley coal merchant, was not a man blessed with compassion. For Alfie there was little to choose between *empathy* and *apathy*. However, as neither word was within his limited vocabulary, he was happy uttering short sentences with clear meanings.

'Ah won't be able t'be in t'panto,' groaned Fred.

'Jus' as well, y'big nancy,' shouted Alfie, who disapproved of his son's theatrical tendencies.

His mother, Edie, pulled up one leg of his trousers. 'Bloomin' 'eck, Fred,' she said with feeling, 'it's swelled up like a football!'

'An' it's 'urtin' like summat else, Mam.'

'Don't worry, luv, it can't be 'elped. Ah'll rub on some goose grease an' then ah'll go round to Doris an' tell 'er they'll 'ave t'get someone else t'play Buttons.'

'Bloody Buttons,' mumbled Alfie.

'Shut y'cake'ole y'useless lump,' yelled Edie.

Alfie knew when to keep quiet. He weighed sixteen stones and was built like a Russian weightlifter, but in the Kershaw household Edie ruled the roost.

The afternoon was bright, clear and cold as Lily caught the bus into Ragley village. She had volunteered to assist

Vera with the preparations for the pantomime. As the bus trundled along, she stared out at the frozen fields streaked with the grey shadows of the bare trees. The hedgerows were rimed with frost and sparkled with a diamond light as the low shafts of sunlight lit up the land.

As Lily stepped on to the frosty pavement outside the General Stores she saw the coal merchant, Alfie Kershaw, delivering to Prudence Golightly. Alfie had bright eyes shining from a face blackened with coal dust and gave a wide, white-toothed smile. He heaved a hundredweight bag of coal on to his shoulders and, with a bent back, staggered round to the coal shed at the rear of the shop.

Miss Golightly came out to pay him and placed a mug of strong sugary tea on the trestle table in front of the shop window. It was a regular arrangement that worked like clockwork and Alfie was always grateful for the kindness of the diminutive shopkeeper, especially as now his son was incapacitated and all today's deliveries had landed, literally, on his broad shoulders.

Neither Prudence nor Lily heard him mumble, 'Bloody Buttons!'

Lily walked up the High Street towards school. There was a box of dressing-up clothes to deliver to the village hall. As she crossed the village green in front of The Royal Oak the clamour of the rooks caught her attention and she stared up into the high elms.

'Penny for 'em, Miss Teacher.' Stan Coe gave her a brown-toothed smile as he climbed out of his Land Rover. It was splattered with mud and dirty snow. The boxy body had been made from army surplus rustproof aluminium and painted Avro-green, and the four-wheel drive was perfect for the rough terrain around his farmhouse. Stan imagined himself as an army general when he drove his powerful vehicle.

The sign 'Spitting Prohibited' on the wall outside The Royal Oak was always ignored by Stan, and he cleared his throat and spat out an obnoxious gobbet of phlegm.

'Better out than in,' he muttered and Lily winced in disgust.

This really was a revolting man and his attentions were becoming unsettling. She unlocked the school door, collected the box of clothes and walked back down the High Street.

On the other side of the village green she heard the familiar hoarse cry of 'Rag-a-bone! Rag-a-bone!', accompanied by the ringing of a bell. Tommy Kettle was a regular visitor to Ragley and he had parked his horse and cart outside the village Post Office. Tommy wore a cloth cap, checked shirt, leather waistcoat, old thick corduroy trousers and boots with steel toecaps.

So began a regular village ritual. Mothers and small children would hurry out with bundles of old clothes and blankets. Tommy would check them with an experienced eye and offer a shiny sixpence or a goldfish. The mothers wanted the money and the children wanted the exotic golden fish. Meanwhile, Maurice Tupham, the champion rhubarb grower, would always appear with a shovel and a bucket to collect the horse manure.

Tommy gave Lily a cheerful smile and a wave as she walked into the village hall.

Outside The Royal Oak, Ruby Smith had arrived at the same time as Deirdre Coe. Deirdre had decided to join her brother for a lunchtime drink, whereas Ruby was about to begin her cleaning in the pub while Agnes looked after young Andy.

Deirdre looked at the departing figure of Lily. 'She's a reight *prima donna* is that Miss Fancy Pants,' she said. 'You mark my words.'

'Well, ah think she's a lovely lady,' retorted Ruby defiantly.

Deirdre turned on Ruby with venom. 'Why don't you sling yer 'ook an' get back t'yer council estate?'

'There's no need t'talk like that, Deirdre. Ah'm jus' doin' a bit o' cleanin' f'Mrs 'Igginbottom.'

Every penny counted for the young Ruby. Her income was a long way short of the £5 per week the newspapers said the average woman earned.

'An' another thing,' continued Deirdre, 'ah wouldn't give time o' day t'that 'usband o' yours.'

'Ah love my Ronnie in spite of 'is faults,' retaliated Ruby.

'Well ah'm not be'olden to any man,' declared Deirdre, ''cause hindependence is a wonderful thing.'

'Anyway, m'cleanin' won't wait, Deirdre,' said Ruby and she walked in.

Deirdre, who always wanted the last word, shouted after her, 'An' ah'll tell y'summat f'nothin', Ruby Smith – ah got a posh new cooker at Christmas for our turkey.' It was well known in the village that Deirdre had taken delivery of a British National Electrics cooker, regarded as a wonder of the modern world. 'It 'as a drop-down door an' it's clean 'cause it's all helectric.'

Mavis Higginbottom behind the bar had heard the

fracas. 'Tek no notice of 'er, Ruby. She's all bosom an' bark is that woman. Wants lockin' up.'

Ruby went to collect her bucket and mop. Mavis called after her, 'Anyway, Pete's been in so there'll be a bit o' lovely stew when you've done, an' y'can tek some back f'your Andy.'

Peter the Poacher had just delivered a squirrel and a couple of partridges. As always, he took his payment in kind and was enjoying his second pint of Tetley's bitter.

Lily had arranged to meet Vera in the Ragley village Tea Rooms prior to helping in the village hall. The dress rehearsal was at three o'clock and many of the schoolchildren were in the chorus line. Vera knew this was a big day for Doris Clutterbuck and had volunteered to act as prompter for the pantomime. It was well known that several of the cast regularly forgot their lines, much to the annoyance of Doris.

Behind the counter was a large poster that read:

Ragley Amateur Dramatic Society
proudly present

CINDERELLA

starring Doris Clutterbuck
in the Village Hall on Thursday, 31st December 1952
commencing 7.00 p.m.
Admission: Adults 6d Children 3d

When Lily walked in the American crooner Al Martino was singing 'Here In My Heart' – still topping the new charts as the UK's first Christmas number one.

Doris smiled when she saw the attractive, well-dressed teacher and felt she added much-needed class to her establishment. Lily unbuttoned her winter coat to reveal a pleated grey skirt, smart blouse with a tiny collar and a red woollen cardigan knitted by her mother.

'Good morning, Miss Briggs, please take a seat and my assistant will take your order.'

'Thank you, Mrs Clutterbuck,' said Lily. 'I'm meeting Miss Evans here in a few minutes, so we'll order then.'

'Yes, that's fine, and I do appreciate you helping out with the children. It can be rather hectic at times.'

She leaned over the counter and nodded towards Nora Pratt, who was polishing a set of dainty sugar spoons by the table in the corner. 'It's Nora's big day. She has a speaking and singing part. I'm so pleased for her – and she's word-perfect of course.'

Lily sat down and looked at the locals, mainly ladies drinking tea and eating cake. Many wore neat little hats and one had a fox fur draped around her shoulders. All seemed to enjoy sharing their news. It made Lily think of the female friends she had had when she was a Land Girl. Now, with the exception of Vera, there was no one she could call a true friend. There was her mother, of course, but that had become a strained relationship in recent years.

She sat back and stared out of the window, then her heart gave a leap as a familiar police car drove past down the High Street towards the York road. Tom Feather was a fine man and she knew she wanted him. She also knew she could never confide in him completely, but, even so, her emotions stirred at the thought of his strong presence.

Her thoughts wandered. Now her dreams were like seeds on the wind, blown to faraway places. All that was left were shadows of a distant past, a secret garden where for a brief time youth had flowered.

Suddenly the bell above the door rang and Vera came in, smart and businesslike as always, and, in the words of Doris, 'my most elegant customer'.

'Good morning, Lily,' she said, sitting down. 'Have you ordered?'

'No, I was waiting for you,' said Lily. 'Is it just tea? It's just that I've seen some tasty crumpets on the far table,' she added with a smile.

'My word, that takes me back,' said Vera.

'Really?'

'Yes, you see Doris is trying to model this place on the famous Bettys Tea Rooms in York. You must try it. It really is a wonderful place. I went with my father back in 1932 as a young girl and you could order a four-course lunch for two shillings. I recall there was a lady dressed just like Doris, in a white apron, and she would bring a three-tier cake stand full of pastries and crumpets. It was such a treat, especially when I finished up with a curd tart.'

'What a wonderful memory,' said Lily. 'Yes, I must go to Bettys.'

Vera looked thoughtful. 'I didn't approve at first because on the shop sign there's no apostrophe in Bettys . . . but life is never perfect.'

Too true, thought Lily.

Vera picked up the menu and began to read. 'Perhaps your policeman will take you,' she added. She had recently purchased some pince-nez spectacles in the style of her fictional hero, Hercule Poirot, and she peered over them knowingly.

'Perhaps,' said Lily quietly. 'Shall we order?'

Vera beckoned to Nora Pratt, as Doris was busy with a feather duster. Three pottery ducks in full flight adorned the wall behind the counter and she dusted them every day. A wedding gift many years ago, they reminded her of her husband, Eric, who had flown the nest with a young and plump professional cheese sculptor who toured the country with her bizarre creations. In consequence, Doris rarely ate cheese and had become an independent and fulfilled lady with her prestigious Tea Rooms and her prominence in the Ragley Amateur Dramatic Society. Meanwhile, she looked upon Nora as the daughter she had never had.

Nora was wearing a smart white apron and a hat that looked like a sailor's. She took out her notepad and licked the tip of her small pencil. 'What would you like, Miss Evans, Miss Bwiggs?' she asked politely.

Vera smiled at Lily. 'Crumpets and tea for two please, Nora – and good luck tonight.'

'Thank you,' said Nora. She glanced up at the clock on the wall above the three flying ducks. 'Dwess wehea'sal at thwee o'clock.'

'We'll be cheering you on,' said Lily.

'Cwumpets an' tea comin' up,' said Nora and hurried off to the kitchen.

Ruby's mother, Agnes, had asked the next-door neighbour to look after Andy while she dragged an old iron bedstead down the road.

''Ere y'are, Tommy. 'Ow much?' Agnes never minced her words.

'T'usual, Mrs Bancroft: sixpence or a goldfish.'

'Sixpence please, Tommy. A goldfish don't buy me a loaf o' bread.'

He handed over a coin. ''Ow's your Ruby?'

'She's in a reight dickie-fit. Ah've never seen 'er in such a state.'

'Why's that?'

''Cause o' that lazy, good f'nothin' 'usband. Spends all their money on beer an' t'bettin' shop.'

Tommy shook his head. 'A shame – she's a lovely lass is your Ruby. She should've tekken up wi' that George Dainty, but ah 'eard 'e's gone t'Spain t'seek 'is fortune.'

'Y'reight there. 'E were broken 'earted when she took up wi' Ronnie.'

'She missed out, Mrs Bancroft,' said Tommy, shaking his head sadly.

Agnes sighed. 'Thanks for t'sixpence, Tommy, an' 'ere's a carrot f'Goliath.'

Tommy's giant shire horse, the lugubrious Goliath, looked up with sudden interest and crunched the proffered carrot with his tombstone teeth while Agnes hurried over to the General Stores.

When Vera and Lily walked across the road to the village hall they met Joseph speaking with the funeral director, Septimus Flagstaff.

'Hello, Joseph,' said Vera.

'Oh, hello, Vera. We're just discussing the funeral of Mr Grimble. It's next Saturday.'

Lofthouse Grimble had been a church bellringer. Sadly, his lungs had been damaged in the Sheffield steelworks and he had only had time for a short retirement before he died. His wife, Pearl, was a member of the church cleaners, the Holy Dusters, and a trusted friend of Vera. Lofthouse and Pearl had lived in a tiny cottage on the Morton road and many mourned his passing.

'Fine lady, is Pearl,' muttered Septimus. 'Tekkin' it all in 'er stride.'

'Yes, I'm sure she is,' said Vera a little curtly.

Joseph looked at his wristwatch. 'I have to go now, Vera. I promised to see Mrs Grimble,' and with that he hurried up the High Street.

'Can I be of assistance, Miss Evans?' asked Septimus.

'No, thank you, Mr Flagstaff,' said Vera. 'We're here to help with the pantomime.'

'My friends call me Bernie,' said Septimus with a shy smile.

'I imagine they do, Mr Flagstaff,' replied Vera. She had no intention of partaking in instant informality with the Ragley funeral director.

In the village hall the dress rehearsal was going well and Lily was looking at the cast list on the revised programme. It had been written on a large blackboard that had been propped on an easel in the entrance. It read:

Cinderella – Doris Clutterbuck
Prince Charming – Ivy Speight
The Wicked Stepmother – Betty Cuthbertson
Buttons & Fairy Nuff – Nora Pratt

Fairy Godmother – Violet Fawnswater
Wicked Stepsister – Valerie Flint
Lord Chamberlain – Ernie Morgetroyd
Baron Hardup – Peter Miles-Humphreys

It was clear from the outset that Violet Fawnswater as the Fairy Godmother was trying to steal the show. However, Doris was used to dealing with theatrical upstarts and soon put her in her place. The plot slowed considerably when Peter Miles-Humphreys, the stuttering shop boy, had to deliver his few lines as Baron Hardup. Valerie Flint, the tall, stick-thin teacher, was as fierce on stage as the Wicked Stepsister as she was in the classroom, while Betty Cuthbertson as the strangely cheerful Wicked Stepmother was simply there for the free tea and cakes. Nora, meanwhile, had been thrilled to discover that not only was she playing her original part of Fairy Nuff, but was now also in the important role of Buttons.

'Let's take five,' said Doris in true theatrical tradition. As the cast sloped off to enjoy a cup of tea, she tapped Nora on the arm. 'Come with me please, Nora,' she said quietly. They walked into the back room behind the stage where old furniture was stored. Doris picked up a small battered suitcase. 'This is for you.'

Nora was puzzled.

'Open it,' said Doris.

Nora knelt down and opened the metal catches. She lifted the lid slowly and stared in awe. It was the Alpine leather corset that Doris had worn for many years.

'It's your turn to wear it, Nora. Your time has come.'

'That's weally kind,' said Nora. She held it up. 'It's the

best Chwistmas pwesent I've ever had. Can I dwess up in it tonight?'

'Yes, it's yours now, Nora. You've earned it,' and she gave Nora a hug.

When Nora repacked the suitcase and walked back into the hall, Doris stared after her with tears in her eyes. It was a symbolic moment, for Doris knew her days as a leading lady were over.

At 7 School View Ruby heard a knock on the door. She stopped feeding Andy and went to see who it was. She was met by a familiar face: it was Barry the Brush.

Barry was born and bred in Cardiff and had lost a leg in the Second World War. Somehow he had finished up in North Yorkshire. A popular, gregarious figure, he would travel around the local villages and come door to door every fortnight with his lilting Welsh accent and a suitcase of assorted brushes.

Ruby could ill afford any extra demands on her meagre housekeeping, but always took pity on the polite young man with one leg. While he was drinking a mug of sweet tea in the kitchen, she stared at a garish hairbrush that she couldn't afford and a practical toilet brush that she could barely afford. Common sense prevailed – at least Ruby's version – and she bought the toilet brush for a few meagre coppers and sent him on his way. She was a good-hearted lady.

Ronnie Smith came into the kitchen and sat down. A familiar cigarette was hanging from his bottom lip and he gave Ruby a bleary-eyed smile. 'Ah jus' need a few bob t'tide me over 'til tomorrow, Ruby luv.'

Ruby picked up her purse nervously and looked inside. 'Ah've not much, Ronnie, jus' what Mrs 'Igginbottom gave me f'cleanin'.'

'That'll do, luv,' said Ronnie, holding out his hand.

Ruby gave him a shilling. 'That's not enough,' said Ronnie. 'Ah need 'alf a crown.'

'Thing is, Ronnie, we need soap powder so ah can wash our Andy's nappies.'

Ronnie gave her a furtive glance. 'Y'know what crossed m'mind this mornin'?'

Ruby was suddenly curious. 'What's that?'

'Ah were thinkin' ah'll tek you t'London one day.'

Ruby's eyes lit up. 'That's where t'Queen Elizabeth lives in 'er palace, Ronnie, an' all t'posh people buy nice things in Hoxford Street. Ah saw 'em in a magazine when ah were 'avin' m' 'air done.'

''Xactly, Ruby, y'spot on there. Y'deserve a treat.' He paused. The moment was right. 'So, can ah 'ave that 'alf crown then, my luv, jus' 'til Friday?'

As Ruby handed over the precious coin, Ronnie never mentioned which Friday that might be.

Lily had spent the remainder of the afternoon with Vera at the vicarage until it was time to return to the village hall for the pantomime.

This was one of the highlights of the Ragley calendar and there was a queue outside on the pavement when they arrived. Elsie Crapper was on the door collecting the shiny sixpences and the threepenny bits, while Florence had arrived with Freddie in Mrs Merryweather's car.

Doris Clutterbuck was on her usual form and there was

a cheer when she made her first dramatic entrance. However, the greatest accolade of the evening undoubtedly went to Nora Pratt.

'This is your opportunity,' said Doris. 'Grasp it with both hands and meet your destiny.' Doris always got a little carried away when she was dressed up like a dog's dinner.

So it was on that cold December night the slim, petite Nora stood on stage in her frilly dress and the treasured Alpine corset. Although it was a little loose on the teenage shop assistant, the strategic addition of baling twine had tightened up the garment and added greatly to Nora's otherwise modest ensemble. She took a deep breath and began to sing the Judy Garland classic from the 1939 film *The Wizard of Oz*.

'Somewhere over the Wainbow,' sang Nora in a sweet voice. Doris, at the side of the stage, sighed. *Not quite what I was hoping for, but perhaps the audience won't notice*, she thought.

There were a few titters from the footballers in the back row, pint pots in hand, but the rest of the villagers thought Nora had done a good job doubling up as the Fairy's assistant plus the demanding role of the cheerful Buttons. So when she sang, 'And the dweams that you da'e to dweam weally do come twue,' you could have heard a pin drop and there wasn't a dry eye in the house. Here was one of their own trying her best, and as one they rose from their seats and applauded.

At the end Doris received a large bouquet and then, as the lights came on, the audience drifted out to their New Year festivities. Following a conversation with Tom, Lily approached Florence. 'Mother, Tom has asked me to join him for a New Year drink in The Royal Oak and then he's offered to drive me home.'

'And what did you tell him?' Florence answered sharply.

'That I would discuss it with you. I told him we usually put Freddie to bed and see in the New Year together over a glass of sherry.'

Florence stared at her daughter and felt the pain of a mother. 'To be honest, I'm rather tired, so you go if you wish. I'll see to Freddie.'

'Are you sure?'

Florence gave Lily a hug and held her hands. She spoke quietly. 'You have a fine mind, Lily, rather like your father . . . but you also have a warm heart. So do take care how you use it.'

'What exactly are you saying, Mother?'

'Merely that I don't want to see you hurt.'

Florence avoided saying more, but the unspoken words hung in the air between them like a sip from a poisoned chalice.

There was a long silence.

Finally Lily squeezed her mother's hand. 'I understand.'

As Lily walked away into the darkness, Florence recognized the eager anticipation in her daughter's confident demeanour and sighed. It brought back painful memories.

Later, in The Royal Oak, Tommy Piercy played the piano and the locals sang along. Eventually Lily glanced at her wristwatch. 'It's almost half past ten, Tom. I ought to be getting home. Thanks for the drink.'

Tom sighed. He had enjoyed the last hour with this

beautiful woman and he didn't want to say goodnight just yet. He took a deep breath. 'My mother is in Scarborough seeing in the New Year with her brother and his wife. You could come back with me if you like – just a nightcap and see in the New Year.'

'No, I need to get back,' said Lily guardedly.

'There's a spare room in the cottage,' he added hastily – perhaps too hastily.

For a moment Lily stood deep in thought and her eyes were soft with sorrow. A night with her handsome police-man was an inviting proposition.

'What is it, Lily?' Tom was concerned.

She sighed. 'Just thinking about this and that. Nothing to worry about, Tom, but thank you for asking.'

When they finally got back to Laurel Cottage they kissed briefly before Lily hurried into the house. The church clock was chiming midnight as Tom arrived back at his empty house in silence, dreaming of what might have been.

Meanwhile, in her tiny room above the Hardware Empor-ium, Nora stared at her Alpine corset hanging behind the door. It was her badge of office and a mark of her new status in the theatrical world.

In the front parlour of the Tea Rooms, Doris was sip-ping tea as the fire burned low. She had unzipped her new body garment and was comfortable in her favourite armchair in the flickering light. She thought back on the day and recognized this important moment in her life, when her Alpine corset had been passed on to the next in line. In a few years she would retire and the mantle of responsibility would go to Nora Pratt, her *protégée*, and the Alpine leather corset would have a new lease of life.

The show must go on, thought Doris as the church bells chimed out twelve times.

A new year had dawned and 1953 stretched out before her.

Chapter Nine

A Tale of Two Televisions

It was Monday, 5 January and the land was still and
sepulchral – a white world, silent and cloaked in snow.
The cold was bitter, almost savage, and all sound was
muted while the creatures of the countryside sought ref-
uge. Lily waited at the bus stop as each unique snowflake
feathered lazily to the ground to join its neighbours, cov-
ering the main street of Kirkby Steepleton in a white
shroud. She glanced up. Above her head the high-pitched
keening of the single telephone wire was a strange, eerie
sound, like the cry of a baby, and Lily pulled her woollen
hat over her ears. An unknown destiny stretched out
before her and she wondered where it would lead.

Soon she was huddled in a seat with a few familiar passengers in the steamy warmth of William Featherstone's
bus, staring out of the window at a spectral vision of sky,
trees and snow. The dawn light revealed a strange world.
During the night the wind had scoured the drifts of snow
to form an alien landscape of curves and ridges. Only the

spiky heads of cow parsley pierced the smooth crust. As she sat there she thought of Tom. He was a regular visitor now at Laurel Cottage, much to the displeasure of her mother.

Eventually the bus arrived in Ragley High Street, a silver ribbon of ice between the desolation of the frozen hedgerows. Inside their homes, the villagers were stoking log fires, while a pall of wood smoke had settled on the pantile roofs, so that when Lily stepped on to the pavement a malodorous mist hung heavy and with every breath icy fingers froze her bones.

As she walked up the school drive she saw John Pruett. The snow on top of his car had settled like flour on a newly baked loaf and he was sweeping it off with a gloved hand. Together they walked into the school office, where Vera was admiring her new calendar. She had cut out a page from her *Woman's Own* magazine. It was a beautiful coloured portrait of the Queen above a calendar for 1953, which she had mounted on a piece of card and hung on the wall behind her desk. 'Perfect for the office, I think,' she said with a satisfied smile.

'I agree,' said John with moderate enthusiasm. 'Very useful.'

'It's a lovely picture,' said Lily, eager to show support for Ragley's most ardent royalist.

'Would you like a cup of tea?' asked Vera. 'I've prepared a pot as I have some exciting news.'

'Yes, please,' said John and Lily in unison. This was clearly something of import.

'It arrived on Saturday right out of the blue,' announced Vera, while John and Lily hung up their coats, scarves and hats. Vera proceeded to draw out the suspense as she poured two cups of tea. Then she added milk from the jug, along with John's regulation two spoonfuls of precious sugar.

'Well, what is it?' asked John, warming his hands on the cup.

'Joseph has rented a television set from a shop in York. It's a trial offer.'

Lily was astonished. 'You have a television?'

Vera smiled. 'Yes. I can't say I was too pleased at first, but it turns out that it has its merits and the news is similar to the cinema.'

John sipped his tea thoughtfully. 'So, along with Mrs Fawnswater, we now have *two* televisions in the village.'

'What's it like, Vera?' asked Lily. 'I've seen one in a shop window in York but never close up.'

'You must come to the vicarage this evening and see for yourself – both of you.'

John and Lily went off to their classrooms to share the news with the children. '*Two* televisions,' said John. 'Who would have thought it?'

It was just before morning break when Vera saw Mrs Violet Fawnswater driving carefully in her Austin A40 over the frozen snow and into the car park. Vera walked out to meet her in the entrance hall.

'Hello, Miss Evans,' she said. 'I'm here to collect Phoebe for the dentist.'

'Yes, Miss Briggs has her ready for collection in the classroom.'

'She was so excited about the circus.'

Vera's response was neutral. 'I'm sure she was.'

As usual, Violet was keen to impress. 'Yes, we went to London and saw the Bertram Mills Circus.'

'Really? It's good, isn't it?' said Vera.

'Oh – so you've been?'

'No,' said Vera with calm assurance, 'I watched it on television last night. It was the programme just before *What's My Line?*'

Violet's eyes opened wide in surprise. 'You have a television set?'

'Yes, Joseph brought it home on Saturday.'

'We have a nine-inch screen,' said Violet proudly.

'Yes, so have we, but Joseph also has a magnifying glass that slips neatly in front of the picture.'

'A magnifying glass?'

'Yes, it increases the picture size to a full twelve inches.'

Violet was aghast at the thought. 'But that's huge!'

'I suppose it is,' said Vera, unwilling to elaborate further but enjoying putting this boastful lady in her place. 'Anyway, must get on. Lots to do.'

Violet looked after her, feeling that since there were now *two* televisions in the village her importance had been reduced by fifty per cent.

At lunchtime Vera called into the General Stores with her shopping list.

'A tin of Nescafé, please, Prudence, and a bag of sugar.'

Prudence looked surprised. 'Coffee, Vera?'

Vera sighed. 'It's for the staff-room . . . and it appears Miss Briggs has a liking for *American* drinks.'

'I see,' said Prudence. 'Changing times.'

'Indeed,' added Vera with a knowing nod. 'And Mr Pruett has taken to preferring it to his usual cup of tea.'

'Where will it all end?' murmured Prudence. She studied the side of the tin. 'It says here that it's composed of coffee solids and powdered with dextrins, maltose and dextrose added to protect the flavour.'

'Goodness gracious, that sounds ominous! Whatever next? It will never catch on and, if it did, poor Mrs Clutterbuck would have a heart attack.' Vera looked down at her neat list. 'And a tin of Cherry Blossom Boot Polish.'

'Would you like to try the new shade, dark tan? It's proving very popular.'

Vera looked surprised. 'Brown shoes, Prudence? I don't think we have any.'

'Is there anything else, Vera?'

'There is something,' said Vera. She lowered her voice. 'Joseph has brought home a *television set*.'

'Goodness me!' It took a moment for Prudence to recover. 'You must let me know how it goes.'

Vera nodded. 'And a packet of Lyons tea, please.'

Prudence smiled wistfully as normality was restored.

Further up the High Street, Fred Kershaw, the local coalman, was delivering to the row of cottages next to The Royal Oak. His swollen knee had recovered thanks to the liberal quantities of goose grease his mother had applied to his leg. Significantly, he had not visited the doctor. As Tommy Piercy had remarked to him in the butcher's shop, 'Who needs a doctor when you've got goose grease?'

There was a rumour that Fred never washed, because even during his first deliveries each morning his face was

black with coal dust. Also, hanging from his bottom lip
was a cigarette. Fred was a chain smoker and he was
happy to share the knowledge that he was addicted to the
best possible cigarette. As a tough member of the Ragley
Rovers football team, he too had seen an advertisement in
the *News of the World* of his favourite footballer, the Blackpool and England winger Stanley Matthews, advertising
Craven A cigarettes. So Fred lit up another of his sixty-a-
day habit, hefted a bag of coal on to his broad shoulders
and scurried round the back of The Royal Oak.

The school cook, Irene Gubbins, was doing some shopping on her way home and had called at the General Stores
for a bag of potatoes. There was a pattern to the week's
meals in her household and if you arrived at her dining
table it would have been possible to know the day of the
week from the food being served. Harry Gubbins liked
routine and his wife obliged. Sundays were a veritable
feast, with a beef joint and giant Yorkshire puddings filled
with delicious onion gravy. On Mondays it was always
cold beef and chips, followed by beef stew on Tuesdays.
After a visit to Tommy Piercy's shop, Wednesdays featured
sausage and mash. Thursdays involved the occasional surprise. Usually it was egg and chips but, on occasions, if
Pete the Poacher had visited The Royal Oak, rabbit pie
appeared on the menu. Fridays never varied. It was always
fish, chips and mushy peas. On Saturdays a large plate of
crab paste sandwiches and slices of Spam were devoured
quickly before setting off to the local football match. It was
a pattern to life much appreciated by Harry.

Sweet courses were rare but enjoyed on special occasions such as birthdays and bank holidays. However, the

selection was limited and included rice pudding, semolina or tapioca, which resembled frogspawn. The *pièce de résistance* was Irene's spotted dick, created from flour, water and a handful of raisins.

Meanwhile, Ruby's mother, Agnes, was in the village Pharmacy. She had a problem and it was there for all to see. Her false teeth lay on the counter.

Eighteen years ago Agnes had been given a special present for her twenty-first birthday. All her teeth had been removed, as her father had said it made sense and would save a lot of trouble in the long run. She had been wearing false teeth ever since.

Herbert Grinchley stared at the teeth and made a decision. 'Try this, Agnes. It's Dr Wernet's Powder. Sez 'ere it gives all-day confidence. Y'jus' sprinkle it on y'plate in t'mornin' an' it meks a sort of a cushion.'

'Sounds right up my street,' said Agnes.

'An' what about some soap?' asked Herbert, never one to miss the opportunity of a sale.

'Soap? Ah've got soap.'

'But this is new an' everyone wants a bar.'

Agnes picked up the tablet of soap. 'Breeze? What's that when it's at 'ome?'

Herbert read the label. 'It sez you're country-fresh from top t'toe wi' cool green Breeze.'

Agnes shook her head. 'No thanks, Herbert, ah'll stick t'me Sunlight.'

'Pity,' said Herbert, ''cause ah'd got a bit o' news.'

Agnes loved gossip. 'Mebbe ah'll try some then,' she said, picking up the bar of soap and smelling the scent.

Herbert leaned over the counter. 'Vicar's gorra telly.'

'A telly!' exclaimed Agnes. 'Can't see Miss Evans tekkin' that lyin' down.'

'Y'reight there, Agnes.'

Back in the vicarage Joseph was explaining to Vera about the wonders of television. 'It's fifty-five shillings per month from Radio Rentals.'

'As much as that?'

Joseph took a step back. 'It includes free tube and valves, Vera, so it's a bargain, or so the man in the shop explained, and it's a trial offer.'

'A *trial* offer . . . I see,' said Vera.

'And servicing is free and I sent off for the free booklet on how it works. You had to send an unsealed envelope with a penny ha'penny stamp on it. There's an option to buy it later.'

Vera frowned. This was not what she had expected.

In her classroom Lily was at her desk preparing for afternoon school. She sat there silent as the grave while above her head dust motes danced in the shafts of winter sunlight. The familiar scurrying of tiny mice could be heard, seeking out warmth and food in the dark recesses of the old Victorian building. Lily stared at her register and counted the names again. Fewer children than usual had returned to school at the start of term following a measles outbreak in the village and she hoped they would soon be well again.

She began to think about the evening visit to the vicarage. John Pruett seemed most enthusiastic about collecting her in his car and driving her back to Ragley. Deep down she wished it could have been Tom.

*

Irene Gubbins had called into the Pharmacy on her way home.

'Hello, Irene,' said Herbert, 'and how are you today?'

'Ah'm fed up wi' toilet paper. We buy that IZAL Medicated.'

'Ah know it,' said Herbert. 'In a box. Tough stuff, like strong tracin' paper.'

'Ah've asked Miss Briggs to only give 'em one sheet each, but does she listen?' She shook her head.

'So what's it to be?'

'Ah jus' need some cream for me 'ands, 'Erbert. All that peelin' an' slicin'.'

'Ah've got jus' the thing,' he said and produced a tube of hand cream as if by magic. 'An' ah've got summat special.'

'Special?'

'It's Snowfire Face Powder. Y'need t'mek t'most of y'nat'ral charm.'

'Ah'm not sure.'

'It'll give you that finishin' touch o' glamour.' Herbert could see he was close to a sale. 'Also, ah've got some *news*.'

'What's that then?'

'Y'can't go wrong wi' a luxury powder for only eightpence.'

Irene opened her purse, dug out a sixpence and two pennies and placed them on the counter.

'They've gorra telly in t'vicarage.'

'Flippin' 'eck! Miss Evans will give that brother of 'ers what for.'

In Violet Fawnswater's luxury bungalow she had closed the curtains and watched a film during the afternoon. It was entitled *The Pluck of the Irish* and featured James Cagney. She had begun to enjoy watching television in the afternoon and looked forward to sharing *Children's Hour* with Phoebe.

In the meantime, she had cut out a coupon from her *Radio Times*. She had decided to send for a sample packet of Weetabix from Mrs Marjorie Crisp in Burton Latimer, plus a free copy of a booklet, 'Ever-Useful Weetabix'. She picked up her copy of the *Radio Times*, turned countless pages of radio schedules and, right at the back, found the small number of television programmes. 'Now, what's on this evening?' she murmured.

Back in Laurel Cottage, Lily had made sure Freddie had finished his meal and she was washing the pots in the sink. Florence came to dry the plates. It was clear she had something on her mind and Lily waited for her to speak.

'I was talking to Mrs Merryweather yesterday, Lily. She's had some business with one of the local solicitors. Nothing dramatic – just thinking ahead to making a will one day.'

'Oh yes? This is news to me.'

Florence gave Lily a searching look.

'Is there a hidden message there, Mother?'

Florence gave a wry smile. 'Perhaps.' She dried her hands on the tea towel and pulled out her diary from the pocket of her apron. 'Anyway, I've written their names in here.'

It was Lily's turn to smile as she wiped her hands and scanned her mother's neat cursive handwriting. She recalled seeing the brass plates of the solicitors on the wall outside their offices in the local market town of Easington.

They would not have filled a prospective client with confidence. Fiddler & Sly specialized in house sales, whereas Crook & Cheatham had a penchant for family discord – or so it was rumoured. The latter triggered some interest for Lily and she copied the telephone number into her own diary for future reference.

At a quarter past seven John Pruett crunched over the snow on Kirkby Steepleton High Street and pulled up outside Laurel Cottage. Florence was in Freddie's bedroom while the little boy put on his pyjamas. She heard the car outside and peered through the curtains. By the flickering light of the street lamp she saw the headmaster pause, remove his trilby hat, smooth his hair and straighten his tie. She recognized the signs and smiled . . . *And he is a gentleman with status*, she thought.

Lily hurried downstairs from her room and Florence was pleased to see how pretty she looked. 'Enjoy your evening with the television,' she said.

Lily paused before opening the door and turned to look at Florence. 'You could go instead of me. I really don't mind. I could look after Freddie.'

'No, not at all. You're expected,' and she opened the door and saw John's eager face.

'Good evening, Mrs Briggs. I'll make sure Lily is home at a reasonable time.'

Lily smiled at her mother. 'Come on,' she said to John, 'let's go.'

Florence stood in the doorway and noticed the attentiveness of the headmaster as he guided Lily into the passenger seat.

What a kind and caring man, she thought . . . *and perhaps* . . .

Within moments she left such reverie behind and went back inside to put Freddie to bed.

By eight o'clock John Pruett and Lily were in the vicarage parlour staring at one of the wonders of the modern age. As usual, television programmes had closed down at 6.25 p.m. following *Children's Television*, which had shown a cowboy film starring Tex Ritter, who had rounded up a gang of rustlers in the Wild West while never once looking untidy. Programmes resumed at 8 p.m. and the first of the evening was called *Newsreel*.

'It's a bit like the Pathé News,' said Lily.

'In your own home,' added John.

Vera seemed pleased. This was a genteel evening, the kind of which she approved, and she served tea in china cups with slices of Victoria sponge.

At a quarter past eight they settled to watch a sporting documentary, *Test Cricketers of Tomorrow*, and Joseph and John shared their expert knowledge. The highlight, however, was a programme called *Ballet for Beginners*, during which Vera came to the fore and made sure her assembled guests knew the difference between a *ballotté* and a *ballonné*.

It was a successful evening and when it came to an end John took Lily back to Kirkby Steepleton. He drove in silence and she wondered if there was something wrong, but then presumed he just needed to concentrate on the treacherous road conditions. For John's part, he loved sitting so close to Lily but struggled to find an amusing anecdote or an interesting comment. As always, in her presence he was almost tongue-tied.

When he had walked her to the front door, Lily thanked him for the lift and wished him a safe journey home. 'See you tomorrow,' she called after him. She was keen to get in out of the cold and closed the door quickly.

It seemed an age later that John Pruett pulled up outside his own cottage. He walked to his front door, stopped under the porch, removed his hat and looked up at myriad stars. The night was calm now and the moon was bright in a clear sky. A feather of breeze ruffled his hair and he flattened it with his palm in that familiar habit of his. Suddenly his eyes were stung with tears and his heart was heavy.

It was balm to his conscience to know that Lily respected him as a professional colleague, but it would never be any more than that. He smiled and shook his head. It had merely been the foolish fancy of an older man and he knew he should have known better.

There was a slow comfort in feeling a few scattered snowflakes against his face and for a while he cherished the pain of the cold as it purged his thoughts and frozen dreams.

'She could never be mine,' he whispered into the empty night.

Then he turned, opened the door and walked into the solitude of his empty home.

On Tuesday evening, shortly before eight thirty, Vera was surprised to hear the doorbell ring and find six men standing outside. They were the church bellringers, led by Archibald Pike.

'Good evening, Vera,' said Archibald. 'We're here for the demonstration.'

'Pardon?'

'On the television set,' explained Archibald. 'Joseph

told us to come along after our bells practice. He said it would be of particular interest to us men.'

'Really?' Vera stood back. 'Well, you had better come in.'

In the vicarage parlour Joseph was busy rearranging the chairs into a semicircle around the television set. 'Joseph, the bellringers are here – and why are you moving my chair?'

'So everyone can see the television set. I want everyone to have a good view.'

Vera did not like her furniture disturbed. 'You failed to mention it to me.'

'Sorry, dear, it must have slipped my mind. It's just that I saw it in the *Radio Times*, so I mentioned it to Archibald and he said the rest of the bellringers were keen as well.'

'Keen? Keen on what?'

'The television cook, Philip Harben, is giving a cookery demonstration. It's called *The Man in the Kitchen*.'

What a waste of time, thought Vera. She knew a lost cause when she saw one. However, with true Christian spirit she breathed deeply and composed herself. 'Would you like some tea, gentlemen?'

Vera's comments over breakfast the next day clearly fell on deaf ears, because on Wednesday evening the Holy Dusters, the church cleaners, arrived to watch *Welcome to City Varieties* from Leeds. It was a lively variety show, the members of the audience were dressed in Edwardian costume and the music was far too loud for Vera's liking.

Thursday was even worse. Vera usually went to bed at ten o'clock, but Joseph had invited members of the Parish Church Council to come back to the vicarage following their monthly meeting in the village hall. They all enjoyed a programme about the Household Cavalry, and even Vera was interested as they were to play a big part in the forthcoming Coronation. However, at 10 p.m. no one was keen to leave when the next programme, *Animal, Vegetable, or Mineral?*, started. It was a fortnightly quiz programme in which a panel of experts, including Sir Mortimer Wheeler, the Professor of Archaeology from the University of London, attempted to identify a series of unusual objects.

Thankfully, Friday was an improvement. Joseph invited the local Girl Guides to watch a programme after school about netball with expert advice from Mary Bulloch of the All-England Netball Association. Vera thought this was a good idea, as the girls were so well behaved and they departed before she had to start preparing the evening meal.

However, the last straw for Vera occurred on Saturday afternoon when she returned from shopping at the General Stores. The parlour was full of local tradesmen, including Fred Kershaw the coalman, and they were all smoking obnoxious cigarettes and cheering loudly. A rugby league match between Bradford Northern and Leeds was being screened and an excitable man with a distinct northern accent was commentating. Vera had never heard of Eddie Waring, the popular voice of rugby league, and had no wish to hear him again.

It was when he was shouting that it was an 'up-an'-under' that she made a decision.

The following week, on Monday afternoon, Joseph returned home to discover the television had gone and the arrangement of furniture was back to normal. 'What's happened, Vera? Where's the television?'

Vera didn't look up from her cross-stitch. 'It's gone, Joseph.'

'Gone?'

'Yes, back to the rental shop. They have just collected it. I thanked them for the opportunity of a trial period and said we would consider it again some time in the future.'

Joseph paced the room searching for a suitable riposte. 'But Vera, it says in the Bible, "Give freely and become generous."'

'Yes, Joseph.' There was irritation in her voice. 'I do know Proverbs, chapter eleven, verse twenty-four.'

Not to be outdone, Joseph searched his memory bank and came up with the perfect response. 'How about, "If you have two shirts, give one to the poor"? The same surely goes for television sets.'

Again, Vera did not look up. 'I am also familiar with Luke, chapter three, verse eleven. Perhaps you should have read on further in St Luke's gospel, Joseph – it's quite illuminating.'

'What do you mean?'

'I'm referring to Luke, chapter six, verse thirty.'

Joseph wracked his brains but couldn't recall. His sister's superiority in Bible studies had always been infuriating.

'Go on, I give up,' he said.

'It says, "Give to anyone who asks you, and if anyone takes what belongs to you, *do not demand it back*".'

Joseph knew when he was beaten. He looked around the room. 'I'll switch on the radio, shall I?'

He didn't notice Vera's smile of satisfaction.

Chapter Ten

Sweet Dreams

It was the frozen dawn of Friday, 6 February when Lily sat in William Featherstone's bus as it trundled along the back road to Ragley village. A pale sun had risen in the east and a line of golden light touched the distant hills. Lily stared out at the monochrome snowscape and thought about her life. Once again she opened the handbag on her lap and studied the old black-and-white photograph. Then she smiled and turned her attentions to the day ahead.

As they passed Coe Farm, trails of wood smoke made drifting diagonal patterns in the sullen sky above a land scoured of life by the bitter winds blowing in from Siberia. A familiar police car stood on the forecourt of Pratt's garage, where Tom Feather was in conversation with Victor beside the single pump. As the bus went by Tom turned to seek out Lily behind the misty windows and waved. She responded with a smile. Their romance had continued to blossom, even though they were both busy with their work, but even so a nagging doubt crossed Lily's mind. *Too fast . . . too soon*, she thought as the bus turned into the High Street.

It pulled up outside the General Stores where a crowd had gathered. A large painted sign outside the shop was causing great excitement and Lily stepped carefully over the frozen forecourt to read it for herself. She smiled. Perhaps this was really the beginning of the end of post-war austerity. The poster read:

SWEET DREAMS

Your dreams have come true!
Sweet rationing has ended.

Sweets will be on sale from 7.30 a.m.
Saturday, 7th February
Prudence Golightly

Sweet rationing had ended officially on Thursday, 5 February, but the supply to small villages in North Yorkshire had taken a day or two longer. Also, Prudence thought that Saturday would be her best day for a bumper sale. Chocolate, nougat sticks and liquorice strips were on her list and she looked out of her shop window at the sea of eager faces. A busy day lay in store.

Deirdre Coe was an early customer. She slapped a penny ha'penny on the counter and picked up a copy of the *Daily Mirror* with its headline 'Sweet Buying Orgy Begins – night queues'.

'Ah'll be in t'morrow,' said Deirdre. 'My Stanley will be wantin' a box o' chocolates.'

Before Prudence could reply, she walked out. The pig

farmer's sister didn't feel like wasting her breath on the tiny shopkeeper.

Betty Cuthbertson and Vera Evans were at the back of the shop and had seen Deirdre's swift departure. 'For two pins ah'd give 'er a piece o' my mind,' said Betty. She glanced in Vera's direction. 'But as ah'm a Christian ah'll 'old m'tongue.'

Vera gave an enigmatic smile and kept her feelings to herself.

'Common as muck that one,' added Betty for good measure. She picked up a copy of the *Daily Mirror* and pointed to a photograph of Derek Bentley, the nineteen-year-old burglar who had been hanged last week at Wandsworth Prison in London for his part in the murder of PC Sidney Miles.

'Word 'as it 'e didn't shoot 'im,' said Betty. 'Alfie the milkman said it were the young lad what did it and 'im only sixteen. Anyway, good riddance I say.'

She continued to flick through the pages.

'Did you want the newspaper, Betty?' asked Prudence, concerned that in its dishevelled state it was no longer fit for selling.

'No thanks, Prudence, jus' m'usual ciggies.'

Prudence shook her head after Betty had gone. 'She doesn't change, does she?'

Vera gave her familiar non-committal smile.

'So how can I help, Vera?'

'I should like to surprise Joseph with a box of chocolates tomorrow. It will be a special treat for him.'

'That's fine. I've got six boxes arriving this evening along with a whole host of sweets. It promises to be quite a day. I'll put a box on one side for you.'

*

In her bedroom over the Hardware Emporium, Nora Pratt was getting ready for school with her own version of sweet dreams.

She had been reading her *Picturegoer* magazine carefully and studying the etiquette of table manners. If she was to succeed as an actress she would have to be confident when dining with important people. In an article by Madame Sokolova of the Royal Academy of Dramatic Art, Nora had read that an actor could reveal the character of someone in a play through their behaviour at the dinner table. For example, a bread roll should be broken, not cut with a knife, and a napkin should be opened to its full extent and spread over the knees. As she packed her satchel she was determined she would carry this new knowledge into her Saturday job in Doris Clutterbuck's Tea Rooms.

Nora stared at her reflection in the mirror. 'A bwead woll should be bwoken,' she said out loud.

When Lily walked across the village green she saw that Tom Feather's police car had pulled up outside the school gate. The tall policeman was wearing a heavy greatcoat and his breath steamed as he blew into his frozen hands.

'Hello, Lily. There's a good film on tonight at the Odeon. Shall we go?'

Lily smiled at his eagerness. 'What's the film?'

'Ronald Reagan and Virginia Mayo in *She's Working Her Way Through College* and it's had a good write-up. Apparently Reagan plays the part of a professor ... and it's definitely not a *war* film,' he added with a grin.

She stared up at Tom's friendly appealing face. 'Yes, that sounds like fun.'

'So I'll pick you up at seven.'

Lily had a spring in her step as she walked up the school drive.

The sight that greeted her in the children's cloakroom was a familiar one now. Straggling lines of snow-covered wellington boots filled the corridor outside the classroom and on the pegs were hand-me-down coats of all sizes, knitted woollen scarves and damp balaclavas. Meanwhile, coughs and sneezes echoed in the Victorian rafters and the bitter wind rattled the wooden casements of the tall windows. Few children owned a handkerchief and many used the sleeve of their thick jumper to wipe their runny noses. In spite of all this, there was a smile on Lily's face as she walked into the school office where Vera was checking registers with John.

'Hello, Lily,' said Vera. 'I saw you talking to Tom Feather.'

Lily smiled. 'Yes, he's invited me to the cinema.'

'That's lovely,' said Vera.

John said nothing, but gave a polite if slightly forced smile.

'It's a Ronald Reagan film.'

'Oh yes, a very handsome man,' approved Vera.

'To be honest, I prefer Richard Burton. It said in *Picture-goer* that he was the hottest thing in Hollywood,' said Lily.

John picked up his registers disconsolately. 'I heard he could have been a Welsh miner,' he said as he set off for his classroom.

'John doesn't sound happy,' remarked Lily.

'It will be his sister,' explained Vera. 'She's staying with him and insists upon tidying everything. It takes him a week to get it back to how he likes it.'

At ten o'clock Lily was working with Sam Grundy, a keen little six-year-old who was progressing rapidly with his reading. Sam had opened his *Janet and John* reader and staring at Book Four, page 3, 'Little Fisher Duckling'.

Lily was using a 'look and say' reading scheme to help Sam with an introduction to less regular key words. There were over three hundred of them in Book Four, a challenge for the curly-haired farmer's son, but he was word-perfect as he read '*wave, gave, flake, lane, snake, like, five, bite, slide* and *white*'.

'Well done, Sam,' said Lily. 'A gold star for you,' and Sam smiled as if he had won the football pools.

However, Lily was still concerned at the quality and content of the reading scheme. It presented to her pupils a simple, middle-class world, a long way from that experienced by the children at Ragley. It was clear that the tale of 'Little Peachling' meant nothing to Frank Shepherd. The incongruous story concerned a baby inside a peach who grows up and leaves home to seek his fortune. He decides to give spiced buns to various animals, including a monkey.

Lily considered asking John for some new reading books, but remembered his manner earlier and decided to wait until another day. It was time for morning milk and as usual the children enjoyed their daily third of a pint. The fact that it was often frozen in winter, with coal tits pecking at the foil tops, and curdled in summer mattered little. In an age of austerity, most of these children were grateful for any sustenance that came their way.

In the distance Lily could hear the church bells making a melancholy, muted sound. It was the funeral of seventy-five-year-old George Icklethwaite, who had served in the army in the First World War and lived the rest of his life in the village. The bellringers had muffled their bells and Ragley folk stopped what they were doing to count out the number of times the bells tolled, one for each year of George's life.

It was well known that the 'killing cold', as it was called by the locals, took away the sick and the weak, and Lily looked thoughtfully at the children in her care, who seemed unconcerned about the freezing weather and couldn't wait to run in the snow and slide on the ice.

Across the road Ruby Smith walked into the General Stores holding an old handkerchief over her mouth. She was coughing.

'Good morning, Miss Golightly,' she mumbled. 'Just some porridge oats, please.' She knew her son needed a hot and filling breakfast on this bitterly cold day. There was no heating in the house and ice had formed on the inside of the windows. Ronnie was still in bed, snoring loudly. He had spent another evening supping Tetley's bitter in The Royal Oak and it was time to sleep it off.

Prudence put a two-pound box of Scott's Porage Oats on the counter.

Ruby, now heavily pregnant, counted the coins carefully from her purse and coughed again.

Prudence looked concerned. 'Whatever is the matter, Ruby?'

'Ah've gorra tickly cough an' a sore throat an' ah'm worried ah'll pass it on to our Andy.'

Prudence pointed to the sign on the wall that read 'VICTORY V gums and lozenges for cold journeys'. Then she opened a packet from behind the counter. 'Have one of these,' she said, 'and take a few with you.' She scattered some of the small brown tablets into Ruby's open palm. 'These will help you through the morning,' she added with a gentle smile.

'Thank you kindly, Miss Golightly,' said Ruby, popping one into her mouth. The bell above the door rang forlornly as she tightened her headscarf and hurried out.

Oh dear, thought Prudence, *whatever will become of that dear young girl?*

It was lunchtime and Lily wrinkled her nose at the nauseating smell of boiled cabbage that permeated every corridor and her classroom. She handed in her late-dinner-money tin to Vera in the school office.

Vera looked up from the admissions register. 'I hope you enjoy your evening with Tom.'

'Thank you, Vera. I'm sure I shall,' replied Lily a little defensively.

Vera sensed the troubled mood. 'He is a good man and I'm sure he cares for you.' She stared out of the window at the skeletal trees etched in frozen snow. 'Have you noticed that he always *thinks* before he speaks . . . remarkable in a man. His words are often measured.'

'Yes, I know,' said Lily quietly.

'He brings to mind Proverbs, chapter sixteen, verse twenty-four.'

Lily shook her head and waited patiently for the wisdom of Vera.

'Gracious words are a honeycomb, sweet to the soul and healing to the bones,' she quoted.

'Wise thoughts, Vera.'

A tired Ruby was followed by Ronnie into the village Pharmacy. 'Ah've come t'collect m'mother's description, Mr Grinchley,' she said.

'Fine lady, is Agnes,' said Herbert. 'Ah 'ope she's not badly.'

'No, jus' summat t'do wi' 'er tubes,' said Ronnie, 'or so she told Nellie next door.'

Ruby frowned at Ronnie. 'We need t'look after m'mam.'

'Rudyard Kipling said God could not be everywhere so that is why he made mothers.' Herbert was proud of his literary knowledge.

''E's right,' said Ruby.

'Does 'e come in 'ere?'

'Who?' asked Herbert.

'This Rudyard bloke,' said Ronnie.

Herbert shook his head. ''Ere's y'prescription, Ruby, an' when's y'baby due?'

'Nex' month, God willin'.'

'Mek sure y'look after 'er, Ronnie.'

Ronnie scanned the shelf behind Herbert's head. 'An' ah need some Brylcreem.'

'Tubs are one an' eight an' a tube is 'alf a crown.'

'Can y'lend us some money, Ruby luv?' asked a plaintive Ronnie, but Ruby was already heading for the door.

*

On Friday evening, while Prudence Golightly was making a tray of oatmeal biscuits, Lily and Tom were enjoying a relaxing evening in York at the cinema. The end of the evening followed a familiar pattern, with a fish and chips supper and a goodnight kiss in the car outside Laurel Cottage. It was clear Tom wanted Lily to stay longer, but he was gentle and patient.

'You must know I care about you,' he said quietly as he held her hand and looked into her eyes.

'Yes, I know, Tom . . . and I care about you.'

'So what's stopping us going steady?'

'It's *complicated*,' sighed Lily.

Tom leaned back in his seat. 'I haven't felt this way before.'

'I'm sorry, Tom.'

'Do you need more time?'

Lily stared out at the frozen world. Her heart said *no* and her head said *yes*.

'What is it, Lily?'

'I can't . . . not yet.'

'Then I'll wait. I'm a patient man.'

He walked her to the door and kissed her softly on her cheek. 'Goodnight, Lily, and thanks for a lovely evening.'

Lily watched him drive away and shivered. There was so much she wanted to share with Tom, but it could never be.

On Saturday morning Lily caught the bus with Freddie to buy him a toffee apple and a bag of liquorice laces in Prudence Golightly's General Stores. The road into Ragley was quiet, but in spite of the bitter cold there was hope for the days ahead. Hazel catkins shivered in the hedgerows and winter aconites brightened the dark patches of the woodland. The icy blasts did not deter the hardy folk of Ragley village and a queue stretched out to the forecourt of the shop and past the bus stop.

Freddie was thrilled with his sweets, and as an extra treat Lily called in to the Tea Rooms to buy him a cake and a cup of tea. As they were leaving, she held the door open for a lady she hadn't seen before.

Agatha Makepiece was frail and elderly, with porcelain skin and hair of winter-grey, and she wore a shabby fur coat and a neat hat with a feather in it. She walked in, upright and elegant like a prima ballerina, and sat alone at a corner table. She lived nearby in a thatched cottage that was now in urgent need of repair and it was a rare occurrence for her to step out and meet the world.

Doris Clutterbuck looked up from the counter, a hint of concern on her face. 'Go and serve Miss Makepiece, please, Nora, and be careful what you say.' Doris lowered her voice. 'Her mind wanders a bit these days.'

'What can I get for you, Madam?' asked Nora, notebook in hand. Doris had insisted she must always be polite.

'A pot of tea, please,' said Agatha.

'Anything to eat? We have some nice cakes and some sausage wolls fwesh fwom the oven.'

'That sounds lovely, my dear.' There was a pause as the elderly lady looked around her. 'I don't carry money because I can't remember what to do with it.'

Nora was puzzled. She had never come across a customer without any money. ''Scuse me a moment.'

Doris sighed when Nora reported back to her. 'Don't worry, she's a lovely lady who has fallen on hard times.

Give her a pot of tea and a crumpet. That's what she had last time . . . and, by the way, Nora, Miss Makepiece used to be an actress.'

Nora served the tea and crumpet, excited at the opportunity to meet such a lady. 'Mrs Clutterbuck says you used to be an actwess.'

Suddenly the vacant look in Agatha's blue eyes faded and she became alert. 'Yes, I was at RADA.'

'Wada?'

'Yes, the Royal Academy of Dramatic Art. I was there in 1923 with John Gielgud and in 1931 when the Duchess of York opened the new building. I remember those days so well.'

'I want t'be an actwess.'

'You must be the girl who sang "Over the Rainbow" at the pantomime. I was there. You performed beautifully.'

'Oooh, thank you, but ah stwuggle a bit wi' m'speakin'.'

Agatha stretched out a hand that resembled ancient parchment and touched Nora's rosy cheek. 'You will be fine. Follow your dream and don't be scared – just live life.'

Nora nodded, recognizing this special moment. 'Do you miss being an actwess?'

Agatha picked up the teapot and began to pour. 'The person I miss most is *me*.'

Violet Fawnswater had been the first to buy a box of chocolates in the General Stores and was luxuriating in her favourite armchair with a port and lemon and a surfeit of chocolate. She was reading her *Blue Cars Continental Holiday Catalogue* for 1953 and considering ten days in Switzerland for 32 guineas. She cut out the advert, filled it in and put it in an envelope. She stuck on a 1½d stamp and addressed it to Shaftesbury Avenue in London. 'Armchair comfort in a Pullman coach,' she murmured to herself. 'You can't say better than that.'

There was a special moment when Doris and Nora had tidied everything away in the Tea Rooms.

'Well done today, Nora, and thank you for dealing with Miss Makepiece so sensitively.' She picked up a shopping bag from behind the counter. 'This is for you for being such a good girl and a wonderful help.'

To Nora's surprise, it was a box of chocolates.

'Thank you,' she said. 'Ah'm weally gweatful.' She stared at the box for a moment. 'Ah'd like to wun over t'Miss Makepiece to see if she would like a chocolate.'

Doris smiled. 'That's a kind thought. Off you go and then go straight home.'

At Coe Farm Stan was not pleased.

'There were none o' them boxes o' chocolates left,' Deirdre told him. 'When ah called in that stupid Prudence 'ad sold 'em all.'

'She wants lockin' up,' muttered Stan.

'Ah'll go back t'morrow,' said Deirdre. 'She might get some more in.'

'An' pigs might fly,' grumbled her brother. 'Anyway, ah'm off out to t'pub so put y'coat on.'

'Oooh lovely, Stan – are y'tekkin' me out?'

'No, y'daft mare. Fire's gone out so you'll 'ave t'get some more logs.'

*

Nora knocked on Agatha Makepiece's door and the old lady was pleased to see the young tea-shop assistant for the second time that day.

'I'm sowwy t'twouble you, Miss Makepiece, but would you like a chocolate?'

'What a kind thought. Do come in.'

Nora stepped hesitantly over the threshold. 'Jus' for a minute.'

Agatha pulled back a curtain that led to a tiny kitchen. 'Now, young lady, do you know what drink goes well with chocolate?'

'Tea,' said Nora. The answer was obvious.

Agatha gave a wry smile. 'No, my dear, it's coffee.'

'Coffee! But ah only dwink tea. Mrs Clutte'buck says coffee is an Amewican dwink and not for us in England.'

'Well, let's be adventurous, shall we? As actresses we need to experience new things.'

'Vewy well,' said Nora, 'ah'll twy some.'

Agatha spooned the Nescafé into two china cups and poured on boiling water, then a little milk. 'Now, let's add a tiny bit of sugar as this is a special occasion,' she said, enjoying the sense of suspense.

Nora sipped it carefully. 'Ah weally like it,' she said, her eyes bright in wonderment.

'I thought you would.'

'Mrs Clutte'buck says it won't catch on an' we'll always be a nation of tea dwinkers.'

'But what do you think?'

'Ah think she would be sad if she knew ah was dwinking coffee.'

'That may be, but we don't have to be sad now.'

'All wight.'

'Remember, Nora, it's the drink of the future.'

And Nora never forgot.

It was late on Saturday and darkness had fallen. In Laurel Cottage Freddie was playing on the hearthrug with his toy train and Lily was curled up on the sofa reading Jane Austen's *Pride and Prejudice*. She looked at Freddie with affection and smiled.

Meanwhile, Florence was reading a book on rug-making with the intention of undertaking an ambitious project to make a deep-pile carpet. It appeared there was a company in Ossett who supplied all you required, including a piece of canvas, a large quantity of wool and a rug hook.

Everyone was warm and content and the radio was playing the number-one record, Perry Como's 'Don't Let the Stars Get In Your Eyes'.

Suddenly there was a knock on the door.

'Oh dear, who can that be?' groaned Florence.

'I'll go,' said Lily.

She opened the door and there stood Tom. 'I thought you would like these to share over the weekend with your mother and Freddie.' He handed over a large box of chocolates. 'Couldn't resist. There were only two left, so I bought these for you and one for my mother.'

Lily held the box in surprise. 'You shouldn't have, Tom!'

He lowered his voice. 'It was also to say thank you for being part of my life.'

She stretched up and kissed him tenderly. 'Would you like to come in?'

He smiled. 'I would love to, but I ought to get back home. I'm expected.'

As Lily watched him drive away she wished her life could have been different, and that night when she lay in her bed there were no sweet dreams. All that was left was a trembling peace.

Chapter Eleven

Do Angels Have Wings?

It was early March and a thin light bathed the waking land. The season was changing and a pallid sun appeared fleetingly beyond the rags of clouds that raced across a pale-blue sky. Vera looked out of the vicarage window and smiled as she recognized the signs. It was a sight to lift the spirits and gave hope of warmer days to come. The earth had shifted and hopes of spring were replacing the bitter winter months. The sprouting leaves of hawthorn had brought new life to the hedgerows and the spears of daffodils thrust their blue-green shoots above the grass. The last of the snow had gone and snowdrops, shivering with balletic tension, were like pearls in the pale sunshine. Aconites and crocuses provided a splash of colour and the sticky buds on the horse chestnut trees were cracking open.

Vera sighed as she thought ahead to a busy day. She had been brought up to have a strong sense of *noblesse oblige* and firmly believed that a person of social rank should be generous to those less fortunate. So it was that she was destined to experience a day of problem-solving – and that included her brother. He was due to take both classes today for Bible stories. Joseph was always comfortable in his pulpit with a congregation of adults. Sadly, where children were concerned he didn't have a clue. Vera knew she loved her brother – he was a kind and gentle man. However, although the Bible had taught her that love was constant, she wondered if this included Wednesdays.

Close to the blacksmith's forge in Ragley village was Badger's Row, a collection of thatched cottages. The one at the far end of the row was no longer weatherproof. The thatch had sagged in places and, whenever the rain was more than a light drizzle, buckets had to be placed around the kitchen floor.

It was here that six-year-old Rosie Finn was filling a heavy kettle from the pump above the kitchen sink. She was cold and had shivered during the night in spite of the old army blanket that had provided a little extra warmth over the winter months.

Mary Finn, a single mother, was frying a thick slice of bread in dripping for Rosie's breakfast. ''Ere y'are, luv,' she said. 'Eat this an' be a good girl.'

Rosie took the bread eagerly as she stared at the calendar on the wall. Each month there was a new picture with a Bible quotation underneath. This month it was a picture of a smiling Jesus with long fair hair, a neatly trimmed beard and surrounded by children. In the sky above his head two winged angels looked down, while the text read 'Suffer little children to come unto me.'

Rosie chewed her bread and dripping and wondered why children had to suffer.

In Laurel Cottage Florence was watching Freddie dip his toast soldiers into the runny yolk of a boiled egg before she took him off to school. The radio was on and Guy Mitchell was singing 'She Wears Red Feathers'. She stared out of the window and was happy to see the spring sunshine. If it wasn't for the situation with Lily all would be well – but her daughter had begun to spend more time with her handsome policeman and Florence sensed no good would come of it.

When Lily walked across the village green that morning she sensed the change in the air. The first primroses brightened the verges, birds were pairing up and claiming territory, while rooks cawed loudly in the elm tops. Soon new shoots of lime and ash would burst into life.

'Mornin', Miss Briggs,' called out a familiar voice.

'Mornin', Miss,' echoed another.

'Good morning, boys,' she called back and looked around, but she couldn't see anyone.

'Up 'ere, Miss.'

Lily looked up into the branches of the weeping willow above her head. Big Dave Robinson and Little Malcolm were sitting on a branch sharing a liquorice shoelace.

'Do be careful, boys – it doesn't look safe.'

'We're playing Tarzan, Miss,' explained Big Dave.

'So it's you who should be worried, Miss,' said Little Malcolm with a mischievous grin.

'Why is that?' asked Lily.

"Cause lions can't climb trees,' shouted Big Dave in triumph.

'Well as long as you're not next to Lake Manyara in Africa, you'll be fine.'

'Why's that, Miss?'

'Because that's where tree-climbing lions live,' and she strode off towards school.

'Bloody 'ell, Malc – tree-climbing lions.'

Malcolm stared after Lily Briggs. 'That's problem wi' teachers, Dave – they know f***in' everythin'.'

The Revd Joseph Evans rode down the Morton road on his 1940s bicycle, which was beginning to show its age. He parked it outside the General Stores prior to buying a bag of biscuits for the staff-room; he wanted to contribute towards the morning tea and biscuits that were part of his regular visit.

As he walked into the shop Rosie Finn was in front of him at the counter.

"Ello, Miss Golightly,' said the little girl politely.

'Hello, Rosie, what can I do for you?'

'Can me mam 'ave 'alf an onion please . . . an' one apple?'

The little girl put two pennies on the counter.

Prudence was used to serving unconventional amounts. She was also mindful that on no account should she provide a *whole* onion, as this would be perceived as charity. The outcome would be that Mary Finn would not frequent the General Stores again. So she cut an onion in half, wrapped it carefully, selected the largest apple and put them in a paper bag. 'Here you are, Rosie, and here's a barley sugar for remembering to say "please". Now run straight home.'

Rosie beamed, picked up the bag, popped the sweet in her mouth and ran out of the shop, pausing only to stare up in wonderment at the doorbell as it rang.

She turned in the doorway and shouted back, 'My mam says ev'ry time a bell rings an angel gets its wings,' and Prudence waved in acknowledgement.

'Children,' said Prudence, 'they never cease to surprise you.'

'Very true,' said Joseph, thinking ahead to school assembly and the two lessons that awaited him.

Morning assembly seemed to go well and Vera propped open the double doors that led from the entrance area to the school hall so she could listen and join in the prayers. However, as always, the children's questions caused difficulties for the well-meaning cleric. Joseph had been waxing lyrical about heaven and guardian angels for about ten minutes when Rosie Finn put up her hand.

'Mr Evans,' she asked, 'why do angels have wings?'

Joseph thought of the Renaissance painters he had studied and the many story books that featured flying angels.

However, before he could answer the practical Sam Grundy called out, ''Cause if they didn't they would fall out of 'eaven, sir.'

'That's right,' said Veronica Poole. 'They need to stay above the clouds.'

'They've got some sense,' said the deep-thinking Norman Fazackerly, who had recently read a book about the weather and cloud formations, ''cause they won't get wet. Y'wouldn't want wet wings.'

Joseph was getting desperate. The logic of young children was beyond him.

'Ah 'ope one falls in our back garden, Mr Evans,' shouted out Bertie Stubbs.

Joseph was taken aback. 'Your garden, Bertie?'

'Yes, sir, then we'd 'ave one o' them garden angels you were goin' on about.'

John Pruett gave Joseph a friendly nod and got up. 'We'll end with the Lord's Prayer, boys and girls.'

Joseph's spirits lifted a little after his lesson in Lily's class with the younger children – that is, until six-year-old Joy Popplewell looked up at him. 'That were a lovely story about God, Mr Evans.'

'I'm glad you enjoyed it,' he replied with a satisfied smile.

The little girl looked thoughtful.

'What is it?' asked Joseph quietly.

'Well . . . did God make Daddy?'

'Yes.'

'An' did God make you?'

Joseph nodded. 'Yes, he did.'

'An' did God make me?'

Joseph sighed at the innocence of youth. 'Yes.'

Joy's face lit up with understanding. 'Well,' she said triumphantly, ''e's gettin' better at it.'

At the back of the class Lily took the handkerchief from the sleeve of her cardigan and held it against her mouth to stifle her laughter.

Daphne Cahill raised her hand. 'Will we *all* go to 'eaven, Mr Evans?'

'I certainly hope so,' said Joseph with an encouraging smile.

Bertie Stubbs called out suddenly, 'My grandad got killed in t'First World War.'

'I'm sorry to hear that, Bertie,' said Joseph with feeling.

'So, is *'e* in 'eaven?' asked Bertie.

'Yes, I imagine so,' said Joseph, although without conviction.

Bertie frowned. 'So 'ow old will 'e be –'cause 'e were twenty-one when t'Germans shot 'im.'

Suddenly there were animated children all raising their hands and calling out in excitement.

'Will 'e allus be twenty-one, sir?' shouted Frank Shepherd.

'An' when ah die will ah be older than m'grandad?' Bertie wanted to know.

'What will we do all day?' asked Daphne.

'That's right,' added Reggie. 'If it's jus' clouds an' sky there's not much t'do.'

'An' will we jus' 'ave t'clothes that we die in, 'cause they'd get mucky after a while,' continued Daphne.

'An' there's nowhere t'put a washin' line,' muttered Rosie Finn.

'Do cats and dogs go as well?' asked Sam Grundy suddenly from the desk at the back.

'Will ah see our 'Arry again, sir?' asked Arnold Icklethwaite.

Joseph had taken a step back, such was the torrent of questions.

'Harry?' he murmured.

'Yes sir, 'Arry.'

'Oh dear, what happened to Harry?'

'M'dad 'it 'im wi' a spade.'

'A spade?' mumbled Joseph. This conversation was getting out of hand.

'Yes, sir, an' 'Arry were t'best 'amster ah ever 'ad.'

'And your father hit him with a spade?' asked an incredulous Joseph.

'Yes, sir, 'cause 'e thought 'e were a rat.'

'Oh dear.'

'But m'dad said 'e were sorry afterwards so everybody were 'appy . . . 'xcept 'Arry, ah s'ppose.'

In John Pruett's class Joseph's Bible story lesson went better than usual. The children were attentive and, with John sitting at the back of the classroom, discipline was total.

'So in conclusion, boys and girls, the children of Israel built a temple and they crossed the Red Sea,' announced Joseph in triumph. It had been a good story, one of his best.

Eddie Brown raised his hand. 'Can ah ask a question, please, Mr Evans?'

'Of course you can, Edward,' said Joseph with a beaming smile.

'Well, y'said *children* o' Israel, didn't you?'

'Yes, Edward, I did.'

'An' they built them temples an' suchlike.'

'Magnificent temples,' purred Joseph.

'An' then these children o' Israel crossed that sea wi' a funny colour.'

'Yes, the Red Sea.'

'Well, ah were jus' wond'ring . . .'

'Yes?'

'What were all t'grown-ups doin'?'

Joseph looked at the clock on the classroom wall. Lunchtime beckoned and he breathed a sigh of relief.

*

The children in Lily's class were in the hall dancing to music in their bare feet. John Pruett had brought in his gramophone and Lily had placed a precious 78 rpm record on the turntable, wound the handle and lowered the needle with extreme care. The chirpy harmony of Edvard Grieg's 'Anitra's Dance' from *Peer Gynt* echoed around the draughty hall and the children interpreted the music in their own way. Some, like Daphne Cahill and Rosie Finn, were quite balletic; others, like Arnold Icklethwaite, ran around dodging left and right like a rugby league player.

At the end the children sat on the bench outside their classroom tugging on their socks and shoes. It was clear that little Rosie Finn was struggling.

'Shall I help you?' asked Lily. She had just finished teaching Sam Grundy how to tie a double knot in his laces. 'Let me have a go.'

Lily tugged on one boot but had trouble with the other. 'These are really difficult to get on. I think you've grown out of them.'

Finally, Rosie managed to squeeze both feet into her boots.

'Thank you, Miss.'

'Rosie, we need to tell your mother your boots are too small.'

'They're not my boots, Miss.'

'Not your boots!' exclaimed Lily.

'No, Miss.'

'Then whose are they?'

'M'brother's, an' m'mam said ah 'ad t'wear 'em 'cause she can't afford new uns.'

'So these are your brother's boots?'

'Yes, Miss, 'e only 'ad small feet before 'e died.'

Lily stared hard at the little girl, taking in the ragged clothing and the knots in her hair.

'I'm sorry, Rosie . . . When was this?'

'Last year, Miss. Our Derek 'ad a poorly chest. 'E's in 'eaven now.' Rosie stared up out of the high arched window at the scudding clouds. 'So 'e won't need no shoes, so m'mam says.'

Joseph was collecting his books from the classroom and heard the conversation. He was silent for a long time while an idea formed.

A few minutes later he was discussing it with his sister. After searching through the 'Emergency Clothing Box', Vera gave him a large brown paper bag. Then she watched him as he walked his bicycle down to the school gate and rode off along the High Street. Not for the first time, she realized that her brother had a kind heart. He simply needed pointing in the right direction.

Joseph cycled to Chauntsinger Lane, past the blacksmith's and on to Badger's Row. He parked his bicycle against the wall of the last cottage and knocked on the door. Mary Finn opened it and the flour on her hands suggested she was making bread.

'Mr Evans,' she said. 'This is a surprise.'

'May I have a brief word, Mary? It won't take long. I have something for you.'

Mary looked suspiciously at the paper bag.

Joseph glanced around the cramped room. The furniture was sparse and the pantry door was open. It had a stone shelf opening to the outside and protected by a wire grille, and it necessitated regular shopping for perishables.

He held up the bag. 'There are some boots in here for Rosie. They're her size, and there's a pair of sandals as well.'

Mary rubbed the flour from her hands on her pinny and folded her arms in a determined fashion. 'Ah don't want no charity, Mr Evans, but ah thank you kindly.'

Joseph recalled his sister's advice and chose his words carefully. 'I'm not offering charity, Mary,' said Joseph firmly. 'I want you to *pay* for them. In fact, I insist.'

Mary smiled. 'You've come to t'wrong 'ouse, Vicar. There's no spare money.'

'I don't want money. I want your *labour*. An hour on Sunday morning working with the Holy Dusters. The team needs a reliable woman like you.'

Mary drew herself to her full height and stepped forward. 'So long as it's not charity.'

Joseph put the bag of footwear on the table and turned to go.

'Eight o'clock, Sunday, Mary – and bring Rosie. She can help my sister make some sandwiches. The ladies always have some tea and sandwiches and cake afterwards. Nothing special – just a little ritual.'

He didn't look back as he strode out.

Mary watched him attach his cycle clips and ride off on his ancient bicycle.

Before she left school Vera called into the kitchen where Irene Gubbins the cook was tackling the pots and pans she had used for today's school dinner of boiled beef, carrots, cabbage and potatoes.

'It's a struggle is this, Miss Evans,' she said, her face flushed with effort.

Vera watched Irene as she sighed and crouched down to clean the kitchen cooker. It was another problem in Vera's busy day, but she had an idea.

At the school gate she met Mrs Riley, mother of eight-year-old Gordon. Her son was a free spirit, reciting his twelve times table in a sing-song voice and ending with a smile that would have melted the heart of the meanest Scrooge.

'Hello, Mrs Riley,' said Vera. 'How are you today?'

'Bit flustered, to be 'onest, Miss Evans. It were a difficult night with our Gordon's breathin' an' ah thought ah'd jus' call in t'see 'ow 'e's gettin' on.'

'It's almost certainly asthma,' said Vera, clearly concerned. 'You need to take him to see Doctor Davenport.'

'Ah'm not comfortable wi' doctors,' said Mrs Riley with a frown. 'Ah've 'ad some bad experiences.'

'The school nurse will be here next week and she will help, I'm sure.'

'Thank you, Miss Evans, ah know y'mean well an' ah want my Gordon to 'ave a better chance than ah 'ad . . . but life's a bit difficult sometimes.'

Vera was concerned at Mrs Riley's reticence to seek medical support. 'Well, I'll mention it to Mr Pruett and Miss Briggs and we'll keep an eye on him.'

Vera hurried across the road to the General Stores.

'Just a few things for now, please, Prudence.'

Prudence stepped up behind the counter to be on a level with the tall school secretary. 'Yes, Vera?'

'A pad of your Basildon Bond writing paper – blue, please.'

'The sign of quality,' said Prudence with a knowing glance at her dear friend.

'And matching envelopes, of course.'

Prudence placed them on the counter.

'Also, I need some of your Ajax Cleanser. Irene in the kitchen needs a bit of help with her cleaning.'

Vera hurried back to school and Irene was thrilled with her new cleaning agent. 'Thank you, Miss Evans,' she said. 'What will they think of next?'

Ruby Smith was in Tommy Piercy's butcher's shop again.

''Ave y'got a bit o' scrag end for a stew please, Mr Piercy?'

'Ah 'ave jus' the very thing.' He slapped a generous slice on the counter and charged the minimum. ''Ow are you, Ruby? Y'mus' be gettin' close now.'

Ruby's face was flushed. 'Mebbe a couple o' weeks, Mr Piercy, but m'mam's keepin' an eye on me so ah'll be fine.'

It should be Ronnie, thought Tommy.

Ruby's next call was to the General Stores. 'Ah need a box o' cereal, please, Prudence.'

'You can't beat Kellogg's Cornflakes, Ruby,' said Prudence, 'with plenty of sugar and milk.'

'Sounds lovely,' said Ruby, but doubted there would be much sugar in the house.

'And here's a treat for young Andrew.' Prudence selected a packet of Rowntree's Sunripe Jelly from the shelf behind the counter.

'That's really kind, Prudence,' said Ruby. ''E'll be thrilled when 'e sees this.'

Ruby was crossing the High Street when Stan Coe screeched past in his Land Rover. She stepped out of the way quickly, put her hand on her swollen tummy and paused while she gathered herself.

Vera witnessed the incident and called out, 'Are you all right, Ruby?'

Ruby had dropped her shopping bag and Tommy Piercy rushed from his shop to pick it up. He looked angrily after the speeding Land Rover as it tore round the bend at the end of the High Street. ''E drives like bloomin' Stirlin' Moss, does that Stan Coe. Wants lockin' up.'

'Shall I walk you home, Ruby?' asked Vera.

'Ah'll be fine, jus' a bit of a shock, that's all.'

'Would y'like t'sit down?' asked Tommy.

'Thanks, but ah'll get off 'ome,' and she crossed the road.

Tommy was annoyed. 'Ah saw 'im through m'window. Gorra face like a blind cobbler's thumb.'

Vera, although puzzled by the description, got the message. She spotted Albert Jenkins, the school governor, coming out of the Post Office. Albert was an intelligent man and always supportive of the local school. He listened intently to what Vera had to say and decided to stop by the school to have a brief word with John Pruett during afternoon break.

John was on playground duty when Albert called to him from the other side of the school wall. The conversation was brief and to the point.

'You mark my words, John,' concluded Albert forcefully, 'one day that Stan Coe will go to hell in a handcart.'

John Pruett gave a wistful smile as Albert turned and set off across the village green. *Let's hope so*, he thought, but said nothing.

Agnes was concerned when Ruby returned home and told her about Stan Coe.

'Sit down, Ruby, an' ah'll mek some tea. Andy's asleep, so y'can put y'feet up.'

'Thanks, Mam,' said Ruby.

She looked at the contents of Ruby's shopping bag and sighed. Their income didn't go far now that Ruby couldn't do any cleaning. Also the house was distinctly chilly – cold enough for Agnes to have to put on a second pair of cotton lisle stockings to protect her legs.

As she picked up the kettle from the trivet in the hearth she muttered, "'E's allus been a wolf in cheap clothin', 'as that Stan Coe, an' 'e were a bully at school as well, so ah've 'eard.'

Lily had finally agreed to join the church choir and after school she walked up to St Mary's Church to join in the practice. Vera was in the process of solving yet another problem. The choir stalls were on either side of the chancel floor and, as usual, Davinia Grint, the lead soprano, was threatening the stained-glass windows with her highest notes. In contrast, Gerald Crimpton was the sole member of the bass section and it was to his eternal misfortune that he suffered from severe nasal problems. In consequence, his contribution had all the subtlety of a creaking door.

An argument had broken out between the two and Vera intervened to introduce Lily.

'Please welcome Miss Briggs, the teacher from our village school.' Vera looked at Davinia with a firm expression. 'Lily is a *mezzo*-soprano and should complement your beautiful voice, Davinia.' The self-important soprano was sufficiently flattered to calm down. 'And Gerald, I've brought a nasal spray for you from the chemist.' Gerald looked delighted and Davinia smiled in triumph while Lily looked bemused.

'You'll like Gerald,' whispered Vera to Lily. 'He's the strong silent type – rather like your policeman,' she added with a knowing glance.

Lily blushed as she recalled the tenderness of Tom's goodnight kisses.

It was late afternoon in the vicarage and Vera had completed a letter to Mrs Riley on her new Basildon Bond writing paper. As a result, Mrs Riley took Vera's advice and visited the doctor and local Pharmacy. From then on, each evening, she opened her tin of Potter's Asthma Cure, sprinkled some of the precious powder into a bowl and then lit it carefully. Gordon stooped over the bowl and inhaled, and, slowly but surely, his breathing became easier.

Vera turned to her next task. She was making a hassock for church and embroidering it with loving care. The date 1952 had been stitched carefully above the name of the late King. She looked across at Joseph, who was preparing his next sermon, and felt a great surge of pride in her younger brother. It had been a demanding day, but he had done well.

Joseph looked up, concerned. 'I'm worried about this sermon, Vera.' He put down his pen in despair.

Vera smiled. 'Don't worry about tomorrow, for tomorrow will bring its own worries,' she quoted.

Joseph sat back. 'Yes, I know that one ... Matthew, chapter six, verse thirty-four, as I recall.'

'Well done, Joseph.' She sat back as the ticking of the

clock on the mantelpiece measured out the moments of their lives. 'I'm pleased you could help Mary Finn and her daughter. That was a job well done.'

'Thank you, Vera. We could celebrate with a glass of my home-made wine.'

Oh dear, thought Vera. 'Perhaps a little later, Joseph,' and she bowed her head to her stitchcraft.

Darkness had fallen on Badger's Row and Mary Finn was preparing a meagre meal. Rosie was trying on her new footwear, first the sandals, then the boots and finally back to the sandals to wear around the house.

She walked over to the window and stared up at the dark sky and the cold moon. 'Mam, is our Derek in 'eaven?'

Mary paused in chopping the half onion. 'Yes, luv, an' God will be watchin' over 'im.'

'Ah 'ope so, Mam. An' will there be angels?'

Mary scooped the onion into the pan. 'Yes, Rosie, lots of angels, an' they're up there in 'eaven lookin' after y'brother.'

'Mam, ah asked Mr Evans a question, but ah don't think 'e knew t'answer.'

Mary stirred the slices of bacon and chopped onion. 'An' what were that?'

'Ah said do angels 'ave wings?'

'Wings?'

'Yes, Mam.'

'Well, ah'm sure they do, luv.' She looked out of the window and recalled the retreating figure of the local vicar as he pedalled down the lane.

And some ride bicycles, she thought.

Chapter Twelve

Husbands and Homemakers

As Ruby Smith stared out of her bedroom window the first light of a pale sun gilded the distant hills and the scent of wallflowers was in the air. It was the pre-dawn of a day when the breath of spring hung in the air, tenuous and tantalizing, the merest hint of a new season. While in the far distance the Hambleton hills appeared bleak against a wind-driven sky, beneath the hard crust of earth new life was stirring. It had been a long, cold winter, but life had come full circle. It was Friday, 27 March and spring had returned once more to Ragley village.

However, the wonder of the seasons was far from the mind of the teenage Ruby. She recognized the pain.

'Mam . . . Mam!' she shouted in anguish. 'Baby's comin'.'

After getting off the bus Lily felt refreshed on this spring morning. In the hedgerows the sharp buds of hawthorn guarded the arrowheads of daffodils and on Ragley High Street the primroses splashed the grassy banks with colour.

It was the end of a busy week and a student teacher was due to arrive today for her preliminary visit prior to her teaching practice in the summer. Lily thought back to her days as a student in training and vowed she would do her best to mentor the newcomer.

She walked across the road to look at the poster on the noticeboard outside the village hall. Tom had asked her to accompany him to the Annual Spring Dance tomorrow evening. This year it was one of the events to raise funds to replace the railings on the school wall, plus contributing to a shelter for the bus stop. The villagers of Ragley were keen to support. Removing the railings had been a symbolic gesture towards the war effort and everyone was keen to move on and return the image of the school to its pre-war days.

The poster read:

Ragley Village Hall Committee

ANNUAL SPRING DANCE

Saturday, 28th March 1953
7.30 p.m.
Admission: One shilling

Lily felt comfortable and smart in her new cardigan suit. Her mother had made it for her and the pleated skirt, now only twelve inches from the ground, was the height of fashion. With her last salary she had bought a pair of Brevitt Casuals, slip-on shoes with a cushioned soft tread and perfect for a busy day in school. It was enough to turn heads as she walked up the High Street towards school.

*

At 7 School View Ronnie Smith had never got out of bed so quickly. Agnes was in no mood to take prisoners. She wanted action . . . and she wanted it fast.

'Ronnie, move y'self and go t'Doctor Davenport!' she shouted. 'Tell 'im t'baby's on its way an' ah'm 'ere but ah need some 'elp.'

Ronnie dragged on his clothes and ran out of the front door and up the Morton road as if the hounds of hell were chasing him.

In the bedroom Agnes mopped Ruby's forehead with a damp flannel. 'Now then, Ruby luv,' she said, 'ah think this one might be comin' a bit quicker.' Ruby groaned and began to breathe fast. Her contractions were already getting stronger, longer and closer together.

'Oh Mam, it 'urts,' she gasped as she gripped her mother's hand.

'Don't worry, luv – ah'm 'ere.'

When Lily walked into the staff-room the student teacher had already arrived and had introduced herself to John and Vera. It was clear that they both approved of this enthusiastic and purposeful young woman.

'Hello, Lily,' said John. 'This is Anne Watson, our student from the college in Ripon.' Anne was a tall, slim brunette, twenty years old and lissom in her movements. From the outset Lily recognized she was keen to succeed.

'Welcome to Ragley,' said Lily, 'and I shall do my best to help. Feel free to ask any questions.'

'I need to get to know the children,' Anne said, 'and confirm my timetable. Then I have to prepare my lessons over the Easter break and present them to my tutor, Miss Trimble.'

'You will be working with the children in my class,' said Lily, 'and they're hard-working and responsive. The summer term will give us the opportunity to do some work outdoors. This is a wonderful place, with the woods, fields and animals. We need to make use of them.'

John was listening intently. 'As well as learning our tables and handwriting,' he interjected.

Anne got the message. 'Of course . . . and Miss Trimble would expect nothing less.'

John smiled. He knew Miss Trimble. Her nickname of the Ripon Rottweiler was appropriate for this fierce lady.

'Let's go into the classroom,' said Lily.

Anne picked up her bulky satchel of children's books and a cumbersome ring-binder of lesson notes.

That was when Lily noticed the ring on the third finger of her left hand.

The arrival of a breathless Ronnie attempting to hammer down his door was something Dr Davenport took in his stride. He asked his wife, Joyce, to telephone the local midwife, then he picked up his black bag and hurried out of the house. As always, Joyce was calm. A friend of Vera's since their school days, she was already admired in the local Women's Institute for the excellence of her sponge cakes and her cold-cure remedies.

Dr Davenport and the midwife, Eileen Goodbody, a buxom, no-nonsense Yorkshirewoman for whom childbirth was like shelling peas, arrived at 7 School View at the same time and set to work in the blink of an eye. Agnes was reassured and answered their calls for hot water and clean towels while keeping an eye on young Andy.

Ronnie remained downstairs in the kitchen, chain smoking and gagging for a pint of Tetley's. 'Another bloody mouth t'feed,' he muttered.

In John Pruett's class all the children were busy copying out a note to take home to their parents.

John had written on the blackboard: 'School closed today for the Easter holiday and will reopen on Monday, 13th April.'

Every child had to write it out twice, with the second copy being taken home by the younger children in Lily's class.

After the first hour Lily soon appreciated that Anne had the makings of a good teacher. She communicated well with the children and responded to their requests for help. It was the beginning of a positive partnership. Lily was even more impressed when Anne volunteered to play the piano in assembly.

However, when Anne opened her songbook to Albert Midlane's popular hymn 'There's a Friend for Little Children' and began to play, Lily stared out of the window. John Pruett observed how she was suddenly in a world of her own. Also, he was sure he noticed a tear in her eye and wondered why.

After morning milk Lily and Anne were on playground duty during break. They were each sipping a cup of tea and watching Reggie Bamforth play the part of Robin Hood with a group of boys. He had been to Phoebe Fawnswater's house to watch the new weekly series of *Robin Hood*. Patrick

Troughton had become the first actor to play the role on television and Reggie was shooting imaginary arrows at Norman Fazackerly, who kept falling down and pretending to die.

Lily and Anne were soon in conversation. Anne lived with her parents on the Easington road and she intended to get married to John Grainger during the summer holidays, as soon as she had qualified. She was proud of her engagement ring, a small opal in a gold setting, and held it up in the morning light. 'It belonged to John's grandmother, so it's been passed down through the generations.'

According to Anne, John was a tall, handsome trainee woodcarver. After completing his National Service he had secured employment with a local furniture maker specializing in oak sideboards, tables and chairs. She said he always took a pride in his work, often adding a finishing touch of a beautifully carved acorn. However, it was when he was in his shed at home on his father's farm carving models of shire horses that he felt like a craftsman of old, creating wonderful shapes from a simple block of seasoned oak.

As the bell rang for the end of playtime, Anne noticed there were no rings on Lily's finger.

It was midday and the doctor and midwife had done their work. Ruby was holding a beautiful baby girl in her arms. 'Ah did it, Mam,' she said.

'An' she's lovely . . . jus' perfec' like 'er mother,' said Agnes. 'C'mon, let me 'old 'er.'

Ruby was too tired to lift the small child, so Agnes picked her up and held her close. The familiar softness and scent of a new-born baby reminded her of Ruby all those years ago. 'You've gorra gran' that loves you, my sweet,' she whispered, 'and a mam who will always be there for you.'

When she looked back at the bed, the exhausted Ruby was asleep and Agnes stood there gazing down at her daughter and listening to her soft breathing. The sibilant sounds brought comfort to her soul.

However, the moment was shattered when Ronnie opened the bedroom door.

'Do you want to 'old y'daughter?' asked Agnes, a little reluctantly.

'Bit later, when ah get back.'

'Get back? Where y'goin'?'

'Pub o' course, t'celebrate . . . it's tradition,' and Ronnie clattered down the stairs.

Anne Watson was sitting next to an inquisitive Rosie Finn and an intrigued Phoebe Fawnswater at lunchtime.

'What's that, Miss?' asked Rosie.

'It's my engagement ring.'

'What's it for?'

'It's to show I've promised to marry my boyfriend.'

'When are you getting married, Miss?' asked Phoebe.

'In the summer holidays.'

Rosie considered the implications. 'And will you have a pretty dress?'

'Yes, I shall – a lovely white dress.'

'I went to my aunty's wedding and she wore a white dress,' said Phoebe. 'Why are they always white?'

Anne considered this for a moment, seeking a suitable

response. 'I think it's because *white* is the colour of happiness and your wedding day is the happiest day of your life.'

Phoebe frowned. 'So why does the groom wear *black*?'

Good question, thought Anne.

When Ronnie walked into The Royal Oak he was disappointed that the tap room was almost empty. A few retired farmers were sitting at the table next to the bay window drinking bottles of stout while playing a fives-and-threes dominoes game. Clarence Higginbottom pulled Ronnie the obligatory free pint to 'wet the baby's head' and Ronnie raised his glass. 'To m'daughter,' he said.

One of the farmers looked up. 'A daughter? 'Ard luck. Y'need *sons* t'earn money.'

There was unanimous approval among the domino players and they returned to their game shaking their heads as if there had been a death in the village.

''Ello, Ronnie, ah saw y'comin' in.' It was Thelma, the local flirt.

''Ello, Thelma. Ruby's just 'ad a baby – little girl.'

'Well, y'better buy me a drink t'celebrate. Ah'll 'ave a Cinzano Bianco – ah like them erotic drinks. Remember, Ronnie, y'bought me one in Morecambe.'

In the summer of 1951 Ronnie had enjoyed an illicit day trip with the voluptuous eighteen-year-old Thelma when he was on leave from his National Service. She had brought a camera and he had taken her photo leaning against the seafront railings and smiling seductively. She had been wearing her new Terylene pleated skirt and had just paid one shilling and ninepence for a pair of Twinco sunglasses.

As she smoked her Capstan cigarette she had felt like a film star.

Back in the staff-room Lily and Anne were discussing projects for the summer term when John walked in carrying his cane and a long leather strap.

'I thought it worth mentioning our policy regarding discipline,' he said. 'If anyone misbehaves, then obviously I would expect you to deal with it immediately and you may send a child to me for punishment.' He held up the cane. 'This is for six of the best, usually for fighting, bullying, swearing and smoking. However, I try to keep that to a minimum and use this instead. It's an old barber's strop and ideal for lashing an outstretched hand.'

Lily pursed her lips and remained silent.

Anne looked concerned. 'I would hope there would be no need for that, Mr Pruett, as I intend to provide a relevant curriculum that excites the children and keeps them interested. That has worked so far on my previous teaching practices.'

Well said, thought Lily.

John sat back a little perplexed, and unsure if there was a hint of implicit criticism.

Anne saw his reaction. 'And as this is such a lovely school, I can't foresee a problem.'

John seemed sufficiently placated. 'Well, you will appreciate it has to be done or they'll think there's no discipline – and, come to think of it, it didn't do me any harm.'

Afternoon school went well for Lily and Anne, though it was clear they were unimpressed by John's old-fashioned style of teaching. Lily kept a professional silence.

During his physical training lesson his pupils stood in

pairs throwing a beanbag to each other across the hall in a desultory fashion. Likewise, his craft lesson comprised the girls making identical peg bags while the boys made long cylinders from thick cardboard for storing spills. It was uninspiring.

In contrast, at the end of the day the children sat in rapt silence during Anne's story time. She read from her copy of Beatrix Potter's *The Tale of Peter Rabbit* and brought the story of the mischievous and disobedient Peter to life. The children held their breath when he was chased by Mr McGregor and sighed with relief when his mother finally put him to bed with a dose of camomile tea.

It was the last day of the spring term and for the children a two-week Easter holiday beckoned, with thoughts of climbing trees, pond dipping and Easter eggs. After school a relaxed John Pruett and Lily met in the staffroom with Anne for a cup of tea.

'Well done,' said Lily when the children had gone home. Then a thought struck her. 'By the way, there's a dance tomorrow night in the village hall.'

By late afternoon the news of Ruby's baby had filtered through to the local Pharmacy and Herbert Grinchley made sure it was soon all around the village.

Meanwhile, Nora Pratt was at the counter with her best friend, Shirley Makin. Fourteen-year-old Shirley was regarded as the best teenage cook in the village and both girls were excited about the Saturday night dance.

'Y'need t'try this, girls,' said Herbert. He held up a bottle of the new Silvikrin Cream Shampoo. 'Ah 'eard it said Britain's up-an'-comin' girls are rushin' t'buy it.'

'Why's that, Mr Gwinchley?' asked Nora.

''Cause it gives you poise an' confidence.'

'Ah'd like t'be confident,' said Shirley, who tended to hide her light under a bushel. She picked up the bottle and studied it carefully. 'Hey, Nora, it says it gives you "sheer beauty".'

''Ow much is it, Mr Gwinchley?' asked Nora.

'One shillin' an' threepence, an' that'll give y'three shampoos.'

Then Herbert produced a large bottle from under the counter like a magician. 'Or y'could get double in t'big bottle for two shillings.'

'That's thwee shampoos each if we spend a shilling each,' said Nora quickly. She was top in mathematics in her class.

Shirley nodded. 'Meks sense t'me.'

On her way home Lily had called in to the General Stores and bought a tin of Ovaltine. That night before going to bed she smiled when she prepared a steaming mug. On the side of the tin it said 'The World's Best Nightcap', and as she climbed the stairs she gave a secret smile and thought of Tom.

There was a watercolour painting hanging above her bed. Painted with care and precision, it showed a village scene in high summer. A beaten track led up to a white-fronted farmhouse with a riot of wisteria clambering up its walls. Two burly farm labourers were leaning against an old Ford tractor, apparently deep in conversation, while the distant fields of barley shimmered in the sun-light. Lily stroked a delicate finger down the side of the wooden frame and studied the picture carefully. It brought back memories of warm summer days in the Land Army, gathering in a bountiful harvest . . . and special times.

On Saturday morning, at the age of twenty, Diane Wigglesworth was thinking about her life. She and her mother were in the hairdresser's shop waiting for their first customers.

Diane had met a suave physiotherapist from the hospital in York and he had suggested that she would make a perfect nurse. He had told her there were training allowances starting at £200 per year, plus twenty-eight days' holiday with pay. A professional career in the arms of the handsome health worker stretched out before Diane. However, all was not what it seemed. He had given her a copy of 'A Nurse's Life' from the Ministry of Labour & National Service and then asked her to sleep with him on their second date.

Unknown to Diane, Bernard was a sexual predator with a string of conquests. Sadly, it was the first disappointment of many that were to befall the Ragley village hairdresser. Her mother offered her a cigarette and some advice. 'Don't trust men,' she said. 'They're only after one thing.'

Their first customer arrived. It was Violet Fawnswater.

'I thought I would try that beauty treatment shampoo you mentioned, Diane,' said Violet.

'White Rain,' said Diane, 'new from America. A sachet f'ninepence or t'economy bottle for 'alf a crown. Meks 'air shiny, silky an' beautiful, an' preserves y'natural oils.'

Diane was better with her products than with her choice of men.

'Ronnie, ah want t'call 'er Racquel,' said Ruby.

'Racquel? 'Ow come?' Ronnie was pleased. He had no recollection of a previous girlfriend called Racquel and it occurred to him it could have been a lot worse. It could have been Thelma.

'Ah were readin' that Gipsy Fortuna what does star signs,' said Ruby. 'She tells y'fortune in t'*Erald* an' she said yesterday were a lucky day.'

'Star signs?'

'Yes, Ronnie. She's called Racquel Fortuna. Sounds posh.'

The new astrologer had started a weekly column in the *Easington Herald & Pioneer* and many of the ladies in the village had become avid followers. The fact that Gipsy Fortuna was actually Brenda from the bread shop in Thirkby who needed extra cash for a new wardrobe was not common knowledge.

The Saturday Spring Dance was a great success. The village hall was full, and chairs and tables had been placed around the outside to leave plenty of room for dancing. Clarence Higginbottom had set up a bar on a huge trestle table stacked high with barrels of beer and soft drinks. Then he returned to The Royal Oak, leaving his wife and daughter in charge. Meanwhile, young men were hoping to catch the eye of one of the girls while old-timers swapped stories.

John Pruett had brought a gramophone and set about selecting appropriate records for the various dances. It wasn't long before Vera gave up trying to guide Joseph through the basic steps of a waltz, but Lily was impressed with Tom. She was a good dancer herself, and he proved surprisingly adept and coped wonderfully with the quickstep.

Unknown to Lily and Vera, John Pruett had been attending Edith Fortesque's Ballroom Dancing Class in Easington and had been practising a wide range of dances. Lily agreed to be his partner for the valeta, which was a demanding ballroom dance in triple time. However, John's feet skipped across the floor with effortless ease.

'That was wonderful, John,' said a breathless Lily, and he glowed with pleasure. This was the opportunity he had been waiting for – a chance to engage his beautiful colleague in stimulating conversation.

'*Valeta* is the Spanish for weather vane,' he said, which seemed a little incongruous to Lily.

'That's interesting,' she said without conviction. 'Thanks for the dance, John,' and wandered off back to Tom.

After a while Tommy Piercy took his seat at the piano and took out a packet of Player's Navy Cut Medium cigarettes. He stared affectionately at the picture of the bearded sailor on the front of the packet and recalled his own days in the Royal Navy. It was a change from his pipe, and he lit a cigarette, puffed contentedly and opened the piano lid. Soon everyone was enjoying a selection of their favourite wartime songs, including 'The Lambeth Walk', 'White Cliffs of Dover', 'We'll Meet Again' and 'Don't Dilly Dally on the Way'.

Lily watched Tom singing along with gusto and wondered if anyone noticed when she didn't join in.

To Vera's surprise, Ronnie Smith made an appearance at the dance. Vera had visited Ruby during the afternoon and delivered a bunch of flowers and a knitted cardigan for baby Racquel. Ruby had been so grateful, and there were tears in her eyes at the acts of kindness from friends and neighbours.

Vera marched up to Ronnie, who had just ordered a pint from Mavis behind the bar. 'How is Ruby?' she asked.

'Fine thanks, Miss Evans,' replied Ronnie, unconcerned. 'Jus' restin'.'

'I'm a little surprised you're here, Ronald. Is there someone with Ruby?'

''Er mother,' said Ronnie and he supped deeply on his pint. 'So ah'm wettin' t'baby's 'ead like ah did wi' Andy,' and he walked away, sat down next to Thelma and offered her a cigarette.

Herbert Grinchley leaned over to Alfie Kershaw and nodded towards Ronnie. ''E ought t'be careful wi' 'er.'

'Y'right there, 'Erbert,' said Alfie. 'She knows all there is t'know in t'bedroom department does that one, so ah've 'eard.'

Towards the end of the evening Lily saw Anne looking a little distressed and walking out of the front door towards the High Street. She followed and saw Anne stubbing out a cigarette with a grimace. When she noticed Lily she gave a wan smile. 'I hate cigarettes.'

'Then why smoke them?' asked Lily.

'Because my John buys them for me. All his favourite film stars smoke.'

'Just tell him you don't like them.'

Anne looked a little forlorn. 'It's difficult.'

'Why?'

Anne sighed. 'He's got set ideas about us. Just a typical man, I suppose.'

'What do you mean?'

'Well, he says after we're married he'll be the *husband* and I'll be the *homemaker*.'

'What about your profession? You'll be a teacher. That must come first.'

Anne shook her head. 'He doesn't see it like that. He'll expect me to be at home tidying the house, making his meals and warming his slippers.'

'Anne – it's not my place to interfere, but you need to tell him how you feel and you need to do it soon.'

'You're right,' said Anne. 'I'll try.'

Lily watched the young student walk away looking thoughtful.

Lily was staring up at the scudding clouds when Tom appeared. 'Here you are,' he said. 'Everything all right?'

'Just trying to point Anne in the right direction.'

'Really? She seems fine to me.'

'Apparently John Grainger has some old-fashioned ideas.'

'Such as?'

'Married life. The roles of men and women. Husbands and homemakers.'

'I see.' He put his arm around her shoulder. 'I wouldn't see marriage like that. You're too good a teacher.'

Lily looked up at him quizzically. 'Sometimes, Tom Feather, you say just the right thing.'

He stroked her cheek gently. 'That's the problem with love, Lily. You can't choose. It picks you.'

212

She stretched up and kissed him, but said nothing.

'One day I'll understand you,' he said quietly.

Lily shivered.

'Shall we go back inside?' Tom asked. 'I don't want you to get cold.'

It was last orders and Mavis was serving John Grainger and Tom Feather, making sure they had every opportunity to admire her prodigious cleavage as she pulled the pints. She looked up at the young woodcarver. 'Ah 'ear y'gettin' married.'

'That's right, in the summer.'

'Ah know t'secret of a 'appy marriage,' said Mavis and she gave a conspiratorial wink in Tom's direction.

'And what's that?' asked John.

'We go out twice a week for a meal.'

'That's nice.'

'Yes, it is. Ah go on Tuesday an' 'e goes on Friday.'

Chapter Thirteen

A Friend for Miss Golightly

It was Saturday, 4 April and spring had arrived in all its glory. Tiny lambs tottered on uncertain legs in the fields and yellow petals of forsythia lifted the spirits. The log fires and long, dark days of winter were but a distant memory and thoughts of playing in the woods and Easter eggs filled the minds of the children of Ragley village. In the flower tubs outside The Royal Oak the daffodils raised their bright-yellow trumpets to the sky and the first swallows had returned to their old haunts to build their nests.

When Lily cycled past the village green Big Dave and Little Malcolm were peering into the village pond and collecting frogspawn in jam jars. They gave a cheerful wave as she rode up the Morton road in the morning sunshine with the soft breeze in her face.

She passed the village milkmen, Alfie Morgetroyd and his son Ernie. They were going at their usual sedate pace, accompanied by the familiar clip-clop of their horse's hooves and the rattle of churns. The horse knew when to stop and women came out with jugs of all shapes and sizes. Ernie would scoop a ladleful of precious milk while Alfie passed the time of day.

Lily smiled. It was a gentle scene that had become part of the fabric of her life. Finally, she turned into the vicarage driveway, parked her bicycle against the wall and went into the church hall. Vera and the ladies of the St Mary's Social Committee were already hard at work preparing for that afternoon's Easter Bring and Buy Sale. Lily removed her hat and gloves and walked over to a trestle table laden with books, toys and knitted dishcloths.

Also, propped against the table leg was the most wonderful teddy bear she had ever seen.

Edith Tripps, the thirty-seven-year-old headteacher of Morton Primary School and a dear friend of Vera, saw Lily's surprise. 'He's magnificent, isn't he?'

'Oh, hello, Miss Tripps,' said Lily. 'Yes, I was just admiring him.'

Edith stooped down and picked up the teddy bear. 'He was left behind by a wealthy American who visited the village with her daughter and he was too big to fit in her luggage.'

'I see,' said Lily. 'Well, we must find him a good home.'

'I said exactly the same to Vera.'

Joyce Davenport, the doctor's wife and treasurer of the Social Committee, appeared carrying two brass candlesticks. 'Where shall I put these, Edith?'

'With the rest of the bric-a-brac, I presume,' said Edith.

Joyce pointed a candlestick at the teddy bear. 'I see you're admiring our furry friend, Lily. Rather than put

him on sale, why don't you take him back to school? I'm
sure the children would love him.'

'What a good idea,' said Edith with a wry smile, 'but we
had better clear it with *our leader*.'

They all turned and looked at Vera, who was checking
the quality of the napkins on the refreshment table. She
called across to them, concerned at their apparent inactiv-
ity, 'Come along, ladies – Proverbs sixteen, twenty-seven.'

Lily and Joyce looked puzzled. 'Don't worry,' whispered Edith, 'that's one of her old favourites: "Idle hands
are the devil's workshop."'

'Right,' said Joyce, 'come on, ladies, back to work.'

The teenage friends Nora Pratt and Shirley Makin were in
the General Stores. 'Good morning, Miss Golightly,' said
Shirley. 'We're goin' t'make a cake.'

'It's for t'Bwing an' Buy Sale,' added Nora.

'That's wonderful, girls,' said Prudence.

Shirley put two pennies and three farthings on the
counter. 'Mrs Clutterbuck said can she please 'ave a dozen
eggs?'

Nora added another two pennies. 'An' two ounces of
lemon dwops, please.'

Prudence unscrewed the top of the jar and with a small
scoop transferred the bright-yellow, sticky sweets on to the
pan of the weighing scales. When it reached two ounces
on the dial she added one more sweet for good measure
and poured them into a blue paper cone, which she folded
expertly at the top.

'Thank you, Miss Golightly,' chorused the girls, and as
they walked out of the shop the doorbell rang merrily.

'Who would have believed it?' Prudence murmured to herself. 'Rationing over – eight years after the war.'

Back in Doris Clutterbuck's kitchen, Nora and Shirley took turns to whisk the cake mixture with a fork for what seemed like an eternity. Naturally, they also took turns to scrape out the bowl and lick the cake mixture from the large wooden spoon.

In years to come they would look back on this time in their young lives and think of these special days. They would remember treacle pudding and spotted dick and the vast array of preserved fruit – rhubarb, apples and plums in neatly labelled Kilner jars on the high wooden shelf in the pantry. It was a private ritual for them that after a plateful of plums and custard they would line up the plum stones around the edge of the plate and recite, 'Tinker, tailor, soldier, sailor, rich man, poor man, beggarman, thief.' Anyone with eight stones would hope for a second helping to begin the recitation once again.

Soon the cake was in the oven and the Bring and Buy Sale beckoned.

Deirdre Coe walked into the General Stores and marched up to the counter. 'Ah want a bag o' sweets f'my Stanley.'

How rude, thought Prudence. 'Which ones, Deirdre?'

'Them,' said Deirdre, pointing to the large jar of liquorice torpedoes.

'How much?' asked Prudence as she unscrewed the lid.

'Four ounce.' And Deirdre slapped a coin on the counter.

Prudence was a Christian lady, but it did not stop her from disliking Deirdre Coe, who was always disrespectful when she came into the shop. It was a relief when she departed. 'Just as bad as her brother,' murmured Prudence.

She remembered that Stanley had continued as a pig farmer during the war, but in the evenings he had been an ARP, or Air Raid Precaution, warden. He had enjoyed shouting at the villagers and banging on their doors telling them to turn out their lights. When Prudence had covered her plate-glass window with strips of tape to reduce the chance of shattered glass after a bomb blast, Stan had complained that she hadn't done it properly.

That was when she had just lost Jeremy, taken from her life by the horror of war. She stared around her shop and felt a keen sense of loneliness. Through the window she saw Ruby Smith walk by pushing a pram and she thought of what might have been.

Ruby was looking well again. Her cheeks were rosy and her chestnut hair fell in waves around her pretty face. She was proud of her baby, and villagers stopped and cooed in appreciation and felt the little girl's soft skin and tiny fingers. 'Jus' perfec',' was the regular opinion.

Ruby enjoyed this time of year. The final wisps of mist had disappeared in the early-morning sunlight. The first warmth of spring had brought new life to the quiet land. It was as if the trees and fields had emerged from a deep sleep. The cuckoo, the messenger of spring, had arrived along with new grass and primroses. On days such as this there was a lightness to her spirit and a spring in her step. She thought it was a pity that Ronnie was still in bed and not sharing this beautiful morning.

*

In Doris Clutterbuck's Tea Rooms the first customers were enjoying their morning cup of tea and a toasted teacake. On the radio Lita Roza was singing her hit record 'How Much Is That Doggie in the Window?' and everyone was humming along to the catchy tune.

Doris was behind the counter reading an article in her *Woman & Home* magazine entitled 'Can a woman run a home and a business?' It featured a lady who ran a hat shop in York. She seemed to have the perfect life and said she owed it all to her nightcap of Cadbury's Bournvita. Doris usually had a cup of tea and a digestive biscuit at bedtime but was now seriously considering changing the habit of a lifetime.

It was late afternoon when Lily cycled from the church hall to school. In the basket attached to her handlebars was a large teddy bear. The Bring and Buy Sale had been a success thanks to the military organization of Vera and her willing team of helpers.

A Land Rover was parked outside The Royal Oak and as she cycled past a coarse voice shouted, 'Who's y'furry boyfriend, sweet'eart?'

It was Stan Coe and, as always, Lily ignored him.

Happily he was inside the pub by the time she had put the teddy bear in the school's store cupboard and set off down the High Street. She decided to call in to the General Stores to buy some sweets for Freddie. However, when she spoke to Prudence it was clear to Lily that there was something amiss.

'You're just in time,' said the petite shopkeeper. 'I was about to close up.'

Lily bought a bag of mint imperials. 'Is everything all right, Prudence? You look a little sad.'

'You're very observant,' said Prudence. 'I'm just lonely. Some days are better than others. It wasn't so bad when I looked after a pair of evacuees, a little brother and sister from Whitechapel. They were lovely children and I enjoyed the company. It was very silent when they returned to London – no one to talk to once the shop door had closed.' She glanced up at the clock. 'Which reminds me . . .'

She walked to the door and turned the sign from OPEN to CLOSED.

Lily decided to take the initiative. 'I'm not in a hurry, Prudence. I could stay a little longer if you like.'

Prudence smiled. 'That would be lovely.'

They walked into a cosy sitting room and Prudence prepared a pot of tea and opened a packet of chocolate biscuits. 'We haven't really spoken much, have we?' she said. 'You seem to be enjoying your teaching.'

Lily felt relaxed in the company of this gentle lady. 'Yes, Ragley is an excellent school. I'm pleased to be part of it and the people in the village are so supportive.' She sipped her tea and looked up. 'Well, most of them.'

'I know what you mean,' said Prudence. 'I heard about Stanley Coe being the likely culprit when you fell off your bicycle.'

'I'm still a little nervous, to be honest, when I approach that bend. Fortunately I haven't seen him on that road for a while.'

Prudence nodded. 'I expect Sergeant Feather had a quiet word. He's good at that. He spots problems before they get worse and deals with them.'

'Yes, I'm lucky to have him as a friend.'

'A friend? No more than that?' asked Prudence softly. She peered over her spectacles.

Lily looked down and stirred her tea.

'Sorry, not my business,' added Prudence with an apologetic and dismissive wave of her hand.

'It's just that affairs of the heart are sometimes difficult to discuss,' said Lily.

'I understand . . . really I do.'

There was an awkward silence.

'Yes,' said Lily eventually, 'Vera told me about Jeremy. You must have loved him very much. I'm so sorry.'

Prudence glanced up at the mantelpiece and the photograph of the young Spitfire pilot. 'I discovered long ago that love can be a fickle companion. Perhaps you need to grasp it while you have the opportunity.'

Lily couldn't ignore the message there. She looked around the room at the clock on the mantelpiece and the various photographs of Prudence as a younger woman and, of course, pictures of her and Jeremy.

'Prudence . . . how did you know you loved him?'

Prudence put down her cup and saucer. 'I knew from the first time I sat next to him on the school bus.' She settled back in her armchair and let her memories wash over her like gentle rain from heaven. 'It's quite a story.'

Lily smiled. 'I've got time.'

'Well, it began in Woodchurch in Kent and as a schoolgirl I used to catch the bus to Ashford. It was an eight-mile journey and I knew every twist and turn. It used to stop in a little hamlet called Stubbs Cross and the driver would call out, "Stubbs Cross . . . and so am I!" We all laughed, even though we had heard it countless times. Then Jeremy would climb on board and he would sit next to me. He was my childhood sweetheart. There was never any other.'

Lily watched the delicate movements and gestures of this considerate lady. She became animated as the fleeting pictures of her past were captured in her reminiscences. 'I remember seeing a doodlebug and thought it was a noisy plane with fire coming out of the tail. Then three of them landed on our farm and I swept up the broken glass outside the cowshed.'

'You were lucky to have survived,' said Lily.

'Petrol rationing meant a ride in a motor car was something very special, but Jeremy took me out to the coast one day in an old Austin Seven Tourer. After that, although the sea was only ten miles away, it was out of bounds. We had a picnic and he asked me to marry him. Of course, I said yes.' Her eyes glistened with the memory of that moment.

'That night Mother had made her speciality, rabbit stew covered in breadcrumbs. We thought it was a feast. It was our last meal together. He went off the next day and I was left behind. I never saw him again.'

In the distance the church clock chimed the hour.

'So what's your story, Lily?' asked Prudence.

Lily smiled and shook her head. 'Nothing like yours. I was in the Land Army and, after the war, I continued my education. I attended Royal Holloway and gained a General School Certificate in Maths and Physics. That was followed by a Diploma in Education at the London Institute, because I always wanted to be a teacher. They gave me a grant, which meant I had to agree to teaching in a southern counties school. Then, after my father died, I secured the vacant post here in Ragley and we moved to Yorkshire.'

'And I'm so pleased you did,' said Prudence. 'The school has gained a wonderful teacher and I have a new friend.'

A new friend, thought Lily as she cycled home. The beginnings of an idea were forming in her mind.

It was late evening when Doris Clutterbuck took out her Ewbank carpet sweeper from the cupboard under the stairs and began to clean the floor of the Tea Rooms.

'Important t'freshen it up,' she said to herself.

Finally, she climbed the stairs to her flat and took a sip of the hot bedtime drink that was waiting for her. She smiled. 'Sleep sweeter . . . Bournvita,' she sang quietly to herself.

Easter Sunday morning was bright and clear, and Captain Rupert Forbes-Kitchener was immaculate in his neatly pressed uniform as he inspected the local Combined Cadet Force. They were forming the guard of honour outside St Mary's Church as the Brownies, Scouts and Guides trooped past carrying their various flags and colours. It was a fine ceremony and supported every year by the villagers of Ragley and Morton – a time for the two villages to come together.

The Cadet Force was a thriving institution; most of the teenagers in the area joined and took part in its many parades. Grammar schools and independent schools had provided the vast majority of officers during the Second

World War and, in consequence, the tradition was continued afterwards. It was a common sight in Ragley, as in other villages, to see young boys dressed in full khaki uniform with Blancoed gaiters and shiny black boots marching up and down and practising drill with .303 rifles. Captain Forbes-Kitchener had a .38 revolver in a leather holster attached to his belt and took pride in the fact it was always fully loaded!

For these teenage boys learning to fire guns on the rifle range was the norm. After all, it was expected they would all go on to do their National Service, so getting used to firearms made sense.

Tom and Lily joined the steady stream of villagers from both Ragley and Morton as they walked through the guard of honour. Soon the church was filled for one of the special services of the year and Joseph Evans was in his pulpit.

After his sermon he mentioned the news that had shocked the nation. In a solemn voice he said quietly, 'We also must continue to remember Queen Mary in our prayers.' On 24 March the country had come to a standstill when the Prime Minister, Winston Churchill, announced on the BBC Light Programme that, after an illness, the Queen had died peacefully at the age of eighty-five.

'Happily,' said Joseph, trying to lift the spirits of his congregation, 'she lived to see her granddaughter, Queen Elizabeth, ascend the throne and soon we shall all have the opportunity to witness her Coronation . . . and what a wonderful day that will be.'

'We're buying a telly,' whispered Aloysius Pratt on the

back pew to Tommy Piercy. 'Once in a lifetime t'see a Coronation.'

'Will y'be invitin' y'friends?' asked Tommy.

Aloysius stared down at his hymn book and smiled. 'Mebbe them that brings some sausages.'

It had certainly been a remarkable event when, in the week following her death, over a hundred thousand people had filed past the late Queen's coffin in Westminster Hall before she was laid to rest at Windsor.

'And may I remind you,' said Joseph, 'that official mourning will last until the twenty-fifth of April.'

After the service the villagers milled around, sharing news.

'Can I give you a lift home?' asked Tom.

'Yes, please,' said Lily, 'but first I need to speak to Vera.'

Tom leaned against the church wall and watched Lily, smart in a new cream suit that emphasized her slim figure. Their relationship had developed during the past few months and they were clearly viewed as an 'item' in the village. However, there was still something holding Lily back. He sensed she loved him as much as he loved her, but she was cautious when he spoke of a future together. A life shared with this beautiful woman was his dream and he knew he had to be patient.

Meanwhile, it was clear that an animated conversation was taking place. He saw Vera nodding vigorously and saying, 'Yes, perfect.'

When Lily returned to Tom she was smiling.

'So, shall we go?' he asked.

'We need to call in at school first, if you don't mind.'

Tom drove into the car park and Lily hurried into school.

He was surprised to see her reappear carrying a large teddy bear. 'What on earth . . . ?'

Lily climbed into the passenger seat. 'Now, please can you stop on the High Street outside the General Stores? I won't be long.'

Tom nodded, perplexed but happy to go along with whatever she was doing.

When Lily knocked on the rear door of the General Stores, Prudence stared wide-eyed at her.

'This is for you, Prudence,' she said. 'Someone who needs a friend and a good home. He was in America during the war, but he can't go back there. I spoke to Vera and she agreed you were the perfect person to look after him.'

For a moment Lily thought Prudence would burst into tears, but she took the teddy bear and hugged him. 'Thank you so much.'

Little did she know then it was to be the beginning of a lifelong friendship.

It was getting dark when Prudence finally found the perfect place for her teddy bear. There was a shelf above the shop counter alongside a tin of loose-leaf Lyon's Tea and an old advertisement for Hudson's Soap and Carter's Little Liver Pills. Here he could watch the world go by and meet all the customers.

Prudence stared at the bear for a long time. *You could do with some smart clothes*, she thought.

Late in the evening she was sitting at her dining table, her Singer sewing machine tapping out its regular pattern as a fine blue jacket took shape.

She sat back and smiled, and the teddy bear appeared to

smile back at her. 'You need a name,' Prudence murmured
to herself.

Then she nodded. She had made a decision. She gave a
deep sigh and her eyes were soft with an everlasting
sadness.

'Yes,' she said, 'I shall call you Jeremy.'

Chapter Fourteen

Shed Heaven

William Braithwaite was a proud man. Today was the day of days. As president of the Ragley Shed Society he was so excited he could barely eat his second sausage sandwich. It was Monday, 27 April and the inaugural Shed Open Week was about to begin. There was also the competition for Ragley's Best Shed – the result of which was destined to enter village folklore.

For a few days the men of the village would be able to explore the secret kingdoms of their fellow enthusiasts. However, today was particularly special for William, as he had recently constructed his *second* shed. The first was for his racing pigeons and the new one was for the committee meetings. So, on this bright April morning, he stood in his back garden and surveyed a wondrous sight – two sheds, side by side.

Predictably, it was the day he became known in the village as 'Billy Two-Sheds'.

*

Joseph was in a good mood. A new day had dawned and the eastern sky was filled with a soft pink light. In the vicarage garden the rooks were building their nests in the highest branches, the sign of a good summer to come. Joseph had left early after agreeing to meet the Shed Committee in William's shed. The men of this esteemed body considered Joseph to be the perfect judge for their competition. He was honest and fair, a man of the cloth. What could be better?

However, the well-meaning cleric had no idea what lay in store. John Pruett had told him to proceed with caution, as the men of Ragley were very proud of their sheds and on no account must he show any favouritism. As he walked towards the larger of William's two sheds, Joseph heard the scolding cry of a thrush as it tried to crack a snail's shell. It was an omen that he didn't recognize.

After being greeted by the members of the committee he was given the list of sheds to visit during the week. The winner of the title Best Shed would be announced on the village green on Saturday morning.

Meanwhile, it never occurred to any of them that a shed might be owned by a woman . . .

As Lily cycled on the back road from Kirkby Steepleton, a gauze of mist covered the distant fields. All was quiet as she sped along, until the harsh shrieking of a pheasant shattered the peace of the beautiful morning. It flapped its wings in fury as it tried to protect its space, then it rushed across the road in front of her. She recognized its anger and understood its intent.

As she turned into Ragley High Street, she once again enjoyed the sight of this little corner of North Yorkshire.

Outside the village hall the almond trees were in blossom, while the closed buds on the cherry trees were waiting for the trigger of life from the arrival of the warm days ahead. Daffodils and tulips brightened the tubs outside The Royal Oak and the weeping willow on the village green was flushed with new green leaves.

Lily parked her bicycle and walked across the playground, where Winnie Pickles and Edie Stubbs were playing two-ball against the school wall. Both their speed and their dexterity were impressive.

'Good morning, girls. I used to do that.'

'Can you show us, Miss?'

Lily put down her bag of books and picked up the two tennis balls. Hesitantly at first, but then with growing confidence, she began to bounce them against the wall.

'Hey, you're really good, Miss!' said Winnie.

'And so was I once upon a time,' said another voice. Vera had arrived.

'Perhaps Miss Evans would like to try,' said Lily with a smile.

'I seem to remember I did it with a partner.'

'So did I,' said Lily. 'Let's give it a go.'

Some skills are never forgotten, and when John Pruett pulled up in his car he saw his two colleagues giggling like schoolgirls amidst a flurry of tennis balls.

'Good morning, ladies,' he shouted from the car park.

Suitably embarrassed, Lily and Vera hurried into school.

'There are some things you just can't forget,' said Vera.

There was a moment's hesitation before Lily nodded and hurried to hang up her coat.

*

230

Big Dave had called for Little Malcolm on his way to school.

'Are y'ready, Malc?'

'Not yet. Ah've got summat t'show you.'

Little Malcolm's aunty Maureen had brought him a present from Cleethorpes. It was a John Bull Printing Set and he looked at it in wonder.

'Dave,' he called, 'come an' look!'

Big Dave peered into the box. There was an inkpad and a stamper with little rubber letters.

'Ah'll 'ave a go,' said Big Dave with the confidence of youth. Then he looked around furtively. 'Where's y'mam?'

'In 'er shed mekkin' 'er Devil's Brew. It's 'er new 'obby. M'dad sez it's like paint stripper.'

'So does mine,' said Dave. ''E were poorly f'two days an' me mam weren't pleased.'

He picked up the letters carefully and thought of a word. Then he smiled and began to insert them on to the wooden block. *Ah'm good at spellin'*, he thought.

Little Malcolm had found his mother's shopping list on the kitchen table. The reverse side was blank. Big Dave pressed the stamper on to the ink pad and stared at the row of letters. Then he pressed it firmly on to the paper, unaware that the letters had to be arranged in reverse order.

The two boys stared at the result.

Little Malcolm was puzzled. 'What's *skcollob*?' he asked.

An angry shout from the kitchen disturbed their concentration. 'Where's my shoppin' list?' yelled Mrs Robinson.

'Bloody 'ell,' muttered Big Dave. 'C'mon Malc, we're off!'

*

Ten-year-old Robin Knutsford was in the kitchen of his house on the council estate. His mother was making him a jam sandwich for breakfast and the radio was blaring away.

'Why do we listen to t'Shippin' Forecast, Mam?'

''Cause it's important for fishermen.'

'But we don't know no fishermen, Mam.'

Madge Knutsford smiled as she recalled how she had known one in the biblical sense on a day trip to Saltburn-by-the-Sea. 'Well, never you mind and gerron wi' y'breakfast.'

'Mr Pruett says 'e wants t'talk t'you, Mam.'

''Ave y'done owt wrong?'

'No, jus' opposite. 'E reckons ah'm very clever.'

Madge stared at her ginger-haired son, who always had his nose in a book, and thought of that red-haired seaman from long ago.

Joy Popplewell and Veronica Poole were in the General Stores staring up in wonder at Jeremy Bear.

'Good morning, Jeremy,' said Joy.

'He was wondering if you liked his outfit,' said Prudence. 'He chose it himself.'

Today Ragley's favourite bear sported a sailor hat, blue coat with brass buttons and white pillow-case trousers.

'I think he looks really smart,' said Veronica.

'I like his shiny buttons,' added Joy, clearly impressed.

Prudence was delighted. 'Jeremy is very proud of his sailor suit. So, girls, what would you like?'

'Well, I couldn't decide between Pontefract cakes and mint imperials,' said Veronica.

'And I was thinking about dolly mixtures and sherbet lemons,' said Joy.

'I can see it's a difficult choice,' agreed Prudence. 'How much money have you got?'

'I've got a penny,' said Veronica.

'And so have I,' said Joy.

Prudence looked up at Jeremy. 'What do *you* think?'

The girls stared up at the bear, expecting him to reply.

Prudence nodded sagely as if Jeremy had uttered private words of import. 'Jeremy has a good idea. He says put some of each in the same bag.'

Prudence opened four jars and put a generous scoop of sweets into two bags.

'Thank you, Miss Golightly,' chorused the girls. They looked up. 'And thank *you*, Jeremy.'

Prudence considered the idea of mixing various sweets in one bag. *I must try this more often,* she thought.

The General Stores was empty when Vera approached the counter. 'Good morning, Prudence,' she said. 'I need a packet of tea, please.'

'I feel I must ask you, Vera, as I've mentioned it to everyone else . . .'

'Yes?'

'These are new. They're Tetley tea bags. Are you interested?'

Vera stared in astonishment. 'Tea in bags!'

'Yes, so you don't need a tea strainer any more. You just pop them in the cup and add hot water.'

Vera composed herself quickly. 'No thank you, Prudence. I'll stick to the *proper* way of making tea.'

She picked up the packet of tea Prudence gave her, paid and marched out. *Whatever next!* she thought.

*

Traditionally Monday was washday in the village and Ruby Smith was busy. It was a routine she had completed many times and involved buckets of water, soap suds and a steamy kitchen. After possing the dirty clothes in the posser tub, she carried the wet washing outside to squeeze each garment through the mangle and remove the excess water. Often she would complete the drying process on the rack in front of the fire, but on this sunny April morning she was able to peg out sheets on her washing line.

While it was hard work for Ruby, it was even more difficult for some. Until recently her neighbour, Betty, would take her washing down to the stream and simply pound her clothes against a rock, then stretch them out on the grass to dry. Betty also used to make her own soap from mutton fat, caustic soda and water, but in recent times had taken to borrowing a bar of Sunlight soap from the generous Ruby. On this morning she arrived in the back garden, smoking a cigarette.

"Ave y'got a bit o' soap t'spare, Ruby?'

'In t'sink,' said Ruby.

'Ta, luv. Them sheets look clean,' said Betty as she puffed cigarette smoke all over them.

'Ah'm using that new Oxydol,' said Ruby. 'Sez on t'box it washes *vivid* white.'

'Y'reight there, Ruby,' agreed Betty as she stubbed out her cigarette and lit another. 'It's proper dazzlin'.'

Ruby laughed. 'Any whiter an' you'll need sunglasses in our 'ouse.'

'Ah've jus' seen that stuck-up Deirdre Coe goin' somewhere posh by t'look of 'er.'

'All net curtains is that one,' said Ruby with feeling, 'an' fruit in a bowl jus' f'show.'

'Y'reight there, Ruby, an' she dresses t'kill.'

Ruby pegged her final nappy on the line. 'Ah've 'eard she cooks t'same way.'

They both laughed and went inside to make a pot of tea.

In John Pruett's classroom he had written a huge number on the blackboard. It was 29,999.

'Now, who can tell me what that number is?'

Robin Knutsford was the first to raise his hand. 'Sir, it's twenty-nine thousand nine hundred and ninety-nine.'

'Well done, Robin,' said John. 'Now, children, this number has been in the newspapers recently. It's the number of pounds Manchester United have paid Barnsley for their twenty-one-year-old centre forward Tommy Taylor.'

Everyone stared in astonishment.

"Ow can anyone be worth that much, sir?' asked Big Dave.

'It's hard to say, David,' said John, 'but Manchester United are a big club with lots of money and they want the best players.'

'Another pound would have made it thirty thousand, sir,' added Robin for good measure.

'That's right,' said John, 'but the manager did not want to burden the footballer with a thirty thousand price tag, so during the negotiations he took a pound note from his wallet and gave it to the tea lady who was in the room at the time.'

'Cor, ah bet she was pleased, sir,' said Little Malcolm.

'Now, I want you to imagine all the players in the Ragley

Rovers football team are each worth the same as Tommy Taylor. So how many pounds would you need if every one of the eleven players was worth twenty-nine thousand nine hundred and ninety-nine pounds?'

A few children scratched their heads, but they were used to doing sums every morning and learning their tables, so long multiplication was fairly straightforward, even with numbers as large as these.

John smiled when Robin Knutsford was the first to raise his hand with the correct answer. He remembered that he needed to speak to Mrs Knutsford as a matter of urgency.

In morning assembly Joseph discussed the importance of praying to God.

'So that's why we say the Lord's Prayer every day,' he concluded.

Through daily practice, the children were word-perfect, with a few exceptions among the younger ones. Five-year-old Arnold Icklethwaite, a little boy with a constantly runny nose, was a case in point. Arnold closed his eyes and recited, 'Our Father, who does art in heaven, Harold is His name. Amen.'

Arnold was destined to presume God had the same name as his uncle and to carry on with this version until he was eight years old.

Veronica Poole put up her hand.

'Yes, Veronica,' said Joseph.

'Mr Evans, if God is watching in church on Sunday I can show him my new shoes.'

'What a lovely thought, Veronica,' said a beaming Joseph.

However, his confidence immediately took a beating once again when he was asked a question he couldn't answer.

It was Arnold's elder brother, Billy, who raised his hand, looking decidedly puzzled.

'Ah've been thinkin', Mr Evans . . .'

'Yes?'

''Bout God.'

'That's good, William,' said Joseph. 'And what were you thinking?'

'Well 'ow did 'e know 'e were God . . . who told 'im?'

John Pruett recognized a soul in torment and moved quickly to ring the bell for morning playtime.

In the staff-room at morning break Joseph was sipping tea and trying to recover from Billy Icklethwaite's question. He looked at his sister with concern.

'What's wrong, Joseph?' asked Vera.

Joseph gave a deep sigh. 'I need a little gentle reassurance. As you know, I've been asked to judge the best shed in the village.'

'Good luck with that,' said John. 'There's a lot of competition.'

'Did you know, Vera,' continued Joseph, 'there are three hundred and sixty-five assurances in the Bible?'

Vera sighed. 'As a matter of fact I did,' she replied pointedly.

For a moment Joseph looked crestfallen and Vera felt a pang of guilt.

'Are you making some more of your delicious home-made wine for the May Day celebrations?' she asked, changing the subject. She smiled as she witnessed the delight on her brother's face.

'As a matter of fact I am,' he said. 'My Honeysuckle Supreme is coming on nicely.'

While Joseph was a humble man, his modesty did not extend to his winemaking exploits.

At lunchtime Mrs Stubbs called in to speak to Lily about Bertie. He was due at the dentist that afternoon. Lily sympathized, as the local dentist's was known affectionately as the Torture Chamber. After his patient had breathed in gas through a rubber face mask, the dentist would get to work with a fierce implement that had the sound and impact of a road drill. Also, Lily recalled, the old brown leather furniture gave off the smell of decay and death.

''E's 'ad ever'thin' that's goin', as Bertie,' said Mrs Stubbs.

Lily reflected that there were always at least two or three children every week suffering from one of the common illnesses, including chicken pox, whooping cough and measles. Regular doses of Herbert Grinchley's cod liver oil and rose hip syrup seemed to help. However, one remedy of which Lily was unaware was that Mrs Stubbs had spent the morning sitting in her front room with her feet in a bowl of urine in the hope it would cure her chilblains!

That afternoon Lily and John worked together with all the children for an activity session. It was John who decided that the girls and boys should be in separate groups. The girls did sewing with Lily, making raffia mats, while the boys did some basic carpentry and set about constructing wooden teapot stands.

Lily thought the tasks were functional rather than inspiring and was unimpressed when John refused to let any of the girls tackle carpentry.

'You can't let *girls* use a saw,' he declared in horror.

It was at times like this that she hoped one day to become a headteacher herself and have the authority to plan her own curriculum.

Ruby was outside the Pharmacy talking once more to her next-door neighbour, Betty. They were smiling at little Racquel in her pram when Deirdre Coe appeared.

'Ah saw you 'angin' out y'washin' this mornin'. Ah've got one o' them new 'Oover 'lectric washin' machines,' she announced. 'Does a whole family wash.'

'But you 'aven't gorra family,' said Betty.

'Ah know, but my Stanley meks up f'that wi' 'is mucky overalls.'

'Ah'm 'appy wi' m'posser tub,' retorted Ruby without conviction.

'Well, no more washday drudgery f'me. My Stanley looks after me – not like your Ronnie,' and she walked away.

Ruby felt as though she had been slapped and had no immediate response. Deep down she knew Deirdre was right, but she pursed her lips and said nothing.

'Never mind,' said Betty. 'Let's go an' see 'Erbert in t'Pharmacy an' catch up wi' t'gossip.'

Ruby nodded, but Betty could see she was still shaken by Deirdre's unkind comments.

'Did y'know 'Erbert were a member o' t'Home Guard?'

'A Local Defence Volunteer?' said Ruby.

'That's right – the LDV,' added Betty and smiled ruefully. ''Cept we called 'em Look, Duck an' Vanish.'

Ruby laughed and they walked in together to collect some castor oil for young Andy.

At the end of school John Pruett was talking to Mrs Knutsford in the school office. 'You'll need to start saving up for a uniform,' he said. 'Robin is almost certain to pass his Eleven-plus.'

'An' pigs might fly, Mr Pruett. Ah'm only jus' gettin' by as it is.'

John Pruett sighed deeply. He hated to see talent wasted and Robin was one of the brightest boys he had ever taught.

He looked out of the window and saw Robin leaning against the school wall reading a book. As usual he was wearing old clothes and hobnail boots. You could always hear him coming from far away. Predictably, he was known as 'Ginger Nut' among the other children, but he accepted this with good grace and was a popular pupil. His regular nosebleeds were counteracted by his mother, who would drop a large key down the back of his shirt. It was an old wives' tale that John could never recall being disproved.

'Perhaps there will be a grant,' he said. 'I'll enquire for you.'

Mrs Knutsford smiled knowingly. 'Thank you for tryin', Mr Pruett.'

The next few days turned out to be a dreadful experience for Joseph. Men he had known for years as valued members of the village community regressed to nothing short of eccentric when they retired to the privacy of their sheds.

Late on Tuesday evening he discovered that Archibald Pike used his shed for weaving bell ropes for the church. When he entered the shed in the cold moonlight, shapes resembling hangman's nooses hung from the rafters and turned Joseph's blood to ice.

'Naturally I would expect to win, Vicar,' said Archibald with a fixed smile, 'as my shed is dedicated to the church.'

On Wednesday he entered the dark and secret world of Maurice Tupham, where in an eerie light he was introduced to the art of forcing rhubarb. Maurice also had high expectations. 'Ah'm presuming ah'll get at least a commendation as ah provide such 'igh-quality rhubarb for t'village. It's a labour o' love, Mr Evans.'

On Thursday Alfie Kershaw's shed stank like a brewery and Joseph recoiled when he opened the door. The stench was like a physical blow. 'Finest c'llection o' beer bottles on God's earth,' announced Alfie. 'If that dunt win, nothin' will.'

On Friday Joseph could have wept following an insight into a man he regarded as a pillar of the local community. Aloysius Pratt waxed lyrical about his collection of nuts and bolts through the ages. They were displayed in old jam jars on wooden shelves that lined his shed. However, it was when Aloysius selected a dome-headed screw and held it up to the light as if it were a thing of beauty that Joseph made a swift departure.

Back at the vicarage, Vera was following a pattern from her *Woman & Home* magazine. She was knitting a cardigan in midnight blue embroidered with Tyrolean flowers – namely her favourite, starry-white edelweiss. Vera was always very precise. She had been into York to purchase seven ounces of Lister's 3-ply wool and was working at a tension of seven stitches to the inch with No. 8 needles. Although the pattern suggested it would fit a bust of up to thirty-seven inches, Vera had made the necessary adjustment and reduced it appropriately. After all, she liked a slim, close fit.

When her brother walked in she could see he was severely stressed. He was staring forlornly at his list. 'Only two more sheds to go.'

Vera put her arm around his shoulder. 'Remember, Joseph, you can't add years to your life with worry – but it can steal life away.'

'I'm in a fix, Vera. I shouldn't have taken it on.'

'God will guide you.'

'Yes, I'm sure he will . . . but He didn't have a shed.'

As Lily left school on Friday, Tom walked up the drive to meet her and stood next to her bicycle. He handed her a brown paper bag.

'I thought you would like this, both for yourself and then for the children.'

Lily looked inside. It was the newest novel by C. S. Lewis, *The Voyage of the Dawn Treader*.

'That's a wonderful gift, Tom. Really thoughtful. Thank you so much.'

'And are we still fine for this evening?'

They had taken to going to the cinema on a regular basis now. Tonight it was *Singing in the Rain* with Gene Kelly. As he walked away, she thought how lucky she was to have found such a fine man, faithful, true . . . and honest.

Honesty, she thought – an important virtue. Perhaps she was close to sharing what was on her mind with Tom. She stared down at the book and felt like a small boat on a troubled sea, not knowing if the next big wave would take her to shore or dash her to pieces.

By six o'clock on Friday Joseph also felt as though he were sinking fast. All the men he met appeared perfectly normal until they set foot in their sheds.

Men and sheds, he thought, as the realization crept over him that tomorrow he would have to choose the winner. He sat down on the bench under the weeping willow on the village green, put his weary head in his hands and contemplated an uncertain future.

'What's t'do, Vicar? Are y'frettin'?' It was Gertie Robinson.

'Oh hello, Mrs Robinson, I'm fine thank you.'

'Y'look proper peaky t'me.'

'It may be a slight migraine coming on,' he said weakly.

Gertie stared down at the frail figure, who looked as though a stiff breeze would blow him away. She made a decision.

'Mr Evans, come wi' me. Ah'll soon 'ave y'fettled.' Gertie had arms like tree trunks and almost lifted him from the seat before frogmarching him down School View. 'Y'need a quick pick-me-up an' ah've got jus' the thing.'

A few minutes later Joseph found himself at the bottom of the Robinsons' back garden, sitting on an upturned box in the corner of an old wooden shed.

'Now, Vicar, try a drop o' this.'

*

Judgment Day arrived on Saturday morning when Joseph announced to the Ragley Shed Committee that the winner of the Best Shed competition for 1953 was Mrs Gertie Robinson. The men retired to their sheds in a state of bewilderment. Their shed world had been turned upside down.

'But she's a woman ...' said Archibald Pike in bewilderment.

'Ah wouldn't allow a woman in my shed,' declared Maurice Tupham defiantly.

'Whatever next?' grumbled Alfie Kershaw. 'A woman Prime Minister?'

Everyone laughed. 'Not in my lifetime,' muttered Aloysius Pratt.

That afternoon the committee held an emergency meeting. Billy Two-Sheds proposed that the vicar should stand down as the judge and that future competition entries should be restricted to members of the committee – comprised entirely of men.

The motion was carried unanimously.

Gertie's Devil's Brew, meanwhile, was suitably named. It was genuinely evil, with a kick like a mule and an aftertaste of red-hot coals with the merest hint of paint stripper.

After one glass there was a feeling of bonhomie. A second glass made you feel distinctly euphoric. After that you were simply floating in the clouds.

However, for Joseph it had been shed heaven.

Chapter Fifteen

The Second Sex

It was a slow dawn and as Lily looked out of her bedroom window the scent of wallflowers and cherry blossom made her feel this was a time of renewal. The flower spikes on the horse chestnut trees gave promise of summer and a preening sparrow stared up with beady eyes full of anticipation for the new day.

It was Wednesday, 20 May and sunlight caressed her skin like a lover's kiss. The distant hills shimmered beneath a ring of fire and a thin band of gold lit up the horizon. Above her head only the cawing of the rooks in the high elms disturbed the peace of this perfect morning.

Lily sighed. It was good to be alive on a day such as this.

As she cycled along the back road to Ragley village, Lily was at peace in her world. In Twenty Acre Field the green unripe barley swayed in sinuous patterns in the gentle breeze. Misty carpets of bluebells and the pale-yellow blossom of wood sage brought splashes of colour to the woodland clearings. The baa-ing of lambs and the distant cry of a curlew were sounds of a familiar countryside.

When she reached the High Street a flock of starlings wheeled in sharp formation towards St Mary's Church and Lily thought of Tom and the words he had spoken last night. She smiled as a day of new promise and expectation stretched out before her.

However, life is full of the unexpected, and as she approached the village hall she saw Vera pinning a poster on the noticeboard and pulled up. 'Good morning, Vera.'

'Good morning, Lily. This should cause a stir.'

Lily dismounted and read the poster. 'I see what you mean,' she said with a smile.

'Definitely a *first*,' said Vera. 'I can't imagine the word "sex" has appeared too often on a poster in Ragley. It will certainly get the ladies of the Women's Institute interested.'

The poster read:

Ragley & Morton W.I.
Wednesday, 20th May 1953 at 7.00 p.m.

'The Second Sex'

A talk by Clarice Culpepper
Based on the book by Simone de Beauvoir
A cream tea will be served.

'It's about time women stood up to be heard,' said Vera. 'The suffragettes did it and now it's our turn.'

With that, a determined Vera and a curious Lily walked side by side towards the school gate.

On the playground Reggie Bamforth and Phoebe

Fawnswater were both reading their weekly comics. Reggie was absorbed in his *Eagle* and enjoying the adventures of Dan Dare, Pilot of the Future.

He glanced across at his friend. 'What y'readin' that for, Phoebe?'

'It's exciting,' said Phoebe. She was clearly engrossed. Phoebe was reading *Girl*, her 'super-colour' sister comic to the *Eagle*.

Each week Phoebe called in at the General Stores, placed four pennies and a ha'penny on the counter and collected her comic. She loved reading about Kitty Hawke and her 'all-girl air crew'. Phoebe had decided she wanted to be a pilot when she grew up. However, there was much to achieve before then. She had to pass her Eleven-plus, go to the Time School for Girls in York and then on to university. It was a pathway planned years ago by her mother.

She thought she would tell Miss Briggs of her ambitions. All she needed was advice and Miss Briggs knew everything.

Anne Watson's teaching practice was going well. She was clearly an exceptional teacher, as even Miss Trimble, the Ripon Rottweiler, agreed after observing her lessons. Her copious file was always detailed and included the time, age group, equipment, aim of each lesson and how it was expected to develop.

Lily and Anne were on playground duty during morning break and Billy Icklethwaite was showing Anne his new belt. It was striped red and green, with a snake clip. He had attached a loop of baling twine and was clearly proud of this new item in an ensemble that otherwise appeared decidedly scruffy.

'What's the twine for, Billy?' asked Anne.

Billy was surprised at such a question, as the answer was obvious.

'For m'sword, Miss.' He held up his hazel branch and ran towards Reggie Bamforth, who had been persuaded to act the part of the Sheriff of Nottingham.

Anne looked at the children playing their various games. 'Fascinating, isn't it?' she said. 'The only limit appears to be the extent of their imagination.'

Two piles of coats represented the goalposts at Wembley Stadium, while a rope tied to the hook on the wall of the boiler house became an opportunity to be Tarzan the Ape Man along with his ear-shattering jungle cry – that is, until Edna Trott shooed you away with her yard broom.

As well as the school playground, all the side roads off the High Street were solely for play, as there were few cars, and here too the children of Ragley acted out their fantasies, often as footballers at a time when English football was the envy of the world, with stars such as Stanley Matthews and Billy Wright. Newsreels at the pictures of the England football team kept everyone in touch with the latest matches.

Few games were shared among boys and girls except hopscotch, which was particularly popular on the High Street, where the flagstones were the ideal size to draw around when marking out the numbered boxes with a stick of chalk. This morning Robin Knutsford and Edie Stubbs were playing the game happily on the school playground.

Dominating the large spaces of the playground, boys were acting out cowboys and Indians or cops and robbers. Little Malcolm was lying on the ground, completely still.

'Oh dear, Malcolm, what's the matter?' shouted Anne.

'Ah've been shot, Miss.'

'Shot!'

'Yes Miss, by t'sheriff.'

It was time for the bell, and Anne and Lily walked back into school.

'You do wonder if it's psychologically damaging for boys to spend their playtimes killing each other,' observed Lily.

In contrast, many of the girls were acting out motherhood with dolls.

'That reminds me,' said Lily, 'why not come along to the talk in the village hall tonight? It's about women and their role in society today. You could get some tips for dealing with your chauvinist husband-to-be.'

Anne grinned. 'Good idea.'

In the village Pharmacy, Herbert Grinchley was serving Mrs Alice Dlambulo, who had arrived in Ragley with her husband from Jamaica three years ago. After taking jobs no one else wanted, her husband had finally found regular employment as a bus conductor in York. Her hard-working son, Clyde, had done better with a job at Morrisey's Motor Cycle Mart.

Mrs Dlambulo was a happy lady with a sense of fun and she was used to Herbert's sales technique. This morning she wanted some hand cream, as her hands were chapped after washing Clyde's overalls twice a week.

Herbert put a jar of Pacquins Hand Cream on the counter. 'This'll do t'job, Mrs Dlambulo.'

'Ah s'ppose so.' She picked up the jar and read the label. 'It might even work miracles,' she said with a quizzical look.

'What might that be?' asked Herbert.

'Well, it says soft *white* hands after washing up.' She held up her black hands and smiled.

'Oh 'eck,' said Herbert and his cheeks flushed.

Next in the queue was Joseph Evans, looking distinctly grey around the gills.

'I need something to settle my stomach,' said Joseph. 'I'm feeling a little queasy.'

'What brought that on, Vicar?'

'Possibly my Honeysuckle Supreme wasn't quite ready.'

Herbert smiled. The vicar's home-made wine had a reputation in the village. He slapped a quarter-pound tin of Andrews Liver Salts on the counter. 'Here y'are, Mr Evans, a refreshing and pleasant fizzy laxative for inner cleanliness. Settles the stomach and tones the liver.'

Joseph didn't need the sales patter – just some relief. 'Thank you, Herbert,' he said and staggered back to the vicarage.

The talk in the staff-room at lunchtime was of televisions. More people in the village were buying or renting them. It seemed everyone wanted to view the forthcoming Coronation in their own homes and sales had rocketed. The ardent royalist Vera had surprised Joseph by sending him to York to make an immediate purchase, and Tom proposed to buy one for his mother this coming weekend.

John Pruett was ahead of them all and had rented one from the store in York three weeks ago.

'Are you enjoying your television, Mr Pruett?' asked Anne.

'I certainly am,' said John. 'I watched the FA Cup Final.'

'So did I,' said Anne. 'It was a wonderful game. I saw it at my parents' house. Blackpool beat Bolton four–three. Stan Mortensen scored a hat-trick and Stanley Matthews was the star of the match – at the age of thirty-eight.'

John looked surprised. 'For a *woman* you seem to know a lot about football.'

'Of course, I enjoy all sports,' said Anne, looking slightly bemused. 'It didn't occur to me that it depended on whether I was a woman or not.'

Lily looked up sharply. It was important to avoid friction in the staff-room. 'I'm sure Mr Pruett meant that these days it is unusual for women to be knowledgeable about sports that have traditionally been supported by men. Isn't that so, John?'

Vera picked up the teapot. 'Another cup of tea, Mr Pruett?'

Ruby was outside the General Stores when Ronnie suddenly appeared.

'Where 'ave you been?' she asked.

'Ah've gorra job,' said Ronnie proudly.

'Flippin' eck, Ronnie, wonders never cease! What's t'job?'

'Racin' pigeons – ah'm lookin' after 'em f'Billy Two-Sheds.'

'But you don't know owt about pigeons.'

'What's there t'know? Jus' a bit o' seed an' water an' mek sure they don't escape.'

'Sounds a cushy job.'

'Cushy job! Ah'll tell you who's gorra cushy job, Ruby. That Peter Brough what you listen to on t'radio wi' 'is dummy, Archie Andrews.'

''Ow come?'

'A *ventriloquist* on t'radio!' exclaimed Ronnie. 'Y'can't see if 'is lips move.'

'But that's *entertainment*, Ronnie, an' you 'ave t'use y'imagination.'

'Imagination, imagination,' said Ronnie. 'What's that when it's at 'ome?' And he went inside the shop to buy a packet of cigarettes.

Well it's a start, thought Ruby.

It was afternoon break and Lily picked up Vera's *Woman & Home* magazine, which she had left behind in the staff-room.

'Anne, have a look at this.'

There was an article entitled 'Marriage Survey'.

'It says here that a successful marriage all depends on the wife creating an atmosphere of happiness in the home. When a wife produces a family, she feels she has achieved her destiny.'

'Oh dear,' said Anne. 'I don't want to have children ... well, not immediately. I want to *teach* first.'

Lily closed the magazine and wondered how Anne's future husband would respond. She also reflected on her own life.

*

Vera had called in to the General Stores. 'We need to give the pews a good polish,' she said.

Prudence rummaged around in the back room and reappeared with a cardboard box full of tins of furniture wax. 'We have a good selection, Vera,' she said. 'There's Johnson's Pride in a large economy size.' Prudence knew Vera well. 'Or you might prefer the scented lavender wax.'

Vera smiled and dreamed of Sunday's congregation breathing in the delicate scent of her favourite flower. 'I'll take the lavender, please, Prudence.' She looked in her purse, selected a shiny shilling and a threepenny bit and placed the coins on the counter.

The till rang with a high-pitched ding and Prudence relaxed with the knowledge of another satisfied customer. She was pleased she hadn't produced the huge bottle of Pride liquid wax at five shillings, as that would certainly have been too *common* for the vicar's sister.

Meanwhile, George Hardcastle, the bank manager from Easington, had taken a different sort of shine to Vera and he was parked outside the General Stores in his Rover P4. It was a car that George believed reflected his solid and sensible image, the epitome of respectability.

Indeed, Vera approved. *Handsome but not flashy*, she thought. While the third headlamp in the middle of the grille looked odd, George was proud that the aluminium body panels were the result of the surplus stock of wartime aircraft.

George clearly admired the slim, graceful Vera and had made hesitant and stumbling overtures in the past. They had, however, been met with an icy calm by the aloof school secretary – not least because Mrs Wilhelmena

Hardcastle, a portly and vociferous lady, was the current president of the Ragley Women's Institute.

A passing AA patrolman on his motorbike glanced at the shiny AA badge on the grille of George's car and gave a smart salute. George nodded back in appreciation. It was good to feel valued as a motorist of note, and he smiled at the recognition of his status in the community.

However, this feeling of wellbeing soon vanished.

'Can I offer you a lift, Miss Evans?'

Vera reflected on his use of the English language. *You can, but you may not*, she thought.

'No thank you, Mr Hardcastle,' she said. 'But thank you for the offer.'

At the end of the school day John Pruett asked all the children to stand quietly and recite the school prayer. Then, after a reminder not to swing on the school gates on their way home, they walked out in single file.

John noticed that Big Dave and Little Malcolm appeared more eager than usual.

'Are you in a hurry, boys?'

'Yes, sir, we're off t'play Subbuteo.'

John's eyes lit up. 'The table soccer game? On that green cloth marked out like a football pitch?'

'Yes, sir.'

'And little footballers that you flick with fingertip control? I've seen the box in the shops. It looks good.'

'Is is, sir, it's great. Tonight it's Ragley Rovers versus Leeds United.'

'Should be a good game.'

'Y'can come an' play if y'like, sir,' offered Dave.

There was a moment when John would have loved to have said yes, but professional restraint won over. 'Another time, boys,' he said sadly.

Sometimes being a headteacher is no fun, he thought.

Prudence Golightly looked up when the bell rang again. She was serving Millicent Merryweather as Deirdre Coe strode up to the counter. For Prudence the gloomy and formidable presence of Stan Coe's sister was unwelcome, but as always she remembered her manners.

'Good afternoon, Deirdre. I'll be with you in a moment.'

Deirdre frowned and glanced at Millicent. 'Life's too short for idle talk,' she muttered, 'an' ah need summat sharpish.'

Prudence ignored the rebuke and began packing Millicent's basket. 'Was there anything else, Milly?'

Millicent checked her list. 'Well, I do need some soap powder, please, Prudence.'

'There's plenty to choose from. We've got Tide, or have you tried Persil?'

Millicent picked up the box. 'Actually, I haven't, although my sister uses it.' She studied the label. 'The *Herald & Pioneer* said that three hundred housewives in London all agreed it was the best.'

'Well, ah'm not convinced,' said Deirdre sharply, 'an' what do southerners know abart cleaning my Stan's overalls after 'e's mucked out t'pigs?'

'Fair point, Deirdre,' said Millicent, although she didn't agree. Her sister lived in London and her smalls were always spotless.

*

At the end of the school day and before the meeting in the village hall, Lily and Anne walked in the sunshine to the Tea Rooms to enjoy a cup of tea and a sandwich.

Both Nora Pratt and her friend Shirley Makin were assisting Doris after returning from Easington Secondary School. They were wearing their navy-blue school uniforms plus the obligatory white apron and sailor hat.

It was almost closing time when most of the customers had departed and Nora and Shirley were able to enjoy a conversation with Lily and Anne.

'How's school, Nora?' asked Lily.

'Fwustwatin', Miss Bwiggs,' said Nora. 'This new GCE's a pwoblem.'

The General Certificate of Education, introduced in 1951, hadn't proved popular with many of those who weren't in a grammar school.

'It's all changed now,' said Shirley. 'We're like guinea pigs. Me an' Nora would 'ave got our School Certificate, but they changed things t'mek it 'arder.'

'Oh dear,' said Anne. 'I know what you mean. Now that they've raised the pass mark from thirty-three to forty-five per cent half the pupils fail.'

Lily nodded. 'Also, you need five GCEs to get into the sixth form, including mathematics and English. It's tough.'

'Weally depwessin',' said Nora.

'So we're leavin' nex' year. Ah'm goin' on a cookery course an' Nora's goin' t'work for Mrs Clutterbuck.'

Lily sat back with her cheese and lettuce sandwich and contemplated opportunities for young women. Only 5 per cent of pupils went on to university and most of them were men.

The forthcoming talk in the village hall should prove to be interesting.

In Morton Manor Captain Rupert Forbes-Kitchener was looking forward to the Coronation. He had been put in charge of coordinating the village celebrations. He had a distinguished team, including Mrs Hardcastle, the formidable president of the Women's Institute; Albert Jenkins, the school governor; and Vera Evans, the school secretary, who without doubt was a woman of substance and rare intelligence.

As he was writing the proposal for a brass band to support the grand afternoon tea in the High Street, he was listening to his new wireless. He had spent the remarkable sum of £16.16s.3d on the latest in modern technology – namely, a portable radio.

The state-of-the-art All-Dry radio used Ever Ready batteries and needed no aerial, earth or mains wires. In its smart walnut cabinet it was sitting on the kitchen worktop while his wife, Alexandra, relaxed and listened to the Light Programme.

Meanwhile, the grocer's boy with the unfortunate stutter had cycled up the long drive that morning and delivered a box of provisions, including a bottle of Lucozade. Rupert considered it to be an expensive luxury, but had kept quiet after Alexandra had declared it replaced lost energy, and there was threepence back on the empty bottle. At least that's what it said on the label and Rupert had ceased to argue over his wife's little idiosyncrasies.

Even so, he was concerned about her failing health and, with a new baby to care for, he was considering hiring a nanny. Someone needed to look after his daughter – and *after all*, he thought, *I'm a man*.

At seven o'clock the village hall was packed and Vera stood up to make the introduction.

'Ladies, it gives me great pleasure to introduce a remarkable woman who describes herself as a disciple of the French writer and philosopher Simone de Beauvoir. Clarice Culpepper was educated here in North Yorkshire and went on to study at Oxford. Much has changed since the war, and perhaps we are approaching a time in our lives when we need to reconsider our role as women. We proved during the war that we could do the work of men . . .' Vera paused while there was a ripple of applause.

'And we were better!' exclaimed Millicent Merryweather from the back row.

There was muttered approval. Clarice liked what she saw.

She lived in Stoke Hammond in Buckinghamshire and during the war had worked in a nearby village called Bletchley, but no one knew what she had done, nor did she ever discuss it. Since then she had been a supporter of women's rights and was currently on a nationwide tour. She liked Vera Evans, recognizing her as another woman who knew her own mind and didn't suffer fools gladly. Vera also had an excellent speaking voice.

'So,' continued Vera, 'welcome to the ladies from Morton who have joined us for an enlightening evening of information and insight. Please show your appreciation for a distinguished lady of our age, the emerging feminist Clarice Culpepper.'

There was sustained applause as the tall, imposing lady stood up.

Emerging feminist, thought Clarice. *I must use that.*

'Ladies of Ragley and Morton, good evening and thank you for the welcome – and, of course, to the equally distinguished Miss Evans for the invitation.'

Vera gave a nod of acknowledgement; her Christian faith permitted no more.

Clarice took a step forward and a silence descended. 'Let me begin by saying, we're *special* . . . we're *different*.'

She held up a well-thumbed copy of a book. 'This is the groundbreaking nineteen forty-nine work by Simone de Beauvoir, *The Second Sex*. It sold more than twenty thousand copies in its first week. It's written in French, but the English version will soon be in all the bookshops and I urge you all to read it.'

Her direct, almost confrontational, style had grabbed everyone's attention. It was also the first time a speaker had used the word 'sex' in a WI meeting since Isaac Crumble explained the mating ritual of tortoises back in 1947. That had been a slow evening in more ways than one.

'Simone de Beauvoir's book describes the treatment and position of women through history to the present day. We have been second-class citizens for long enough and it's time to do something about it.'

There were murmurs of 'Here, here!' and it was immediately clear the audience was captivated by this dynamic woman.

'In the interest of the propagation of the species, we are biologically different to males.'

Starting Over

'What's she mean?' whispered Sylvia Icklethwaite to Gertie Robinson.

'Men 'ave bits an' we don't,' said Gertie, who always told it how it was.

'For example,' said Clarice, extending her slim arms in a pose like a ballerina, 'females have a more difficult time building up muscle mass.'

Gertie Robinson looked down at her massive biceps. *Well, some of us don't*, she thought.

For the next thirty minutes Clarice held the audience spellbound with her detailed analysis of women's oppression. She described a work of anthropology and sociology, a modern feminist upsurge. It was so captivating that Joyce Davenport almost forgot to switch on their recently purchased Baby Burco boiler, another wonder of the modern age.

Clarice had reached the grand finale. 'Let me be honest, when I first read this book I thought that it rambled on a bit, but the message is powerful.' She paused for dramatic effect. 'Remember this, ladies – one is not born, but rather *becomes* a woman.'

The applause was tumultuous.

The talk afterwards over a superb cream tea was of the countless hours of housework every week. Gertie Robinson was telling Clarice that all her washing was done in the sink with the occasional drop of Lux liquid to clean the dirty pans.

'Problem isn't so much us,' said Gertie. 'It's *men*.'

How true, thought Clarice.

*

Tom was waiting to collect Lily after the meeting. She had arranged to leave her bicycle at school. After climbing into his car they set off for Kirkby Steepleton.

'How did it go?' he asked.

Lily was cautious with her reply. 'Fine, simply discussing the role of women.'

Tom was astute enough to read behind the neutral statement. They drove on, each with their own thoughts, until Tom suddenly opened up. 'I think society is changing. Women showed during the war what they can do. They drove ambulances and kept the factories running.'

'And worked the land and drove tractors,' added Lily.

Tom nodded as they reached Kirkby Steepleton and pulled up outside Laurel Cottage.

'It will take time, but eventually society will see that women are equal to men – or does that sound too patronizing?'

'No, Tom, you're making sense and I'm hopeful you can spread the message.'

'You mean with Neanderthals like Stan Coe?'

'He's a lost cause, but perhaps you could nudge John Pruett a little.'

Lily could see that Tom was searching for the right words. 'John is a fine man,' he said at last, 'but simply a product of his generation. He's more than ten years older than me.'

'Sorry, I didn't mean to criticize my colleague. It's unprofessional, and John has been very helpful to me.'

'He's a lucky man to have you alongside him.'

Lily smiled, then leaned across and kissed him on the cheek. 'You say all the right things.'

'Not always.'

'What do you mean?'

'Occasionally my sense of timing is poor.'

'In what way?'

'Well, there's something I want to ask you and it's been on my mind for a long time.'

Lily stared up at his honest face. 'Go on, just say it.'

'Well . . . I was wondering what you thought about . . . you know . . . *marriage*.'

Chapter Sixteen

Crowned at Last!

It was Tuesday, 2 June, Coronation Day, and Ragley village was decked out for a carnival. Union Jacks hung from every upstairs window on the High Street and colourful bunting stretched across the road as Lily cycled into school. She had agreed to meet John Pruett and Edna Trott in the school hall to collect all the dining tables and carry them outside for the party tea on the High Street that afternoon.

Lily had arranged with her mother that she would help with the preparations in Ragley during the morning and then return to Kirkby Steepleton to spend time with Freddie at his school party during the afternoon. The evening was another matter, and she hoped it involved Tom. A busy time was in store, a national holiday and a day of celebration.

Little did she know it was destined to be a day of surprises – a day she would never forget.

*

In the vicarage Vera was enjoying an early-morning cup of tea as she listened to the radio. Billy Cotton and his Band was playing 'In a Golden Coach', their new record to celebrate the Coronation.

As she sipped her tea, Vera thought of the day ahead. She was about to set off for the village hall to assist the ladies of the Women's Institute prepare the grand party tea. Trestle tables were to be lined up on the High Street and Tom Feather had ensured the road would be closed to motor traffic. She and Joseph would be together in the vicarage from half past ten onwards, watching the Coronation on their new television set. She checked the timings in the *Radio Times* and the route of the royal coach.

Around the country an extra one hundred thousand television sets had been sold so that people could watch the event. Vera glanced at her radio and then at the television set that was destined to become the focus of family entertainment. The world as she knew it was changing.

Meanwhile, in London thirty thousand people had been drenched overnight. Following heavy rain and a drop in temperature, they huddled under blankets and umbrellas in Whitehall and Piccadilly, determined not to miss out on a chance to see the Queen in her coach of burnished gold.

Princess Elizabeth had been proclaimed queen in February 1952, immediately after the death of her father, King George VI, but the British public had had to wait for over a year for her actual Coronation, which had required months of meticulous planning. Now three million people lined the streets of London while in Ragley village Vera checked the quality of her scones.

*

In the General Stores Elsie Crapper had bought a copy of the *Daily Express*. There was a reminder that to celebrate the Coronation everyone was allowed an additional pound of sugar and four ounces of margarine.

'A special day, Elsie,' said Prudence, as she handed over the extra allowance.

'It is indeed, Prudence,' said Elsie, 'and may I say how distinguished Jeremy looks this morning?'

Jeremy Bear was wearing a Union Jack waistcoat, white trousers and a bowler hat.

'Thank you, Elsie,' said Prudence. 'He's so excited about watching a television for the first time. Captain Forbes-Kitchener has arranged for one to be set up in the village hall, so we're closing the store at ten o'clock.'

In Morton Manor Rupert Forbes-Kitchener was clutching the copy of the *News Chronicle* that had just been delivered.

'Look at this, Alexandra,' he said.

The headline read, 'The Crowning Glory: Everest is climbed. Tremendous news for the Queen'.

'It says here that Edmund Hillary and his Sherpa guide have climbed Everest.'

'That's wonderful,' said a weary Alexandra.

'But this is the best of it, my dear,' and Rupert pointed to the text in bold print. 'It was conquered by men of *British* blood and breed.'

'I thought he was a New Zealander,' said Alexandra quietly.

'That's as good as being British,' insisted Rupert, becoming red in the face.

Alexandra seemed unconvinced. 'Surely his little friend is from one of those Gurkha places?'

Rupert was getting hot under the collar. 'But he was just the *guide*. It was Colonel Hunt's expedition. He was the brains behind it all. So it's a British triumph and just in time for the Coronation.'

'Yes, dear, I'm sure you're right, and no doubt our new Queen will be told, but she will have other things on her mind.'

Rupert looked puzzled. 'What do you mean?'

'Well, for a start, that dreadfully heavy crown she will have to wear.'

Rupert shook his head, folded the newspaper and headed for the hallway.

Violet Fawnswater had watched the programme *About the Home* and had taken advice from television chef Marguerite Patten with regard to refreshments to be enjoyed during the Coronation. She was expecting a dozen family members to descend on her home and it was important to cater for the discerning palate. With this in mind, she began to prepare melon cocktails and salmon mousse to eat while watching the television.

Violet was unaware that Vera had seen the same programme and her response had been quite different. Vera had shaken her head in dismay and announced, 'Standards are slipping, Joseph. How dreadful to eat off one's lap in front of a television set.'

It was a quarter past nine and Tom Feather was in the village hall. He fiddled with the dials on the Bakelite television with its nine-inch screen. It was the set provided by Captain Forbes-Kitchener and he knew a large crowd would gather. This was one of an astonishing 2.7 million television sets in the country, with an average of between seven and eight adults plus countless children watching each one. BBC TV had opened earlier than usual with the Test Card to allow viewers to tweak their aerials to achieve a better reception.

When Tom was satisfied with the grainy black-and-white picture he stood back to admire his work. He looked at his wristwatch and hoped Lily might join him later.

Across the road, Diane Wigglesworth and her mother were each smoking a cigarette while taking turns to do each other's hair.

The shop was closed and today the conversation was different. It made a change from the usual talk of liberty bodices, suspender belts, nylons and roll-on girdles, along with lusting after Richard Burton. Instead they analysed the various men in their lives and agreed that, just like a game of snakes and ladders, when the dice was rolled they would undoubtedly end up with a snake.

'Ah pity t'Queen,' said Diane, 'marryin' that Prince Philip.'

''Ow come?' asked her mother.

'Well, 'e's a *man*.'

Lily had helped John Pruett decorate the tables with red, white and blue crêpe paper and was now returning home on her bicycle. As she cycled out of the school gates flower candles on the horse chestnut trees gave notice of the summer days ahead. On the High Street bluebottles buzzed in the hedgerow where bracken was uncurling among the cow parsley, and the magenta heads of fox-gloves waved as she swept by. On the back road to Kirkby Steepleton sycamore and ash keys hung in the trees above her head and the fluffy seeds of willow drifted on the heavy, still air.

It was a time of renewal and Lily felt good to be alive, particularly as she was expecting to meet Tom later and give him a long-awaited answer to his proposal of marriage. She knew it was a decision that would please Tom and anger her mother.

Back at Laurel Cottage, Florence was picking flowers in the neat little garden. She had offered to decorate the tables for the afternoon party at Kirkby Steepleton Primary School.

On the High Street outside her gate she could hear a group of excited boys playing cricket with dreams of representing Yorkshire. 'Ah'm Freddie Trueman,' shouted an aspiring fast bowler. 'An' ah'm Len 'Utton, t'best batsman in t'world,' yelled another.

Florence had collected bunches of marigolds, sweet peas and roses when Lily arrived. 'How lovely, Mother,' she said. 'Let me help.'

As they gathered flowers, bright-winged butterflies hovered above the buddleia bushes, while the drone of bees could be heard in their never-ending search for pollen. Cuckoo spit nestled in the lavender leaves, sparkling like bright foam, while the scent of roses hung in the air like a lover's embrace.

Meanwhile, Florence gave Lily a sharp glance and wondered why she appeared so elated.

At half past ten everyone settled down to watch the Queen and the Duke of Edinburgh leave Buckingham Palace for Westminster Abbey, then two hours later the world held its breath at the moment of the crowning. By two o'clock the villagers of Ragley and Kirkby Steepleton were opening their curtains and emerging bleary-eyed into the open air as the celebrations began.

On Ragley High Street dozens of children wearing party hats made of folded newspaper sat down for their party tea outside the village hall. Vera put down a tray of North Yorkshire County Council glass tumblers filled with lukewarm home-made lemonade on one of the trestle tables, and Nora Pratt and Shirley Makin served the drinks to each child. There were crab paste sandwiches and biscuits, followed by a special surprise when Prudence Golightly appeared from the General Stores after her huge delivery of Wall's ice cream. Each ice cream was in a brick-like carton and there was a choice of raspberry or vanilla. Prudence had also wrapped them in two sheets of newspaper to make sure the ice cream lasted for another two hours.

Another collection of tables, covered in snow-white cloths and decorated with bright bunting, had been prepared under the guidance of Vera and the ladies of the Women's Institute. These were for the adults, and an impressive tea appeared with military precision. Cold meats, pork pies, pickles, dainty cucumber sandwiches, hard Wensleydale cheese and freshly baked bread were laid out, along with jugs of home-made elderflower cordial. A few bottles of Joseph's home-made wine also made an appearance, but were carefully avoided. Then Joyce Davenport and Edna Trott served tea and cake, including a huge plateful of Audrey Poole's raspberry tarts. It was a veritable feast.

Meanwhile, on the village green in front of The Royal Oak, the Ragley Brass Band, by now well lubricated with Tetley's bitter, were playing some rousing tunes, including 'On Ilkla Moor Baht 'At' and 'Jerusalem'.

Three miles away in Kirkby Steepleton a similar party was taking place and, after the children had eaten their fill and were playing games, the adults sat down in the giant marquee to enjoy a well-earned drink.

Florence was chatting with some of her friends and Millicent Merryweather came to sit with Lily. 'You must come round for tea sometime, Lily,' she said.

'That's kind,' said Lily, 'and I do love your cottage.'

She had first visited Millicent's home with her mother, following introductions from Vera, and they had been made most welcome. The sign on the gate read 'BILBO COTTAGE' and the house had a red front door with a shiny brass door knocker in the shape of a roaring lion. The kitchen had leaded windows and there was a spacious study full of books. In the lounge was an oak-beamed ceiling, and a photograph of Millicent's husband, Roger, an army captain complete with military moustache, stood on the mantelpiece. They had sat on a wrought-iron seat in the large garden next to a bed of floribunda roses. Blackberry and redcurrant bushes bordered an immaculate lawn and they had enjoyed tea and scones in the sunshine.

Milly was a dear friend of Vera's and together they attended the twice-weekly Ragley Cross-Stitch Club, on Tuesdays and Thursdays. Florence had become their latest member and Milly would put her large canvas bag full of materials into the boot of her car and collect her new friend from Laurel Cottage.

It was during these journeys that they shared stories of their lives during the war. Milly had joined the Auxiliary Territorial Service, or the ATS as it was known. She had driven a lorry and operated searchlights and anti-aircraft guns. 'However, we weren't allowed to pull the firing lanyard, worse luck. That had to be done by a man, even though I was better qualified.'

'Too true,' agreed Florence.

'We also operated a sound locator unit that could identify enemy aircraft, which meant we could guide the searchlights and anti-aircraft guns. However, the result was we were exposed to the full force of German bombing. Scary times,' she mused, 'but somehow we survived.'

Lily recalled Tommy Piercy saying to her, 'Brave lady, that Milly Merryweather. No bigger than two penn'orth o' copper, but she gave them Germans what for.'

Secretly, Milly had found the war to be liberating and she had achieved tasks that in the past were only in the domain of men. During those times, her husband, Roger, had listened in awe when he returned on leave. However, he knew not to dissuade his feisty and confident wife from her sense of duty.

'So what was the war like for you, Lily?' Millicent asked her as they chatted after the Coronation party.

'Not as exciting as yours, I'm afraid. I was in the Land Army and simply worked the land.'

Millicent smiled. 'I was courting a farmer once – long before Roger, of course. He was quite a catch. In fact, he asked me to marry him, but I didn't fancy being a farmer's wife.'

Lily smiled and said nothing.

'So, Lily, were there any men in your life?'

'Now there's a question!'

'Well?'

Lily sighed. 'There was a man once . . . but that's another story.'

Millicent, although intrigued, recognized the closure of that line of conversation and moved on to a lighter topic. 'Has anyone ever told you just how much you look like Vivien Leigh? She is one of my favourite actresses.'

'It's been mentioned,' said Lily, her cheeks flushing slightly.

Millicent looked at Lily and came to a decision. 'Why don't you go and meet up with your young policeman. I'm sure he would love to see you. I'll clear up here.'

Lily accepted her offer gratefully, said goodbye to Florence and gave Freddie a big hug before she left.

She arrived back in Ragley as the brass band was playing 'God Save the Queen' and everyone stood to attention while they sang. Tom Feather beamed when he saw her and she went to stand next to him to join in the National Anthem. When the band moved on to a medley of popular dance tunes, couples were soon on their feet dancing in the street.

'Would you like to dance, Miss Briggs?' asked Tom with a wry grin and a formal bow.

'Yes I would, kind sir,' replied Lily with a mock curtsey.

As they waltzed the moist air caused her hair to fall in damp tendrils over her high cheekbones and she flicked them back over her ears with a swift movement. Tom held her closer. He admired her profile and the smooth skin of her neck, wanting to kiss it gently . . . but not here . . . perhaps later.

Deirdre Coe was further up the High Street in the public telephone box. She was coming to the end of a brief conversation with her rich cousin Donald in Richmond. Donald was determined: he had no intention of loaning even more money to her brother, the infamous Stan, regarded by Donald as the black sheep of the family. Stan had persuaded Deirdre to telephone him on the assumption he would be in a good mood on this special day.

'The pips are going, Donald,' shouted Deirdre. 'Ah'll 'ave t'put some more coins in but ah've no change left.' The telephone went dead with a buzz like an insect and the call ended.

'Oh 'eck,' said Deirdre. ''E won't be pleased,' and she headed miserably back to The Royal Oak.

On one of the benches outside the pub, Ruby and Agnes were watching over Racquel in her pram while Andy sat on the grass with a tumbler of orange juice. Agnes had been inside to find Ronnie. ''E's past carin' again, Ruby. On 'is fourth pint, said Clarence.' She was holding two packets of Smith's crisps. ''Ere y'are, luv,' she said and gave one to Ruby.

'My lucky day,' said Ruby. The packets of crisps each contained a little blue waxed-paper twist of salt and Ruby had found two of them. She was rejoicing at the unexpected good fortune when a drunk Stan Coe staggered past and bumped into the pram.

'Watch where y'goin', y'big lump,' shouted Ruby.

Stan was too far gone to notice, but his sister had heard the remark. 'Shurrup, y'skivvy.'

'Skivvy, y'self, Deirdre Coe,' retorted Agnes, 'an' tek y'brother 'ome.'

Deirdre glowered at Agnes and led her brother away. There was a heated conversation between them and Agnes overheard Deirdre shout, 'Problem is, Stanley, if y'go on like this you'll be t'richest man in t'graveyard.'

Then Deirdre hurried back down the High Street, leaving Stan slumped on a bench against the wall.

'That Deirdre Coe is a reight sourpuss,' grumbled Agnes. 'She never 'as a kind word for anyone.'

'Ah jus' 'ope 'er Stan gets 'is comeuppance one day,' said Ruby.

'Y'reight there, Ruby. 'E should be 'ung, drawn an' quoted.'

It was early evening and the party was coming to a close for the children. Families were making their way home and Lily and Tom were sitting on the bench under the weeping willow tree. Tom was wearing his best suit and had put his jacket over Lily's shoulders as the temperature began to fall.

'So, have you given it more thought?'

Lily felt comfortable leaning on the shoulder of the giant policeman. She could feel the heat of his body and luxuriated in its warmth.

'About what?' she murmured.

'Marriage,' said Tom. 'You know how I feel . . . I thought you felt the same.'

'It's a big step, Tom. But you know I'm keen.' She was torn between her past and a possible future, but deep down she knew she wanted this man. She had looked into his eyes and seen his soul.

'I can wait a little longer if you want,' he said, but she could see the disappointment on his face. Tom recognized the signs. It was as if she was so close to saying yes and relaxing in his arms, but then a door closed.

'In that case, Tom Feather . . .' said Lily with a smile . . .

It was then that little Rosie Finn shattered the moment. She ran across the green towards her clutching a small bunch of buttercups and shouted, 'Do y'like butter, Miss?'

Lily smiled and crouched down as Rosie thrust the buttercups under her chin. A golden glow reflected on her skin.

'Y'do, Miss!' shouted Rosie in triumph. 'Yes, y'do. Y'like butter.'

She ran off to make a daisy chain and Lily sighed at her innocence.

"Scuse me, Sergeant.' It was PC Dewhirst, looking anxious. 'We need to open the road t'traffic.'

The spell was broken and Tom stood up. He had moved smoothly back into professional mode. 'I had better go.' He glanced at his wristwatch. 'We can talk later.' Lily handed him his jacket. 'Keep it for now,' he offered.

'No, I'll collect my coat and bag from school,' she said.

Tom slipped on his jacket and smiled. 'Fine, I'll be back soon.'

He set off briskly back down the High Street and Lily walked slowly towards the school gate.

She was unaware that she was being watched.

A few minutes earlier a car had parked on the outskirts of the village outside St Mary's Church and a tall, fair-haired man had got out and looked around him. He stretched. It had been a long journey.

Although he was a stranger to Ragley he had studied the various locations on an Ordnance Survey map. He knew where the village hall stood, the local public house and, in particular, the school. The day of the Coronation had seemed an ideal time to visit. There would be crowds and he could stand in the shadows and watch. He walked along the Morton road, looking wistfully at families as he passed them. They appeared happy, relaxed and content. In the distance he could hear music and laughter. There was a shady alleyway next to the village Post Office and he paused there and lit up a cigarette.

Then, when he saw what he was looking for, he watched silently from the shadows.

Lily put on her coat and picked up her bag from the staff-room. The school was silent apart from the creak of the entrance door as it swung on its hinges. As she closed the staff-room door and stepped out into the gloomy corridor, a hand gripped her shoulder and she screamed.

''Bout time you 'ad a real man instead o' that snobby do-gooder of a copper.'

She could smell the beer on his foul breath.

''Ow 'bout a nice kiss f'Stanley?'

Lily struggled as he pushed her against the wall and she shuddered with distaste that this man was so close to her.

Then suddenly Stanley Coe was no longer there. A pair of strong hands had dragged him off his feet and punched him in his bloated stomach. As Stan doubled up in pain, he was pulled outside and a single powerful blow under his chin sent him crashing against the boiler-house doors. He lay there in a crumpled heap, unconscious but still breathing.

Lily stepped back in astonishment and looked up at the tall, fair-haired man. 'Rudi! Rudi! Where did you come from?'

He was still for a moment, drinking in the sight of her. 'It looked like you needed saving again.'

Lily was overcome with the shock of being attacked by Stan Coe and confronted by her past.

'Rudi . . . that man . . . he's a dreadful person, but how is he?'

'Yes, yes, he's fine. Just winded and he will be dazed for a while. I've seen it many times.'

'How did you know where I was?'

'The village postmistress in Amersham always found it hard to keep a secret for too long, as you may remember.'

Lily smiled, recalling fragments of an earlier life that she had tried so hard to forget.

'You shouldn't have come.'

They gazed at each other for what seemed like an eternity. It was Lily who broke the tension between them. 'Rudi – you promised.'

He moved closer and rested his hands gently on her

shoulders. There was a long pause and his grey eyes were full of sadness. *'Ich wollte mich verabshieden.'*

'Wohin gehst du?' replied Lily.

He smiled at her response. 'You remembered my teachings.'

She nodded. 'Why do you need to say goodbye? Where are you going?'

'To Hamburg to start a new life.' There was barely a trace now of his German accent.

'When?'

'Soon – in August.'

'And why are you here?'

'I wanted to see Freddie before I go.'

Lily considered this carefully. 'Mother must not know you're here.'

'I understand.'

Lily's thoughts were racing. 'She's going away for a week at the end of the month.'

They spoke quietly for a while and then he took his leave. As Lily watched him go she knew it was the end of trust, a time of despair and heartache. Then finally realization dawned and she thought of Tom. She knew now it was a road that she should never have travelled.

Rudolph Krüger was back in her life.

Chapter Seventeen

Stolen Waters

It was Friday, 1 July and, after a night when dense clouds lay heavy on the sleeping earth, a humid summer day was dawning. Early-morning mist covered the distant fields like a cloak of secrets. It had been a stifling night and Lily had tossed and turned. She had made excuses to Tom, saying there was a lot on her mind, and they had seen little of each other during the past few weeks. Tom was puzzled, but said he understood. *After all*, he thought, *marriage is a big decision*.

Slowly she climbed out of bed, opened her bedroom window and breathed in the summer air. The scent of roses drifted up to greet her as a pink dawn crested the horizon and the clouds cleared.

The cottage was quiet. Freddie was sleeping and Florence had left the previous day to spend a week with her cousin Ingrid in Pickering. Millicent Merryweather had volunteered to take Freddie to school and then on to the junior cricket practice afterwards. Apparently Freddie was showing great promise. 'They start them playing cricket young in Yorkshire,' Milly had announced.

However, it was Rudi who dominated her thoughts. She had arranged for him to visit Laurel Cottage that evening at 6.30, an hour before Freddie's bedtime. Then in early August he was due to return to a new life in Germany.

She closed the window and selected the lightest of her summer dresses from her wardrobe as the heat of the morning touched her skin. An eventful day lay ahead.

Vera had risen early and collected sprigs of mint from the vicarage garden. In her kitchen she chopped it carefully and added equal parts of sugar and brown vinegar. It was intended to create a tasty accompaniment to the lamb chops that were to be the centrepiece of the evening meal.

'Joseph deserves a treat,' she said to herself.

Outside the leaded windows, wisteria clung to the window frame and butterflies spread their lace wings on the stems of the buddleia bushes.

A perfect summer morning, thought Vera. Then she looked at the distant clouds over the Hambleton hills and frowned. *But I fear a storm is coming our way.*

She finished her preparations and set off for school. As she walked across the village green Tom Feather appeared from the Easington road driving his police car. He seemed preoccupied and gave Vera a brief wave as he drove past. She stopped to watch his car travel down the High Street and turn on to the York road. She had seen little of Tom recently and she wondered why.

Tom was excited as he drove down the A59 and past the Rowntree's chocolate factory on his way into York city centre. Today was a special day in his life. After saving for several years, finally he had enough to purchase the car of his dreams, an Austin A30. Soon he would be the proud owner of a four-door family car and, although his relationship with Lily had appeared to be on hold in recent weeks, he was keen to surprise her. He hoped there could be days out with her, perhaps to the coast or the Yorkshire Dales.

A new world was about to open up for the Ragley policeman and he wanted to share the experience with the woman he loved. But on the rare occasions they had spoken since Coronation Day, Lily had been cool, reticent and distant, and Tom did not understand why. Gradually the realization was dawning on him that perhaps she did not want him in the way he wanted her.

As she cycled along the back road to Ragley, Lily reflected on the past few weeks since the incident with Stan Coe and the surprise appearance of Rudi. The events of that day had made it clear to her that a relationship with Tom was now out of the question – sadly, a life that could never be. Tom deserved better. She knew it was a love that was lost and it saddened her.

In the meantime, for both of them, a day of decisions lay ahead – decisions that would determine the rest of their lives.

Little had been seen of Stan Coe since the day of the Coronation. Deirdre had said that in the days that followed he had been sleeping off a hangover. However, Herbert Grinchley in the village Pharmacy had let it be known that Stan had been seen later that night propped up against the school's boiler-house doors before staggering back to Coe Farm. It was a mystery that remained unsolved for the gossipmongers of Ragley, and the talk soon turned to the hot summer days and the American teenage tennis player, Maureen 'Little Mo' Connelly, who had won Wimbledon and looked set to take all four of the Grand Slam titles.

At the school gate Lily leaped from her bicycle and walked up the drive, where Vera was talking with Miss Valerie Flint. Valerie was teaching John Pruett's class during the morning while John attended a headteachers' meeting in York. Her tall, imposing figure often sent shivers down the spines of the children in her care. Lily had met her on several occasions but had never warmed to this severe woman. She was a firm disciplinarian and, from John Pruett's point of view, a 'safe pair of hands'. As always, Valerie's conversations with Vera tended to involve the deterioration of standards in modern life.

'Good morning, Vera. Hello, Valerie,' said Lily. Her hair was dishevelled and her summer skirt had blown high in the summer breeze when she dismounted her bicycle. She wondered why Valerie was frowning.

'Good morning, Lily, and what a beautiful day,' replied Vera.

'I've always thought that *posture* is so important for young girls who want to go anywhere in life,' said Valerie rather pointedly. 'Don't you think so, Vera?'

'I suppose so,' said Vera, wondering where this conversation might be heading.

'*Correct deportment* is vital when you ride a bicycle, don't you think, Lily?'

Lily looked bemused.

'You mean as *we* were taught, Valerie?' said Vera. 'Perhaps that's a little old-fashioned now.'

'*Standards*, Vera,' said Valerie. 'They are important in our professional life.'

Vera caught Lily's eye and winked. 'You mean a straight back and ankles tucked in?'

'Exactly, Vera,' said Valerie.

Lily was irritated by Valerie's chilly manner, but did not let it show. She pushed her bicycle into the cycle shed and wondered why a woman only a few years older talked to her as if she were a teenager.

George Postlethwaite, the one-armed postman, parked his bicycle outside the General Stores and took Miss Golightly's mail out of his leather satchel. He sorted the letters and, as he always did, read her postcard. It was important to keep up to date with village affairs.

He was so preoccupied that he failed to spot his arch-enemy – namely, the rough-haired and very lively Yorkshire terrier belonging to Billy Two-Sheds. Monty had always enjoyed barking at the curmudgeonly postman and took the opportunity to bite him on the ankle.

'Gerrof y'little bugger!' shouted George. He saw Miss Golightly looking up in alarm from behind the counter. 'Beggin' y'pardon,' he added as he hopped into the shop. 'Here's y'mail, Miss Golightly. Y'Aunty Maud says she's 'avin' a nice time in Morecambe but 'er leg is playin' up again.' He looked down ruefully at his torn sock. 'A bit like mine.'

'Thank you, George,' said Prudence, 'and here's your paper.'

Prudence always gave George a free newspaper each day as it was important to keep the purveyor of local information on one's side.

He glanced at a front-page article. 'Ah see the papers are still full of those Christie murders.'

John Christie had been sentenced to death for the murder of his wife, Ethel, and was believed to have been responsible for seven other killings. In total, six bodies had been found at his home, 10 Rillington Place in London's Notting Hill.

'Yes, a terrible case,' said Prudence.

'They'll 'ang 'im,' said George. As he left the shop Monty was baring his teeth at him again. 'An' ah wish they'd 'ang that bloody dog as well,' he muttered.

It was morning break, Valerie was on playground duty and Vera was drinking tea in the staff-room when Lily walked in looking preoccupied.

'How are you, Lily? You seem quiet.'

'Fine, thanks, Vera, just a few things on my mind.'

'Tea?'

'Yes, please.'

Vera picked up the tea strainer and glanced up at Lily. 'How is Tom these days? I've not seen him for a while.'

'He's fine ... I think,' said Lily. 'To be honest, Vera, we're both busy and we haven't seen much of each other lately.'

Evasion, thought Vera and fell silent as she poured the tea. 'A little like Joseph and myself,' she said eventually.

'We only meet at mealtimes. I sometimes wonder what he gets up to all day. It must be difficult. His flock share their secrets with him and he has to keep them hidden. It reminds me of stolen waters.'

Lily frowned. 'Stolen waters?'

'Yes, one of the earliest Bible quotations that Joseph and I had to learn many years ago.'

'And what was that?'

Vera stared out of the window, 'Proverbs, chapter nine, verse seventeen: "Stolen waters are sweet, and bread eaten in secret is pleasant."'

'I understand,' said Lily quietly.

Vera stood up. 'I'm always here, Lily, if you need a good listener.' She poured another cup. 'I'll take this to Valerie. She's a dear friend but tends to keep to herself. One day I'm sure she will share whatever it is that troubles her.'

Lily was left alone in the staff-room.

Stolen waters, she thought . . . *but there are some secrets that can never be shared.*

Ruby was in the General Stores while Agnes looked after Andy and Racquel.

'Ah thought ah would mek some scones – m'mother loves 'em.'

'That's thoughtful, Ruby,' said Prudence. She put two tins of Bird's Baking Powder on the counter. 'They're on offer.'

'Ah'll tek 'em, please.'

She looked at a pile of multicoloured kitchen cloths. 'What's these, Prudence?'

'They're new,' said Prudence. She showed her the label.

It read: 'Old Bleach kitchen cloths. The perfect cloth to encourage a husband to dry the pots.'

'I think they thought the stripes would appeal to men.'

Ruby laughed. 'They could mek 'em all t'colours of t'rainbow an' my Ronnie wouldn't stand near my sink.'

'That's a pity,' said Prudence. 'Mrs Buttershaw has just bought some.'

'Ah know the one,' said Ruby. 'Sez she's a modern woman but allus gets crumbs down 'er cleavage.'

Prudence smiled. *I know just what you mean*, she thought, but kept a respectful silence.

Meanwhile, in the Tea Rooms the radio was playing and Doris was humming along to Frankie Laine's number-one record 'I Believe' while she served Joyce Davenport and Wilhelmena Hardcastle with tea and Yorkshire curd tarts.

A disgruntled Deirdre Coe was at the next table and not happy at being made to wait.

Wilhelmena gave Deirdre a caustic look and spoke in her usual foghorn voice. 'We were just reflecting on the war, Doris.'

'Oh yes,' said Doris, replacing the ash tray with a clean one, as the president of the Ragley Women's Institute was a chain smoker.

'I was just saying to Joyce that our husbands did their bit for the country, Joyce's husband as an army doctor and my George as a captain in the West Yorkshire regiment.'

Deirdre looked up from her custard cream and glowered in their direction. 'Well, my Stanley couldn't go off t'fight. 'E 'as a 'eart condition an' t'country needed farmers, so Mr Churchill said.'

'It didn't stop him getting drunk like he did on Coronation Day,' said Wilhelmena pointedly. 'It was all round the village the state he was in.'

Deirdre stayed quiet. Stan had kept the events of that day to himself.

Meanwhile, in the staff-room Lily was beginning to think there was more to Valerie Flint than met the eye. Her views of education were particularly perceptive and Lily was warming to this outspoken lady.

'Before the war only ten per cent of children at state schools left with any qualifications and most left at fourteen, so the situation today is clearly better,' said Valerie.

'I agree,' said Lily, 'but we have a long way to go to encourage them to have a love of learning, particularly with the stock of reading books we have available.'

'That's why I insist upon the children in John's class writing their own stories and we read them out at the end of the day.'

'I do exactly the same,' said Lily, greatly encouraged.

'Also, I tend to avoid the books he suggests for class story time.'

'What are those?' asked Lily.

'Richmal Crompton's *William* stories, where the mother doesn't cook or do housework or prepare meals. Then there are the *Jennings* stories – he and his friend, Derbyshire, live in a parents-free world at a boarding school.'

'Yes, I've heard those on the radio,' said Lily.

'Also there's Billy Bunter in his public school and, of course, there's Enid Blyton's Famous Five.'

Lily was surprised. 'Enid Blyton is very popular.'

'Yes, but her characters live in a middle-class world. During a time of food rationing the children enjoy ham sandwiches, strawberries and cream, and drink copious amounts of ginger beer.'

'You have a point,' conceded Lily.

'Also, the police are often portrayed as bumbling simple-tons and it is left to the children to solve problems and catch the crooks.'

Valerie sat back and gave Lily a penetrating stare. 'Your Sergeant Feather wouldn't approve.'

'He's just a friend, Valerie.'

'That's good to hear.'

That afternoon, after John had returned, Lily used her box of drawing pins to mount a series of pictures of vari-ous birds for the children in her class. She was impressed that these country children recognized every one. They identified a house sparrow, starling, greenfinch, chaf-finch, blue tit, great tit, blackbird and a robin in quick succession, before choosing one to draw.

It was a successful lesson, but Lily's mind kept wander-ing to the after-school event that was fast approaching – a meeting with Rudolph Krüger.

Rudi's car pulled up outside Laurel Cottage and he stepped out and looked at the garden gate and the neat flowerbeds beyond. He paused as if he wished to capture the memory. Lily was waiting at the window and he waved. She opened the front door and looked left and right before beckoning Rudi inside.

'You came,' she said. She stepped back and suddenly they were face to face in the hallway.

'I wanted to come,' he said quietly.

'I think I knew that one day I would see you again.' Her voice was quiet and her eyes were filled with sadness. She looked up into the handsome face of the tall, blond German. 'You look well, Rudi.'

He nodded briefly. 'How are you, Lily?'

'I'm fine.'

'You look beautiful. You always did,' and he gave that smile she remembered so well.

There were memories that were tender to the touch and Rudi was caressing them fingertip softly. It was easy to see why her younger self had fallen in love with this quiet and soulful man. There had been gravitas in his words and she had listened to them eagerly.

Rudi looked towards the kitchen. 'Florence is away?'

'Yes, she left yesterday.'

'So we can talk.'

'For a short while.' Her voice was neutral and calm. Once he had consumed her life, but now he was a stranger. It had been a love of fire and ice. Finally, in the cool light of her new life, she knew it was over between them and had been for many years.

'May I see Freddie?'

'He's playing in the back garden. Come and see.'

Freddie was hitting a tennis ball against the wall with his cricket bat. He was engrossed and showed great skill. Tall for his age and athletic, he had the makings of a fine sportsman.

He stopped when Lily walked out with the tall stranger.

'Freddie, this is the friend I told you about. He's come to say hello.'

Freddie stared up, full of curiosity. 'Can you play cricket?' he asked.

'Cricket? I have never played.'

Freddie was puzzled. 'I thought everyone played cricket.'

'Not in my village,' said Rudi. 'But perhaps you can teach me.'

Freddie passed him the ball and stepped back to the chalked set of cricket stumps on the wall. 'You bowl, I'll bat.'

Rudi threw the ball gently and Freddie hit it back to him.

'What's your name?' asked Freddie.

'Rudolph.'

Freddie grinned. 'Like the reindeer?'

'Yes, like the Christmas reindeer,' replied Rudi. 'But my friends call me Rudi.'

Freddie nodded sagely. 'I'm Frederick, but my friends call me Freddie.'

'I know,' said Rudi quietly.

Tom had finished his shift and was showing off his new car to PC Harry Dewhirst. He had parked outside York railway station alongside a 'Go by Train' poster. 'Only works out at a penny three farthings a mile,' it read. 'Quick, comfortable and convenient.'

Harry tapped a finger on the metal plate of the advertisement. 'Y'won't need British Rail now, Serge', wi' y'new Austin Seven.'

Tom beamed with pleasure. 'You take our car back to the station – I'm driving home in this.'

As he climbed into the smart leather driver's seat he knew where he wanted to go first. He headed north out of the city.

Twenty minutes later Tom slowed as he drove down Kirkby Steepleton High Street. Fifty yards from Laurel Cottage he stopped under the shade of a copse of sycamore trees. He could see a tall stranger speaking to Lily by her garden gate.

Something was not quite right.

He turned off the engine and sat quietly, watching the scene that unfolded before him.

Lily stood at the gate at the front of the house with Rudi and Freddie.

'It's your bedtime now, Freddie,' she said. 'Say goodbye to Rudi.'

''Bye, Rudi,' said Freddie.

'Thank you for showing me how to play cricket,' said Rudi.

Freddie looked up eagerly. 'I play after school on the village cricket field. You can come and see me if you like.'

Rudi smiled, but said nothing. He stretched out his arms to the boy and looked at Lily as if seeking permission. She gave a brief nod and he picked up Freddie and for a brief moment held him close. 'Be good, Freddie.'

The boy ran off back into the house, still clutching his cricket bat.

Finally, Lily and Rudi faced each other and he put his hands on her shoulders. A wisp of her hair shivered in the light breeze and he tucked it tenderly behind her ear.

'Goodbye, Lily. Thank you for letting me see Freddie.'

'It was important you had the opportunity. You can see he is happy here.'

'I see that now. I did wonder.'

'Good luck with your new life in Germany, Rudi. I hope all goes well for you.'

There was silence – the moment of parting had arrived.

Finally Rudi stepped closer and hugged Lily tenderly. 'It was good between us.'

'Yes, it was, but that's in the past. I loved you once, Rudi, but that was the love of a young impressionable girl. I'm a woman now and I understand more about life. We each have a life to live – but not together. It's taken years to heal, but I'm not the girl you once loved.'

'I know,' he said and kissed her forehead.

'You must go now, Rudi, and never come back.'

Then he whispered in her ear, 'Thank you for letting me see my son.'

He climbed back in his car and wound down the window.

'Goodbye, Lily.'

'Goodbye, Rudi.'

'Look after our boy.'

'I will.'

Tom watched the two people in front of him. He stared in shocked silence as the tall, faired-haired man pushed a lock of hair behind Lily's ear. It was an act of intimacy and in that moment he knew they were lovers.

Also, he could not help but see the similarity between

the boy and the man: the same high cheekbones, long limbs and blond hair. *Surely it can't be*, he thought.

Anger surged through his body and he reversed the car, turned and drove away.

He had seen enough.

That night Tom lay in his bed while lightning flashes were followed by the roar of thunder. He could not sleep, tormented by a need he could not fulfil. The heat was unbearable, close and oppressive.

Thoughts of Lily raced through his mind.

A great deception had come between them.

It had come at a cost.

He had lost the woman he loved.

In Laurel Cottage Lily heard the rain beginning to beat against her bedroom window. Heaven's giant army was on the move. The storm was close now, a great storm, and she was in its path. For a moment she felt the echo of a life that had once filled her waking dreams. That life' had gone now. It was a passing memory, frozen in time.

When her baby was born she had wept until there were no more tears left inside her. She remembered that young woman for whom love was intoxicating, an adventure under the stars. Now she had to live with the inner truths that filled her waking dreams. Tom's love was different, steadfast and true, unwavering in a sea of secrets . . . but it too was over.

There was a force in Tom that echoed in her sleeping thoughts. A giant wave had crashed over her and shattered her dreams. Only scattered pieces remained, shifting pebbles on silent sands. Deep down, Lily knew that life at

Starting Over

Ragley School was transient. It would pass by like a summer breeze and one day she would move on.

However, secrets had a habit of being discovered – often at the most unlikely moment.

Chapter Eighteen

White Lies and Wishes

It was Wednesday, 22 July and the first soft kiss of sunlight brushed Lily's bedroom window. Beyond the Hambleton hills a golden glow shimmered on the horizon where the earth met the cloudless sky.

Lily awoke to a new dawn. A shaft of light shimmered on the empty pillow beside her head and, for a moment, she imagined Tom was there. Then she stretched, stepped lightly out of bed and opened the window. In the distant fields sheep munched contentedly on the dew-covered grass, while the branches of beech trees stirred with a sibilant whisper. A breathless promise hung over the land on this perfect morning.

It was also a perfect day for cricket.

Lily smiled as she heard Freddie's excited voice in the next bedroom. That afternoon it was the annual Easington & District Small Schools Cricket Tournament on the Ragley cricket field and Freddie was one of the boys representing the Kirkby Steepleton under-eight team. Lily thought back to the day Freddie had played cricket with Rudi in the back garden. Soon Rudi would be back in Germany and that chapter of her life would be over, closed for ever.

She also thought of Tom. It was clear he must be busy with his life and she had avoided him during the past three weeks. She missed his companionship and caring manner and wished it could have been different. He was a wonderful man and she knew she loved him.

However, wishing and reality were a world apart and she had to accept the life she had chosen. With a heavy heart she stared once again at the empty pillow beside her own.

At 7 School View a heated conversation was taking place. Agnes had left for the chocolate factory, Ronnie was sitting at the kitchen table and Ruby was feeding Racquel while Andy tried to climb into the posser tub.

'Ah wish you'd get a job, Ronnie.'

Ronnie lit up another cigarette. 'Ah've gorra job.'

'Ah don't mean jus' lookin' after them pigeons f'Billy Two-Sheds. Ah mean a *proper* job. One where y'go out t'work on a Monday morning and bring y'pay packet 'ome on a Friday.'

'There's not many jobs like that.'

'Well that Clyde Dlambulo got one repairin' motorcycles an' 'e's from Africa.'

'But they don't pay 'im much.'

'An' 'is dad gorra job as a bus conductor.'

'Ah couldn't do that 'cause of m'vertigo.'

'Vertigo! What's that when it's at 'ome?'

296

"Igh places, Ruby. Y'go all wobbly. Ah'm gonna tell Doctor Davenport ah've gorrit so ah couldn't go up to t'top deck t'c'llect fares.'

'Well we need more money t'feed our children, Ronnie, so gerrof y'backside.'

'What will t'neighbours think wi' you shoutin'?'

'Probably same as me – that you're a lazy so-an'-so.'

'Ah'm off,' said Ronnie.

'Where to?'

'Doctor's – wi' m'vertigo,' and the door slammed behind him.

In the school office Vera had typed out a list of new admissions. It was lengthy, as the number of children on the roll had grown rapidly.

'I've spoken to County Hall, Mr Pruett,' said Vera, 'and they have confirmed that our growing school population qualifies us for a new full-time teacher from next spring term onwards. They said they would write to confirm it.'

'That's wonderful news, Vera. Three classes – who would have thought it?'

'So I'll draft a letter to the governors, shall I?'

'Yes, please, and I'll go and tell Lily.'

Vera was surprised at his eagerness.

Lily was in her classroom writing a list of farm animals on the blackboard.

'Exciting news,' said John.

Lily was startled by his sudden appearance. 'Oh, hello, John. What is it?'

'County Hall have said we qualify for another full-time

teacher from next January. So we can look forward to another member of the team.'

'That's wonderful! Well done.'

'It's you I have to thank, Lily. Parents on the borders of our catchment area are choosing us instead of Morton or Easington. You've brought new life into Ragley.'

Suddenly he was tongue-tied again in her presence. There was so much he wanted to say, but he could not find the words.

Lily seemed to sense his shyness.

'No, John, you're the headteacher so you should take the credit.'

'Well, we're a team – a good team.' There was a time when he had thought it might be more than that, but not now . . . not ever.

Morning surgery had begun at Dr Davenport's and the waiting room was almost full when Ronnie walked in. It was a gloomy place, with wooden chairs lining the walls. The unwritten rule was that only adults sat down while children remained standing. Ronnie sat and lit up a cigarette to add to the thick pall of smoke that already filled the room.

The woman next to him coughed loudly as Ronnie leaned back and blew a smoke ring. It was meant to impress, but he could see his talents were falling on stony ground. Eventually the youthful, clean-cut Richard Davenport popped his head round the door and said, 'Next patient, please.'

Ronnie was out of his seat like a rat out of a trap and settled in the visitor's chair on the other side of Dr Davenport's desk.

'So, what seems to be the problem, Mr Smith?'

'Vertigo, Doctor, summat awful.'

'*Vertigo?* What makes you think you have vertigo?'

'Ah get dizzy when ah stand up quick.'

'Well, there are other reasons for that. Let me check your blood pressure.'

Richard was thorough as always, but had soon worked out there was little wrong with Ronnie apart from a nicotine addiction and his regular intake of Tetley's bitter. He gave him a prescription for a simple tonic and advised him to moderate his lifestyle, knowing full well that Ronnie would take no notice.

Ronnie trudged off to the Pharmacy, where he proceeded to tell Herbert he was at death's door.

It was morning break and Winnie Pickles was playing tennis with a stick and a tennis ball. The ball bounced off the school wall and rolled towards Lily. She picked it up and threw it back.

'I want to be like Little Mo,' shouted Winnie and Lily smiled at her exuberance.

Big Dave and Little Malcolm were deep in conversation outside the boiler house. There was no pile of coke there any more, simply the memory of exciting times at Ragley School.

Lily approached the intrepid duo. 'How was your visit, David?'

Big Dave had gone with the other school leavers up to Easington Secondary School for an introductory visit. He paused before responding, as he knew he would be leaving his cousin behind. 'It were fair t'middlin', Miss.'

'So are you looking forward to it?'

'Well, they do woodwork, Miss, an' ah like woodwork an' buildin' things.'

'That's wonderful, David, and they will have work-benches and proper tools.'

Little Malcolm was staring at his scuffed sandals. Two green candles of snot were dripping from his nose, but he was too full of regret to wipe them away with the sleeve of his torn pullover.

'Malc is upset, Miss. 'E wants t'come to t'big school an' all – but 'e's got t'wait 'til 'e's eleven.'

Lily crouched down and spoke softly. 'The good thing, Malcolm, is that David can find out a lot about Easington and when you start you'll know all about it.'

'That's right, Miss, an' ah'll look after 'im.'

Little did they know it at that moment, but Big Dave would spend the rest of his life looking after his cousin. In a future they could not comprehend, they were destined to be friends for the rest of their days; for this one year only would they be parted.

'There you are, Malcolm,' said Lily, 'things aren't so bad after all.' She offered Malcolm her clean handkerchief. 'Now wipe your nose and enjoy your playtime.'

Little Malcolm looked curiously at the spotlessly clean and neatly ironed handkerchief as if it was a strange, for-eign object and then wiped his nose as he always did – with his sleeve. Some habits were simply ingrained.

'Thanks, Miss,' he said, handing back the handkerchief, 'an' ah'll allus remember you givin' us t'chance t'do that drawin' when we could 'ave got caned.'

Lily gave a knowing smile. *Another long sentence*, she thought.

At lunchtime Anne Watson made a surprise visit, clutching her teaching certificate. Vera and Lily chatted to her and shared her excitement over her marriage to John Grainger next month, then Lily suggested she stay for the afternoon and work alongside her. Vera also mentioned that a new teaching post for the next academic year would soon be advertised and Anne showed clear interest.

At the end of school there was a surprise for Ruby Smith. She had received a message that Mr Pruett wished to speak to her.

When she arrived, the caretaker, Mrs Trott, was standing outside the office door and gave her a reassuring smile. She tapped on the door and a voice called out, 'Come in.'

'Y'wanted t'see me, Mr Pruett,' said Ruby.

John Pruett put down his pen and looked up at the attractive but clearly downtrodden young woman standing before him. 'Please sit down, both of you, and thank you for calling in.'

Puzzled, Ruby sat down, Edna beside her.

'Our school numbers are growing,' said John, 'and I've heard there will be another class next year. We could do with an assistant caretaker to help out for a few hours per week. Mrs Trott speaks very highly of you, Ruby.'

'An' m'leg is playin' up again, Ruby, an' m'back,' added Edna for good measure.

John Pruett decided to stop the school caretaker there

before it became too personal. 'So I should like to offer you the job of assistant caretaker. Are you interested?'

'Oooh, yes please, Mr Pruett!' said Ruby, and Edna Trott and John Pruett shared the knowing smile of a job well done.

A crowd had gathered at the Ragley cricket field. A few fathers had left work early to watch their sons playing cricket, while mothers looked after the refreshments and shouted encouragement to their children. Tom Feather was off duty and supping the last dregs of a glass of warm beer outside the refreshment tent. Albert Jenkins arrived carrying two more glasses of Chestnut Mild.

'Plenty of future Yorkshire talent here today,' said Albert. He sat down in the deckchair next to Tom and handed him a glass.

Tom smiled. It was good to relax, even though his waking dreams were still filled with thoughts of Lily. 'Thanks, Albert. You're right – some of these lads show promise.' His eye was drawn to Freddie Briggs, who had just hit the ball to the boundary, and he scanned the crowd to see if Lily was there.

It was then that he recognized a figure standing alone in the deep shade of a weeping willow on the far side of the ground. It was the tall, fair-haired man he had seen with Lily a few weeks ago. Tom remembered their embrace.

He stood up quickly. 'Excuse me, Albert.'

He skirted the field at a cautious pace and approached the stranger from behind. The man was engrossed watching the cricket and almost hidden from view behind the arching branches of the willow.

Tom knew he must remain calm even though rage was

building up inside him. The only outward signs were the twitching of his cheek muscles and the clutched fist behind his back.

'What are you doing here?'

Rudi was startled, but quickly regained composure. 'I'm here to watch the cricket.'

Tom heard his accent. He was shocked. 'Are you German?' He could barely utter the words.

'Yes, I am,' said Rudi quietly.

Tom was trying to control his anger. The betrayal seemed complete. 'A German . . . dear God!'

He turned his back on the man and stepped away. He was rigid with hatred. Then, in an instant, he turned again, walked forward and grabbed Rudi by the shirt collar. 'I think you know why.' His voice was cold and his blue eyes were chips of ice.

Rudi took a deep breath. 'I know who you are – Lily told me. So, can we talk?'

'There's nothing to say,' said Tom, releasing his hold and stepping back. 'I've seen all I needed to see.'

'There's a lot you don't understand.'

'I know enough.'

Rudi weighed his words carefully. 'No you don't . . . I know she loves you.'

'What?'

Rudi stepped closer to Tom and spoke quietly. 'So, if you love her you need to listen to what I have to say.'

Tom shook his head. 'Why should I? It's obvious that Freddie is your son.'

Rudi gave a brief nod of acknowledgement. 'Yes, he is, and Lily is his mother.'

'I knew it the moment I saw you together.'

'Tom, in a week or so I am going back to Germany once and for all, but before I go you need to know the truth – the truth about Lily.'

Tom was in despair. 'The truth! It's been a lie from the start.'

Again, Rudi measured his words. 'We have a word in German – *Notlüge*.'

'What's that?'

'In English you would say a "white lie".'

'A white lie is still a lie.'

'Tom, she had no choice.'

'Choice? She chose you as her lover.'

'We were young and it was a long time ago. We were both trapped, her as a Land Girl knowing no one and in a difficult family, and me as a prisoner-of-war working on the farm. We were drawn to each other.'

'So why was it a white lie?'

'Because it was Florence who made the decision to hide the truth. She was so deeply ashamed. She thought it would protect Lily from what people would think of her as an unmarried mother.'

There was a silence between them as realization began to dawn for Tom.

'I can understand that,' he muttered. 'That's how people think.'

Rudi could see the tension starting to fall away from Tom and he stepped closer. 'I don't want to leave without giving Lily a chance of happiness. She is a wonderful woman.'

'That's what I thought, but she has been living a lie with me.'

'Please give her the opportunity to make things right.'

'How can I? Everything I believed to be true has gone.'

'But not your love for her.'

Tom sighed, knowing this was true. 'What about Freddie? Does he know?'

'No, and he mustn't know for his own protection.'

'Yes, I can understand that – he's half German.'

'I know, but is that so bad?'

'I spent five years fighting Germans. If we had met I would have tried to kill you.'

'And I you.' Rudi breathed deeply and nodded towards the boys playing cricket in the sunshine. 'I want Freddie to have a good life here in England.'

Tom shook his head. 'So why are you going? Why run away from your responsibilities?'

'I ran away from them because I could not give my son what he needs most of all.'

'And what is that?'

'A stable home, security and a loving family.'

'Perhaps you ought to try.'

'It's too late.' Rudi stared up at the sky. 'Tom, she loves *you* – and if you have any sense you will see that.'

Tom's shoulders slumped. He felt beaten. 'I don't even know your name.'

Rudi looked around. 'Can we go somewhere else, somewhere more private?'

Tom hesitated, then nodded towards the woods to the east of the village. 'There's a path,' he said, and they set off together.

*

Back in the school office, Vera had completed the end-of-year attendance registers and John was writing the total in the school logbook. Through the open window Vera could see children playing on the school field and Lily and Anne Watson walking in the sunshine. The office was quiet and Vera decided to seize the opportunity.

'I was just saying to Miss Watson that there's a teaching post coming up at Ragley in January.'

'Yes,' said John, 'I'm sure she would be an asset to any school.'

'Most certainly. Her teaching practice was excellent and, of course, she is now familiar with *our* children.'

'She would need to apply through the official channels,' said John with a note of caution.

I've already mentioned that to her, thought Vera. 'Of course, Mr Pruett.'

'The school governors would have their say,' added John.

'Naturally,' said Vera, in the knowledge that her brother, Joseph, as chair of governors, would do as she told him.

'Thanks, Vera,' said John, 'that's very helpful,' and he closed the logbook, locked it in the bottom drawer of his desk and set off for the Ragley cricket field to umpire one of the games.

Vera watched him go and smiled, pleased with her tactical acumen and with the thought that, like all good school secretaries, she could manipulate the headteacher to her way of thinking.

Rudi and Tom walked in silence through the woods until they reached a stile that led to one of Stan Coe's fields, and they sat down. Wild honeysuckle grew among the brambles, filling the air with its heavy scent. Rudi took a crumpled cigarette packet from the top pocket of his shirt. 'Cigarette?'

'Thanks, no – I don't.'

Rudi leaned back against the fence and lit his cigarette. Tom looked at him curiously. 'So, tell me about you.'

Rudi stared down at the ground and drew on his cigarette. 'I'm Rudolph Krüger, but my friends call me Rudi.' He paused, searching for the right words. 'I was born in nineteen twenty-four.'

Tom gave a forced smile. 'So was I.'

'My childhood was in Pomerania on the Baltic coast and then in nineteen forty-two I was conscripted into the *Wehrmacht*, the German army. All my friends joined. There was no choice.'

'Same for me, I suppose,' said Tom. 'We had to crush Hitler.'

Rudi nodded. 'They sent me to the Eastern Front. It was a cruel winter. Minus thirty. Somehow I survived. Then suddenly we were in retreat from Russia. It was chaos.'

'I read about it,' said Tom. 'It must have been hard.'

Rudi looked thoughtful. 'It was.'

'So what happened?'

'I was captured in Belgium by American soldiers. It was a relief to know it was over. I was given food and drink and we marched seven hundred miles to Marseilles.'

'Marseilles? What then?'

'We were put on a troop ship to Maryland in West Virginia and then there was another ship to Liverpool. I was transported to a prisoner-of-war camp in Hertfordshire, near a village called Much Hadham. By then my name was changed to "Krueger" as there was no umlaut key on their typewriter.'

Tom shook his head. 'What a journey.'

'Labour was in short supply, so prisoners were needed to work on the land. I was sent to Amersham in Buckinghamshire and I lived in a wooden hut on a farm. It felt like home to me. You will have guessed the rest. I met a Land Girl called Lily, fell in love and she had a baby. I had no say in what happened next. Her mother, Florence, took her away. Before she left she told me I had shamed her daughter and her family. I carried on working on the farm.' He sighed and stubbed out his cigarette. 'Finally I have saved enough to return to Germany.'

On the High Street Vera cut a striking, elegant figure as she strode towards the Morton road. Another school day was over and she was pleased she had spoken with Edna Trott about getting some help for her with the school cleaning.

Parked outside the church was George Hardcastle, who had delivered his wife to Joseph's 'Care in the Community' seminar. When he saw Vera walking towards him his stomach knotted in anguish.

I wish I had a Vera in my life, he thought. *Instead I've got a Wilhelmena.*

He hoped Vera would notice his new car. It was a low-slung two-seater Austin Healey 100. At £1,064 it was the world's cheapest 100 mph sports car. Red with a black interior, a 90 bhp four-cylinder engine, rakish wire wheels and fold-flat windscreen, it could reach 60 mph in ten seconds. With nine out of ten being exported to the USA, it was rare to see one in the UK, so when George had pulled up all heads had turned. Sadly, there was not a flicker of recognition from Vera. Extreme displays of extravagance did not appeal to the vicar's elder sister and George was left to wonder why he had chosen Wilhelmena as his wife – *or had it been the other way round*?

Tom and Rudi had walked back to Rudi's car, parked in a shady spot on the Morton road near the church.

'I am pleased we have spoken,' said Rudi.

Tom had come to appreciate the efforts of this strange German. It was clear his experience of war had been traumatic, and he had emerged older and wiser. Although Tom could not imagine leaving behind a child to begin a new life, he understood the logic behind the thinking of this articulate man.

'So am I,' he said.

Rudi was insistent. 'Freddie thinks Florence is his mother and it has to stay like that.'

Tom considered this carefully. 'That will be for Lily to decide.'

'Of course.'

Rudi stretched out his hand – a significant moment for both men. Tom recognized the gesture of an enemy who had become a brief acquaintance and he grasped Rudi's hand in a firm handshake. 'Good luck, Rudi.'

Rudi's grey eyes were unblinking as he returned the young policeman's searching gaze. He opened his car door, but then he turned again. There was a final thought he wished to share. 'Tom . . . Lily wants to be in your life, but because of the mistake we both made she will not allow herself to accept happiness with another man. She's a wonderful woman and does not deserve to suffer because of one silly mistake she made as a teenager in wartime. It's tragic, because she deserves a life. She would like it to be with you, but believes she is not good enough.' He climbed into the driver's seat, started the engine and wound down the window. 'You and I both know that is not true.'

After he had driven away, Tom stood there for a long time staring at the empty road.

For Lily it was a restless night, and as she lay awake in the early hours she saw there was no moon, only backlit clouds that covered the land with shadows of confusion. There were tears on her face as she stared at the empty pillow beside her. Many years had passed since she had known joy with Rudi. As time went on it had been replaced with a constant pain and emptiness.

Her mother had told her that what she had done would ruin her life and that she, Florence, knew the best way forward. She recalled the bitterness that had spilled from her mother's lips and how she had wilted before the onslaught.

Finally she fell asleep and in her dreams she saw Rudi and Tom – two good men, side by side . . . but a world apart.

Chapter Nineteen

Starting Over

It was a false dawn as a thin ambient light cast a ghostly shadow on Lily's bedroom wall. She had been awake for many hours and knew she had to face the world and accept her destiny. The time of renewal had arrived. It was Friday, 24 July, the final day of the school year. There were children to teach and they relied on her. This was her life; Ragley had become her home. Her past would remain a secret.

Finally she slipped out of bed and opened her bedroom window as a sliver of sun crested the horizon and dawn raced across the land. It was another perfect morning in this beautiful part of the world. The air was warm and humid, only the slightest breeze wafting the fields of ripening barley that stretched to the horizon.

Lily heard the stairs creak as Florence crept down to the kitchen to prepare a pot of tea – a morning ritual that never changed.

She reflected on her relationship with her mother. It

had altered over the years and she knew her father's death had taken something from Florence that could never be replaced. The doctor had said he would have felt no pain, but that provided little solace. So Florence had carved out a new life with Lily and Freddie; it was the best she could hope for. Lily, meanwhile, had settled for what she considered to be the only decent solution – an outcome that meant Freddie was with her, part of a close-knit family, but never her son . . . never her very own.

In life there was always a price to pay.

She walked to the chair next to her dressing table and picked up her handbag. She opened it and took out the black-and-white photograph that she always kept there. Then she smiled. It was Freddie when he was a baby. For Lily it was balm to a troubled soul and provided her with comfort and strength to face another day. Last night had been like many others, her dreams filled with echoing ghosts. Looking at this photograph always gave her solace.

Perhaps one day it may be different, she thought, *but not now . . . not now.*

Lily ate her breakfast with Freddie while Florence busied herself in the kitchen. It was a special time of the day, when she watched the young boy with deep affection and talked to him about the day ahead.

'Good luck on your last day, Freddie,' she said. 'When you go back after the summer you'll be in the juniors – one of the big boys.'

Freddie grinned and pushed his empty cereal bowl to one side. 'I'm a big boy now,' he said defiantly.

'Well, be good and enjoy today, and then it's the holidays and we can have fun together.'

Lily made sure he had a clean handkerchief in his pocket, then she prepared to go and leave him with Florence.

'Good luck, Lily,' said Florence guardedly. 'Hope today goes well,' she added, but there was no warmth in the message.

'Thanks, Mother,' replied Lily. She gave Freddie a hug and set off on her bicycle.

A refreshing breeze blew in her face and, as always, she slowed on the bend where she had been forced off the road many months ago. In contrast, on this quiet morning the scene was a peaceful one, with cattle in the fields chewing the cud under the welcome shade of a copse of sycamores. Honeysuckle and wild roses intertwined among the hedgerows as she passed Pratt's garage and Coe Farm before Ragley village came in sight.

Lily slowed as she reached the top of the High Street. To her surprise there was a brightly painted gypsy caravan parked on the village green. It was causing great interest and a few curious children were trying to peer through the windows, but the blinds were drawn and no sounds could be heard from within.

Edna Trott was at the school gate, leaning on her yard broom and talking to John Pruett. They were staring at the caravan. Lily dismounted and propped her bicycle against the school wall.

'Good morning,' she said. 'This is interesting.'

'It's Seaside Gladys, Miss Briggs,' said Edna.

'Seaside Gladys?'

'She comes every year during the school summer holidays,' explained John. 'The children are always excited.'

'Ah've no doubt she'll be out sellin' lucky 'eather an' clothes pegs,' said Edna. 'She goes door to door an' if y'cross 'er palm wi' silver she'll tell y'fortune.'

'I've never had my fortune told,' said Lily.

'Perhaps you should,' said John with a gentle smile. 'You never know what might be in store for you.' He glanced up at the clock tower. 'Anyway, things to do,' and he set off up the cobbled drive.

'Mebbe you ought t'give it a try, Miss Briggs,' said Edna with a grin.

'Perhaps,' said Lily.

Edna could see the doubt on Lily's face. 'Talk t'Ruby. Seaside Gladys is 'er aunty from Skegness. Ruby told me that Gladys were born on t'day Queen Victoria died in 1901 an' that it gave 'er some sort o' special power.'

'And what might that be?' asked Lily with a smile.

'She knows what's goin' to 'appen before it 'appens.'

Lily stretched out her hand to the wicker basket on the front of her bicycle and rested it on her handbag. 'I'm not sure I would want to know,' she said quietly.

'Mebbe not, Miss Briggs,' Edna nodded sagely. "Cause ah've 'eard she tells it 'ow it is.'

In the staff-room Vera was holding forth while John and Lily listened intently.

'Now don't forget you are all invited to this evening's soirée at the vicarage. It's to celebrate the end of another successful school year. Joseph and I have invited staff, governors and one or two special friends. So we'll expect you at half past seven for drinks and nibbles.'

'Thank you, Vera,' said John, 'we shall look forward to it.'

'I've asked Millicent to come along, Lily, so she can give you a lift.'

'That's helpful,' said Lily. 'You seem to have thought of everything.'

Vera looked down at the list in her pocket notebook. 'Well, yes, I hope so. This evening should be fine.' She gave John a demanding stare. 'However, there is much to do today, as I'm sure you are aware. We have notes to parents to send out informing them that school reopens on Monday, the seventh of September, plus the advert for the new teaching post to be forwarded to County Hall.'

John nodded and looked at Lily. 'Also the children's reports have to be taken home at the end of school,' he said. 'We shall need those in sealed envelopes.'

'All in hand, Mr Pruett,' said the ever-efficient Vera. 'Lily has already completed hers.'

John, slightly nonplussed, hurried off to prepare the morning assembly and ring the school bell.

Joseph arrived for assembly along with Elsie Crapper, who accompanied a rousing rendition of 'When a Knight Won His Spurs'. This was followed by Lily's school choir singing a sweet version of 'All Things Bright and Beautiful'. John told the children his own version of Oscar Wilde's tale 'The Selfish Giant' and Lily realized that perhaps she had misjudged him, for he was clearly a gifted storyteller.

After Joseph had led the children in the Lord's Prayer,

John wished the school leavers every success when they moved on to Easington Secondary School. It was then that Phoebe Fawnswater looked around with curiosity as she realized that when it was her turn to leave Ragley School she would be separated from all her friends. She would be driving into York with her mother to commence her secondary education at the Time School for Girls, with its smart uniform, straw hats and hockey sticks. Phoebe suddenly wasn't sure she liked the idea.

Malcolm Robinson looked sadly at his giant cousin and Big Dave nodded back knowingly. School would be different for them for the next academic year until Malcolm moved up to the big school. However, as their two families always went on holiday together each summer, a week at Butlins in Skegness beckoned and thoughts of schooldays to come were quickly forgotten.

At morning break Lily was on duty and was surprised to see David Robinson talking to Winnie Pickles, watched by a bewildered Malcolm. Big Dave always prided himself on never talking to girls, but today was clearly different.

'So are you looking forward to secondary school?' asked Lily.

'Yes, Miss,' said Winnie. 'We'll learn 'ow t'cook wi' proper ovens.'

'An' ah'll probably do an apprenticeship when ah'm fifteen or sixteen,' said Dave confidently.

'Well, good to see you are discussing it,' said Lily.

'Yes Miss,' said Winnie, 'an' we were jus' talkin' about t'white lines.'

'White lines?'

'Yes, Miss,' said Dave. 'They 'ave t'biggest playground

you've ever seen, but right down t'middle they 'ave two parallel white lines about ten yards apart painted on t'tarmac.'

Lily was pleased with the word 'parallel'.

'T'keep boys an' girls sep'rate, Miss,' explained Winnie.

'I see,' said Lily. 'And does it work?'

Dave grinned. 'We don't like bein' *told* y'can't talk t'girls. Seems a daft rule – so we're practisin'.'

'Practising?'

'Yes, Miss,' said Winnie. 'Jus' in case we 'ave something t'say to each other when we get there.'

'Ah've never really bothered before,' said Dave.

'Why is that?' asked Lily.

Dave pondered this for a while. 'Well girls are ... *different*.'

'Very true,' said Lily. She smiled at Winnie. 'We *are*.'

With that they both stood up, walked to the school field, sat ten yards apart and tried to conduct a conversation. Little Malcolm, puzzled at his cousin's strange behaviour, wandered off to the playground to read Reggie Bamforth's comic.

The familiar face of Anne Watson suddenly appeared on the other side of the school wall and she waved to Lily.

Lily went over to meet her. 'Hello, Anne, how are the wedding plans going?'

'Fine, thanks. It all seems to be happening so fast now.' She leaned over the wall and spoke in a conspiratorial whisper. 'And I'm definitely applying for the teaching post here.'

'That's excellent news!' said Lily. 'Good luck.'

'My other half is not pleased, but I persuaded him it was

for the best, as we would have *two* incomes. That seemed to swing it, particularly as he was on about buying a state-of-the-art workbench and lots of tools. I've noticed he's started reading DIY magazines and has plans to transform our new home with cupboards and shelves.'

'Sounds as if it's working out for you,' said Lily.

'Hope so,' said Anne. 'Anyway, shopping to do. I'm catching the bus into York to try on my dress.'

She waved again and strode off confidently towards the High Street.

Lily was deep in thought when she was startled by the beeping of a motor horn. She looked up to see Stan Coe leaning out of the window of his Land Rover and leering at her as he drove past the school and round the village green. He gave a wave and shouted what might have been an obscenity before driving up the Morton road to meet his friends at the Pig & Ferret.

Lily trembled at the memory of his hands on her shoulders on Coronation Day and considered mentioning his continued attentions to John Pruett. She knew, eventually, this would reach Tom and hoped he might intervene.

It was after lunch in the staff-room that Vera mentioned Tom.

'Sergeant Feather has been invited this evening, Lily,' she said. 'I thought you would like to know.'

John Pruett looked up cautiously from his *Times Educational Supplement*, while Lily's cheeks reddened slightly.

'Thank you for mentioning it,' said Lily, but she did not progress the conversation.

During the afternoon John organized an extended playtime and the children gathered on the school field to play cricket and rounders. It was while Lily was supervising one of the outdoor sports that she saw Tom drive past in his police car and she wondered about the distance between them.

As they went back into school Reggie Bamforth was walking beside Lily looking thoughtful. 'Ah'm not goin' any more to Phoebe's house t'watch television, Miss,' he declared.

'Oh dear, Reggie, why is that?'

'Las' time ah went with m'mother an' we watched summat really scary.'

'Scary?'

'*Quatermass*, Miss.'

Lily remembered reading about *The Quatermass Experiment*, which had recently begun on BBC television. While it gripped the nation, many terrified children were hiding behind the sofa.

Reggie ran off to join in a cricket match on the school field while Lily leaned against the wall and watched a group of carefree five-year-olds playing ring-a-ring-a-roses in the sunshine.

At the end of the school day Lily and John met in the staff-room and enjoyed a cup of coffee together.

'I don't think Vera would approve,' said John as he added milk to the two mugs.

'Most certainly not,' agreed Lily with a smile. 'I suspect Vera will always serve us tea.'

John settled down in one of the chairs and sipped his coffee thoughtfully. 'Thank you for all you have done, Lily, and I do hope you enjoy your holiday. Have you any plans?'

'My mother mentioned a week in Whitby, but that's all at present. I'm sure there will be days out. What about you?'

'I'll be in my garden, I expect. My sister occasionally visits, but nothing really apart from that. I can't say I'm looking forward to it. She's very disruptive – enjoys tidying up.'

Lily could see the disappointment on his face and realized the headteacher probably led a lonely existence out of school. 'You must come round for tea one day, John. My mother enjoys making a fuss of visitors. Call in when you're passing and we can arrange a date.'

John became animated. 'Thank you so much! That would be lovely.' He wanted to say more, but the words wouldn't come. He was also aware that Lily's relationship with Tom Feather appeared to have gone strangely quiet and he wondered why.

As they parted, Lily felt as though she had gained a small insight into the life of her colleague.

When Lily pushed her bicycle down the drive Ruby was standing by the gate.

'Hello, Ruby,' said Lily. 'How are you?'

'Fine thanks, Miss Briggs. Ah've jus' come t'say 'ello t'my Aunty Gladys. She's a lovely lady an' she 'as a great gift.'

'So I heard.'

'She's got them sidekick powers.'

Lily nodded and smiled. 'So did she tell your fortune, Ruby?'

'Yes, Miss Briggs, she did. She told me ah'd meet a tall

stranger an' 'e would look after me an' ah'd be 'appy an' blessed wi' children.'

Lily couldn't think of an appropriate reply. 'I see,' she said.

'But instead ah met Ronnie,' said Ruby with a shrug. 'Mind you, ah've got two beautiful children. So there are some blessings in life ah s'ppose.'

'Miss Evans told me you had been invited to her evening soirée.'

Ruby looked puzzled. 'Y'mean 'er party? Yes, ah'm goin' wi' Mrs Trott. She's thrilled t'be invited. Sounds a posh do. Ah'm puttin' on m'best frock.'

'That's lovely, Ruby,' said Lily. 'See you there.'

A small lady with colourful clothes appeared by the steps leading up to the caravan. 'There she is now,' said Ruby. 'Come an' meet 'er.'

They walked across the village green and Lily propped her bicycle very gently against one of the shafts of the caravan.

'This is t'teacher ah were tellin' you about,' said Ruby.

'Miss Briggs,' said Gladys, 'I'm very pleased to meet you. I know you are always kind towards my favourite niece.'

Lily was fascinated by her birdlike movements and bright-blue eyes. 'It's a pleasure to meet you,' she said.

Gladys studied Lily intently. 'Tell me, would you like to know a little more about your life?'

Lily was curious. 'How would you do that?'

'The simple way is for me to read your palm. It will only take a few minutes.'

Lily looked around her. The village green was empty

and the High Street seemed strangely quiet. *Why not?* she thought.

Inside the neat caravan there were two chairs on opposite sides of a small round table covered in a blue tablecloth. They sat down and Gladys reached for Lily's hand.

'May I?' she asked and then studied her palm, tracing the lines with a delicate finger. 'You will have a long life, my dear,' she said, 'and there is a strong love line.'

Gladys went very silent for a few moments. Lily realized in this quiet cocoon of space the outside world seemed far away.

'What you seek is within reach, but only after you solve the problem that is troubling you,' said Gladys softly.

Lily said nothing, but felt the import of her words. She thanked Gladys and a few minutes later said goodbye and cycled home.

Solve the problem that is troubling you, she thought. *Easier said than done.*

Back at Ruby's house, Ronnie arrived with unexpected news.

'Ah've gorra job.'

'Flippin' 'eck, Ronnie! Yer a wonder. Jus' when we needed some extra money. What is it?'

'Deliveries.'

'What – in a van?'

'No.'

''Orse an' cart?'

'No.'

'What then?'

'Mebbe a bike.'

'A bike?'

'Yes, but that would be provided as a perk.'

'So what is this job?'

'Communications.'

'*Communications* – that sounds impressive!'

'Yes, ah'll be keeping t'public up t'date wi' current affairs.'

'So who's y'boss?'

'Miss Golightly.'

'Y'mean Prudence at t'General Stores?'

'Yes, an' ah get paid ev'ry Sat'day mornin'.'

''Old on a minute,' said Ruby. The penny had dropped. 'Y'deliverin' papers, aren't you?'

'In a manner o' speakin'.'

'Well what else is it?'

'Ah 'ave t'go in early t'write address on t'top o' each paper – an' there's magazines an' comics as well. It's a big job.'

'Ah thought that young lad, Timothy Pratt, delivered papers.'

''E did, but he's packed in t'concentrate on 'is dad's 'ardware shop.'

Ruby looked at Ronnie and thought *Ah've got a twenty-one-year-old paper boy for a 'usband.* But she realized she needed to be thankful for small mercies. 'Well, it's a start, Ronnie . . . well done,' and Ronnie drifted off to The Royal Oak to celebrate.

When Agnes arrived home from the chocolate factory Ruby shared the news.

'Ronnie's gorra job, Mam,' she said.

'Ah've 'eard it before, Ruby,' said Agnes. 'What is it this time? Road sweeper?'

'No, it's workin' f'Miss Golightly.'

'What, in t'shop?'

'No, deliverin' papers.'

'Flippin' 'eck,' Ruby! When will 'e get a proper job? We've 'eard all this time an' time again.' Agnes shook her head in disgust. 'Mark my words, Ruby, it's that *déjà vu* all over again.'

Ruby simply looked sad. Whatever *déjà vu* was, it didn't sound promising.

In Laurel Cottage Freddie was playing in the small sitting room while Lily and Florence tidied the kitchen.

'Millicent is giving me a lift to the end-of-year party at the vicarage,' said Lily, 'so I'll be leaving shortly after seven.'

'I see,' said Florence quietly. She seemed preoccupied.

'What is it, Mother?'

'I was wondering how you can sing in church knowing what you have done.'

'That's a hurtful thing to say, and you know I enjoy singing.'

'Nevertheless it concerns me.'

Lily threw down her tea towel. 'You see, Mother, that's the difference between us. It doesn't shock me and there will be a day when what has happened to me won't be seen as a great sin.'

Florence looked at her daughter with utter disdain. 'That can never be.'

Lily closed the door and spoke quietly but firmly. 'Mother, understand this: I'm a different person now. That impressionable young Land Girl has grown up. You call it shame, but for me at that time it was my first taste of what

I thought was love. That silly girl has gone now. I'm a woman who knows her own mind, while your generation are ashamed of an illegitimate birth.'

Florence recoiled in shock and put her hand to her mouth. 'Don't say that word.'

'Oh Mother, can't you see the world is changing?'

'Not now, not ever. We have a chance of a new life here in Yorkshire. As you well know, down south the neighbours were beginning to talk about who Freddie's mother might be. We *had* to move on.'

'And we have – it's fine here.'

'Yes,' said Florence bitterly, 'a life without *shame*.'

The words were hurtful and cut like a knife. 'I don't see Freddie like that. He is not someone I associate with shame.'

Florence shook her head, white with rage. 'Your father never recovered from the shock. It probably helped to end his days.'

Lily stepped back. 'That's a cruel thing to say. Father died of pneumonia. It was an *illness* that took him from us – not the so-called shame of which you speak.'

She left the room and went upstairs to get changed while Florence sat down, shaking with anger.

Lily and Millicent Merryweather arrived at the vicarage shortly before half past seven, both wearing their best summer dresses. Vera was a keen gardener and rambling blackberry canes and a riot of raspberries covered the walls of weathered brick. She was standing in the porch and came out to greet them.

As Lily walked across the crushed gravel of the courtyard her fingers lightly caressed the mauve flower spikes in a neat border of lavender and she paused to enjoy the scent.

'My favourite,' said Vera.

'You have a beautiful garden,' said Lily.

'One of my passions,' replied Vera with a smile, 'and aren't we lucky having such a lovely evening?'

There was still over an hour's sunlight before darkness began to descend and everyone stayed outside enjoying the early-evening warmth. Albert Jenkins was talking to Valerie Flint and Elsie Crapper while admiring the fragrant honeysuckle and the bright colours of the climbing clematis. Irene Gubbins and Edna Trott were standing next to Ruby, who was pointing out a spectacular border of Victorian roses.

Ruby waved as Lily walked over to join them. 'Ah love roses, Miss Briggs,' she said. She looked happy and relaxed in a cotton dress and a straw hat covered in summer flowers. She sniffed a deep-yellow rose appreciatively. 'An' that's a Bobby Dazzler.'

'An' 'ave you 'eard t'news 'bout that Stanley Coe?' asked Irene.

'That's right, Miss Briggs,' said Edna. 'It's all round t'village.'

'What's that?' asked Lily.

''E's gone an' been arrested by PC Dew'irst,' said Irene.

'Arrested!' Lily was shocked. 'What for?'

''E got drunk in t'Pig an' Ferret,' said Ruby, 'an' 'e were boastin' 'bout knockin' you off y'bicycle.'

'An' t'landlord rang t'police,' added Edna.

'I see,' said Lily cautiously, but secretly pleased. *Everything comes to he who waits*, her father used to say.

It was then that Lily saw Tom. He was wearing an open-neck white shirt and a lightweight grey suit and thoughts of Stan Coe getting his comeuppance were dismissed.

Tom was speaking with Captain Forbes-Kitchener and both were drinking warm beer. The captain, as always, was impeccably dressed in his regimental tie and three-piece suit; the vagaries of the weather rarely influenced Rupert's attire. Meanwhile, Tom was aware of Lily. While he was driving to the vicarage he had decided what he must say to her.

Edna Trott pointed out Prudence Golightly. 'Lovely t'see Prudence 'ere t'night,' she said. 'She's certainly been through 'ell an' 'igh water, poor lass. It were terrible sad 'bout 'er Jeremy. Shot down in 'is Spitfire over t'Channel. 'E were a lovely man by all accounts an' they were due t'get married. Ah doubt Prudence will ever get over it. She loved 'im t'bits.'

'Y'right there, Edna,' agreed Irene. 'Ah can't imagine what she's thinkin' on a lovely occasion such as this.'

Suddenly there was a tinkling of a spoon tapping a glass and, to Vera's concern, Joseph appeared from the kitchen carrying a tray of celebratory drinks. He placed it carefully on the old wooden table outside the kitchen window and proceeded to distribute a glass to each guest.

'Time for a traditional end-of-school-year toast, everybody. As a special treat I've opened my home-made lavender wine.' He looked around at the impassive faces. Everyone was aware of the reputation of Joseph's winemaking.

'Now, while this may not to be to everyone's liking,' he continued, 'I can assure you it is perfect for a hot summer's evening. Lavender is of course my dear sister's favourite

327

flower, so I do hope you will enjoy its distinctive zesty fla-vour. I've no doubt you will agree it certainly has the edge on my potato wine and I'm sure you will appreciate its fine bouquet. So, ladies and gentlemen, friends one and all, and with thanks for your support during another success-ful school year, the toast is – Ragley School.'

'Ragley School,' echoed the throng.

Sadly, Joseph was still a novice winemaker, unaware of the wild yeasts that can abound on fruit and taint the air with an unpleasant aroma. Consequently, a bouquet simi-lar to rotting mushrooms and damp dishcloths swiftly met the nostrils of those assembled, and not surprisingly the generous quantities in the tall glasses found their way in rapid and surreptitious succession into a variety of flower beds and plant tubs.

Throughout the evening conversations ebbed and flowed until a relaxed and happy occasion came to its close. It was almost time to leave when Tom approached Lily.

'I wondered if you had heard the news about Stan Coe? We've got him at last for dangerous driving and he will certainly lose his licence.'

'Yes, I've just heard. Thank goodness. He deserves whatever is coming to him.'

Tom studied her face and took the plunge. 'Lily . . . I was hoping you might be free for a drive.'

'A drive?'

'In my new car.'

Lily could sense the eagerness in his voice. 'So you finally bought your car?'

'Yes, and it's still a beautiful evening.'

'I'm not sure . . .'

He leaned forward and whispered, 'It's important.'

Then he went off to offer his thanks to Vera.

The observant Millicent Merryweather had spotted the close attentions of Tom Feather towards Lily and came over and spoke softly to her.

'Lily, do you want a lift – or have you other plans?'

Lily looked thoughtful. 'Thank you, Milly, but Tom has just asked me to take a drive with him.'

Millicent smiled. 'That's fine. See you soon.'

When Tom returned he saw Millicent walking towards her car and glancing back at him expectantly. He looked at Lily and smiled. 'So you're coming with me? Thank you.'

They walked across the courtyard towards the vicarage gate. 'It's here,' he said.

Lily saw his new car and felt a great sadness. She knew he was so proud and wished to impress her, but it was wrong to encourage this fine man.

'Do you mind if we walk instead – just for a little while?'

There was a moment of disappointment, but Tom seemed undeterred. 'Very well.'

They strolled slowly down the Morton road towards the village green under a vast red sky in which the stars, like celestial fireflies, held steadfast in the firmament. They didn't hold hands as they used to do, and Lily realized that a life of unfulfilled promises was complicated.

When they reached the village green the orange lights of The Royal Oak shone brightly, and they stopped and breathed in the balmy night air.

'So, the end of your first year, Lily. You've certainly made your mark.'

'I've grown into the job, I suppose – and I've loved teaching these children. So, yes, there's a sense of satisfaction. Ragley School is a special place and the village has become my new home.'

She looked down the High Street where the lights of the shops gave out a reassuring glow: the General Stores & Newsagent, Piercy's butcher's shop, the village Pharmacy, Pratt's Hardware Emporium, Doris Clutterbuck's Tea Rooms, the Hair Salon and the Post Office – all silent now.

Tom gestured towards the old bench beneath the graceful canopy of the weeping willow tree. 'Do you mind if we sit down? There's something I want to say.'

Lily sensed he was searching for the right words. In the distance the familiar sounds of the night could be heard – a hooting owl, the rustlings of small creatures in the grass and the distant bark of a farm dog. She allowed him to take her hand as they walked across the green and the gentle twig-combing breeze was soft in her hair.

When they sat down there was silence between them as they leaned back and took in the shapes of the pantiled roofs, the school bell tower and the moonstone hills beyond. It was a view painted in heaven.

Lily began to relax. Suddenly in this cocoon of private space she felt secure.

'What did you want to say, Tom?'

He took a deep breath. 'You're a wonderful woman and I love you . . . and I believe you love me. I want to spend the rest of my life with you.'

'But I can't.'

'You can. I met Rudi.'

'Rudi – you spoke to Rudi?'

'Yes, two days ago, after the cricket. I learned a lot.'

'Oh, Tom!'

'And I know about Freddie.'

'Freddie – my Freddie?'

'Yes, so I know that is what has stopped you saying yes.'

'But Tom . . .'

'No – let me finish. The past is in the past. That was wartime.'

Suddenly Lily's shoulders shook and tears ran down her cheeks.

'How can you accept me?'

He stroked her cheek gently. 'Sshhh,' he whispered. And he put his arm around her shoulders. 'You don't need to say any more.'

There was a strained silence until, like the bursting of a dam, they both began to speak at once.

'Sorry – you first,' said Tom.

'We did what was right for Freddie. He deserved married parents, not a single mother. After Father died my mother was in a terrible state. Her world had collapsed around her. A new beginning for us all up here in Yorkshire seemed ideal. I knew then that I loved teaching – and I'm good at it,' she said defiantly. 'If they had known the truth I wouldn't have got a teaching job here as an unmarried mother, especially in a Church of England school. The school governors would have been horrified, but no one has ever known the truth until now.'

Tom held her closer. She was shaking with emotion. 'Lily, I really do understand, but there must be a way to make it right.'

'Don't you see? If the school governors knew they

would insist on my resignation. They would demand it. It may be 1953, but it may as well be 1923. Society still treats a single mother like an outcast.'

'They don't need to know, and, anyway, I don't care what people think. I still want us to make a life together and be happy.'

Lily knew it was a rare show of strength for Tom to swallow his pride.

'But do you really want me in spite of all you know?'

Tom sighed and stared up at the sky. It was changing from purple to black and the stars shone down like sentinels.

'I've always wanted you, Lily . . . for better or worse. I love you . . . always have . . . always will.' The brief pauses gave weight to his words. These were the measured thoughts of an intelligent and sensitive man.

Lily looked up at him. 'Tom, I don't want to live a lie and be scared for the rest of my life. That's how it was,' she murmured to herself. 'Rudi was gentle and kind, but our time together was always in secret, away from prying eyes.'

'Yes, that's how things were then and they still are now, but they won't be in the future. It doesn't have to be like this. Times can change . . . we can change.'

Lily wanted to believe him. In the silence of the night the thunder of her thoughts was overwhelming.

She stood up and walked a few paces, then turned. 'Then there's Freddie. He will need to know one day.'

'One day, yes, but not now – not now. I don't think he would fully understand.'

'But would we stay here in Ragley? I love teaching here at the village school.'

Suddenly her secrets had scattered in the wind like sycamore keys and there was a new lightness to her thoughts. The weight of worry had been lifted.

Tom stood up, walked towards her and held her hands. 'And I enjoy being a Yorkshire policeman. We could stay here. I just want to be with you for the rest of my life.'

'Oh, Tom.' There were tears in her eyes. The shadows of the past had flown. The old world was behind her now and it was time for starting over.

He held her close. 'So, Lily . . . will you marry me?'

Lily looked up at Tom and saw there was no weakness in this man . . . only love.

She smiled and said simply, 'I will.'

And in a heartbeat her new life began.

'If you loved *Starting Over*, why
not see where it all began?'

TEACHER, TEACHER!
Jack Sheffield

It's 1977 and Jack Sheffield is appointed headmaster
of a small village primary school in North Yorkshire.
So begins Jack's eventful journey through the school
year and his attempts to overcome the many
problems that face him as a young and
inexperienced headmaster.

The many colourful chapters include Ruby the
20-stone caretaker with an acute spelling problem,
a secretary who worships Margaret Thatcher, a villager
who grows giant carrots, a barmaid/parent who requests
sex lessons, and a five-year-old boy whose language
is colourful in the extreme. And then there's also
beautiful, bright Beth Henderson, who is irresistibly
attractive to the young headmaster . . .

PLEASE SIR!
Jack Sheffield

It's 1981, the time of Adam and the Ants, Rubik's Cube, the Sony Walkman and the Falklands War, as headteacher Jack Sheffield returns to Ragley-on-the-Forest School for another rollercoaster year.

Vera, the ever-efficient school secretary, has to grapple with a new-fangled computer – and enjoys a royal occasion – while Ruby the caretaker rediscovers romance with a Butlin's Redcoat. And for Jack, wedding bells are in the air. But the unexpected is just round the corner . . .

EDUCATING JACK
Jack Sheffield

As September 1982 arrives, Jack Sheffield returns to
Ragley-on-the-Forest village school for his sixth year
as headteacher. It's the time of *E.T.* and Greenham
Common, Prince William's birth, *Fame* leg warmers and
the puzzling introduction of the new 20p piece. Nora
Pratt celebrates twenty-five years in her coffee shop,
Ronnie Smith finally tries to get a job, and little Krystal
Entwhistle causes concern in the school's Nativity play.

Meanwhile, for Jack, the biggest
surprise of his life is in store . . .

SCHOOL'S OUT!
Jack Sheffield

As the new school year begins, Jack Sheffield prepares
for an even more eventful year than usual.
A new teacher is appointed, and before
long tongues start to wag.

Meanwhile, five-year-old Madonna Fazackerly
makes her mark in an unexpected way, life
changes dramatically for Ruby the caretaker and,
in the village coffee shop, Dorothy Humpleby
plans a dirty weekend.

It's the era of the new CD player, the McDonald's
McNugget, the threat of a miners' strike and a final
farewell to the halfpenny piece.

Jack has to manage a year of triumph and tragedy . . .

SILENT NIGHT
Jack Sheffield

1984 – the time of the miners' strike, Trivial Pursuit, Band Aid, Cabbage Patch dolls, and a final goodbye to the pound note as Jack returns for a new school year.

Christmas is an important time for the children of Ragley-on-the-Forest school . . . They are to sing a carol in a church in York, and are actually going to be on television! Keeping his excited children, not to mention their parents, under control during these momentous events taxes Jack and his staff to the limit. But little Rosie Sparrow's singing brings some special Christmas magic, and the lives of several people are transformed as a result.

STAR TEACHER
Jack Sheffield

It's 1985, and as Jack returns for another year
as headteacher at Ragley-on-the-Forest village school,
some changes are in store.

It's the year of Halley's Comet, *Dynasty* shoulder
pads, Roland Rat and Microsoft Windows. And at
Ragley-on-the-Forest, Heathcliffe Earnshaw decides
to enter the village scarecrow competition, Ruby the
caretaker finds romance, and retirement
looms for Vera the secretary.

Meanwhile, Jack has to battle with some
rising stars of the teaching profession to
save his job and his school . . .